PHANTOM HOOF PRINTS

PHANTOM HOOF PRINTS

Kathleen Parker

iUniverse

PHANTOM HOOF PRINTS

Copyright © 2014 Kathleen Parker.

All rights reserved. No part of this book may be used or reproduced by any means, graphic, electronic, or mechanical, including photocopying, recording, taping or by any information storage retrieval system without the written permission of the publisher except in the case of brief quotations embodied in critical articles and reviews.

This is a work of fiction. All of the characters, names, incidents, organizations, and dialogue in this novel are either the products of the author's imagination or are used fictitiously.

iUniverse books may be ordered through booksellers or by contacting:

iUniverse
1663 Liberty Drive
Bloomington, IN 47403
www.iuniverse.com
1-800-Authors (1-800-288-4677)

Because of the dynamic nature of the Internet, any web addresses or links contained in this book may have changed since publication and may no longer be valid. The views expressed in this work are solely those of the author and do not necessarily reflect the views of the publisher, and the publisher hereby disclaims any responsibility for them.

Any people depicted in stock imagery provided by Thinkstock are models, and such images are being used for illustrative purposes only. Certain stock imagery © Thinkstock.

ISBN: 978-1-4917-4669-1 (sc)
ISBN: 978-1-4917-4670-7 (e)

Library of Congress Control Number: 2014916411

Printed in the United States of America.

iUniverse rev. date: 10/14/2014

CHAPTER 1

A Determined Current

Oh, how I miss that glorious feeling, the turf springing under my hooves, like I was a colt again! That day I was unbeatable, unstoppable. None of the others rivaled me. I was like a bird sailing with the wind. That is, till the very end.

I reveled in the challenge of his breath on my flank. He was a dark shadow of a nuisance. I let him keep up for a while, until I saw the last jump. My feet barely touched the ground as I drew off for home. Alas, just before takeoff, the ground came out from under me. I was down, but Oliver flew from me as if he were jumping the hedge himself. He rolled across the turf and lay silent, unable to tend me.

But she did, as always. She hated to be away from me, even when I raced. Her body quaked as she cradled my head in her lap. Her hair caressed my cheek; its softness matched my fiery, sleek coat. Her voice carried me into the warm, welcoming light and through the endless blue sky.

The worn tread of Karen Mulligan's shoes slid and then gripped the pedals. Each push was an effort to propel the bargain-store ten-speed up the western Pennsylvania slope. Elevated above the seat, concentrating her power, Karen managed to shift the bike into an easier gear. The tension in her quadriceps was only temporarily lessened, though, as the road steepened. Heaving, she pushed onward, eyes focused on her friend Mindy York ahead of her.

Mindy appeared unaffected by the effort. Her longer, stronger legs pumped the pedals rhythmically all the way to the top of the hill. Karen caught a glimpse of Mindy's red bandana waving from her neck, as if it were taunting her. *We beat you!* Then her slim form disappeared over the crest of the hill, wavy blond locks mimicking the bandana in the wind.

Relief finally came for Karen as she topped the crest. She relaxed her feet on the pedals, letting the bike carry her down the other side. The warm air of June whizzed past her face, drying some of the sweat and invigorating her. Torrents of air fluttered through her golden-brown hair, despite the heavy application of hair spray. She hoped the hour of blow drying, curling, and teasing would not be in vain. Tasting the salty sweat forming on her upper lip, she wondered how her makeup was faring. She had carefully applied the plum and purple eye shadow, since *Cosmopolitan* proclaimed they were the best hues for green eyes. At the bottom of the hill, Mindy slowed her bike, and her thick hair settled on her shoulders.

"Whew," Karen said as she rode up beside her. "I'm glad we're almost there. I can barely keep up with you!"

"You're doing fine," Mindy said. Her porcelain skin was slightly pink from the air and exercise. "Is this the turn?"

A sign on their right read "North Fork Dam Road."

"Yes, this is it," Karen replied.

The girls made the right and pedaled on. The flatness of this section relieved Karen's aching muscles. The girls breathed the cool, damp air and enjoyed the vista. Welcoming trees shaded the road from both sides. A stony creek bubbled from below the bank to the left. Its passage seemed to cool the whole hollow. There was a steep wooded hillside to the right. Dense leaves gave way to a narrow trail that appeared to go up the hill, and Mindy remarked it was a nice place for a gallop. This area, just outside the city of Johnstown, spoke to Karen's soul. She wouldn't mind riding the four miles from her parents' house. At the age of fifteen, she yearned to escape the doldrums of a dying industrial town.

Serene as this area was, the hills to the east were scarred from the brutal, grinding teeth of machinery. The luscious green canopies of hardwood trees had succumbed to the strip mines, leaving nothing but the dull brown of dirt and stone. Karen marveled at the beauty of this hollow, yet an image of devastation lingered in the folds of her memory. She fought to keep the memory at bay, but acknowledging the loveliness of this area sparked a realization. It reminded her of the precarious balance between nature and industry in this area.

Now, with each casual push on her pedals, she drifted back to a time when she was small enough to hold her father's hand as they walked along a river. Visions of the sun glistening off the dancing current flooded her mind. She remembered being hoisted on her father's shoulders and him pointing across the water to an emerald hillside, where a bald eagle roosted high atop a tree. The twitch of its head and the downward point of its beak remained clear to her, but a strange scraping noise distracted her. Her father quickly placed her on the ground. He wore an expression of confusion and concern. They walked along for some time, the noise growing ever stronger as they went. They stopped when they could see huge clouds of dust sprouting from the hillside, which was bare and nothing like where the eagle had been. She could still recall her father's gasp of disgust as a gigantic tree fell with what sounded like an explosion. The sky immediately erupted with rain, and she was hoisted again upon her father's shoulders. She gripped his forehead as he sprinted to the safety of his Chevy Nova. As she looked at her father from the passenger's seat, despite being very young, Karen knew her father's face was wet not only from the rain.

Karen cringed at the memory and shook off a strange and sudden chill.

"Hello, earth to Karen," Mindy teased. "Where do we turn next?"

Karen snapped from the past and into the promise of the present. "She said it was the first driveway on the left."

Mindy turned into the dirt driveway and descended into the yard. Karen followed but was quickly distracted by a nicker coming from the small stable several yards away. Plagued with clumsiness, she threw herself off balance by quickly turning her head, and her bike hit the uneven ground of the driveway with a hard bump. Startled by the jolting, she slammed on the brakes, sending the bike skidding on its side. Torrents of laughter erupted from both girls as Karen struggled to her feet.

A shabby house trailer sat to the right. The girls saw the front door open, but then their attention immediately focused on the sleek, dark figures bounding toward them. Deep barks announced the girls' arrival. Dobermans were scarce in town, yet the girls were not afraid. The noble beauty of the dogs captivated them. A command from the porch stifled the barking.

"Quiet!"

A woman descended the steps from the house trailer and strode toward the girls. Her aura matched that of her dogs, not the trailer. She was tall, with a lean, muscular build. Her high cheekbones were accentuated by her ponytail of vibrant strawberry blond hair. The tanned skin of her face emphasized her large dark eyes. She was the epitome of hard work and strength. Stable work had sculpted her, rivaling any workout plan.

She looked serious as she approached them. She commanded the dogs to come and sit beside her. She called the larger black male Master and the rust-colored female Aries. They obeyed her commands instantly.

Mindy was still amused by Karen's clumsy fall, but her giggles were stifled as quickly as the dogs' barks. It took just a glare from the woman. Karen's folly was not dismissed either.

"I hope you can ride a horse better than you handle that bike," the woman said. "My name's Ginny. Follow me." With the Dobermans trotting beside her, Ginny headed for the barn.

How did she know I'm the trained rider? Karen wondered. She hadn't described herself over the phone to Ginny, yet the woman had identified her as the one applying for the stable's riding position. She followed close behind Ginny. For once, Mindy lagged behind.

Roles were now reversed. Instead of Karen feeling slow and inadequate compared to Mindy, she felt confident. Having had three years of riding lessons, she yearned for more riding time. She had grown tired of the lazy lesson horses at J. T. Acres, although she appreciated them for teaching her how to ride. Now excitement welled up in her. This situation was almost too good. The stable was close to her house, and Ginny had several horses in training. Karen was willing to do anything to secure a position as Ginny's rider.

The little barn exuded a simple charm. It wasn't painted, and the wood's character gave it a rustic, homey feeling. The blue summer sky met the green mountains that surrounded the little valley. As simple as it seemed, it was heaven to Karen. As they entered the barn, four sets of ears pricked forward. Ginny made introductions.

"This is Cajun. She's a reliable old girl, a quarter horse who I use for lessons." She patted the horse's kind face.

Mindy's bravery returned. "She's a liver chestnut, isn't she?"

"Yes. She isn't the most beautiful mare, and her trot is a bit rough. She's been a saint, sometimes giving two or three lessons a day. I hope you girls work out. It will free me up to look for more clients and hopefully buy more lesson horses."

Ginny moved to the next stall. "Next is Legend. He's a Thoroughbred. I buy them cheap from the racetrack. They need retraining after being racehorses. We try to get them quiet and rideable. Then I sell them as show prospects. I agreed to meet you today because I need a rider. My cousin Mary was helping me with the horses, but now she's going back to school. On top of that, I've been very busy trying to start up a dog grooming business. Also, I have a son." She paused, as if she needed to choose her words carefully. "He's a handful."

Karen detected a softening in Ginny's tone but was more interested in the sleek bay gelding than Ginny's problems. Legend had a bright, intelligent eye, and his expression was soft as he nuzzled Karen's hands. His head was refined and beautiful, highlighted by a large star on his forehead. An intricate system of veins streamed about his head, pronouncing nobility and heart. Karen knew she was gazing upon a horse like none she had known before. Centuries of select breeding had created the ultimate equine. She had always been fascinated by the racing breed when she watched races on television. Gazing at the majestic beast, almost in a trance, she imagined galloping full out in a large field. She studied his long, elegant legs, perfectly engineered to gobble up the miles.

While in her trancelike state, Karen ignored Ginny's furrowed brow and look of impatience. She couldn't ignore the woman's biting tone as she said, "Don't get too attached to that horse. If we train him right, he should bring me a nice profit."

Karen's shoulders tensed. She blinked quickly, refocusing on Ginny and leaving her dream world. She didn't know what to say or how to react. She didn't understand how Ginny could sell such a beautiful horse. Mindy didn't have a problem asking the question Karen couldn't voice.

"How can you sell them?" Mindy's eyes were lit with outrage, emphasized by her blue eye shadow and liner.

"I can't afford to keep them all," Ginny stated. She looked at the two girls, and her tone softened. "Besides, the more horses I sell, the more I can rescue from the track. Bad things happen to them when they don't run well. You know?"

The girls didn't know. They looked at each other in confusion and concern. Ginny walked on to the next stall. Inside, an emaciated steel-gray horse flattened his ears. He swished his tail and tossed his head, as if to say, "Stay away, I don't trust you."

"This is Dorian," Ginny said. "You have to keep your eye on him. He's been mistreated, and he sometimes bites. I don't know if he'll ever trust people again. My old trainer bought him out of some race tracker's field. He felt sorry for the horse. He thought they were trying to starve him to death. He's a big project."

A worthy one, Karen thought. Despite his bony appearance and sour attitude, the gray sported a fine dished head. It was reminiscent of his Arabian ancestors, who were foundation stock for the Thoroughbred breed. He stood over a lot of ground, and his head was only about a foot from the ceiling.

"Let's get down to business," Ginny said, continuing on to the next stall. "Karen, this filly will test your riding skills."

She nodded toward a small rose gray. The filly put her head over the stall door, allowing Karen to rub her face. Then, as if to say, "Hurry up, let me out of here," she pawed at the door, banging her hoof against the bottom of it.

"This is Dawn," Ginny said. "She's two years old and only green broke. I don't know how her owner ended up with her. Kirsten is a beginner and barely able to ride Cajun. I wouldn't have recommended this pairing, but it is a boarder for me. I need this filly to be trained so that Kirsten can handle her." She looked at Karen. "We don't have much time. Kirsten's parents aren't going to pay for her much longer if their daughter can't ride her. Let's get her saddled."

Karen snapped to at the direct order. She led Dawn from the stall and placed Ginny's old Stubben saddle on the filly's back. Dawn wiggled under its weight, prompting Ginny to hold her head steady. Karen tightened the girth slowly, giving Dawn a chance to get used to it. She took the bridle from Ginny and gently opened the filly's mouth by putting a thumb into the interdental space of her mouth. Again the filly tossed her head as the cool steel was pulled over her tongue. Karen checked the bridle for fit and shortened the cheek pieces.

"She has such a petite head. Is she an Arabian?" Karen asked Ginny.

"That's part of her problem," Ginny said dryly.

With Dawn tacked correctly, Karen stood tall and squared her shoulders. She grasped the near rein and led the filly into the riding ring. Ginny followed, bending over to pick up stray rocks that sprawled around the entire arena. Traditional footing was nonexistent, not even the barely passable sawdust that cushioned the arena of J. T. Acres. Ginny's riding ring was lined with nothing more than the dirt and stone of a once green Pennsylvania meadow.

Karen stood Dawn beside a mounting block. Ginny held the filly's bridle as Karen mounted. Dawn skirted sideways as she felt the rider's weight. Karen spoke softly and gave the filly a reassuring pat and then took hold of the reins.

"You better shorten your reins a bit," Ginny said as she walked to the center of the ring, Mindy beside her. "She needs to feel you're there. It's good to be easy on her mouth, but be ready to steady her if she spooks."

Dawn pranced off nervously. Karen sat quietly, unruffled by the show of nerves. Any slight noise or movement distracted the filly, causing her to lift her head and gawk in its direction. Karen made give and take movements with the reins to reposition Dawn's head. This helped to refocus her as she trotted around the ring. Karen posted with the rhythm and drove the filly forward with confidence. Dawn trotted willingly at first, but tension built again in her small frame. She began to rush around the ring's perimeter.

"If she gets too quick, steady her and do some figure eights and serpentines," Ginny said.

The technique worked. Dawn began to lower her head and round her back, signs of relaxation and submission. After twenty minutes, Ginny suggested they stop on a good note. "Relax your reins and let her walk around twice."

Karen took a deep breath and smiled at Mindy as Dawn slowed to a walk. Mindy gave her a thumbs up. *Surely Ginny will ask me back*, Karen thought.

To the left of the ring, the Dobermans lay stretched out in the sun. Karen admired their athletic bodies and obedient demeanor. Yet in an instant, they leaped up, ears pricked and eyes fixed on the house trailer door. Dawn sensed their tension, flicking an ear toward them and snorting softly. Karen wasn't concerned. She gripped Dawn's sides lightly, reminding her that she was there.

Suddenly, the trailer door was flung open, banging against the outside wall with a terrible clatter. Karen had no time to see who came out, as Dawn wheeled and bolted away from the racket. Karen reeled in the reins and pulled back, bracing against the unwanted motion. Behind her, she could hear boots pounding on the trailer's deck. Glancing at Ginny, she saw her eyes widen as she started toward the trailer.

"Brad! Don't you dare!" Ginny yelled to a skinny sandy-haired boy. He ran behind the trailer. The Dobermans trotted after Ginny's son, seeming intent on getting his attention. Reaching the end of the trailer, they peered around the corner. In the next instant, they cowered to the ground as a loud engine roared.

A dirt bike exploded from behind the trailer and raced through the yard, tearing toward the riding ring. Dawn had just started to pull up, but this new onslaught of noise was too much. Seeing the roaring metal beast careening past her, the filly bolted again. Karen was no comfort to her now. She just wanted to flee, and Karen was holding her back. Dawn flung her head down between her knees, bucking wildly. Karen gulped for air as her heart jumped to her throat. She must stay on. She braced her feet against the metal stirrups, allowing her torso to lean against the movement. She planted her seat in the saddle and pulled firmly on the reins. Dawn continued around the ring at a torrid clip,

Karen bouncing and struggling to center herself in the saddle. Finally, the filly tired, and Karen was able to pull her up.

Ginny stared at Karen in disbelief, and then her attractive face tightened with anger. She whipped around toward the perpetrator, her fists clenched. The faithful Dobermans stood at attention and watched her as she started toward the edge of the ring. Past the ring, the dirt bike spun to a stop. Its rider peered from beneath his helmet's rim, admiring his dirty work.

"Wow, you sure look scared!" he called to Karen.

Karen was still catching her breath and tried to stay upright on her shaking legs as she dismounted.

Mindy, on the other hand, could talk just fine. "You little turd, are you trying to kill someone?"

Ginny kept walking toward her son. With each step, her fists relaxed and her gaze softened. The corners of her mouth relaxed into a pout. By the time she reached him, it seemed like she was the child, trying to plead her case to an uncompromising parent. Even her voice was meek as she spoke.

"Brad, I asked you to wait until we were done with the horses. You could get someone hurt."

"She stayed on pretty good. You wanted to test her anyway." He picked at a hole in his faded jeans where his bony knee protruded.

Karen and Mindy's jaws dropped at the same time. They were speechless.

"I'll take that bike from you," Ginny said, her voice stronger. "You'll have to ride a horse. Maybe you'll learn to respect them then."

"Ha, I'd like to see that happen. Hey, Mom, welcome to 1986! Who wants to ride a nag when you can have one of these?"

With that he yanked the steering wheel around and drove off, the dirt bike screaming as he disappeared into the distance.

Karen watched as Ginny inhaled deeply. Her shoulders drooped, and her hands hung limp at her sides. A few seconds passed with Karen holding Dawn, who stood quietly chewing the bit, and Mindy looking between Ginny and the trail of dust settling in Brad's wake. Suddenly, Ginny's back straightened and she pivoted toward them with military precision. She looked past the girls to the barn door and gestured for them to follow her.

"At least he won't be bothering us for a while," she said as she walked to the barn. "Since his dad left, he's been nuts. He just needs to blow off some steam." She waved Karen and Dawn into the filly's stall. "Mindy, will you get a bucket of cold water? We need to sponge this horse off. You have to get it from the creek. My uncle built this barn bare bones for me. I haven't been able to put in the water line yet."

Karen saw the look of bewilderment on Mindy's face and was surprised when Mindy picked up a bucket and went off to fetch the water. She had expected at least a complaint. When Mindy returned with the bucket, she took the tack from Ginny and returned it to the tack room. Karen and Ginny tended to Dawn. The filly was none worse for wear. Comfortable in her stall, she munched hay as if nothing had happened.

When they were done with Dawn, the girls and Ginny stood at the back door of the barn, facing away from the house trailer. The hollow was at peace again. Birds chirped in the surrounding trees and a light breeze filtered through the tall grasses. An unfinished wooden fence extended away from the barn along the left bank. Above, North Fork Dam Road ran parallel to the fence. Karen thought the area looked as though Ginny had started a turnout paddock.

"I guess I'll show you the rest of the place," Ginny said. She looked at Karen with approval and added, "By the way you can ride for me all day, every day."

Karen's heart swelled with pride, and her soul soared. This was a dream come true.

"You'll start with Dawn and Legend," Ginny continued. "Dorian is still very tough, so you better not try him yet. Many people can't handle Thoroughbreds, so Legend will give you an introduction to their nuances. If you can handle him, we'll see about you riding Dorian."

"Thanks for the opportunity!" Karen said.

"Don't thank me yet. I expect a lot of work from you. You'll have to help with stalls and feed sometimes if I'm busy in the shop. We have to finish this fence so the horses can be turned out here." She nodded toward the meadow.

"No problem." Karen paused. She met Ginny's eyes and glanced at Mindy, silently asking if she could ride too.

"Oh, yeah." Ginny turned to Mindy. "You seem helpful too." She patted the girl on the back. "Come help and you can take Cajun on the trails. It will be good for Legend and Dawn to go with a quiet horse."

"That's music to my ears," Mindy said. "This ring stuff gets boring anyway."

Ginny continued the tour, following the bubbling creek that had welcomed the girls into the hollow. As they walked, the tension melted away from Karen's shoulders. She forgot about Brad and her harrowing ride. She breathed the freshness of the leaves, nurtured by the moist air rising from the creek. It meandered and twisted toward and then away from the road, but maintained a parallel course with it. The future grazing paddock took up about an acre and ended at a thickly wooded area. A concrete bridge traversed the creek and beyond it, a lane cut through the woods, going east. It met with the Somerset Pike, which the girls had taken from Johnstown.

This side of the property had a different feel, Karen noted as she stepped off the bridge. A palpable chill crept over her. It moved slowly across her face and enveloped her entire body. Involuntarily, she shuddered. On her right, something large caught her attention. Almost lost in the shade of the surrounding oak trees was an old manor house. There was a strange presence about the house. The closer they got to it, the colder Karen felt. She lagged behind Ginny and Mindy as a sense of dread washed over her, striking at her core. The hair on her arms stood straight up. Everything in her told her to turn and run.

Mindy and Ginny stopped close to the house, staring at it, but Karen remained on the rutted gravel driveway that led to the house. It circled around the remains of a large fountain. In more fortunate times, it must have welcomed the owner with the exuberance of rising and cascading water. Now its crumbling stones formed a barrier at the front door.

Karen had no desire to cross the barrier. The manor's state of disrepair projected a sense of foreboding. Window frames were windowless from the first to the third floor. They revealed peeling, decrepit walls inside. Yet remnants of the house's former grandeur remained. Even from where she stood, Karen could see an ornate fireplace with a large chimney in one of the front rooms on the first floor. Her gaze rose to the third floor room to the left of the chimney. Its black, scorched walls made her heart skip a beat. She couldn't fight the urge to leave anymore. As if stepping out of a bog, she forced her feet to move and started walking backward. The sound of her feet scuffing the gravel caused Ginny and Mindy to spin around.

"What are you doing?" Mindy asked. "You look like you've seen a ghost."

"Don't you feel that?" Karen's voice shook.

"Feel what? It's a beautiful day."

"That chill," Karen replied.

"Don't let this place scare you," Ginny said. "It needs a lot of work, but everything's fine. Man, I hope the locals don't get in your head. You'll never want to cross the bridge again."

This did not comfort Karen. "What do you mean?" she asked, although she really didn't want to know. Like a nervous horse, she just wanted to return to the barn.

"Come on," Ginny said, sounding amused. "The ghost stories aren't real. Do you think I'd put my dog grooming shop in here if it was haunted?" She nodded toward the right corner of the first floor. A modern door of dark wood with stained glass in the middle stood in a side entrance to the house. Above it hung a mahogany sign with the words "Delightful Dog Grooming" etched in black. "The shop is almost ready to go. I'm going all in. With the amount of advertising I'm going to do, I have to be successful. In time I'll have this place looking brand new. If there are ghosts, the Opies will want to come back here for sure!"

"Who are the Opies?" the girls asked simultaneously.

"Only one of the richest families in Johnstown. Old man Opie helped found Bethlehem Steel. This town wouldn't be the same without the mills."

Again, tightness gripped Karen's chest, this time from real-life anxiety. She thought of her cousin Jessica and how her father had been laid off from the steel mills. Jessica was unable to go to the movies or hang out at the mall anymore. Her family had to save every penny to make ends meet.

"It looks like the Opie house went the way of the mills," Karen said.

"I don't know what happened to this place," Ginny said. "Rumor has it that old man Opie and his daughter lived here. Years ago, a fire broke out in the house. Opie and his daughter disappeared without a trace. Most everyone believed they died in the fire, but their bodies weren't found. The mystery surrounding their disappearance was very controversial. There were so many conspiracy theories that the family name became scarred. Supposedly, no one showed up to claim the estate, and the state put this place up for auction. Only me and one other man showed up for the sale. I narrowly outbid him, and the Opies' misfortune turned me into a property owner." Ginny was clearly proud of her bargain purchase.

"That's great," Karen said, "but if it's okay with you, I'd rather spend my time across the creek and in the barn."

"Okay, scaredy-cat, let's get going," Mindy said.

They started back, not noticing the flit of a pink sleeve in the glassless window of the charred room on the third floor. The fleeting sun caught the green of a dangling emerald, but then it disappeared into the shadows as the sunlight shifted west.

Karen gladly led the way, the icy sensation pushing her over the bridge. Upon stepping on solid ground on the other side, her tingles melted away. The tension left her chest, and she breathed easily. The nickering horses greeted her inside the barn. Now her body tingled with excitement. *My little piece of heaven*, she thought. *I'm going to treat these horses like my own.*

As she and Mindy rode home, Karen decided to invite her cousin Jessica out to the barn. It would be a nice escape from reality for her. It costs nothing, just some sweat and pedaling.

The girls bounded into Karen's house with such exuberance, it was obvious Karen's mother thought something was wrong. To the contrary, the teens greeted Colleen as warmly as Karen's cockapoo/beagle mix greeted them. Karen's normal teenaged angst had retreated, and she told her mother about their adventure. Tucking her chin length reddish-brown hair behind her ears, Colleen abandoned her kitchen work to listen intently. Tim, Karen's father, also discarded his book in the living room and joined them in the kitchen. Karen finished the story by telling her parents she could ride for free anytime. Colleen smiled and congratulated her daughter. As she looked into her mother's blue eyes, Karen was struck by memories of her Irish grandmother. When her grandmother Meg was alive, her stories had kept Karen, her athletic brother Scott, and their many cousins captivated.

"Great," Tim said. "It's by the North Fork Dam, and as long as the golf course is there, the developers will keep away. You'll have plenty of riding area. That's one part of town that hasn't been razed."

His gray eyes clouded, and Karen knew he was remembering the destruction they had seen that day along the river. Her enthusiasm waned with the echo of those monstrous machines in her mind.

"You should see it, Dad," she said. "It's beautiful."

But her English teacher father had already buried his nose back into his book.

Karen snapped back into jubilance. "Mom, I hope we have goo goo cluster ice cream. It's time to celebrate." She flung open the freezer and crowed triumphantly at the sight of the carton of Galliker's ice cream. "Can I have the video card?"

"All right, all right," Colleen said. "I can't keep up with you." She got the rental card from her purse.

Karen and Mindy went to bed with stomachs full of chocolate, caramel, marshmallows, and peanuts and the ridiculous images of evil tomatoes from the movie *Attack of the Killer Tomatoes* adding fuel to their natural giddiness. Yet as Mindy slept soundly, Karen tossed and turned all night.

The mythical white oak stood in solitude atop the bare hillside. Fanning its dense branches upward and outward toward the heavens, it beckoned the buck and doe, the woodland squirrels, and the eagle to its haven. The hillside rumbled under the obscene encroaching machinery. Noxious fumes choked the air and the remnants of the surrounding trees crunched under huge tires. The deer spooked and galloped away, and the squirrels scattered wildly. The eagle clung to the oak's upper bough, staring into the black smoke until it scorched his lungs. With a sharp cry he soared away, leaving his screams in the wind.

Two braves approached the oak. Using a magical chant, they evoked a cloud of warm mist. In tandem they spun their arms like windmills, pushing the mist around the oak to form a protective shroud. They tiptoed amongst the enormous roots and found a particularly large one to kneel against. The ground shook around them, and a dark, hulking form ripped the misty cover. The braves sat facing each other. They held their hands out to each other and pressed their palms together. With eyes closed in concentration, they chanted to the heavens. The mist thickened around the oak as the sky blackened. Lightning cracked overhead, streaking the braves' long black hair with static. The wicked engine pierced the envelope of mist. The braves stayed in intense meditation until the giant root cracked under the weight of a tire as tall as a man. Finally, their coal black eyes met in sorrow, and they fled.

The iron sides of the machine opened, releasing something much smaller but even more sinister. Steel-toe work boots stomped through the mist. A horrible buzz cut into the oak's base on the uphill side, joined by another saw on the downhill side. The oak shuddered in rage, sending a gigantic branch to the earth and crushing the first saw into shrapnel. The remaining saw tore onward until a sea of pebbles slithered under the leather work boots. The boots slipped on that angry sea, and with the saw they plummeted down the hillside to be engulfed by the swirling rapids of the river below. Its whitewater smashed the saw against the boulders of the river bed.

Yet, like an insidious cancer, the boots returned, always bringing a freshly sharpened blade with them. The white oak dropped all of its branches through the fight, until finally it crashed to the ground in submission.

Karen's pounding heart wakened her as deafening thunder roared.

CHAPTER 2

Unlikely Hero

Birds chirped joyfully with the rising sun. Opening the grain bin, Karen smiled as four sets of pricked ears swiveled toward her. The horses' excited nickers rose with the aroma of molasses, enveloping her in warmth. Mindy opened the stall doors one by one as Karen dumped the grain into feed tubs. Muzzles plunged into Karen's buckets, stealing bites before the grain reached the tubs in the corners of the stalls.

"C'mon, you silly boy, you can eat easier out of your tub." Karen pushed Legend's shoulder, reminding him to give her space. "Eat up. We're going to ride out today."

"Finally, I'm going to let Cajun stretch her legs," Mindy said.

Karen's heart fluttered as she gazed at Legend's sleek frame and noted his soft eyes, blinking in delight as he rummaged through his feed. He picked out the molasses-clumped oats first, devouring them with a nod of his head. He proceeded to the corn, breaking its hard exterior methodically. Karen smiled at the gelding's particular eating routine. Noticing his half-empty water bucket, she frowned.

"We better get the watering done first," she said.

"Oh, man, I was afraid you were going to say that," Mindy said.

The girls grabbed two buckets each and headed toward the creek. The morning dew dampened their sneakers and the grass squeaked under their feet. They approached the worn path that led down the bank to the creek bed. Karen paused to study their "standing stones." These were two flat stones about a foot apart. The spacing provided a good base of support for scooping the five-gallon buckets into the moving water.

However, thanks to the previous night's rain, the rocks were almost entirely underwater.

"Not much standing room there," she said as she started gingerly down the muddy bank.

The words had barely escaped her mouth when she heard buckets rattling along the stony bank behind her. Mindy was sliding on her rear end, her feet digging into the mud in vain as she tried to stop.

"Whoa!" Karen skirted out of the way just in time, almost falling herself as she jumped to the side.

Mindy thrust one leg out, aiming for a boulder sitting at the edge of the creek. Her foot connected with its solid side and she braced herself, stopping just short of the water's edge.

Karen erupted into laughter. "I'm not the only klutz around here!"

She helped her friend up. The two brushed Mindy's bottom, hoping to remove the mud. They quickly realized there was no point, and the denim remained smeared with a souvenir from the North Fork Creek.

Valiantly, Mindy had held onto her buckets. The girls collected them and prepared to venture onto the standing stones. Karen stepped onto the nearest, planting her foot in the center. Precision was a must for her next step. She studied the second stone; only a small dry spot remained at the top. She lifted her right leg, pointed her toes at the evasive target, and stepped. Her aim was true. She pivoted lightly and faced downstream. She dunked her buckets into the lively current, filling them in no time. She heaved them one at a time over to Mindy, who stood almost as precariously at the creek's edge. Mindy handed the other two buckets to Karen and the cycle continued. Just as Mindy placed the fourth bucket down, they heard the jingle of dog tags. The girls looked up the bank and saw the muscular form of Master standing at the top of the bank. His eyes brightened with recognition of the girls. He lowered his head and trotted down the path toward them. Although just a stub, his tail wiggled with happiness.

Mindy greeted him with enthusiastic pats. "Hi, boy. You didn't have any trouble getting down here." The noble dog sat beside her, enjoying the attention.

"I guess four legs are better than two," Karen said.

She prepared to join Mindy at the creek's edge, but Master whipped his head around and leaped to his feet, staring up the bank. In a flurry, the female Doberman, Aries, ran down the bank. Karen smiled and prepared to greet the other dog, but her eyes widened with apprehension as she saw a third figure racing down the path. Brad hurtled full speed at Mindy, the devil alive in his hazel eyes. Karen knew what was coming but was helpless to stop it. Brad's outstretched hands connected with Mindy's torso. The pencil-thin girl stood no chance, and she crashed into the creek with so much force, she ended up toward its center. This was fortunate, as the running current cushioned her. Her braced hands barely saved her head from hitting the unforgiving rocks of the creek bed. She pulled herself from the bubbling water and held up her hands muddy in disgust.

Karen eyed Brad with contempt. She remembered his sneering expression from the episode with the dirt bike. Now he was on foot, just like her. She leaped from the stepping stones and surprised herself by landing solidly on the bank. She glared at Brad. He only laughed and ran up the bank. Karen dug in and chased him, but her moment of brilliant coordination was short-lived. She slipped and fell face first onto the bank. Exasperated, she lay there, head lowered in defeat. Master and Aries crowded around her, licking her face in consolation. Brad was long gone.

Mindy hauled herself out of the creek and helped Karen to her feet. The girls looked at other in amazement as Karen asked how that little twerp could get the best of them every time.

Mindy shook her head. "At least we're both a mess."

The girls collected the water buckets and continued with the morning chores. The summer sun was rising, and its welcome warmth dried their clothes. Cleaning stalls and dumping wheelbarrows drove off the creek's chill. The busy morning forced the girls to forget about Brad and his antics. It was time to ride.

Armed with two weeks of ring work with Legend, Karen was confident about riding him in the woods. She was officially in love with Thoroughbreds. Unlike Dawn, who remained skittish, Legend was brave. He never turned a hair when Brad roared past the ring on his dirt bike, and she was amazed at his composure. Legend lived up to all the tales Karen had read about his breed, the stories of the incredible heart and drive of the great racehorses of the past. Legend was Karen's idol. He seemed tuned in to every thought or movement she made. The slightest touch elicited a response. With barely a tickle to his sides, he powered forward, covering the ground like a finely tuned machine. He crossed the ring in no time, and even at a trot she felt like she was floating. He never tired, always holding his head high with his neck bowed, barely sweating during the warmest days. His ears constantly flicked back and forth, waiting for her next cue. Karen loved and appreciated the gentle lesson horses of J. T. Acres, but this was a whole other animal. She felt magical when she rode this horse, who could only be compared to the fictional the Black, the amazing stallion in the book *The Black Stallion*.

Legend and Cajun were almost tacked when Ginny walked into the barn. "What happened to you?" she asked when she saw the girls' dirty jeans and flat hair.

"Your son is what happened to us!" Karen said.

"Oh, come on. Are you kidding?"

Reluctant to complain about Brad to his mother, Karen chose her words carefully as she told Ginny about Brad's prank.

"Sorry." Ginny paused. "Don't worry. He's going with his dad for a few days. " Changing the subject, she said, "So, you're ready to trail ride Legend. Karen, you'll have to keep a hold of him. Mary has been galloping him back there, but I want him to settle down. He needs to learn to relax, walk most of the ride. We really need to get the racehorse out of him to sell him. You'll probably be in front, because he walks faster than Cajun, but if he gets nervous, try to keep beside her or even behind her. Her presence should help calm him."

Karen acknowledged Ginny's instructions. Grudgingly, the girls donned hard hats at Ginny's insistence.

"I guess it really doesn't matter," Karen said. "My hair is ruined anyway."

Ginny stood by as the girls mounted, and then had once more comment before they left.

"By the way, the neighbors reported a strange guy walking through their yards. They saw him yesterday and a few other days. He hasn't done anything wrong, but just be cautious. The phone in the barn works now. I have to go take care of some business, but call the police if you see anything suspicious. I'm going to tie the dogs, but you can let them loose after your ride. No one will trespass here with two Dobermans patrolling."

"Okay," Karen and Mindy answered in unison.

Legend strode up the driveway and crossed the road enthusiastically. Relishing his smooth, powerful strides, Karen breathed deeply of the fresh air. They entered the woods across the road, following the trail up the hillside. The Thoroughbred snorted, lowering his head against the light hold Karen had on the reins. She surveyed the darkened peace of the forest. A light breeze whispered through waving branches. As they wound upward through the woods, the noise of the road faded. Karen turned and looked back at Cajun and Mindy.

"Isn't this great?" she asked.

"Really cool," Mindy replied. "I don't have to push Cajun like I do in the ring."

Karen smiled. "What a good old girl."

After a prolonged climb, the trail made a gradual left turn and leveled off. Legend tossed his head and started to prance, his legs springing under him. He arched his neck and braced against her hands.

"Easy, boy, steady now." She tightened the reins and leaned back. Squeezing her seat bones and releasing the pressure on the reins, she asked the horse for a half halt. Legend did not respond as easily as he did in the ring. It took several attempts for him to relax into a walk.

Karen turned to Mindy; she and Cajun had fallen several yards behind. "This must be where Mary lets him run. He definitely wants to go."

"Hold on, I'll try to get beside you." Mindy urged a reluctant Cajun along Legend's near side. She grabbed Karen's left rein, steadying the anxious gelding against Cajun's solid frame. The pair continued in tandem along the ridge, and Legend slowly relaxed.

"Nice move," Karen said to Mindy.

"I saw it on TV. Before the races they lead the Thoroughbred and jockey from a calm horse. It seems to keep the Thoroughbred from getting too excited before they race."

After two miles, the trail descended toward the road. It became difficult for the horses to walk side by side. Mindy allowed Cajun to fall behind Legend. Aware of the change in terrain, Legend lowered his head and the gentle snorting started again. He picked his way among the rocks that littered the path. With ears angled sideways and back in concentration, he never stumbled. Karen gave him his head, sensing the anxiety had left his body. He was so relaxed he didn't falter as they came upon a ragged tent pitched along the path. Cajun turned a suspicious eye toward the shelter, but the steady old mare kept her course too.

The front flaps open, the tent was dark inside, revealing only a sleeping bag spread on the ground. A circle of stones in front of the tent formed a fire pit. It was lined with charred wood and ash and a faint odor of smoke lingered in the air. Sharpened sticks leaned against the stones.

"Maybe there is a vagabond around here," Mindy said.

A shudder ran up Karen's spine. "Let's not stick around to find out."

Their muted hoof beats turned to distinctive clip-clops as the trail merged with North Fork Dam Road. The girls headed east toward the barn. Legend lowered his head even more. He seemed to enjoy the rhythmic clang of his hooves on the pavement. His ears flicked forward and back as his head bobbed with each stride. Occasionally cars passed. Some slowed in consideration of the horses; others whizzed by as if they didn't exist. Either way, Legend was unbothered by them. He just strode on, at times causing Cajun to trot to keep up.

As they turned into Ginny's driveway, Master and Aries greeted them with excited barks. They strained to the limits of their chains, eyeing the horses and riders intensely.

"Hold on, guys," Karen said. "We'll untie you soon."

In the barn, they tied the horses in the aisle, Legend toward the front and Cajun a few yards behind. As they untacked, Karen ran her hand over Legend's back. A slight dampness traced where the saddle had been. His coat was dry other than that.

"Wow, buddy, you barely turned a hair in this heat. I think you'll be okay while I let the dogs loose. Can you keep an eye on him, Mindy?"

Suddenly, the Dobermans erupted into aggressive barking. Karen's heart rate quickened and her body tensed. With apprehension, she walked toward the heavy rolling barn door. Slowly she pushed it aside, peering out at the doghouses. Her breath caught in her throat as she came face to face with a bearded man. He smelled worse than the school gym after a volley ball game. His eyes were as wild as his beard, staring out under heavy brows. As he rushed toward her, Karen clung desperately to the door handle, trying to push back against him, but he was too strong. Rabid barking roared through the hollow. He flung the door open and stalked toward her, a stout branch in his hand. Karen yearned for the last five minutes back. Why hadn't she freed the dogs immediately?

Terror roared through her body, causing her to tremble and hyperventilate. She backed away, hands up, unsure of what to do. The man raised the branch over his shoulder like a baseball bat, his eyes squinting with anger. Legend snorted and pawed nervously, tossing his head against the restraint of the cross ties.

"Give me the keys to that bike!" the man growled, motioning to the house trailer.

Karen was almost at Legend's shoulder now, her body shaking. Breathless, she could barely speak.

"I don't know where they are," she managed to say.

"Well, you better find them!" the man shouted. He swung the branch and Karen scooted back, narrowly avoiding the impact. The branch slammed into the thousand-pound frame of Legend, who sprang into action.

Legend reared high, breaking the chain and bumping Karen to the side with his shoulder. He lunged toward the man, who scrambled away, dropping the branch, his eyes wide in shock. With ears pinned, Legend lunged again, knocking the vagrant down. He slammed his head on the dirt floor. Legend galloped past, barely missing his body with stampeding hooves. Karen staggered to her feet, watching Legend's flagged tail as he raced out into the ring.

The man lay motionless on the barn floor, and the ground under his head was red with blood. She forced herself to take a step closer. His chest rose and fell; he wasn't dead. The phone was at the front of the barn, so she'd have to walk past him to call for help. Every muscle in her body tensed as she shifted her weight to take another step. An agonized groan escaped from the man. Karen jumped back, ready to run. Suddenly, Mindy's slim form whizzed past her. Like an Amazon warrior, she held a pitchfork like a spear. She thrust it at the man's throat, stopping only inches from his skin.

"Don't move!" she screamed.

Her shrill voice snapped Karen from her state of fear. Eyeing a shovel along the wall, she grabbed it and rushed at the man. He was surrounded by a shovel on one side and a pitchfork on the other. Adrenaline coursed through Karen, and she started to tremble. For the first time since the man appeared, she and Mindy looked at each other, wide eyed and open mouthed, identical expressions on their faces that said, *"Now What?"*

They both jumped when a man spoke from behind them. "It's okay, girls, I'll take it from here."

Both girls looked slowly over their shoulders, keeping their weapons fixed on the vagabond. A tall man approached, carrying a shotgun over his shoulder. His striking icy blue eyes peered intensely from under his ball cap. Striving to achieve the man's height, a boy their age matched the man stride for stride.

Another moan escaped from the vagabond. He moved his arm as if trying to push up from the ground. The icy eyed man strode forward, aiming the gun at the struggling man's head.

"Hold it right there! I'll use this, so help me God!" the armed man said. "Shane, there's a phone over there. Call the police."

The boy ran back to the door and picked up the barn phone.

The man turned to Karen and Mindy. "Girls, go ahead and back away. You don't need to be near this guy."

Karen nodded at Mindy and exhaled. Locking her eyes on the now still form on the ground, she backed away to the unrattled Cajun. The old mare stood half asleep in the second set of cross ties. Mindy stroked the mare's shiny coat from the opposite side.

A quiet voice startled Karen. "Don't worry. The cops will be here soon."

She jerked her head around, meeting a second set of icy blue eyes. The teenaged boy was at her left shoulder. He looked down at the ground as he continued. "We've seen this guy lurking around. We knew he was trouble." He scuffed the ground with a work boot, sending dust over the bottom of his blue jeans.

His father agreed, still facing away from the teens with the shotgun trained on the man. "I knew this guy would try something like this. He was sneaking around my shed the other night. Shane has a few four-wheelers, and it looked like this creep was eyeing them. He got away from me then, but I knew he was still around. Those Dobermans are good watch dogs, but they can't do much tied up. I knew something was going down by the way they were barking. We live on the other side of the hollow, on North Fork Country Club Road, second house on the left. My name's Jack, and like I said my son's name is Shane."

"Thank you, sir," Karen said. "I don't know what would have happened if you hadn't shown up."

Karen spoke to Jack, yet her eyes were on Shane. He placed his hands on his hips, squaring his well-developed shoulders. His thin blue T-shirt revealed lean but toned biceps and a slim waist. His legs were long and thin. He caught her looking, and embarrassed, she looked down at the ground. Yet she noticed the attractive contrast between his thick dark brown hair and tanned skin and bright blue eyes.

Jack spoke again, grabbing Karen's attention. "How in the world did the two of you take this guy down?"

"Legend!" She had forgotten about the horse. She ran past the men and looked into the ring. The Thoroughbred was scouring the ground for scattered tufts of grass. "Oh, thank God, he's okay. The horse is the real hero." She told Jack and Shane how Legend had broken free and knocked the man down.

"He knew what he'd done," Mindy said. "You should have seen him prance around out there afterwards. He was so proud of himself!"

"I don't know about that," Jack said, "but this guy is going to have a hell of a headache." The vagabond's eyes were glazed. He was still breathing, but had stopped trying to stand.

Master and Aries announced the arrival of the police. The whine of an ambulance followed shortly behind them. The police secured the vagabond and allowed the paramedics to tend to him. Officers took statements from the girls and Jack and Shane. Karen stood with an officer in the center of the ring, Legend at her side, as the paramedics carried the vagrant out on a stretcher. Blood smeared his face, obscuring his eyes and any expression. An intense sense of pity came over Karen. She wondered what had happened in this man's life to put him in such a place.

Suddenly, the man lifted his head and scowled at her. "Opie! Opie! You're a no-good Opie!"

The policeman looked at her in concern. "Is your last name Opie? Do you know this man?"

"No, no," Karen stuttered. "I think the Opies owned this place before my instructor did. That's all I know."

Terrified that he thought she was an Opie, she started after the stretcher. "Hey! I'm no Opie. I have nothing to do with them."

The policeman grabbed her arm. "Please don't go near him."

Karen called to the vagabond once more, telling him she wasn't an Opie. As the medics lifted the stretcher into the ambulance, she heard the man say, "Opie, Opie, Opie!"

They were not allowed to enter the barn as the police investigated the crime scene. After putting Cajun in her stall, Mindy joined Karen in the ring. They looked after Legend as the police finished their work. Shane and Jack approached the girls.

"You girls did good," Jack said. "Sorry we had to meet under these circumstances, but if you ever need anything, you know where we live."

"Here's our number." Shane handed Karen a wrinkled piece of paper. It looked like a part of a feed bag.

"I like that, recycling at work," she said, teasing. He half smiled and nodded.

Just then, Ginny's 1970's baby-blue Cadillac sped into the driveway. It slid on the gravel as she slammed on the brakes.

"I wish you hadn't called her," Mindy said to Karen. "She is going to flip out."

"That's our cue to leave," Jack said.

Jack and Shane hustled past the barn and disappeared over the bridge. Ginny stormed past the girls. "What is going on?" She didn't wait for an answer as she continued toward the barn. A policeman tried to calm her at the entrance.

"We've been ignoring our guards, "Karen said to Mindy. The girls went to Master and Aries, showering the dogs with pats and praise. Being beside the large dogs comforted Karen as she struggled to get the sound of vagabond wailing about the Opies out of her head.

"I'll never keep you tied again." She hugged Master's broad shoulders and stroked Aries. She only wished the Dobermans could be by her bed and protect her from her dreams.

CHAPTER 3

Sisters and an Irish Man

An August dawn burned away the fog of a humid night. Karen jumped out of her parents' Pontiac LeMans, leaving Mindy to bid Colleen goodbye for the day. Butterflies turned Karen's stomach as she approached Legend's stall. He greeted her with a gentle nudge from his fine head. She took a deep breath, and her stomach settled as his velvety nose touched her skin.

She rubbed his forehead. "Are you ready, boy? It's your first horse show."

Mindy dragged herself into the barn, shoulders slumped, eyes squinting. "You've got to be crazy. We got up at six in the morning for you to go prancing around trying to win a dumb ribbon. Ginny's not even up yet."

"There's more to it than prancing around for a ribbon. Horse shows test the rider's skills and the horse's manners. You find out whether all the training you've done with them has worked or not. Besides, we have to give him a bath, feed him, and let him digest for an hour before we leave. C'mon, you like watching horse shows. The saddle club show has always been the highlight of our summer. I'm so glad I get to actually participate." She elbowed Mindy playfully in the ribs.

"Ouch. Come on. I'm half dead as it is." Still, Mindy managed a crooked smile.

Karen led Legend through the ring toward Ginny's house trailer. The only running water came from a spigot behind it. Mindy followed with a bucket, sponge, and soap. The girls continued through Ginny's large yard. Mindy said, "Now I understand why we get water from the creek. It takes forever to walk up here."

"I'll sure be glad when Ginny gets that water line installed." Karen said.

To the right, Karen noticed Ginny's rusty horse trailer hiding among thick weeds. "You'll be out of hibernation soon, old trailer," she said.

Mindy grunted a half-hearted giggle.

They found the water spigot with attached hose behind the house trailer. Karen cringed as the facet squeaked to life.

"Let's hurry and keep it down. Brad's in there somewhere. I don't want to wake the beast," Karen whispered.

"Too late for that!" Brad flung open his bedroom window. Normally an abrupt movement and noise would startle a horse, but Legend simply cocked an ear and stomped the ground with his hind leg in annoyance.

Karen glared at the young face peering out the window. Brad's hair sprang from his head in all directions, like a burst of sand blown by a gust of wind. His hazel eyes gleamed with mischief, and Karen braced herself as she saw him raise his hand. He banged on the window frame, staring at Legend, waiting for a reaction. The horse merely pinned his ears and tossed his head.

"Guess he's too smart for your foolishness. Go back to bed." Karen downplayed her irritation.

She watched the starfish of hair rise and fall sharply. The thud of his body on the mattress told her that it was too early to be up, even for Brad.

Karen put a sparkling Legend into his stall for breakfast. She grained him first, then the other horses. The girls picked through the stalls and gave the horses staying behind hay and water.

"Good thing I told you to bring your riding pants to change into there," Mindy said. "Imagine doing all this work in your clean breeches."

"I guess you were right. My jeans are dirty already." Karen looked at her watch. "Where is Ginny? It's eight o' clock. We have to get going!"

As she glanced toward the house trailer, hoping to see Ginny, a black Dodge Ramcharger rolled down the driveway. A tall thin man with wavy sandy hair got out and strode toward the door. The girls both recognized him and his truck. It was Brad's father, Joe. Ginny emerged from the trailer, pushing a reluctant Brad in front of her. She barely looked at the man as she held her hand out, exchanging something with Joe even as she pushed Brad closer to him. Joe put his arm around Brad's shoulders and steered him toward Ginny's old Cadillac. Ginny bounded toward the Ramcharger and jumped in the driver's seat.

"I guess we're using Joe's vehicle," Karen said. "At least we're going now."

Joe and Brad took off in the Cadillac. Karen turned to gather Legend's tack, but looked up in dismay as she heard the truck ascend the driveway and start down the road. The horse trailer remained parked in the weeds. Karen stood with her mouth agape.

"What in the world is going on?" Mindy asked.

"I hope she's not chasing Joe. You should have seen them the other night, arguing in the yard. Why would she do this to me now?" Karen said, fighting back tears.

"It makes no sense. He got Brad. Why else would she follow him?"

Deflated, the girls sat on overturned water buckets. Karen stared at the ground and scraped mindless shapes in the dirt with her heel. Mindy propped herself along Legend's stall door, her eyes shut. Several minutes passed. Karen pondered calling her mother to pick them up.

Suddenly, the crunch of gravel caught her attention. She looked toward Ginny's driveway to see the Ramcharger descending from the road. It pulled straight through the yard and started to back up to the horse trailer.

"Mindy! She's back, let's go." Karen shook her friend from dozing.

Hurriedly, Karen hoisted the old Stubben onto her right forearm, with girth and saddle pad on top, and threw the bridle over her left shoulder. Mindy grabbed two buckets in one hand—one for Legend to drink from and the other with soap and a sponge to bathe him as needed—and with the other hand picked up the grooming box with brushes, a comb, and hoof pick. The two started across the ring toward the horse trailer, where Ginny was turning the crank to attach it to the truck. There was a rustling behind the trailer, and the surrounding weeds started to shake. Suddenly, two teenage girls emerged from behind the trailer and headed for Karen and Mindy.

"You must be Karen," the taller of the two girls said. "I got the hay net. Ginny told me to fill it in the barn. Wow, you're so lucky! You get to ride in the horse show today. I bet Legend will win! I can't wait to start riding. Ginny said you'd teach me how. I'm Ivy."

She was slightly shorter than Karen, about five feet two inches tall. She had a sturdy but lean frame, her legs strong beneath her navy athletic shorts. Her ash-blond hair brushed her shoulders. Stunned by the onslaught of statements, Karen wasn't sure how to respond. Yet as she met Ivy's brown eyes, she recognized a yearning for approval.

"Oh, sure, I can work with you," she said. "Thanks for the hay net. There's a bale in front of Legend's stall if you want to fill it."

"Of course, right away." Before leaving, though, Ivy glanced at Mindy, who didn't hide her expression of confusion and annoyance. "You must be the sidekick. Look at your hair. It's gorgeous!" Ivy grasped one of Mindy's locks, twirling it between her fingers. "It's the color of spun gold. My mom says I'm a dirty blond, but not you. You're so lucky."

As Mindy's brow furrowed and her lips tightened, Karen braced herself for Mindy's reaction.

"Thanks, I guess," Mindy said. "Your hair is nice too. Mine is a pain, it takes forever to dry." She paused. "But the name's Mindy, not sidekick."

"Sure. Now let me get that hay." Ivy rushed on to the barn.

Karen looked at the second girl. She had the same compact frame as Ivy, but was more petite. A dusting of freckles decorated her porcelain shoulders, her collarbones apparent under her tan tank top. Black nylon shorts hung loosely around her waist. Her catlike eyes under shapely arches were hazel brown with splashes of green around her pupils. Auburn waves of long hair framed her well-defined cheekbones, matching a speckling of freckles on her nose.

"Don't mind my sister," she said to both Karen to Mindy and then spoke to Karen. "Ginny told us you're a good rider, and we've both dreamed of getting lessons too. Ginny keeps us pretty busy helping in the dog grooming shop. I'm sick of it, but at least I have some extra money. With my dad being laid off from the coal mines, I never get to do anything. I'll pay you what you want to teach us how to ride. My name is June."

Something about June resonated with Karen. She was obviously younger than Ivy, but she emitted a calm, confident aura. She knew what she wanted and was willing to work for it.

"You don't have to pay me, and I don't think I'm that great of a rider. I just work with Ginny's projects. You'd be better off with a real instructor, but I'll help you if I can."

The catlike eyes widened. "Anything to get me out of the house," June said.

She took one of the buckets from Mindy and the trio walked on to the horse trailer. Ginny peered at them from behind the truck.

"What's going on?" Karen asked. "I thought we were going to miss the show."

Ginny laughed. "I'm not that late. Besides, I had to get reinforcements. Ivy and June only live a few minutes away."

Ivy rushed up to them with the hay net. "Yeah, we live right on the corner, where Somerset Pike meets North Fork Dam Road."

With all the equipment, teenagers, and horse loaded, Ginny drove west through the Conemaugh Gap to Route 22. After forty-five minutes they pulled into the rutted driveway of the Clyde Saddle Club. Large trees shaded the way, leading them to a clearing. The show ring was beyond a slight incline. Dozens of horses and riders were warming up before the first class. Ginny pulled the trailer into the last shady spot available.

The sun's warmth cast out of a clear blue sky. A few cottony clouds hung overhead. A pleasant breeze carried the sounds of horses schooling. Hooves sent clouds of dust over the dry surface of the show ring. Karen had been here before. She had shown with J. T. Acres. She had appreciated the experience, although she hadn't won a ribbon. J. T.'s lesson horse had been lazy that day, and combined with Karen's weak driving leg, the pair had completed a slow canter transition. She expected a different response this day from Legend. He wouldn't let her down.

Legend was anything but lazy. He stepped off the trailer with flared nostrils. His eyes were ringed with white. His head rose high until each vertebra could stretch no more. Barely able to control him from the ground, Karen tightened her hold on the lead rope. She patted his neck, trying to calm him. He threw his head and circled nervously.

"He thinks he's at the track," Ginny said. "You better lunge him. I don't know if this will work today."

"Please, Ginny, I can handle him. I know I can."

"I don't know," Mindy said. "I've never seen him like this."

Ivy and June paid no attention to Karen's plight. Dazzled by the beauty and spectacle of the horse show, they scattered like hunting dogs. Ivy high tailed it to the show ring with a more subdued June on her heels. The sisters stood at the rail, commenting on the horses enthusiastically. A few riders gave them looks of surprise or annoyance.

"Oh, look how beautiful." Ivy pointed to a Saddlebred who was high stepping by.

The quick movement of her hand spooked the horse. He jumped to the side, almost unseating his rider.

"Hey! Watch it!" The young saddle seat rider glared at Ivy from beneath her navy derby.

Like a flash, Ivy spun and ran toward a group of horses tied to trees. Startled, the horses threw their heads, straining against the ropes that held them. This time June tried to temper her sister's enthusiasm.

"Ivy, c'mon. You're scaring them."

Ginny held her head in embarrassment. "Karen, you'll have to be on your own. I need to prevent those two from causing a disaster."

A man's voice came from behind Ginny. "Go on. Maybe I can be of assistance to the lass."

The man who spoke was tall with broad shoulders, wearing a white T-shirt. His face was robust with a large, prominent nose, yet his blue eyes were soft and kind. Wavy, barley colored hair sprang from his head.

Karen noticed his Irish accent, like the singsong tones of her grandmother, who despite being born in the United States, always told her grandchildren Irish legends with a lilt. Karen felt an instant connection with this man.

"My goodness, John!" Ginny hugged the Irishman. "It's been a long time."

He smiled at Ginny in admiration. "I wondered when you'd ride out with the hunt again. I heard how that unmentionable man up and left you. But you're doing well, I hear, a grooming shop and everything. I knew you had it in ya to shine. You don't need any lousy man!"

"Oh, John, you're too kind. We'll have to catch up over a drink. For now I would appreciate your help with the horse. I need to gather those other two."

She gave John a hurried account of Legend's history and Karen's skill level. John nodded and assured her that things were under control. Ginny set off to find the sisters.

John turned to Karen. She felt him sizing her up with those shining blue eyes. He had an amused look on his face. "Now, lass," he said, "you're not timid, are ya?"

Karen felt challenged. "Of course not. I've spent a lot of time with this horse."

"Good. Now, what you've got to remember is that he thinks he's back at the races. We're dealing with adrenaline here. Nothing we do is going to take that away. So we have to make him think he's doing what is familiar. If we try to hold him back, we'll upset him. If we try to work him in circles and figures, we'll frustrate him."

Karen was dismayed. "But what else can we do? That's how I school him at home."

"Now, now. Don't you become frustrated on me already. See that field down there? You're getting a crash course in riding with a cross and racing seat." John smiled. Then you're going to let him gallop a while."

"Now that's what I'm talking about!" Mindy exclaimed.

With John's help, they tacked the horse. "Now, you need to raise your stirrups a good four holes," he instructed. "That will help you balance and hold yourself off his back. We don't want to bother the horse. We just want to give him the opportunity to settle down. To ride with a cross, take one rein and put it on top of the other. Now you'll hold them together like that with both hands. This gives you a stronger grip. Hold each hand on either side of his withers. Push down into the base of his neck for balance. Don't move your hands. Cue him to go in a big circle by rotating your shoulders slightly inwards. Use a bit of inside rein. Just let him roll, stay with him, and watch out for everyone else!"

Karen swallowed her apprehension, thinking, *If I blow this, Ginny won't let me show again.*

Contrary to the normal routine, John instructed her to take a canter immediately. She felt Legend's tension. His body felt like a gigantic springing coil underneath her. He shook his head aggressively, and she heaved back on the reins. Legend braced against her, tossing his head again. His pace quickened.

"Relax, lass!" John commanded. "Let his head go!"

She dug her knuckles into the horse's neck for balance and released the tension in her hands. It seemed like they were flying. They approached the end of the field, and she had to turn. Other horses were schooling quietly at the field's perimeter and she had to avoid a collision. Remembering the cue for turning, she rotated her shoulders inward and took just a bit of rein. This time she didn't snatch his mouth. He banked the turn with the grace of a grand prix jumper. Exiting the turn, he let out a playful buck. Karen was surprised she held her posture. The racing seat was more secure than she'd expected.

Ten minutes passed. Karen and Legend got into a zone. It was the timeless rhythm of a smooth gallop, the same gait that carried warriors into battle. Karen felt like she was in a battle, and if she won, she'd conquer any empire. Legend took that magical stride that all riders strive to feel. She felt the tension leave his body. He was coming back to her.

"Okay now, lass," John called, "half halt a little. Give and take with that inside rein. Let's get him to round his back."

Legend slowly took a frame. He bowed his neck and slowed his pace to a canter.

"That's fine," John said. "It's time to quit while we're ahead."

John took the horse and offered him small sips of water. He loosened the girth and hand walked him back to the trailer. Karen was glad for the help. Her muscles felt like rubber. She had never used so much strength in her life.

Ginny approached with June walking beside her. A sheepish Ivy followed. Ginny quickly scanned the scene and then looked at Karen. "What are you waiting for? You're a mess. You better change if you want to show."

Ecstatic, Karen started toward the trailer to change into her breeches and jacket. Ivy popped out from behind Ginny and said, "Let me know when you need your boots shined."

"Yeah, sure." Karen hurried off. She had been annoyed with Ivy for pulling Ginny away, but now she felt blessed to have spent time under John's tutelage. She felt empowered and confident.

I'd be excited too, she thought, *seeing my first horse show at age fifteen. Who can blame her?*

Karen changed quickly into riding breeches, tall boots, a sleeveless collared shirt, and riding jacket. She pulled the longer part of her hair into a ponytail. The top and sides had flattened during her schooling session, but she was able to tuck it under her riding helmet to give a neat appearance. She returned to her group and Legend, who was munching grass a few yards from the ring. Occasionally he looked up at the horses competing, studied them for a moment, and then went back to munching. Mindy was holding his lead and she and June talked. Ginny and John laughed from beside the ring. A feeling of belonging and satisfaction came over Karen, and she smiled.

"I'll shine your boots now," Ivy said, approaching Karen with a small brush in one hand and polish in another.

Ginny turned from her conversation. "Ivy! Wait till she gets on the horse. She'll just get them dusty walking around." She paused as they announced the next class. "Okay, let's run a brush over the horse and get the bridle back on. You're up next."

Mindy jumped into action as June watched carefully. Legend looked handsome in the fancy stitched leather bridle. Ginny kept it separate from the other equipment at the farm. The softness was back in his eye. Karen climbed aboard. Her right leg had barely settled at the horse's side when Ivy started shining her boots.

"How's that?" Ivy asked, looking up at Karen.

"Great, thank you so much," Karen replied.

Legend and Karen competed in two flat classes. The first was equitation. The rider's ability to administer the aids, control the horse, and her general position was judged. Although Legend had calmed down considerably, his canter was a bit fast. Karen had to pull inside slower horses, which brought more attention to the horse's sharp attitude. The pair was able pick up the correct lead both times. Legend's first ribbon was yellow for third place. Karen beamed with pride. It was her highest placing in a show to date. Their second class was hunter under saddle.

Judging was focused more on the horse, taking into account manners and movement. The horse had to canter on the correct lead going both directions and the rider had to post on the correct diagonal at a trot. Karen was able to get her diagonals right, but Legend had become very relaxed and picked up the wrong lead going to the right. This knocked them down to sixth place.

Ginny greeted Legend and Karen with a smile after the class. "Hey, kiddo, that was good. He really calmed down at the end."

"Maybe he was too calm. I can't believe we missed that lead."

"Still a good accomplishment," John said. "Look what you started the day with. He wanted to run to the next county! Next time, hold your outside rein just a bit tighter. The off-track horses need a little help balancing when picking up the right lead."

"Okay, thanks, I'll try that." Karen looked into Legend's big brown eyes and stroked his forehead. "What a good boy," she whispered to him.

Karen asked Mindy to get the liniment. She mixed it with water and rubbed a sponge all over Legend's tired muscles. June and Ivy gathered the equipment and loaded the trailer as Ginny and John talked. Ivy lingered within earshot of the adults. Giggling, she reported every tidbit of information to Mindy and Karen. Karen giggled with her. She was intrigued by John, but only because of his horsemanship skills.

"Notice how we get stuck doing all the work," June grumbled as she passed by.

The summer sun was low by the time they left, but energy was high inside the Ramcharger. Ginny was accosted by a barrage of questions involving John. She explained that he was a whipper-in at the prestigious Rolling Rock Hunt Club of Ligonier, Pennsylvania. That meant he controlled the hounds from horseback during a foxhunt.

"Don't you think that's cruel to hunt a fox?" Karen asked.

"In America they just chase them," Ginny said. "It's all for sport. They don't kill the fox. Once the hounds lose the scent, they leave it."

"I guess that's better," Karen said.

"The important thing is that John's a world-class horseman," Ginny said proudly. "His reputation precedes him all over Ireland and England. He was a steeplechase rider and he competed on grand prix jumpers. I had the honor of riding with him at the hunt. You should see this man ride! He jumps things in the field that you wouldn't imagine. He is really something!"

Karen got the chills. She had dreamed of meeting a master horseman like John. She fought back tears of emotion.

After all the work was done at the farm and the horses were settled in, Karen, Mindy, Ivy, and June stood behind the barn.

"You two should come over sometime," Ivy said. "Want to see where we live?"

"I don't know," Mindy said. "We have to get going."

"Oh, come on," Ivy said. "It will just take a minute."

June backed up her sister. "It's just a five minute walk."

Karen held her breath as Mindy rolled her eyes. Trying to draw attention away from her volatile friend, she said, "Okay, where?"

"Follow me!" Ivy joyfully skipped away toward the bridge.

Karen's heart sank. She did not want to go anywhere near that old house. "Wait. I'm not walking past that place."

June turned, her catlike eyes narrowed. "Don't tell me you're afraid. We work in that house every day. She won't hurt you."

Karen got that same tingly feeling she'd had on the first day, when Ginny showed them the old house. "What do you mean, *she?*"

Just then, the sound of gravel crunching announced her mother's arrival. Karen was never so glad to see the blue Pontiac.

"Sorry, my mom's here. Thanks to both of you for today. We'll talk about lessons soon. See you later." Karen nodded to Mindy and the two jogged to the waiting car.

CHAPTER 4

A Common Thread

Karen stood in the center of the ring, watching her new pupil. "Okay, June, for the downward transition, sit deeply in the saddle and squeeze the inside rein."

June trotted by on Cajun, bouncing awkwardly in the saddle. Karen elaborated on the transition technique. "She's extra bouncy, so you really have to squeeze your seat bones to stabilize yourself. It also protects her back from your movement, allowing her to relax into a walk."

A look of concentration on her face, June followed Karen's instructions. The awkward bouncing subsided, and Cajun slowed into a walk. Ivy joined Karen in the center of the ring, analyzing her sister's ride.

"It took her too long to get the walk," Ivy said.

"She's doing just fine. Give her chance," Karen whispered.

"Ivy, be quiet," June retorted. "You're just jealous that it's not your day to ride."

"Well, tomorrow is Sunday, my day. I'll show you how it's done!" Ivy said.

Karen felt like she was watching a tennis match. But the girls' words could sting worse than a ball.

"Speaking of that," she said, "let's stop there. We can't overwork Cajun."

As if on cue, Mindy emerged from the barn. She held Cajun as June dismounted and then led her into the barn, where Karen knew she had already prepared a liniment bath and had carrots waiting. She watched

Mindy with pride and concern. Her riding time had decreased sharply, now that school had started and Ivy and June were using Cajun. Karen imagined Mindy was becoming frustrated with the lack of riding time. Frowning, she lagged behind the three other girls.

A loud clap of thunder shook the hollow. Static electricity shot up Karen's spine, jolting her back to reality. Her surprised scream made the others laugh. They greeted her at the barn's entrance, the sisters each grabbing an arm and yanking Karen inside just as the heavens burst open with rain.

Watching the water drip from the barn's awning, Karen sighed. "Good thing I rode Legend earlier. This puts a damper on Dawn's schooling, though."

"Maybe it won't last long," Mindy said.

Thunder erupted again, and a gust of wind pushed rain into the barn aisle. A mist sprayed the sweat from the girls' skin, enforcing the storm's dominance.

"It's not stopping anytime soon," Ivy said over another roar of thunder. "Come to my house. We'll wait it out there."

"I guess we have no choice," Karen said, looking at Mindy for approval.

Mindy only nodded. As the sisters turned to put Cajun in her stall, Mindy nudged Karen's arm and whispered, "I guess she's finally suckered us in."

Karen laughed uneasily. The rain pounded the barn roof with a relentless clang. "We're gonna have to run," she said loudly.

June turned to Karen with mischief in her eyes. "The quickest way is over the bridge and past the old house. Don't worry. I'll keep the ghost away."

"Great."

The four lined up at the back of the barn. Ivy took charge, saying "Ready, set, go!"

With that the quartet charged through the paddock and toward the bridge. Water splashed over Karen's boots as the rain flattened her hair. The old house loomed on her right as they sprinted across the bridge. Eyes burning as melting hairspray ran down her face, Karen squinted at the ground. She was glad for an excuse to look away from the house.

After a slight pause for traffic on the Somerset Pike, the girls crossed the highway and ran through a small front yard. With June and Ivy in front, they leaped up the steps of a dingy white house.

Karen followed as Ivy pushed June aside and dove into the front door. Her feet crunched on a clear plastic mat inside. The dining room was on the right, and a stairway was directly in front of them. She could see straight through to the kitchen at the other end of the house. A short, stocky woman appeared from there, a welcoming smile on her face. Her long wavy hair could have been June's, except that it was black with random strands of white.

"Oh, you poor dears. You're soaked. Take your shoes off and come in," the woman said.

"Mom, can we have some popcorn?" Ivy asked in a sing song voice.

"Sure, I'll make it now." The woman came closer, her dark eyes studying Karen. "You must be Karen. I've heard so much about you. My girls really look up to you."

"Oh, thanks, Mrs. Hausemann. By the way, this is my friend Mindy."

Mrs. Hausemann smiled and nodded at Mindy. Her gaze shifted back to Karen and she said, "Please, call me Stella."

"Okay, Mom, June said. "We'll be upstairs." Her cheeks were unaccountably flushed.

An indiscernible grumble came from beyond the kitchen. Stella's eyes widened. She turned abruptly, saying, "I'll bring the food right up."

Her shoulders hunched, Ivy whispered loudly to her mother's back, "Keep Dad down here."

Stella nodded and she disappeared into a room to the left of the kitchen. Ivy led the way up the stairs, followed by June, Mindy, and Karen. Hearing a louder grumble, Karen resisted an urge to push past everyone.

They topped the steps and turned right down a short hallway to a bedroom. It was a good size, but apparently the sisters shared it. Two single beds stood across from each other along the long walls. Rain continued to spit against two large windows, one facing directly out to the highway. Looking out the other window, through the gray of the storm Karen could see part of the old house through the trees. A third floor window peered back at her.

Shuddering, she joined the others. They sat in a circle on the floor. The gold shag rug was worn but clean, and fluffy enough to provide a soft seat. The mood lightened as they chatted. Karen felt more comfortable than before, seated Indian style among this circle of kindred spirits.

After talking about the joys of horses and riding, Karen said, "Does anyone else ride in your class? In my school it's just me, Mindy, and this other girl, Wendy, who ride. The other kids think we're some kind of freaks. They never let us forget about elementary school. They were always busting on us because we'd be playing by ourselves at recess, jumping around and pretending to canter like horses. To us it was a lot more fun than playing ball with them."

"Some of the other kids come from farm families," Ivy said. "I think they work so much that they don't care about riding the horses they have. I always think how lucky they are, having horses right in their backyards. They have these big pastures and land to use, but they never talk about it."

"They'd ride western anyway," June said. "I'd much rather ride English. I can't wait to jump!"

"That's the next step with Legend," Karen said. "I wonder if John would give me some jumping lessons."

Stella arrived with a bowl of buttered popcorn and grape Kool-Aid. The girls thanked her and dug in hungrily.

Changing the subject, Ivy asked, "Do you like any boys from your school?"

Mindy coughed on a kernel of popcorn. "Ugh! All the boys at our school are gross and stupid!"

A wave of giggles drowned out the thunder.

"Well, there is one boy," Karen said. "His name is Sean, and he's tall with dark hair. He's kind of cute, but I'd never say anything to him."

"Forget him," Ivy said. "I know someone who's tall with dark hair too. His name even sounds the same. The best part is his eyes. He has awesome eyes. He's even asked about you." Ivy was obviously delighted to gossip.

Butterflies rippled through Karen's stomach. She had thought about the boy with the striking blue eyes throughout the summer. She'd caught herself on several occasions peering across the creek through the trees, hoping to catch a glimpse of Shane. Somehow she didn't mind hearing his four-wheeler start up and watching him ride up the hill beside his house. It was in stark contrast to the disdain she felt for Brad's dirt bike.

Playing dumb, she asked, "Who?"

"It's Shane, silly," Ivy said. "You know the one who helped you with that bum? He asked how you were the other day, you lucky duck. We ride the same bus."

"Oh, really?" Karen said nonchalantly. "Tell him I said hi."

June interrupted. "Okay, enough boy talk. Let's do something interesting. Karen, I'm gonna break your fear of ghosts!"

She jumped up and pulled the blinds down at both windows. Combined with the gray of the day, it sent the room into darkness. A flit of light appeared in the middle of the circle as June lit a candle.

"Whoa, what are you doing?" Karen asked.

"Relax. Nothing is going to hurt you." June placed the candle on a piece of aluminum foil on the floor. "Now, everyone be quiet, close your eyes, and take each other's hands."

The four joined hands—June, Ivy, Mindy, and Karen. Karen looked nervously at Mindy, who had a crooked smile on her face. Realizing the silliness of it all, Karen took a deep breath.

June spoke in a low voice. "Everyone, focus on the candle. Is the ghost of George Washington here?"

The flame stayed true. The room remained silent. June continued, "Is the ghost of Benjamin Franklin here?"

Mindy snickered, and Karen relaxed. Listening to the diminishing rain, she yearned to look out the window, thinking she should get back to the stable to ride Dawn.

June spoke again, this time in a stronger voice. "Grandma Kakowa, are you with us?"

A splatter of rain thrust against the window; a fresh downpour pelted the roof. An odd coolness settled over Karen. Afraid to move, she stared at the flame. It fluttered and danced, its glow reflecting behind Ivy on the back wall.

June sat with her eyes closed, a peaceful smile on her face. "I feel you with us, Grandma. Please be our protector."

Karen let go of June's hand, trying to stand. It felt like a November morning rather than a September afternoon. Goosebumps prickled her, urging her to leave.

June grasped Karen's hand with surprising strength, pulling her back. She never opened her eyes.

"Now, Lady Luminess," June said, "do you exist?"

Karen asked a question that she knew the answer to. "Who is Lady Luminess?" Her body felt like a load of concrete. June maintained her strong grasp.

"Lady Luminess of the old house, are you here?"

A loud clap of thunder startled the girls. Karen ripped her hand from June's and jumped to her feet. She was about to leave, but a cold gust of wind froze her feet. It whipped through the circle, extinguishing the flame. Through the dimness in the room, Karen saw a soft glow flash across the entire opposite wall, and then it disappeared.

She rushed to the windows, jerking the blinds open. She shook the closed panes, searching for cracks or drafts. The windows were sealed tightly. She turned to the others. They were all standing too. Mindy's smile had disappeared and her expression was one of confusion, while Ivy was watching Karen with concern. June stood leaning to one side with her arms crossed, a look of satisfaction on her face.

"They didn't hurt you, did they?" she asked.

"This is too much," Karen said. "You're opening a whole can of worms here. I don't want to be haunted!"

"That's why I called my grandma. She was an Indian and my family's spiritual guardian. Even though she married my grandfather, who was white, she held onto the customs of her ancestors. Before she died, she told my mom she'd always look out for us. She's just a thought away."

Ivy walked over to Karen. "You're not mad, are you?" She put a hand on Karen's forearm.

"Not mad, just freaked out." Karen's tone softened. "That's kinda cool about your grandma."

"We miss her, but my mom really took it hard when she died."

As if on cue, Stella knocked on the door. "Girls, Ginny called. She needs your help in the shop. Something about two dogs getting sprayed by a skunk."

June groaned. "Oh, man, just what I wanted to do on a Saturday night."

"At least we'll make a few extra bucks," Ivy said.

The rain had stopped and a late afternoon sun fought through the clouds. Karen and Mindy parted ways with the sisters at the old house.

"I'm glad we don't work in the dog grooming shop," Mindy said to Karen as they crossed the bridge. "What a smelly job they'll have today."

Karen barely acknowledged the statement. She no longer felt the urge to run past the old house. She even turned to look back at it. Everything was quiet.

As they neared the back door of the barn, Karen started to speak, but the sound of a girl's voice distracted her. She cautiously peered into the barn. A teenager was talking on the phone, her back to Karen and Mindy.

The girl's voice shook with sobs. "You always ruin it for me, Mom. You just dropped me off. Now you're saying I have to be ready in an hour? How am I ever going to learn to ride my horse?"

There was silence, and then Karen heard an angry voice coming from the phone. She couldn't make out what was being said, but the girl's reaction told enough of the story.

"I don't care what Dad wants to do! He's just going to leave us again anyway. When are you going to stop letting him break our hearts?"

Karen looked at Mindy. "That must be Kirsten, Dawn's owner," she whispered. "Maybe that storm stopped me from riding her for a reason."

Finally, Kirsten hung up the phone. She turned around, tears streaming down her cheeks. She was startled to see the other girls.

"Oh, shoot! I didn't know anyone else was here," she said.

"Sorry." Karen stepped forward. "You must be Kirsten. I'm Karen and this is Mindy. We've heard a lot about you. You have a nice filly. She just needs some work and TLC."

"Oh, that's right. You've been riding her. Thanks. I swear my family is determined to make my life miserable. They never bring me to ride her. Now I have to leave again. All of a sudden, my dad is going to pretend to be a father. His expensive dinners and family matinee days don't cut it with me. He'll get bored again and go back with his girlfriend. Then my mom will struggle with the bills. She'll get depressed again and take it out on my brothers and me. I should just sell my horse. By the time I get to come out again, I'll forget how to ride." Kirsten fought back the tears.

Kirsten was a beautiful girl. Her short light brown hair was feathered away from her face in waves, sweeping over her ears. Though reddened, her large aqua-colored eyes were striking. Her porcelain skin had a pink glow. Heart-shaped, her face was reminiscent of a classic Eastern European look, reminding Karen of models in fashion magazines. However, sadness radiated from Kirsten's soul.

"Oh, don't say that," Karen said. "It sounds like Dawn is the best thing you have. Now listen. We can tack her up quick. I'll ride her first and show you some things. Then you can get on and practice. We can do that in an hour."

The three worked quickly. Kirsten's tears disappeared as she brushed Dawn. "You're such a pretty girl. You're getting so much calmer," she crooned to the Arabian.

Karen mounted Dawn to warm her up. Kirsten and Mindy stood in the center of the ring and watched as Karen described what she was doing with Dawn and why. A light breeze had brought some clouds back. With them came a light rain, but it bothered none of them. A light steam rose from Dawn's warm body. A feeling of silence and peace came over the valley. Karen noted Kirsten's relaxed posture and decided she was ready to try her filly.

Kirsten mounted without incident. Dawn had learned to stand while being mounted. Kirsten took up the reins, holding them tautly, her hands behind the withers. The reins were too long for good contact. Karen spotted this problem right away.

"You need to fix your hands. She'll take advantage of you like that. Shorten your reins. Your hands should be on either side of her withers."

Kirsten adjusted her hand position. However, she tensed her shoulders and slouched. Dawn took a nervous step forward.

"Okay, you have to work on relaxing. I'll walk with you. Take some deep breaths. Relax your hands. Sit tall and follow the motion of her head and neck. That's better. Now relax your hips. You need to let them move with her back. That's the only way she will trust you. She has to feel free to move, even though you're in control."

Karen stayed at Dawn's shoulder while Kirsten worked on her position. They practiced circles and figure eights. Dawn finally relaxed her head and neck. Kirsten looked more confident.

"She used to scare me," Kirsten said. "She'd startle so easy. I was always waiting for her to spook. This is so much better."

"She's come a long way. You need to work with her consistently," Karen said. "Dawn will make a nice little horse. You'll see."

They progressed to a trot. Kirsten's posting was wobbly, and Karen instructed her to sink her weight into her heels. "Tighten up that calf," she said.

Kirsten eventually got the hang of it, but when Karen noticed that Dawn was tired, she suggested they end on that note. Kirsten turned to them, patting Dawn's neck. Her smile was in stark contrast to her earlier tears. Karen felt great. She knew this girl would find happiness with her horse.

That theory would be tested sooner than later. The door to the house trailer slammed open and they all heard hurried footsteps clamoring across the porch. Karen turned to see Brad running toward his dirt bike. Before she could process the information, he was sitting on it. She reached for Dawn's reins as the vehicle roared to life. Her ears pricked, Dawn raised her head beyond Karen's reach. Brad zipped past, the bike spitting loads of mud at them. For a finale, he spun around, churning up more earth. Karen was holding her breath. She stepped toward Dawn again, moving slowly to avoid startling her. Dawn simply snorted, as if to say, "What a noisy beast!" Then she dropped her head as if nothing happened.

Brad's visor tipped low. The helmeted figure grumbled something in disgust, spun the bike around, and roared away.

"My gosh, what a good girl!" Kirsten exclaimed. "I've been afraid to ride around here because of Brad and his bike. I think she's used to it now."

"Yeah, these horses have to get used to him," Mindy said. "He just doesn't care if he scares them."

"Exactly," Karen agreed.

"As strict as Ginny is with us, she seems to have no control over Brad," Kirsten said.

Karen nodded. "Yes. It's up to us to protect ourselves."

"Let's make a pact to always look out for each other," Kirsten said.

The three girls touched their right hands together. The pact was made.

Kirsten smiled the entire time they cooled Dawn out and the girls chatted.

"So, what school do you go to?" Karen asked. "I haven't seen you around Johnstown."

"I go to Richland," Kirsten replied.

"Cool, you're up on the hill where all the action is. We'll have to meet at the mall sometime."

Kirsten laughed. "Sure, but I don't know how much action there is. Everyone just cruises around the parking lot or walks around inside."

"I heard they're putting a pool hall up there," Mindy said.

"Between that and the horses, we'll hang out," Karen said.

"Definitely!" Kirsten glanced at her watch. "Uh-oh, my mother expects me out by the pike. I gotta go, but I'll see you soon. When she hears how well Dawn and I did today, she'll have to bring me out more often."

Kirsten's body language showed her reluctance to leave. Her carriage changed from proud and tall to slouched and dejected.

"Great job today," Karen called after her, "Come back as soon as you can."

Kirsten waved as she crossed the bridge.

"I think we should make another pact," Karen said to Mindy. "We need to make her happy when she's here."

Watching Kirsten walk past the old house, Karen was reminded of the day's earlier events. She noticed that Kirsten paid the house no mind. *Maybe it was nothing today, just coincidence*, she thought. *It's dumb for me to worry about that old dump.*

Yet as Karen looked bravely to the third floor, a flash of light in a window winked back at her.

CHAPTER 5

THE DISCOVERY

From his upstairs bedroom, Shane heard the clip-clop of hooves moving down the road. Putting down his book on Indians of Pennsylvania, allowing it to precariously straddle a book on geology and another on the Revolutionary War, he looked out his window. Two horses and riders were on the road. He admired the female form of the girl riding the tall lead horse. Her dark denim Gitanos hugged her curves like a glove. The late September sun cast a golden haze onto her brown hair as her horse turned down the back entrance to Ginny's property. A smaller, slower horse followed, carrying a slim blond girl with a red bandana.

Shane picked up his phone, which he had proudly installed with some help from his father, and called his friend Lance.

"Hey, man, they just got back from riding. Come over." He paused, listening to Lance's response. "Hey, Ivy said that Karen told her to tell me hi. I'm telling you, the other one's pretty too, real skinny. Come on, man, the Atari will be there when we get back."

Shane went down the stairs and made a right into the spacious kitchen. His father sat at the head of the table as his mother placed a sandwich in front of him.

"Where are you headed?" she asked, turning to Shane. "I thought you were reading."

"Lance and I are just going for a ride. That's why I mowed the grass early."

His father looked up from his lunch. "Okay, but tomorrow we have to cover the pool. It's getting too chilly to swim now."

"Sure, Dad." Shane hurried out the door and crossed in front of the large gray house. He glanced at the white trim around the windows, noting they had become dingy.

Oh, great, he thought. *Painting that trim will be the next project before winter.* But he knew he shouldn't complain. A few chores around the house weren't so bad.

He crossed the front yard and passed a few pine trees. He surveyed the three-acre lot, which had become a motor-cross course. Several mounds of dirt served as jumps, and the steep grade of the land provided challenging terrain for the four-wheelers. Turning left, he walked a few yards up the hill to a shed. He mounted his scraped but freshly washed four-wheeler and carefully backed it out of shed. Lifting the seat, he checked the flashlight stored underneath. Its powerful beam shone brightly, despite the sunshine. From below on North Fork Country Club Road, another four-wheeler turned up his hill.

The rider's blond hair blew back under his blue dew rag. He worn a Mopar T-shirt with the sleeves cut off. He stomped the brake with a work boot and turned his machine off.

"What have you been up to?" Shane asked as his friend dismounted. "It looks like you've actually been lifting weights, not just your game controller. You've got some biceps going on there."

"Yeah, you might want to try it too, skinny boy." Lance grabbed Shane's sinewy arm and spun him down the hill.

"Some of us actually have to do chores. I still beat you in height, short stuff." He looked pointedly at Lance's hair. "You're telling me your mom hasn't made you cut that hair yet?"

"She's tried. I just blow her off. When will yours get below the collar?"

"I don't think that would go over too well." Shane ran a hand over his thick dark hair. Its natural wave kept it place, short at the top and feathered at the sides where it blended into the back, stopping at the nape of his neck. "I'll let the girls have the long hair."

"Speaking of that, let's go meet these chicks."

As they both got back onto their vehicles, Shane said, "We have to keep the speed down and park our rides at the bridge. Ginny doesn't want the four-wheelers close to the barn. If she sees us speeding through, we're toast."

"I hear Brad whizzing through there all the time. That's kind of messed up," Lance said.

"Don't ask me, man. The kid has her wrapped around his finger. Anyway, tone it down. She pays me to help out sometimes."

"Hey, I could use some extra cash too. Can you say something to her? I'll help out with the grass or something. I don't wanna babysit, though. I'll leave that for you."

"It's not really babysitting," Shane said defensively. "Brad's only a year younger than us. She just tells me to keep him from killing himself. But no problem. I'll let you do the hard stuff while I watch movies and ride with the kid."

Apparently satisfied with this, Lance led the way. They pulled slowly into Ginny's back driveway and in front of the fountain by the old house. Shane looked up to the third floor windows.

No lights now, he thought.

The boys parked at the bridge and started across the back paddock of the barn. Two horses grazed on the rich grass in its center. They barely flicked an ear as the boys walked past. Their hides still damp from being bathed after their exercise, they munched happily in the warm sun.

Two wheelbarrows sat across from each other in the barn. Every few seconds, pitchforks threw hunks of manure and sawdust into them. Shane led the way, pulled forward by the buzz of a radio. Nearing the barn door, he was blasted by Bon Jovi's "You Give Love a Bad Name," accompanied by the two girls singly along loudly.

> Shot through the heart and you're to blame,
> You give love, a bad name
> I play my part and you play your game,
> You give love, a bad name.

The boys exchanged smirks as they entered. The chorus blared from the radio. Shane clutched his ears and peered into the stall on the left.

Karen stumbled into silence mid lyric. Her eyes, enhanced by dark eye liner, widened in surprise. Her jaw dropped, her cheeks reddened, she looked down quickly.

Trying to ease her embarrassment, Shane said, "Oh, you must be Karen Bon Jovi."

Karen grinned and then laughed. She let her pitchfork rest at her side. She wore a yellow crop top that hovered just above her bellybutton, exposing defined abdominals and the small waist that led down to nicely rounded hips. She was still giggling when she spoke.

"Man, you really busted us. I didn't think anyone else was around."

She glanced over his shoulder at Lance. Lance waved a greeting and turned to Mindy across the aisle.

"Walking in on your singing is better than seeing you holding a bum down with that pitchfork," Shane said.

"No, that wasn't cool," Karen replied.

Shane glanced over his shoulder to see Lance had already walked over to the other stall and was talking in a low voice to Mindy. *That part of the plan is working*, he thought.

He turned back to Karen. "It's kind of loud in here. Can I talk to you outside?"

"Sure, you can walk with me while I dump this wheelbarrow." She thrust it out of the stall, nearly bumping into him. He laughed while he moved out of her way.

He walked beside her as she went to the manure pile. She walked with quick powerful strides, her lean arms flexed with just a touch of muscle tone. The beige of a fleeting summer tan still glazed her skin, the tones providing a nice backdrop for the silver guitar earrings dangling from her ears. She strained ever so slightly against the wheelbarrow's resistance.

"Here, let me take that for you," he said, touching her arm.

"No, I got it. I don't mind," she said.

Amused, he continued alongside of her. She seemed more comfortable talking this way.

"So anyway," he said, "my friend Lance and I were wondering if you two wanted to go for a ride." He spoke slowly at first, and then blurted out the last part quickly.

She dumped the wheelbarrow at the manure pile and paused, looking over the bridge at the ATVs.

"On those things?" The green of the surrounding grass reflected in her eyes. They glowed like emeralds under long, curly eyelashes.

"What's wrong with them?"

"Those things are scary."

"Those things are a lot easier to control than a thousand-pound animal with a mind of its own. Believe me, I know. The first and last time I rode a horse was on Lance's sister's palomino. I ended up on the ground with the horse nibbling my hair. I swear he was laughing."

Her eyes gleamed with amusement. "I would have too."

"Ha ha," he said sarcastically. At ease, he continued, "This trail is kind of rough for horses. I just started working it, but I guarantee once you see what's at the top, you'll want to help clear it so you can use it too."

"Really? You sound pretty confident there, buddy. I'll be the judge of that. You better just take it easy."

"Fine. Do you think Mindy will want to come?" he asked, as they turned and headed back to the barn.

"Definitely. She's the daredevil."

Mindy and Lance were making their way into the paddock. They were having a lively discussion. Mindy seemed to be stopped in midstride, holding her wheelbarrow tightly.

"Looks like those two are getting along just fine," Karen said.

As Karen and Shane approached, they heard Lance say, "C'mon, Bon Jovi isn't real metal. Listen to Metallica or Megadeth. They'll blow you away."

Mindy frowned. "I've never heard of them. How good can they be?"

Lance chuckled and gave Shane a sideways look. Shane said, "You may have met your match, man."

Shane gritted his teeth as Karen squeezed his sides. The four-wheeler strained up the hill beside his house. Lance's machine groaned from behind, and Mindy shouted something into the wind. Karen buried her head into Shane's back. Promptly, he decided it was worth the pain. He accelerated to the end of the lot and into the woods of the surrounding mountains.

As he proceeded up the trail, the wood's cool shade enveloped them, and the gnarled finger of a branch scraped his face. The treacherous terrain demanded intense concentration from the drivers. The trail rose steeply up the mountainside, following a serpentine route ever upward. The four-wheeler groaned with the effort, spewing dirt whenever it lost traction. Shane looked behind to see Mindy pressing her face into Lance's back too. Noting Lance's wry smile, he continued on, angling between trees and warning Karen of potential bumps.

After fifteen minutes of this relentless ascent, the trail narrowed. The sun was promptly blotted out by the overhanging branches of hemlock and white pine. The branches brushed together, forming a tunnel that was both inviting and foreboding. Shane welcomed the cool darkness. The thicket felt like another world.

He finally stopped the ATV. Lance parked behind him. Prying Karen's fingers apart, he said, "We go on foot from here."

"What?" Lance said. "You didn't tell me that."

"Because I knew you wouldn't come," Shane said. "And now you've come too far to go back." He winked at Karen as she dismounted the ATV.

"That's not right, dude." Lance dismounted in a huff.

Shane opened the storage compartment of the four-wheeler and pulled out the flashlight. "Follow me, kids."

Karen walked beside him, matching him stride for stride. Mindy followed close behind with a winded Lance trailing. The woods continued to darken.

"The shades of death," Shane said.

"Dude, what are you talking about?" Lance demanded.

"That's what the Europeans called these clusters of closely knit trees. They tried to avoid routes like this when exploring the new world. They believed the darkness would gobble them up, holding them prisoner forever. The shades didn't scare the Indians, though. Their paths used to cut right through these areas."

"How do you know that?" Lance said impatiently.

"I'll show you."

He led the group through the dark maze. The terrain leveled through a pine forest. He came to a tree on the left side of the path and stopped.

"Look at this. Imagine how many centuries this has been here. I didn't feel right about removing it, but I found another one we can actually look at."

There, sticking into the side of a tree was an arrowhead. Although deeply imbedded into the wood, its triangular shape was unmistakable. Lance and the girls huddled around the artifact.

"I can barely tell what it is," Karen said.

"Don't worry. I found another one. I stashed it here. You can see what it looks like."

He knelt at the tree's base and pushed some pine needles aside. Underneath was another arrowhead. He admired it as he held it up for the others. They crowded around him. Even Lance studied it intensely and took it from Shane for a closer look.

Shane grinned, feeling like Indiana Jones.

The piece of flint seemed untouched by time. It was one inch broad and one and a half inches long. Its irregular surface revealed how it had been made. The maker used stones to pound the flint into shape. The design was simple, yet the instrument was effective. Native Americans survived for centuries using arrowheads to hunt.

"Wow, let me see that." Karen snatched the arrowhead from Lance. "It's hard to imagine making that."

"Yeah," Shane said. "They had no machines. They used what nature provided—rocks, wood, animal bones."

"I wonder what they were shooting at," Lance said. "To penetrate that tree, that arrow had some serious torque behind it."

"That's what makes it cool," Shane said. "You can use your imagination. Maybe that was meant for a deer. On the other hand, Indian tribes used to fight among each other. Maybe one tribe was trying to protect itself from another. Or they could have been fighting with or against the French or the British."

"You claimed we'd see something cool," Karen said. "That's awesome."

"Oh, that's not all. It's just for starters. Follow me."

They continued through the tunnel of branches. As Shane led the way, his eyes strained against the darkness. He scanned the ground for hazardous roots, sometimes taking Karen's elbow to support her. Finally, sun burst through the tunnel, and the teens emerged into a grassy meadow. They squinted against the sudden brightness. Karen grabbed Shane's forearm to steady herself while she caught her bearings. They paused, the four standing in a line, all of them appreciating the light breeze that played with the meadow's tall grasses. It made a soft rustling noise that relaxed the senses. Karen took a deep breath and relaxed her grip on Shane's forearm. She stepped into the meadow and gazed around its borders. Mindy joined her, and the girls looked at each other incredulously.

"Can you believe all this was just a hillside away?" Karen said.

"I can't wait to ride the horses up here. We can give them a rest at the top here and let them graze," Mindy replied.

"Look, it almost has a natural fence. There are trees on each side."

She scanned the lovely tree-bordered meadow from left to right. Shane prepared for her reaction as her gaze halted at the sight ahead. Looming just to the left of the meadow path was a gigantic rock formation. Its outer and lower walls were solid gray rock.

"Wow! What *is* this place?" She led the way now.

"Dude, this is so cool!" Lance said. "Why didn't you tell me about it?" He lowered his voice. "You're taking all the glory. These girls are pretty into it."

"I told you to come out more often," Shane replied.

The boys hustled to catch up. The rocky walls were a quarter mile across the meadow from the wooded thicket. The awe of this place was not lost on Shane. All four of them were silent as they stared with curiosity and awe at the formation. It thrust at least ten stories skyward. Toward the top, the color changed. Instead of gray, the rock took on a reddish hue. At its highest point, the red rock blended with the shade cast from the pine trees along the upper ridge.

"How can trees even grow up there?" Karen asked, still gazing skyward.

"I know pine trees are sturdy," Shane said. "They need less nourishment than other trees, but still, I don't know how they grow up there either."

The sheer walls of the formation created a formidable wall. Shane looked down its long side and noted where light crept through the narrow space between the formation and the tree line.

"It's cool," Mindy said to Shane. "We'll have to hang out with you more often."

"That's not all. I have more to show you." He chuckled quietly as Lance placed himself squarely beside Mindy.

"Okay, showoff," his friend said. "What more could there be to see?"

"Let's keep going. I'll show you everything," Shane replied. "This passage goes the whole way around."

"Are you sure?" Karen said. "It looks kind of narrow."

Shane led them through the path. Spouting from various points on the cliff walls, tiny streams cascaded into waterfalls. Misting the teens as they walked past, they formed little pools at the formation's base. As Karen lifted her face to the mist, Shane noticed the wonderment in her eyes. Surely she'd be interested in his theory on the formation's genesis. The path continued on for at least half a mile, barely separating the rock from the woods. Finally, they came around to the front of the formation, and Shane gave his mini lecture.

"The mountains, rolling hills, plateaus, and sharp ridges of Pennsylvania were formed when, millions of years ago, Africa collided with North America. All that force caused the ground to thrust upward. Only the force of two continents smashing together can form such stout cliffs. What I don't understand is how it formed in such a complete circle."

"You're such a dork," Lance said. "It's just part of the mountain."

"No, it's more than that," Karen said in a low, almost distant voice. It feels different up here. I don't know why."

The group continued to survey the area. The formation sat on a broad plateau. Behind the plateau was another stout mountain range. The path between the formation and the woods was the only thing that separated its walls from the foot of the next mountain. It extended even farther skyward, shading the formation and the western side of the meadow.

"It is like a fortress," Lance said. He turned around, walking toward the tree-shrouded hillside facing their homes.

"Don't go too far buddy," Shane warned. "There isn't much room between us and a steep drop."

"No kidding!" Lance exclaimed. He had gone just beyond the tree line in front of the formation. Pebbles from under his boots plummeted over a vertical hillside.

"I have one more thing to show you," Shane said. "It's the best part," he assured them when they all sighed.

He followed the formation's walls toward the meadow and stopped at a large, dark opening in the limestone. He took the flashlight from his pocket, winking at Karen, whose face had become pale.

"I don't know about this," she said.

"Yeah, you're pushing it, man," Lance agreed.

"Don't worry. I've done this before. It's not very deep, and the walls are solid. The flashlight helps." Shane had to share a spectacular discovery.

"Man, who are you trying to be, Lewis and Clark?" Lance asked.

"I'm surprised you know who Lewis and Clark are," Shane retorted.

"Okay, chickens," Mindy said. "Let's go." She stepped up to the cave entrance.

The group proceeded into the cave. It was wide enough for two people to walk abreast. Shane pointed the high-powered flashlight on the floor. It was damp. He had just reached out to steady Karen when her feet slipped, sending a shock of cold water splashing up their legs.

"That doesn't feel so good now," she said, her voice taking on an edge. "Can we go back in the sunlight?"

"No way! You're not missing this," Shane insisted.

"C'mon, clumsy," Mindy said.

They proceeded along the smooth cave floor, placing each foot carefully. Seventy-five feet inside, Shane said, "Okay, let's stop a minute."

He shone the flashlight to the ceiling. The walls of the cave were grayish white. Tiny crystals twinkled in the light.

"Hey, we're rich," Mindy said. "Those are diamonds, right?"

"No," Shane said. "Sorry to say, they're just aragonite. They're really tiny and worth nothing, but they sure look pretty in here."

"This is incredible," Karen said. "I can't believe how high the ceilings are. I thought for sure I'd hit my head at any moment."

"I think the ceiling is about seven feet high. It stays consistent like that to the end," Shane said. "There's something else on the wall. Follow my light."

He flashed the light on the right wall, reveling a cave painting. The scene depicted Native Americans. They appeared to be hunkered down in brush and were shooting arrows at a fearsome target. White men, clad in red, pointed what appeared to be rifles at the natives. Fallen warriors from both sides were depicted in the scene.

"Some people say," Shane explained, "that the Indians took refuge in caves from the elements or just to hide. They were known to draw scenes from life on cave walls. This scene is pretty straightforward. The white man dominated this land. They eventually drove the Indians out. But the Indians put up a heck of a fight."

"That's really sad," Karen said. "Imagine living in a wonderful place like this, and being driven out."

"That does stink," Lance said.

Shane grinned at him. "What, sympathy coming from you? Now I've made a breakthrough." He pointed the flashlight ahead again. "And for the grand finale …"

"How much more could there be?" Karen asked.

Shane proceeded forward another twenty-five feet. He switched the flashlight off as the cave was illuminated with outside light and he led the group out of the cave and into a whole new world. The huge formation had an inside. Amazingly, its walls protected a vast meadow. Acres of lush grass stretched before them. Cliff walls surrounded them on all sides. They formed a canyon, protecting the meadow from the world. Sunlight sprayed between the expansive cliff edges. It warmed the canyon floor, nourishing the grass from above. Rain could easily saturate the vegetation too. It was a complete ecosystem, as evidenced by the monarch butterflies skirting across the meadow. Antlers popped into view from a distance. A young buck snorted and disappeared from sight.

"Holy cow!" Karen exclaimed. "What a place!"

The others remained in silent reverence.

"Is anyone thirsty?" Shane asked.

He led them to the center of the canyon. A bubbling stream of fresh spring water traversed the canyon floor. The teens cupped their hands to drink, exhaling their satisfaction with the mineral water. They all gazed around the beauty of this seemingly undiscovered world and then looked at each other as if in a trance. Almost telepathically, they promised to never spoil this paradise.

The young buck appeared again. He dropped his head and grazed on the rich grass. Shane broke the silence.

"I think the deer made the path around the outside. It's too narrow to be made by modern man. I suppose the Indians hid out here. They certainly had plenty of fresh water."

"This is a great place to hide for man or beast," Karen said. "I don't think the deer worries about hunters. Good for him."

"Yes," Shane said. "I don't think anyone knows about this place. Do you see how the cliffs seem to turn inward at the top? The trees at the top also seem to lean inward. They cast shadows around the inner perimeter of the canyon. Notice it's the only place there isn't grass. It's like camouflage. It would be hard to spot from the air too. Furthermore, we're not in a flight zone. It's backed by an impenetrable mountain range. From the valley end, most of the frontage is private property. As far as I know, the trail from my house is the only way up here."

"What a great place," Lance said. "We have to be very careful about who we bring here. Select only those who won't ruin it."

The group agreed, with Mindy adding, "We'll have only peaceful picnics here, no loud parties to disrupt the animals. Make sure you take everything you bring back with you. Don't leave any garbage."

"This will be a great place to bring the horses," Karen said. "They can graze while we have a picnic. We can ride them the whole way. They can tiptoe through that narrow path of hemlock and pine. We just might have to duck from the branches. I'm sure they'll go through the cave with a little coaxing. It's certainly high and wide enough." She grinned at Shane. "I told you horses are a superior form of transportation."

The teens lingered for a while longer in reverence of the area. Reluctantly, Shane initiated their departure. "The sun's starting to go down."

As they emerged from the cave and stepped onto the path for home, one more surprise greeted them. A light wind had picked up and it carried the unmistakable sound of human voices. The four heard it simultaneously. They looked at one another in confusion. They scanned their surroundings up and down, across and back. No one was to be seen. As the voices became clearer, the teens understood why.

The voices were not speaking English. Instead, they chanted softly, using simple interchanging syllables. The faint rhythm of primitive drums accompanied the voices. The chanting rhythm remained unchanged. It was intense yet peaceful, as if the speakers were in deep meditation. Despite this, there was a ghostly, eerie quality to it. The girls looked at each other in fear. Communicating in a silent language, they sprinted into the meadow and headed toward the hemlock thicket.

Shane whipped his head around, seeking an explanation. He saw nothing out of the ordinary, except for Lance, whose face had gone white and his eyes wide. His expression begged Shane to follow the girls' lead.

"Go if you want," Shane said. "There's got to be an explanation for this."

"Man, you're killing me!" Lance gritted his teeth and shouted into the darkening sky, "Who's there?"

The only response was the continued chanting.

Shane felt a chill run up his spine, raising the hair on the back of neck. "I don't see anyone, do you?"

"No one. Let's go!" Lance sprinted toward the hemlock thicket, never looking back.

The chanting grew more intense. Shane felt the drums rumbling in his chest. A wave of energy surrounded him, chilling him to the bone. Finally, he fled to the thicket.

Plummeting into the encroaching darkness, he could barely see. Branches scraped across his face, feeling like tentacles snagging him with a thorny grasp. The thicket devoured the remaining slivers of daylight, sending him into a panic. Finally, headlights pierced the path. Lance roared up on his four-wheeler.

"Jump on, man! The girls are about to hightail it out of here!" Shane jumped on the back of Lance's seat. "Keep your eyes peeled. I want to nail the jerks that are messing with us," Lance yelled over the motor.

"You got it," Shane replied distantly. Yet he knew he could not reason or lecture the chanting or war drums away. The cave drawing had left a physical imprint of the native people, and it was clear a spiritual one remained as well.

CHAPTER 6
An Offering

June crept down the stairs, pausing as she peeked over the railing into the dining room. Her mother stood under the archway between the dining room and kitchen. She gave June a silent nod. June hurried the rest of the way down the stairs with Ivy close behind. The front door creaked as June opened it, despite her best efforts to turn the handle and pull it gently. She hurled the screen door open, pushing it wide for her sister. Before Ivy pulled the door shut behind her, she heard her father's grumbling and her mother's response: "Leave them alone, Earl! They're going to the barn."

June jogged across Somerset Pike and toward Ginny's back lane. Ivy rushed to join her.

"I wish he'd go back to the mines," June said angrily.

"Well, that's a mean thing to wish upon your father," Ivy replied.

"At least he couldn't drink *all* day."

The farther she got from the house, the lighter June felt. The barn came into view as they crossed the bridge. A feeling of exhilaration came over her. She was set to start her new project today. She couldn't wait to ride the new palomino pony Ginny had bought.

"It's so cool we get to ride Blondie," Ivy said. "Why did Ginny leave you in charge of her, though?"

"I'm a stronger rider. She wants to get Blondie jumping right away. She's going to push to sell her for a profit."

"Sell her? I love her already. You're going to let me ride, aren't you?" Ivy asked.

"Yes, for God's sake. You can warm her up and cool her down."

As they approached the back of the barn, June noticed the door was pulled halfway closed. She recognized the dark rump of Legend standing in the cross ties. Karen stepped behind the horse. Focused on conversation, Karen whisked a brush across his rump.

"Hmm, it's kind of early for Ginny to be up," June said. "I fully expected to wake her when I'm ready with Blondie. Mindy's visiting her grandmother, so who else is there?" She slowed her pace and motioned to Ivy to do the same.

Silently, the sisters eased toward the closed side of the barn door. There they knelt, listening intently. Another voice emerged from inside. June saw her sister's eyes widen in recognition. Ivy gasped, and June promptly covered her sister's mouth. "Shhh."

They heard Shane say, "I just wanted to make sure you're not too freaked out over the whole thing."

Karen replied, "It's a fabulous place, and I'd love to ride up there, but what in the world was that? I didn't sleep for two nights. I kept hearing the drums and chanting in my head. I can barely go past this spooky old house without running. Now the hills are haunted too?"

"It's just uncanny how it happened after I showed you guys the cave paintings. Could we have awakened the Indian spirits? I admit it freaked me out too. I don't know how happy they were with us. I know one thing, though. I want to keep going there. I wish there was a way to pay our respects without angering them."

"Okay, the minute you say angry spirits, I'm out!" Karen replied.

June stood tall and squared her shoulders in a confident posture. She practiced fluttering her freshly blackened lashes and smiled. She pulled her long hair over one shoulder, fluffing the ends into a pile of waves, and then stepped inside the barn.

Karen flinched in surprise, looking at her incredulously. Shane jerked his head up, his icy gaze piercing the morning shadows. June met his gaze with equal intensity, sending his glare back. His face softened. He did not speak.

With Ivy stepping in behind her, June said, "I know what you need to appease the spirits."

Karen and Shane looked like children caught with their hands in the cookie jar. "You were eavesdropping," Shane said.

"When it comes to native spirits, I have a right to know. It's my mother's legacy. You forget she's half Delaware," June said in a low tone.

"My mother has Indian blood too," Shane said. "So as far as I'm concerned, I have a right to travel these mountains in peace too."

"Are you going to listen to my sister or not?" Ivy said. "She's trying to help, you know?"

June saw Shane's jaw tightened. Karen released Legend from the cross ties and led him to his stall, and then she walked to the front the barn where a small dog was tied. She untied the dog and picked him up, returning to Shane's side. Shane crossed his arms and leaned against the stall door, glaring at Ivy before looking back to June.

"Okay then, what *do* you suggest?" he asked.

"You plant a holly tree. It's a gesture of peace. It will signify reciprocity. Our white ancestors took away their land. Now you're giving back to nature." She skipped over to Karen and scratched behind the dog's ears. "And who is this little guy?"

Karen inhaled and paused, a look of confusion in her eyes. "Umm, this is Ashes. My aunt's cockapoo had puppies. I don't know what his dad was, but he has a heck of a nose and bays like a beagle. He'll go anywhere. He keeps up with the horses, no problem."

The dog had black and brown interspersed evenly through his coat, except for a patch of gray on his chest and on the bottom of his fluffy tail.

Suddenly, Ginny flung the front barn door open, and Master and Aries bounded in. Karen put Ashes down, and Master rushed to greet him. Soon, they were playing together, jumping up and chasing one another through the aisle way.

"Aww, you brought that mutt again," Ginny said. "You better hope my dogs don't eat him for breakfast."

"Look at them, they're playing like old buddies," June said.

Ginny turned to her. "What are you doing standing around anyway? Why don't you have Blondie tacked yet? I don't have all day."

June could only muster a faint, "Okay, come on, Ivy." She and her sister stepped into the golden pony's stall and prepared her for the lesson. June could hear Ginny talking to Karen.

"So you're going to give Kirsten a lesson when she gets here, right?" Karen assured Ginny that she was waiting for Kirsten and that Legend had already been ridden. He was jumping two-foot in and outs. "Good," Ginny said. "Keep him going. John will come with more jumps next week and help you progress him. Thanks for working with Kirsten. Now that she can ride Dawn, her mom is going to keep her. That's a boarder I get paid for."

There was a brief pause before Ginny addressed Shane. "I'm surprised to see you here. I don't need you to hang out with Brad until later." She paused again. "I think I have it figured out though." June saw Ginny wink at Karen.

Well, Karen sure is Ginny's little golden girl, she thought. She looked into Blondie's big brown eyes and stroked her neck. *No matter, girl. You and I are going to show them.*

With Blondie tacked up, Ivy grabbed the reins and led her out of the stall. "Me first," she said. "You said I could warm her up."

"Whatever," June said. She started out of the stall and came face to face with Shane. She was normally not intimidated by boys, but his steel blue eyes pierced her with an intense glare.

"I hope you're not joking about this holly tree. If I get one, you'll have to show me how to plant it. More importantly, you can't tell anyone else about this place. No one from school, your family, no one."

"Don't worry. I won't tell anyone about your rendezvous point."

He scowled at her for another moment and then started out the back of the barn. June heard him greet someone, and a reply came from a girl's voice. A pretty girl with blondish-brown hair and dressed in riding boots and breeches walked past. A light pink blush highlighted her chiseled cheeks. June heard Karen greet the girl, addressing her as Kirsten.

June walked past Dawn's stall, where Karen and Kirsten were starting to tack the horse, heading for the ring. Karen called to her and introduced her to Kirsten.

"Hey, nice to meet you," Kirsten said, smiling. Her eyes were the color of water.

"Hi," June muttered, and hurried past to the riding ring.

She watched as Ivy struggled to steer Blondie in a figure eight at a walk. Ginny bellowed commands, with Ivy snapping to attention with each one. Yet Ivy needed constant reminders for correct follow-through, and June was getting impatient. She sighed in disgust. Glancing toward the barn, she noticed Kirsten leading Dawn to the mounting block. Karen held Dawn as Kirsten awkwardly mounted her. The Arabian tossed her head.

Kirsten better not get heavier, June thought, *or that little horse won't carry her too far.* She had heard Kirsten was from Richland. Anyone who lived up on the hill had to be rich. It certainly didn't look like Kirsten had ever missed a meal. She continued to watch Kirsten and Dawn and was almost disappointed when Dawn settled into a nice forward trot. Karen was full of compliments for both horse and rider.

Finally, Ivy had progressed to a trot and was getting the hang of posting. Yet June noticed subtle signs of agitation from Blondie. The pony's ears were back, and she swished her tail as Ivy pushed her through the corner.

"Ok, that's enough for you," Ginny snapped. "June will take it from here."

June grabbed Blondie's reins and mounted the second Ivy's feet hit the ground.

"Give her a few turns," Ginny instructed, "then come up over the trotting poles."

June asked Blondie for a trot. The little palomino tossed her head and wrung her tail harder. June gave her a firm kick, and the mare skidded off into a quick trot.

"Easy now, not so rough," Ginny said. "You'll have to steady her before you do the poles."

June looked at Kirsten at the other end of the ring. She was relaxing Dawn at a walk and appeared to be watching June. Ignoring Ginny, June yanked Blondie's right rein and drove her up the center to the trotting poles. She looked through the center of the four white poles, set a few feet apart. Blondie started to veer sideways. She tossed her head again, popping her shoulder out to the right. June yanked her left rein and kicked the pony with both legs. Reluctantly, the palomino trotted through the obstacle. Ginny gave her a dirty look, but didn't reprimand her. She passed through the poles two more times. Ginny instructed her to walk.

"Give her a loose rein and relax a few minutes. You're ready to jump."

Ginny and Ivy set up two small vertical jumps, one on either side of the ring. They placed a pole about twelve feet in front of the jumps.

Curious to see what Kirsten was doing, June watched her at the bottom end of the ring. Dawn was cantering a large circle. Despite Kirsten's slightly unsteady seat, the Arabian carried her effortlessly, her small ears flicking back and forth, waiting for her next cue. Karen smiled broadly as she watched from the circle's center.

Spoiled brat, June thought. *Must be nice to have a perfectly trained horse.*

Ginny's instructions snapped her back to the lesson. "All right, the purpose of the pole is to make her slow down and think about where to put her feet. We don't want her rushing too much. Keep her trotting till you're over the pole. If she wants to canter after that, fine. Just stay with her over the jump."

June picked up a trot and circled both jumps once. She opened her left rein and pointed Blondie to the obstacle on the right side of the ring. Blondie stretched her neck downward as she trotted over the pole. She snorted and hesitated when she saw the small vertical.

"Close your leg, push her!" Ginny commanded.

June kicked the pony's sides and yelled, "Get up!" Blondie stuttered in front of the jump and then hopped it awkwardly. June flopped down over her neck on the landing. Ginny was yelling instructions before June recovered her balance.

"Come around again! This time sit back and wait a bit with your upper body. Drive her between both legs. When she jumps, let the motion of her takeoff close your hips, hold yourself just inches off the saddle. You'll keep your balance better if she goes awkward again."

June barely had time to process this before she crossed the pole again. This time, Blondie jumped it smoothly and cantered away briskly.

"Okay, this time, after you land, bring her back to a trot and go for the next jump."

The first jump faced the top of the ring. June had to turn left and guide Blondie in the opposite direction for the second jump. She would be going toward the bottom of the ring. June noticed Kirsten had stopped Dawn at the bottom of the ring, and she and Karen watched her go past.

June sat proudly in the saddle, driving Blondie strongly forward. Blondie rushed over the first pole, knocking it with anxious hooves. She had picked up a canter before the jump and came to the jump at a long stride, taking off too far from it. June wasn't prepared and got left behind the motion, accidentally yanking Blondie's reins as she tried to stay on. Blondie rushed away with pinned ears. June hauled on the reins, trying to slow her into the next pole.

"Skip it this time, June," Ginny said. "Circle around and steady her."

June felt Karen's and Kirsten's gazes fall heavily on her. She yanked Blondie's head to the inside, pointing her to the second jump. Blondie shook her head, stepping out to the right and skipping the pole. June kicked her with an insistent right leg and drove her between the pole and the jump.

"June, what are you doing?" Ginny called.

Blondie stuttered again, but June was ready for it. This time the horse got too close to the jump. Without enough room to take off gracefully, Blondie popped up and over like a bunny rabbit. June was lifted high from the saddle, and braced herself against Blondie's neck, clinging desperately to her mane. She centered herself as Blondie galloped toward the bottom of the ring, toward Dawn and Kirsten. June saw Kirsten's eyes widen and Dawn's head lift. The Arabian's nostrils flared. June looked directly at them, angling Blondie inward. She buzzed past Dawn with inches to spare.

Dawn snorted and spun a half turn. From the corner of her eye, June saw Kirsten snatch at the reins. Karen jumped into action, moving to Dawn's head and taking the reins. June looked between Blondie's ears and cantered to the top of the ring.

"June, stop right now!" Ginny demanded. "That's enough, you're out of control!"

"That was a little too close, June!" Karen said.

Feeling outnumbered, June reluctantly pulled Blondie up. Ginny's glare blazed into her eyes.

"You need to apologize to Kirsten," Ginny said through gritted teeth.

June felt the blood run into her cheeks. Fury pumped into her veins, and she thought her head would explode. She swallowed hard.

"Sorry, Kirsten. I didn't mean to scare you," she called down the ring.

Kirsten said something to Karen, who nodded in response. Dawn received two pats, one from Kirsten and the other from Karen. Karen turned Dawn around and headed to the barn.

"Okay, the pony has had enough," Ginny said to June. "You need to listen to me next time. Take her in."

"Hey," Ivy said. "I'm supposed to cool her down by riding her at a walk!"

"Not today. She's had enough for now, okay?" Ginny said gently.

June stopped Blondie, fighting back tears. She patted the pony's neck, saying, "I'm sorry, girl. I just wanted to show them I can ride too."

"Make sure you wipe her down with a sponge and give her some hay," Ginny said. "When you're done come to the shop. We have a lot of dogs to bathe." She and Ivy left the riding area to start the work day.

Upon entering the barn, June heard sniffling and a shaky voice. In front of Dawn's stall, Kirsten stood with tears streaming down her face. Karen stood in front of her, concern wrinkling her forehead.

"It's just so hard," Kirsten was saying. "My dad has been in and out of my life so much in the past two years. He'd run off with some younger woman for a few weeks, and then he'd come back. I hated him for it, but at the same time I yearned to see him walk through that door. When he'd come home, things would be okay for a while. This time is different, though. My mom has had enough. She kicked him out last night."

"I can't imagine how he could do that to you," Karen said.

"You know, the best thing about coming here is that I don't have to deal with it. I get to be out in the fresh air, get to hang out with cool friends, and ride my beautiful filly. She's come so far. She was so good today, I almost wish she wasn't." Her voice broke. "My mom told me

I better enjoy her while I can. We might not be able to keep her. My mom doesn't make much at the bank."

Guilt swallowed June. Kirsten wasn't rich after all, and she had plenty of problems. June crept forward toward the other girls, a softly blowing Blondie beside her. The pony's ears flicked at the sound of Kirsten's sobs.

"Kirsten," June said, "Don't give up hope. Talk to Ginny. Maybe if you work around here, she'll give you a discount on the board. Ivy and I help her in the shop, but I know she hates stopping to feed the horses at night after working all day. On weekends, she likes to go out at night. Maybe you can feed for her when you're here."

The hopelessness left Kirsten's face. Her eyes widened and she smiled slightly. "Yeah, maybe. I'll ask her."

June exhaled. Despite the close call with the horses, Kirsten voiced no animosity toward her. The mood lightened when Ashes jumped playfully at Kirsten's legs. He carried a hoof clipping in his mouth and tossed it directly to her. Laughing, she picked up the clipping and tossed it outside the barn. Ashes tore after it, grabbing it and bounding back for more. Giggles replaced tears as the girls took turns throwing the clipping.

June's hands were full as she approached the old house late in the afternoon. Activity in the shop had waned, and it was quiet except for some muffled voices coming from behind the fountain. Lance had his back to her. He was talking to Shane, with Karen standing close by. Two four-wheelers were parked beside them. Her arms tired from the day of lifting dogs into and out of the tub, June hurried toward them. She needed to put down the bag of mulch to avoid poking herself with the hoe she clung to. Her grandmother's small book of Indian chants was safely tucked into her jeans.

Again she came upon a conversation she was not meant to hear. The morning's discussion had been interesting and exciting. However, now she bristled, realizing she was the topic of discussion. She slowed her gait, concealing her footsteps so as not to alert the group.

"I still can't believe you're letting her get involved," Lance said. "We agreed to keep the haven a secret. You know she and Ivy are pains."

"June's not that bad," Shane said. "Ivy's the clingy one. Besides, she promised to keep quiet. She knows how to plant the tree, and she's going to recite a chant. We don't know what we're dealing with up there. She knows more about the native customs than all of us."

"You guys are harsh," Karen said. "Give the girls a chance."

"You didn't grow up with them," Lance retorted.

June emerged from the shadows of the tree-lined driveway. Clearing her throat, she said, "Glad I'm so welcome. I can leave right now if you want."

"No, don't go," Karen said. "I want to hear your grandma's chant. Let me help you with that." She took the bag of mulch from June.

Lance stared at the ground and kicked at the loose rocks. Shane walked past him, elbowing him in the side. "Be nice."

Shane showed her a small potted holly tree. "The guy at the nursery said it's better to plant them in spring. Do you think this will work?"

June stared at him. This time he averted his gaze. "I think the native spirits will take care of it," she said. "I brought that mulch to mix with the soil. It will help drain the water through to the roots."

"All right, let's get going," Lance said. "This is half crazy anyway. I still think someone was pulling a prank on us."

"Like who?" Karen said. "They'd have to be pretty good to carry drums, know those chants, and hide in the bushes." She took the holly tree and sat on the back of Shane's four-wheeler.

"Whatever." Lance scowled at June. "Hop on."

The early autumn sun sat low in the sky. Its fleeting light filtered through the trees, setting the leaves of the surrounding maples alight in blood red. June climbed behind Lance in silence. Instantly, he gunned the four-wheeler. She wrapped her arms around him, digging her nails into him ever so slightly, just enough for him to feel their bite.

CHAPTER 7

An Answered Prayer

Saturday's brilliant autumn sun coaxed away the crispness of dawn. Kirsten opened the door of her father's roadster and inhaled the day's arid glory. She said a hurried thank you for breakfast and walked happily from the Somerset Pike drop-off point toward Ginny's back driveway. Looking across the road to the left, she noted a humble white-sided house. *That must be June and Ivy's house*, she thought.

Crossing the bridge and walking through the back paddock, she saw two horses in the cross ties. Karen and Mindy were busy brushing them. Saddles and bridles lay in wait beside them in the aisle way. As Kirsten got closer, she heard Karen speaking in excited tones.

"I couldn't get Ashes within twenty feet of the cave. He just stood there with his fur bristled. He was staring at something and growling. We couldn't see anything to make him do that. I got chills all down my back. Every bone inside me told me to run. I think Shane knew it. He put his arm around me and held me there."

"Are you sure *that's* why he put his arm around you?" Mindy teased.

"I don't know." Karen paused as if thinking. "Anyway, the drums and chanting started up again. Ashes started barking like crazy. You should have seen Lance. His face was white as a ghost!"

Mindy laughed. "Sorry I missed it."

Karen continued, "I have to give June credit. She was amazing. She wasn't scared at all. She dug a little hole for the holly, filled it with dirt and mulch, and told Shane to get some water. He filled a bottle from one of those little waterfalls coming from the outside of the rock formation. He watered the tree, and we all joined hands around it, except for June. She stood in the middle, beside the holly. She took out this small, really old-looking book. I guess it was her grandma's. June recited something from the book. I couldn't make out what she was saying, it wasn't in English. When she was done, she flung both hands up in the air. Suddenly, the chanting and drums stopped."

"You're kidding," Mindy said.

Kirsten stood awkwardly at the barn door, unsure if she wanted to know what the girls were talking about. Just when she thought she had met some nice friends ...

Suddenly, Ashes popped out from between the horses and announced Kirsten's presence. Karen peeked around Legend's substantial body. She bit her bottom lip, looking guilty.

"What kind of freaky stuff are you guys into?" Kristen asked.

Karen and Mindy both laughed. "Come here," Karen said. "You might as well know too."

Karen explained about Shane's discovery of a magical place on top of the mountain that was untouched by modern man. She said it was exquisitely beautiful, and if the trail was cleared a bit, they could ride the horses there. There was one problem—it appeared to be haunted by the spirits of Indians, and that their story was painted on the wall of a cave. Karen stressed that its whereabouts had to be kept a secret.

"So the holly was a peace offering," she finished.

Blinking away her disbelief, Kirsten said, "Okay then, where are we going riding today?"

The front door of the barn opened and a tall, thin woman stepped inside.

"Oh, hey, Mary," Karen said. "We were just deciding where to go riding today."

Ginny's cousin Mary was friendly, talkative, and entertaining. She liked to tell stories of working on a racetrack as an exercise rider. She possessed real-life knowledge of how to handle difficult, excitable Thoroughbreds. Her above-average height and long legs enabled her to keep a secure seat when they acted up. She had a quiet way about her in the saddle, and Kirsten admired the way she handled Dorian. Yet Mary fiercely discouraged the girls from getting involved directly with the racetrack, telling them about the mistreatment of horses and young girls. Mary had suffered a back injury while schooling a horse in the starting gate. When she told the trainer she would need time to heal, he fired her.

Mary pushed her dark brown hair behind her shoulders, revealing a unique but elegant profile. A tiny bulb of cartilage perched midway down her nose, above which vibrant blue eyes contrasted with her tanned skin. She pointed a slim finger up the road and said, "Follow the Dam Road the whole way to the top of the hill." She ignored the girls' giggles at the name of the road. "It will cross in front of the North Fork Dam. The views are great. The road will bear to the left. You'll come upon Mountain View Road to the left. Go about a mile and you'll hit North Fork Country Club Road. Make that left and you'll be heading home on the other side of the creek. You know, Shane's road." She smiled at Karen.

Kirsten watched Karen's face redden at Mary's teasing. *I'll have to meet this Shane*, she thought.

June rushed in. "Hi, sorry I'm late. Ivy was arguing with me because she's jealous I'm riding today. She's supposed to work in the shop. I promised she could ride tomorrow to get her off my back."

Kirsten studied the fragile-looking auburn-haired girl. It was hard to believe she could calm restless spirits.

The girls thanked Mary and finished tacking their horses. They turned left out of Ginny's driveway with Legend in the lead, followed by Dawn, Blondie, and Cajun. Ashes accompanied Legend. The little dog trotted effortlessly, keeping up with the Thoroughbred's long strides.

Kirsten had been nervous about taking Dawn out of the ring, but the filly seemed completely at ease. She looked back to the riding ring, where Mary was schooling Dorian. He kicked up his heels at a canter, and Mary crouched centered on his back, unaffected by his shenanigans. Kirsten patted Dawn's neck, saying, "You just keep looking ahead."

The clip-clop of hooves echoed through the valley. It was difficult to hear each other, but Kirsten didn't mind. She breathed in the fresh air and admired the evolving gold, reds, and oranges of fall. They were riding parallel to a golf course. Its pristine green rolled along the creek endlessly. Kirsten caught Karen's comment about what a waste of space a golf course was, and how great it would be to have it as horse pasture and a cross-country riding course. Kirsten agreed absentmindedly. She could stay just like this forever.

They started up a large incline at a trot. Dawn was spritely on her feet, staying just behind the confident Legend. Kirsten mirrored Karen's two-point position, lifting her weight and holding it slightly off Dawn's back. The North Fork Dam sat atop the hill. A collective gasp escaped the girls, and they stopped to admire the beauty of the reservoir. The sparkling water reflected the blue sky. A majestic red-tailed hawk glided overhead. Fish jumped intermittently from the water. A refreshing breeze lifted Dawn's forelock and flipped her mane back. The filly tossed her head lightly, as if to say, "That feels good."

"Wow, this is neat," Karen said. "Can you believe we get our drinking water in Johnstown from here?"

They followed the road along the reservoir until they met Mountain View Road. It provided its own spectacle, boasting views of the mountain ranges to the south and east. The road was surrounded by rolling farms on each side. They passed several pastures filled with dairy cows, sheep, and the occasional draft horse. The ride could not have been better, and Kirsten decided to make an announcement.

She spoke loudly over the hoof beats. "So this week has been rough. My dad was in and out all the time getting his things. My mom was freaking out, screaming at him constantly. But some good came of it. She told him Dawn is good for me and that Ginny is letting me work some of the board off. She insisted my dad pay the rest. I just have to clean his apartment once in a while. So, thank God, my prayers have been answered. I can keep Dawn!"

Hoorays and congratulations momentarily deafened the hoof beats. Kirsten turned to June and thanked her for suggesting she help Ginny feed.

"I just want to break out in song," Karen said. "That new Bon Jovi tune will do."

She started singing "Livin' on a Prayer." The others joined in, reciting the inspirational rock song about a couple facing hard times and fighting for their dreams.

Feelings of camaraderie brought tears to Kirsten's eyes, which washed away memories of her stress-filled home life.

The horses crossed from the Mountain View Road to the North Fork Country Club Road. It was steep at the top, and they were headed downhill. The road turned from macadam to a combination of dirt, gravel, and rock. The horses had to be careful with foot placement, but it was wide enough for them to feel comfortable. Legend was in the lead and quite relaxed. He easily descended the hill into the valley, and the road changed back to macadam.

They approached a small red house with a charming brook glistening in the sunlight behind it.

"What a quaint little house," Kirsten said.

The words had barely left her mouth when the garage door rumbled open. The horses merely cocked an ear toward the commotion. That is, all the horses except Dawn. Kirsten felt her tense like a coil, ready to spring. Her fear heightened as three teenage boys came bounding out of the garage, wrestling each other for a football. They rolled and tumbled across the yard toward the road, oblivious to the iron-clad hooves approaching. Kirsten struggled to steady Dawn as the Arabian pranced and snorted alongside Legend. The ball broke loose from the mass of arms and legs. It bounced onto the road and, as if precisely planned, hit Dawn squarely in the neck. She spun wildly. Kirsten lost her seat and clung to her neck.

Karen turned the unimpressed Legend into Dawn, blocking her from completing a full spin. The Arabian stopped abruptly as her shoulders met Legend's. Dawn's tantrum ended with wide eyes and a snort, and the horse stood still. She stared down her nose at the boys. Kirsten removed herself from the filly's neck and followed her lead with a piercing stare.

The three boys stared back, mouths agape and faces reddening.

"Leave it to you to cause a near catastrophe, Shane," Karen said flatly.

"Sorry, we didn't know," the boy with brown hair and intense blue eyes said.

Another boy detached himself and walked over to Cajun. "Hey, Mindy," he said, and started chatting as if no one else was there.

"Don't blame, Shane," June said. "It's Gage's garage they came tumbling out of." She nodded to the third boy, who continued to stare at Kirsten, his face still red with embarrassment.

"You're so charming, June," Shane said. "We have to put up with you on the school bus. Now you're reading us the riot act on a Saturday."

Finally, the staring boy spoke to Kirsten. "I—I'm sorry we spooked your horse."

"No problem." Kirsten regained her composure. "You just made my heart skip a beat or two."

Gage's eyes were dark and almond shaped. His hair was a light reddish brown, and his skin almost matched it. Along with the broad structure of his cheekbones, Kristen guessed he had a unique ethnic background.

"You did good to stay on," he said.

Shane introduced Gage to the group. "Maybe we can all hang out later?" he said, smiling up at Karen.

"We'll be done by four o'clock," she said. "Wait a minute. Ginny's going out tonight. Are you watching Brad?"

There was a collective groan from the girls. Shane smirked. "He's not that bad. With us guys down there, he'll leave you alone. And for the last time, I don't watch him. I keep him out of trouble."

"No, you're a babysitter, dude," Lance said.

Laughter erupted from all sides, cutting any remaining tension. Even Gage high fived Lance.

"Okay, dummies, we'll see you at Ginny's," Karen said.

The girls continued down the road, with Mindy reporting an exchange she'd overheard between Gage and Lance before they were out of earshot. Gage asked Lance if he thought Kirsten was all right.

"Yeah," Lance had replied. "Don't be a dork."

The girls mocked the boys' voices and mannerisms the rest of the way home.

CHAPTER 8

Capture the Flag

Four o'clock came, sending Ginny to town and her mother's house to prepare for a night out. Mindy and Karen sat on the base of the old fountain, fresh clothes and a dab of makeup applied. Karen turned to her reflection in the window of the dog grooming shop. Grumbling, she got up and stood closer to the window, turning her head upside down and flipping her hair higher and wider from her face. She grabbed her purse and applied a second layer of hair spray.

"I like those jeans," Mindy said, admiring Karen's new Jordache jeans. Her own Sassoon jeans definitely did not have that brand-new look.

"Thanks," Karen said. "They took up a lot of school clothes budget."

Mindy rubbed the chill of the late afternoon from her arms. The silver tank top she wore might not be enough for an autumn evening.

Suddenly, a sarcastic voice came from behind the house. "Eww, I like your jeans. Eww, does my hair look okay?" Brad walked into view, smirking from beneath a long lock of sandy-brown hair.

"So it's true," Mindy said. "Your mom really did leave you behind to torture us."

"At least we get to leave," Karen said. "Shane is stuck with him all night."

"You know you'd miss me if I wasn't here," Brad said.

"I don't know about that." June, Ivy, and Kirsten emerged from the back driveway. "We see enough of you on the bus."

Brad ran past the sisters, pinching Ivy's and then June's bottoms as he blitzed past. Sounds of disgust came from all the girls.

Finally, the three other boys came down from the Country Club Road. Lance and Shane walked side by side with Gage trailing behind. Mindy went directly to Lance, saying, "It's about time. Brad is driving us nuts."

"Then let's get the game underway," Lance said. "We're playing capture the flag. Boys against girls." He took two rags from his back pocket, one blue and one red. "These are the flags. Each team hides their flag, somewhere behind the old house or the yard. You have to leave a little piece showing. Both teams search for their opponent's flag. If you find it, you run back to your base. The runner can have guards, because the opposite team can take their flag back if they can get to the runner. The guards can do whatever's necessary to protect the runner. If the runner gets back to their base without getting tagged by the opposite team, they win that round. Best of five rounds wins the game. Girls' base is the fountain; boys' base is the porch."

"Bring it on," Mindy said.

"But no one tackle me," Karen said. "I don't want to ruin my jeans."

Why would she say that with Brad around? Mindy thought. *He'll target her for sure.* She took the red flag and went behind the house. She heard comments coming from the front like, "No peeking," and "Stay back here!" She searched the large backyard for a good hiding place. Midway across the yard, on the left was on old well. Its stone sides stood about three feet high. It had a tattered black-shingled roof supported by timber. Flecks of red paint remained on the decaying wood. The top of the well was boarded over, making it nonfunctional. She approached the well eagerly, but stopped herself, thinking that it was too obvious. She continued around the yard, which extended from the house for about an acre and ended at another tree line. She walked parallel to the tree line for several yards. Toward the left corner, a dark path led into the woods. It seemed to run along the creek. As she walked toward the path, a gush of cool air blasted her, popping goose pimples from her arms. *Okay, I won't go down there,* she thought. The gust was followed by an eerie quiet. She couldn't even hear her friends anymore. She was prompted to get out of there. She eyed a small junk pile of steel and wood barely covered by weeds to the right of the path. Hastily, she placed the flag on top of an old board, with most of it covered by the weeds.

Mindy rejoined the group. With a nod, Lance marched past with his flag and went behind the house. He returned after a few minutes, expressionless. The teams sequestered briefly, with Mindy and Lance telling their teammates where their flags were hidden.

"Okay," Lance called, "girls by the fountain, boys on the porch." When everyone was in place, he said, "On your mark, get set, go!"

The boys stormed down the porch steps and toward the backyard. Instead of following them, Mindy led her team across the front of the house and then turned to the backyard. The well was directly in front of her. She sprinted toward it, flanked by June and Ivy. Karen and Kirsten were right behind them.

Closing in on the well, she saw just a bit of blue dangling from a wooden rafter.

"I knew it, silly boy," she said aloud.

Suddenly, Lance came out of nowhere, barreling toward her. He cut in front of Ivy, causing her to trip. Mindy accelerated to her fullest. She could hear Lance breathing behind her and felt June's presence a few feet behind. Catching movement from the corner of her eye, she saw a red baseball cap headed toward June. It was Gage. He grabbed June in a bear hug, as if plucking her out of the air. Mindy looked back to see a smiling, giggling June grab for Gage's cap. Lance continued to press her, and Mindy regretted glancing back. His footsteps were directly behind hers. His fingers clutched at her shoulders. Knowing she was done for, she yelled, "Karen! It's hanging from the well!" As Mindy hit the ground, the Jordaches streaked past her.

Mindy was the first to sit up. Lance lay beside her on his side, heaving for air. She decided to take a break and enjoy the show. Brad and Shane were along the tree line, no doubt searching for the girls' flag. They were oblivious to Karen, who yanked their blue flag from the well with a triumphant smile. Karen turned and dashed to the left, cutting across the yard toward the porch. Mindy yelled, "No! Not that way!" It was too late. Karen was on her way, the longer way.

Gage gave up on getting his hat back from June. He yelled to his teammates, "Brad, Shane! She's getting away!"

Brad's head snapped up. Focusing on his prey with a deadly scowl, he raced after Karen. Shane followed in close pursuit.

"There goes those jeans," Mindy said. Lance finally sat up beside her.

Brad angled diagonally across the yard, like a cheetah flanking a gazelle, and then he paused and flexed his knees.

"What's he gonna do, jump on her?" Mindy said.

Karen spotted him and tried to duck to the right. Brad launched himself at her but suddenly was knocked over. Shane had blocked him. Now both boys lay on the ground in a tangled mess. Karen skipped away smiling. She disappeared around the house.

"Shane!" Lance yelled. "What the hell! Whose side are you on?"

Mindy sat on the ground laughing, unable to get up. Kirsten joined her, gasping for air and bent in half with laughter.

"Not funny!" Lance stormed off.

The red flag remained at the junk pile for another round. This time Ivy snagged the boys' blue flag from the yoke of a large oak tree at the wood's border. She waved it in front of Shane playfully, prancing in front of him instead of tearing off to the base. Shane was more interested in blocking Karen, who was guarding Ivy. As Shane wrapped his arms around Karen, Ivy pouted and jogged to the safety of the fountain.

Lance called a time out before the third round and demanded that the girls wait by the fountain. He gathered the boys on the porch. Mindy heard him grumbling commands to Gage and Brad and telling Shane to get his head in the game. She stifled her giggles, trying to hear every word.

"Who knew he was so serious," Karen said.

"Karen, it's your fault for distracting Shane," Mindy teased.

The third round began with Mindy focused on Brad. His interest in the junk pile during previous rounds put her flag in imminent danger. With the game at stake, her strategy was to send Karen, Kirsten, and Ivy to look for the boys' flag. With Shane intent on chasing Karen and Gage focused on all of the girls' movements, Mindy would contend with Brad and Lance. Although he was mad, Lance was tiring. If she kept him moving, only Brad was left to sniff out their flag. She decided the scrappy June was best suited to tangle with him.

From the word go, Lance bee lined for the junk pile. Brad was near it, searching the tall weeds. Mindy gestured to June, placing her between Brad and the junk pile. Creeping toward Lance, Mindy positioned herself directly behind him. She reached his shoulder and tapped it. Quickly, he turned to her with an expression of satisfaction. He saw the red flag.

"Brad, to your right!" Lance yelled. "In that junk pile."

Brad leaped into action, smashing through the weeds. June was right behind him. Courageously, she dove at his legs, taking him down hard.

"Wow! What a tackle!" Mindy exclaimed.

Lance bolted for the junk pile, sacrificing his own skin under Mindy's clawing fingertips as he broke free. Mindy stumbled after him, but was stopped in her tracks by a human blockade. June had Brad pinned, both hands around his neck. She was banging his head on the ground.

"Don't you ever call me a bitch again!" she screamed.

Brad was smiling bravely, but there was concern in his eyes. He gripped her arms and tried to push her off. She wouldn't budge.

Mindy approached with apprehension. "June, maybe you should stop."

June wasn't going anywhere. "I want to kill him!"

Mindy was grateful to see Shane running up. He pulled June off Brad and took her aside, talking in low tones. Karen and Kirsten stared at Mindy in bewilderment. Mindy could only shrug.

Lance called from the porch, "Ha ha! Come on, guys, we're back in the game!" He waved the red flag jubilantly.

Brad sat up, pounding the ground with both fists. His face was red, and he jumped to his feet in a huff. Mindy held her breath, waiting for Brad to go after June again. Yet he struck off toward Lance, swinging his arms in irritation. June charged away from Shane, yelling something at Brad's back. Shane grabbed her waist and spun her around, demanding she calm down. Ivy and Gage joined the group from the creek side. Karen and Kirsten inched past the commotion and then scurried to Mindy's side. A temporary silence overcame the teens as they walked to their bases.

Kirsten opened the lines of communication by crossing her eyes and sticking her tongue out at the boys. The others burst into uneasy giggles, and everyone seemed to sigh at once.

Gage sidled up to Kirsten. "So what happened?"

"I guess Brad called June a bitch," Kirsten replied.

"Okay, thanks." Gage patted Kirsten on the shoulder and then rushed over to walk with Brad. They weren't so far ahead that Mindy couldn't hear what they said to each other.

"Man, how did you hold it together?" Gage asked. "You must have wanted to kill her for doing that."

"My dad told me, never hit a girl," Brad replied.

Everyone stood around the porch. Shane looked at both June and Brad. "This is supposed to fun. Can you all handle this without killing each other?"

"Yeah, fine," Brad said.

"Okay, let's go," Lance said. "It will be dark soon."

The fourth round went to the boys, despite Mindy's best effort of placing the flag halfway up a tree. To her dismay, Brad spotted it and scaled it in no time. Gage and Lance put up a heavy defense, and Brad was able to sprint to the porch unchallenged.

Round five would take the game. Mindy strategized silently, piecing together observations of the boys' behavior from the previous two rounds. She deduced that the boy's flag was somewhere in the left corner of the yard, close to the creek. Gage seemed particularly anxious to protect that spot, and Lance frequently looked in that direction.

She was barely concerned about the new hiding spot for her flag. The key to the game was for the girls to get the boys' flag immediately, before they had an inkling of where the girls' flag was. She placed the red flag inside a small alcove at the back of the old house. There were nails underneath the overhang, and she was able to hang it across two of them. She instructed Karen to lure Shane away toward the tree line. Kirsten would stick to Gage like glue, and the sisters would search the creek corner for the boys' flag.

"I'll linger around the alcove," she added. "Maybe Lance will realize I'm protecting our flag. The wild card is Brad."

Predictable Shane followed Karen along the tree line. The sly smile on Karen's face seemed to say, *This is too easy.* With Shane handled, Mindy noted Lance's location to the left and brushed past him. She made no eye contact and, running backward, acted like she was watching the others. She steadily backed up toward the alcove, Lance subtly watching her. With his head twitching like an eagle's, he surveyed the others to the left. The girls commenced their assault. Kirsten hovered in front of Gage, faking him out by trying to run by from one side and then the other. Ivy angled toward the creek edge. June backed Kirsten, a second guard between Gage and Ivy. Noticing this, Lance shuddered as if struck by lightning. He tore toward Ivy, leaving Mindy by herself.

Afraid to leave her own flag completely vulnerable, Mindy screamed, "Ivy! Here comes Lance!"

Suddenly, Mindy's feet went out from under her as Brad's arms wrapped around her knees. He looked up at her like a bratty child that continually pulls on his mother's sleeve for attention.

Before she could kick him off, he looked to the back of the house. His eyes widened with realization. He jumped up and ran toward the alcove.

Mindy leaped to her feet and started after Brad. A commotion from the opposite direction distracted her. Ivy was lifting something heavy from the weeds. She flung it aside and yanked the blue flag overhead.

"Yes!" she cried, only to be bowled over by a charging Lance. The blue flag disappeared in a sea of bodies and limbs. June joined the heap. A squall of limbs and arms shook the weeds. Suddenly, a head of auburn waves emerged from the huddle. June broke free and sprinted across the yard, her hair like the tail of a comet. She surged toward the fountain, blue flag in hand. Mindy grinned, but quickly remembered Brad.

He was at the alcove, his hand on the red flag. He jerked downward, but the flag resisted with a ripping sound. The flag was caught on a nail.

"Crap!" Brad yelled.

As he fumbled to free the flag, Mindy closed in. She put him in a bear hug, clutching his writhing body at the waist. He twisted and turned, weaseling away from her. He was off toward the boys' base of the porch.

Panting and alone, Mindy felt surrounded by an eerie silence. Half afraid, she crept around to the front of the house. A concerted roar greeted her, a combination of male grumbling and female celebration. Lance kicked the fountain in disgust. Brad let the red flag drop to the ground. Shane and Gage stood with hands in pockets, looking snubbed.

Mindy laughed at the scene. Ivy and June ran up to her, hugging her simultaneously. "You were like a rocket," Mindy told June. Karen came forward to high five Mindy, with Kirsten right behind her. The girls basked in glory for a moment, cheering for themselves.

"All right, don't rub it in," a dejected Lance said. He extended his hand to Mindy. She took it, and he held it gently.

"Pretty good game, captain." he said.

She hid a smile as Lance kept hold of her hand.

Shane led the group up the driveway toward Country Club Road. Animated, he told Karen some kind of story. The others shuffled behind, with Mindy and Lance trailing. Ivy and Brad walked shoulder to shoulder, but silently. On the other hand, Gage and Kirsten were boisterous, with Kirsten razing him about something. He gave her a sideways smile as she punched him on the arm. June came trotting up beside Gage, stealing his hat again. He barely acknowledged her. Shaking his head, he turned back to Kirsten. June was left with an empty hat to escort her up the hill.

There were grassy knolls on either side of the driveway. Shane cut to the right and guided Karen to a vantage point overlooking the old house. Lance squeezed Mindy's hand, as if assuring himself she was still there. They settled behind Karen and Shane. The others filed in around them, sitting scattered about the hillside.

The sun sank behind the trees. Red rays cast about their tops like brilliant crowns, boosting the stunning color of the leaves. The teens sat quietly for a while, breathing deeply and admiring the evening. After a few minutes, Lance broke the silence.

"So, between the haunted hills and this house, what is up with this area? I mean, I understand how the native spirits are restless." He looked at Mindy. "Did you know that Iron Maiden has a song about the plight of the Indians? I just thought it was cool metal, but if you listen to the lyrics, you get a sense of the fear and hardships they experienced, being driven out of their homelands."

"You should play it for us sometime," Mindy said, and Lance smiled.

He continued, "So, Shane, you say there are weird lights coming from this house at night?" He gestured to the house, whose black interior stared back at them.

"Yeah. I look down here a lot from my porch. I see lights flashing on and off through that top window." He pointed to the third-floor window where the fire had been.

"Okay, okay. You guys are creeping me out," Karen said.

"You chicken," Brad said. "There's no such thing as ghosts."

Lance looked at Mindy and put a finger to his lips. "Shhh." With a mischievous look, he stood quietly and crept away.

Dusk began to envelop the hollow. A streetlight buzzed to life, startling Karen. The group laughed at her, but not for long. Mindy watched as jaws dropped and gazes fixed on the third-floor window. A flashing light appeared, ducking from one corner of the window to another. Karen stiffened, and she gripped Shane's hand, causing him to flinch. The flashing darted from corner to corner. Karen leaped to her feet and ran headlong down the road toward the Somerset Pike. Laughing, Shane started after her.

"Hold on, hold on! It's a joke." He finally caught Karen, grabbing her shoulders and bringing her to a standstill. He guided her around to face his house, catty-corner to Ginny's property. Mindy and the others faces turned to look as well. Lance stood at the top of Shane's front steps with a mirror. He used the mirror to angle the glow from the streetlight into the window. He doubled over in laughter, unable to continue the prank.

"You jerks!" Karen promptly punched Shane in the ribs. She shook an angry fist at Lance, who scuttled down the steps, across the road, and behind Mindy for protection. The others broke into laughter, with Karen quickly joining them.

"I was about a second from following you, Karen," Kirsten said.

"You're fine," Gage said. She smiled in reply.

"Okay, smarty," Ivy said to Lance. "If you think it's that funny, I dare you to go in there. I've seen those weird lights myself. I know it's not you all the time."

"No problem," he said. "But only if Mindy goes with me."

Mindy shrugged. "Fine." The others made a collective gasp.

"I'll get a flashlight from the dog grooming shop," Ivy said.

The group headed back to the house and the front door. Most of the house was in desperate disrepair, so Ginny hadn't bothered installing locks except at the grooming shop.

Lance took the flashlight from Ivy. "Nobody better fool around. We need to seriously see if this is really haunted."

Surprisingly, even Brad agreed to stay quiet.

"The porch is as far as I get," Karen said. She stood at the edge of the steps, waving to Mindy as she stepped inside.

Lance took Mindy's hand. The place smelled musty. The dry wooden floor creaked loudly under their feet. The flashlight did little to cut the darkness. Lance ran his hand along the wall and found the doorway that opened into the living room. Following his lead, Mindy noted Lance's familiarity with the layout.

"How do you know where you're going?"

"Please," Lance said. "As if I could ignore the temptation of exploring this place. I've been in here before."

The living room was in the east end of the house, with large windows looking out toward the fountain. Mindy glanced at it, imagining the fountain shooting water to the sky. An ancient but solid brass curtain hanger remained at the top of the window. Lance guided her to the right. There was a square outline barely discernible on the dark wall. The brick of an old fireplace extended outward and upward from the square.

"This must have been a nice fireplace at one time," Lance said. "Feel the design on the woodwork." He took her hand and ran it over the fireplace's trim.

She traced an elaborate design of circles and scrolls. "Yeah, that seems pretty fancy."

"Not as fancy as you." He brushed her hair from her face and cupped her jaw in his hand. He kissed her softly.

Pleasantly surprised, she embraced him, and they lingered for several minutes in front of the ornate fireplace. Mindy felt strangely comfortable in the large, dark room. She only felt the warmth of Lance's embrace.

Suddenly, a commotion from the porch disturbed them. "I guess the natives are getting restless," Lance said. "We better go."

Lance and Mindy walked back through the foyer. Mindy saw her friends' curious faces peering at them through the glass door. Annoyed, she prepared to chastise them for ruining her moment. Yet as she opened her mouth, a force took her voice away. It hit her with a thud from behind, pushing her forward. The heat from an overwhelming furnace flogged her back. Trying to look behind her, she squinted against a blazing light. Terrified, she ran for the door, dragging Lance with her. It felt like a fire was chasing them down. Desperately, they clawed at the door handle. It wouldn't open. The heat bore down on them. Mindy screamed.

Suddenly, darkness fell. The intense light disappeared as quickly as it had started. The cool night air filtered through the cracks in the glass. The door opened and Brad let them out. He was the only one there.

Mindy tried to slow her breathing. She couldn't stop shaking. Lance was beside her, hyperventilating. His eyes rolled to the back of his head, and he crumbled to his knees. Holding on to him, Mindy knelt in front of him. She lifted his head, uncertain if he had fainted. Brad grabbed Lance's arm and pulled him up. Lance shook his head, as if he had been splashed with cold water. He wrapped his arm around Mindy's shoulders, and with Brad on the other side, the trio stumbled down the porch steps.

Karen ran toward them. "Mindy!" she yelled. "I'm so sorry. The heat was unbearable. It practically blew us of the porch. Are you okay?"

"Don't worry about it," Mindy said. "I would have been right behind you, but the door wouldn't open." She looked at Brad. "I can't believe it. Brad, you really helped us. Thanks."

"It's all right," he replied.

"What in the world was it?" Mindy asked Karen.

"It was a lady, or the form of one. A lady surrounded by incredible light," Karen said incredulously.

Shane emerged from the darkness. "Come on, guys. Everyone else is down by the barn."

Mindy scurried over the bridge first, with Lance directly behind her. Brad, Shane, and Karen followed, talking in low tones. As Mindy approached the barnyard, June, Ivy and Kirsten ran to greet her. Their hugs and reassuring words comforted her. Gage stepped forward and patted Lance on the back.

The hollow buzzed with their exclamations of disbelief and amazement, causing the horses to snort in their stalls and Master and Aries to bark from the trailer. Mindy shook away remnants of flashing light from her eyes. She wiped sweat from her brow and rubbed her throbbing temples.

"That's why she's called Lady Luminess, but I never saw that much power before," June said.

"There's got to be an explanation," Gage said. "An electrical short or something. It's crazy to say that was a lady's ghost."

"Hey, genius," Ivy said. "Ginny doesn't have electricity hooked up in that part of the house. Why would she? You can't live in there."

"That was definitely a woman," Karen said. "I saw the outline of her head, long hair, her shoulders, and a flowing skirt. I won't sleep for weeks."

"Whatever it is," Lance said, his fear still clear on his face, "we're not welcome in there. I don't get it. I never saw that when I was in there before."

"It felt like we were about to be devoured," Mindy said, "then she stopped at the last second. What does that mean?"

"I don't know," Shane said, "but it's going to be an interesting Halloween."

CHAPTER 9

HAPPY HALLOWEEN

The crisp air of the October morning crept into Karen's bedroom, waking her from a deep, dream-filled sleep. Shivering, she blinked away her drowsiness and closed the window next to her bed. She sat back down on the bed, reluctant to leave the pleasantness of her dreams. Emerging slowly into reality, she pondered the unlikely scenarios of those dreams.

Curiously, she had been the lady of the old house. Surrounded by the peace of a hazy mist, she had felt as if she were floating. She sat astride a magnificent chestnut stallion, looking out over his finely arched neck, between his pricked, inwardly curved ears. Her hands rested upon broad, muscular shoulders, providing the perfect balance for her to follow his floating movements as one. They galloped in midair, past the old house and up the grassy knoll toward Shane's. Yet there was no road and no house. The entire area was a vast meadow. The stallion streamed past whispering, waving trees, which rustled their leaves in response. Continuing on, he glided up the hillside to where Shane's yard should have been and ran on into the woods that led to the haven.

Fully awake, Karen thought of how the dream had been awesome, not scary or evil at all. Maybe that old house wasn't so bad. Craving that feeling of tranquility and oneness with a horse, she decided to go riding early.

"It will be just me and Legend," she said aloud, looking down at the expectant eyes of her dog. "And you too, Ashes."

Legend climbed eagerly up the back driveway toward Shane's side yard. Ashes's bannered tail led the way into the grassy lot, where he stopped to smell and track the scents of nature. Karen held her breath, as if this would quiet the sound of Legend's strides ascending the hill. A strange desire to be alone had overcome her. She guided the horse under the autumn canopy at the yard's far border.

Entering the forest, Legend snorted. He lowered his head, tossing it gently on occasion. He picked his way over roots and stones, his ears rotating laterally and angling outward in concentration. His long strides carried them up the path. Karen almost wished he'd slow down. She wanted to savor these moments. She couldn't mess with his natural rhythm, though, and gave the horse a loose rein. Ashes panted ever so slightly, and Karen knew he'd like to drink from the crystal pools of the haven.

The "shades of death" enveloped them with damp coolness. The only noise came from Legend's hooves. The tunnel of branches formed a dome just above Karen's head, as if it had been created to her and Legend's specifications.

No need to bring those noisy machines up here again, she thought.

They emerged into the meadow with its colossal haven. Legend lifted his head and stopped abruptly. Ashes flanked him, and the two stood at attention, still as statues. The only movements came from their nostrils as they tested the wind. Karen sat still in the saddle, allowing the horse to observe the unfamiliar territory. Legend's ears flicked forward and back, and he lowered his head, snorting again. Karen took a deep breath. The fresh air filled her lungs, but it seemed to expand through her whole body. Suddenly, she felt lighter, as if she were hovering over the horse's back. A sense of peace descended, and she felt as if she was only half inside her body. Legend proceeded forward. Without guidance, he went straight to the newly planted holly tree at the base of the haven. Ashes lingered behind for a moment, whining in protest. Karen simply looked back at him, holding his gaze. Promptly, the little dog followed the Thoroughbred onward.

Karen gaped at the holly. Planted only a month before, it already stood four feet high. Its evergreen leaves shone with luster, and bright red berries bulged from its branches. Legend stopped beside it, took a deep breath, and lowered his head in relaxation.

The mysterious lightness lingered through Karen's body. A month ago, she would have dodged the strange feeling by running away down the path screaming. Yet now she felt at total peace. The lightness filtered through the air, bringing the faint echo of flute music in small gusts. It soothed her soul, and the trio remained in silent meditation for a while.

With a thud, time returned weight to Karen's body. Her arms and legs felt like bricks, and her head was foggy. Her labored breathing ignited her senses again. She shook her head and blinked as if coming out of a trance. Clouds rolled across the sky, intermittently revealing the brightness of the sun. The crispness of morning gave way to a pleasant October afternoon.

The sun's rays prompted Legend into action. He took the bit and started off toward the opening of the cave where Shane had discovered the paintings. Ashes ran alongside, stopping and starting as his nose picked up interesting smells. Legend reached the cave, sticking his head into its blackness. Fearlessly, he started through the passageway.

"Whoa, buddy, I won't fit through if I'm on your back."

Karen halted the horse and dismounted. She saw only a glimmer of light at the other end. The floor felt solid under her feet, but she hesitated, debating the safety of going through. Legend made her mind up for her. He tugged at the reins, practically pulling her alongside him.

"Okay, okay, we'll go then."

She walked alongside him, calling for Ashes to follow. Only his nails clipping on the granite floor assured her that the dog was following. She held Legend's withers, using them as her guide.

As they reentered the light of day, Karen shielded her eyes from the sun. After blinking away the discomfort, she gazed upon the pristine beauty of the secret meadow inside the haven's protective walls. Legend dropped his head and devoured the lush grass, bit and all. Ashes bounded through the center of the meadow to the crystal waters of the creek. He lapped the water enthusiastically, as if he'd never tasted anything so good. Legend followed his lead, meandering toward the creek between bites of grass. He too took a good long drink of water. He lifted his head between sips, pricking his ears at a movement in the center of the meadow. Karen followed his gaze and saw the beautiful buck who called this place home. Farther in the distance, three does dotted the fringe of the meadow. The buck snorted and shook his head, and then sprang away.

"Don't worry, big boy. Your secret's safe with me."

As Legend grazed, she admired the deer from afar and listened to the songbirds. Finally, she looked at her watch. It was going on three o'clock.

"Oh, man. We better get going." It was trick or treat night and she had to have the barn work finished before she changed.

Karen remained in a state of bliss as she rode home. Her consciousness seemed to drift somewhere above her, looking down from the treetops and gliding along with the horse. Legend descended into the grassy lot beside Shane's house, and Karen was jolted back into reality.

Standing in the middle of the lot were Shane and Ivy engaged in intense conversation. Ivy stood in front of Shane, clutching his arm and talking close to his face. Shane moved back as if to distance himself, but Ivy moved with him. He shrugged her arm away. Ivy let go briefly, but then placed her hand on his forearm, not clutching but maintaining contact.

A flood of anger welled inside Karen. Initially, she was annoyed to see anyone, aching to hold her connection to serenity. However, seeing Ivy so close to Shane infuriated her. What could they possibly be talking about?

Legend's hoof steps alerted the pair. They looked up, startled by the large creature stepping through the grass. Shane's eyes widened and his mouth opened in surprise. Ivy greeted Karen with a smile.

"Karen! Where have you been? We've been looking all over for you. You've been gone since this morning and Ginny's worried sick. She thought you lost the horse or something."

"More importantly, we thought you were hurt," Shane said. "You shouldn't just take off like that and not tell anyone where you are."

He looked dead serious, glaring at her with those ice-blue eyes. If Karen didn't know him, she might have been intimidated. Instead she brushed off his concerns. Her anger dissipated, and her suspicion of Ivy's intentions crawled to the back of her mind.

"What? I'm not allowed to enjoy a ride by myself to the haven?" she asked.

"The haven?" Shane said. "I didn't think the trail was clear enough for a horse and rider to pass through. That's why I didn't look there."

"Obviously, you have a lot to learn," she said shortly. Her jealousy refused to release her. She stuck her chin up and continued to ride past the others.

"Hey, I want to talk to you before trick or treating," Shane said.

She halted Legend and looked at him. "I don't have time. The stalls need to be finished before we change. I better get the horse back before Ginny kills me."

"Don't worry about the stalls," Ivy said. "Mindy and Kirsten are working on them. June is helping Ginny finish up in the shop. The only other thing we have to do is feed before we change. I can lead Legend back for you. Why don't you talk a while? Just meet us at my house to get ready." She took Legend's reins, looking for Karen's approval.

"Well, okay, I guess." Karen again pushed her feelings aside. Ivy had only tried to help her since they met. "Just take the reins over his head, in case he spooks. You'll have more control that way."

Karen dismounted and thanked Ivy, and then watched nervously as Ivy led Legend along the short section of road. The horse remained calm. Karen relaxed as Legend and Ivy made it across the road and started down Ginny's driveway.

She looked at Shane, who was greeting Ashes. As the dog rolled onto his back, letting Shane scratch his belly, she asked what he wanted to talk about.

He looked up, his eyes soft. "Well, a lot, but first I wanted to show you something I found."

"Oh, here we go again. The last time you found something, we got chased away by Indian spirits. Besides, why should I go anywhere with you? You and Ivy looked pretty chummy there."

"Oh, come on now. I told you Ivy was clingy. We were trying to find you. Anyway, you must not be that scared of Indian spirits. You were hanging out with them all day, alone."

"Compared to Lady Luminess, who apparently wants to incinerate us, the Indians are pretty peaceful."

"Speaking of that, what I want to show you may be connected to her."

"Okay, but how far is it? I'm in breeches and boots, not exactly climbing gear."

"Don't worry, I'll help you. It's practically in Ginny's backyard." Taking her hand, he walked down the hill and crossed Country Club Road. They shuffled down the bank on a narrow path that took them to the creek beside Ginny's. Trees lined the bank behind them and the creek. The corner of Ginny's house trailer was barely visible in the distance. To their right, a grassy trail continued along the creek toward the old house.

A few large boulders surrounded by smaller scattered ones overlooked the creek. He led her to the biggest one and they sat on it.

Karen became nervous. This was the first time she and Shane had been truly alone. She felt her heart rate quicken. "So, this is what you wanted to show me, some big rocks?"

He smiled. "They're not just any rocks. They came the whole way from Canada in a glacier during the last ice age. They're well-traveled."

She laughed, expelling the pent-up air from her lungs. She looked at their interlaced fingers, noting a tan remained on his skin. Her lighter Irish tone had settled in for the cooler months.

"And no," he continued, "that's not what I wanted to show you. But first ..." He let go of her hand and put his arm around her shoulders. With the other, he cupped her chin and drew her to him.

Her eyelashes fluttered as she felt the warmth of his arm around her. Her breath caught in her throat as they kissed. He stroked her cheek, and she started to relax. They parted briefly and kissed again.

Yelling from across the creek interrupted them. Karen pulled back, sure someone had seen them. Shane looked exasperated. They strained to make out what was going on, but over the sound of the bubbling creek, the other voices were indistinguishable.

"I think it's just Brad up to his tricks," Shane said. "He said something about starting the *trick* part of trick or treating early." He rubbed her back. "I guess we better get going, but first, here's part of the reason I brought you down here."

He helped her down from the rock and walked a few yards along the grassy path. A cold breeze rushed at them, blowing their hair back.

"I was checking out this area for next summer. I heard there was a swimming hole here, and I thought that could be fun. We could hang a rope from that tree"—he pointed to the other side of the creek—"and swing out, jumping in the middle. It's pretty deep in the center. Anyway, when I was looking around back here, I came across this."

He knelt to the right of the path. Brushing weeds aside, he uncovered a flat stone about four inches thick.

Shivering, Karen crossed her arms and gazed at the stone. There was an inscription on it. Leaning in closer, she made out an outline above the inscription. It was the shape of a horse's head. In wonderment, she strained to read the inscription.

Loyal Pal

My Beloved Partner
Cherished in Life
Your Death Avenged
Stairway to Truth

A shudder ran down her spine. "Is this a grave?"

"It has to be the grave of a horse. Ginny wasn't the first to have horses on this property."

"It's a nice burial site. This horse was obviously well loved by someone. But how creepy is that inscription, the part about his death avenged? What do you think happened?"

"The last part is some kind of clue," Shane said. "Those aren't some random words. They mean something."

The chilling breeze intensified. Karen rubbed her arms for warmth. She saw Ashes a few yards ahead. He stood stock still with his tail pointing straight out and his right front paw held in the air. He whined and ran down the path.

"Ashes! Where are you going?"

Karen ran after him with Shane close behind. Ashes sprinted to the old house and jumped up the porch steps. He stared at the door, whimpering and scratching at its bottom, anxious to get inside.

Karen stopped at the bottom of the steps. She looked to the west, noting how low the sun was. Ashes insisted that she open the door, but the fiery image of Lady Luminess chasing Mindy and Lance was etched in her brain.

Shane came behind her. "It's okay. She wants us to go in there. *Stairway to Truth*. The southern stairway wasn't damaged by the fire." He took her arm and coaxed her up the porch stairs.

The door creaked open at Karen's lightest touch. Ashes sprang through the doorway and past the living room to the center of the house. He paused briefly at the foot of a wide, curved stairway. Head high, his nose quivered. He bounded up the stairs, impossible for the teens to keep up with.

Karen and Shane rounded the ascending curve of the stairway. Breathless, they reached the third floor. At the top of the stairs, Ashes sat in front of an old roll top desk. A chill ran down Karen's spine again, but she did not want to leave. Something important was in that desk. To the left of the desk was a hallway. She could see at least two doorways along it, presumably leading to bedrooms. The upper walls and ceiling of the hallway were charred in black. If she breathed deeply, she smelled the remnants of smoke. A sense of dread filled her. She averted her eyes from the hallway and focused on the desk. The wall behind it was charred, extending from its left side to the ceiling. Although blackened with soot, the desk was not damaged.

The only sound was her and Shane's breathing. Karen started toward the desk, and in the same instant, Ashes bolted over to it. He took the pointing stance again, his nose directly under the middle drawer. Karen stood beside him, her hand placed tentatively on the drawer.

"Go ahead, open it," Shane said.

She pulled the drawer open. Inside, was a pile of handwritten letters. She rolled back the desk top and carefully placed the letter on top, old and frail, on the desktop. Shane stood beside her. They strained against the diminishing light to read it.

Daughter Dear,

I regret the necessity of this letter. Deep down, you must realize the folly of your ways. Your beloved Pal is gone, and my business continues to run and profit as it has for decades. You have learned that some things are better left as is. From now on you are either with me or against me. I trust you will choose my side.

Sincerely,
Your Father

Karen and Shane stared at each other, eyes wide with shock.

"Loyal Pal," she said. "The horse on the headstone! It sounds like the father sabotaged him. What could a daughter possibly do to make this guy hurt an innocent animal?"

"Sounds like some serious stuff. She must have had something on him. Imagine how heavy it was, to make her mess with his business. Brave woman, I'd say. What does the other letter say?"

A second letter was in the same writing.

Dear Mr. Oliver Milland,

I trust you are doing well. I am writing to assure you that the injury to Loyal Pal was only minor in nature. He will be fit and ready to run in the North Fork Steeplechase. Under your skilled guidance, he should give us something to celebrate, in addition to the pending nuptials between yourself and my daughter.

Respectfully,

William Opie

"The North Fork Steeplechase?" Karen said. "I've never heard of it. I know they used to have them in Ligonier, but I can't believe they had them around here."

"Isn't that when the horses race and jump over obstacles?" Shane asked.

She nodded in response. Something told her that Loyal Pal did not fare well during the race. Her heart sank with sadness.

Voices came from outside the house—an argument between Brad and June. Karen heard her and Shane's names mentioned.

"We better get going," she said. "They're looking for us. I wonder how we can find out what happened to Loyal Pal."

"I don't know," Shane said, "but we'll work on it. Let's keep this between us for now."

Space at the mirror in June and Ivy's bedroom was tight. That night, it did not reflect blackened eyelashes, rouged cheeks, and high-blown hair. It was trick or treat night, and, in contrast to the usual quest for glamour, the reflections yielded a ridiculous curly red clown wig on Kirsten; the lifeless white complexion and bloody mouth of vampire June; the classically dressed equestrian Ivy, complete with stick horse; the eye patch and shredded skirt of pirate Mindy; and the pillow-enhanced gut and filthy cheeks of the bearded bum Karen. Ashes wore an orange collar with arched-back black cats on it. Unaffected by his earlier jaunt to the haven, he wagged his tail and went to the bedroom door often, ready to go on another adventure.

The mismatched crew descended the stairs to be greeted by Stella, the sisters' mother. She was all smiles, handing each of the girls a hollow plastic pumpkin for candy.

"Oh, Mom," Ivy said. "These are for kids."

"It's okay," Karen said. "We're getting a little old for trick or treating anyway. We might as well do it up right." She thanked Stella and clipped on Ashes's leash.

"Don't forget these." Over moans of protest, Stella handed the girls small flashlights. "It's dark. I want these on as you're going house to house."

A crisp, clear evening welcomed the teens as they crossed the main road and headed to the old house.

"How appropriate, we're meeting at a haunted house on Halloween." Kirsten strained to breathe and talk beneath her red plastic clown nose. "Is anyone else nervous about this? Karen? You're usually skittish about this place."

"Oh ... umm ... For some reason I'm okay with it," Karen said.

"What?" June said. "You hate ghosts. We know for sure there's one in there. Just ask Mindy."

The old house loomed dark and silent before them. Mindy hesitated ever so slightly before sitting on the fountain wall at a spot farthest from the house.

"If I'm coming back here," she said, "you should all be okay with it." She turned to Karen and whispered, "Hey, are you okay? You're being really quiet."

"Yeah, I'm fine. I'll tell you later."

"She should be fine," Ivy said. "She spent enough time with Shane this afternoon."

The group giggled, pressing Karen for information. She was tight lipped, saying only that Shane was a nice guy.

Suddenly, a white streak raced toward them from behind the house, screaming, "Boo!" The girls leaped to their feet, scrambling every which way. Ashes strained at his leash, barking a ferocious warning to the sheet-clad form. Promptly, it doubled over in laughter, satisfied with the havoc it caused.

June rushed at the figure, ripping the sheet off and revealing a tousle of sandy hair. "Brad! We should have known."

"Don't drink my blood, vampire," he said.

Laughter came from the driveway. The girls' flashlights revealed three figures walking toward them. Clad in overalls and a flannel shirt, with blackened eyes and drenched in blood, Shane wielded a fake axe at the others. Lance's face was ghostly white, tinged with ghoulish green and blue veins. Gage looked as if he had just gotten off work, wearing a blue mechanic's suit, his face smeared with what looked like grease.

"Way to be original," Kirsten teased as she walked over to him.

"Oh, hey, Kirsten."

Lance greeted Mindy. "Wow, that's some pirate outfit. You can't kill me for my gold, though. I'm already dead."

"Good," she said. "More candy for me."

As a group they streamed along the darkened Country Club Road, the sounds of their talking and laughter were bound to scare away any denizens of the night.

Karen took a deep breath. The smell of fallen leaves and a distant wood stove relaxed her. Shane playfully dug his axe into her distended belly.

"Man, I've never seen a worse transformation in such a short period of time. You've gained fifty pounds and grew a black beard. You obviously didn't bother showering."

"I had to gain enough weight to fit into my dad's jeans, and no, solving mysteries leaves no time for showering." She smeared some of the black from her face onto his.

The group made out like bandits, despite complaints from an elderly lady that they were too big for trick or treating. Despite Lance's ghoulish face, his blue eyes remained charming. He saved the day with a wink, assuring the lady that this was their last year.

"Well, all right," she said, giving each of them two pieces of candy instead of one.

The teens swung their buckets and bags in triumph, digging into their sugary treasure on the way back.

"You guys can come to my house," Shane said. "My mom made some kind of Halloween punch. She said we can hang for a while."

As they neared Shane's yard, Karen hesitated. "I'll meet you guys in a minute. I forgot something in the barn."

"Are you nuts?" Mindy said. "It's dark. Can't it wait till tomorrow?" Mindy asked.

"Really, it won't take me long. Shane showed me this short cut anyway. I can go right down the bank here."

"I'll go with her," Shane said. "You guys wait on the porch."

Karen and Shane descended the trail leading to the creek at the back of Ginny's property. "You didn't have to come," Karen said.

"I don't know what you forgot that's so important, but I wasn't letting you go alone."

"I didn't forget anything. I just want to say a prayer for Loyal Pal. He was stuck in the middle of a family war and he paid the price for it." She stopped in front of the horse's headstone. Silently, she prayed that Loyal Pal was at peace.

"You're pretty nice for a bum," Shane said.

Karen gasped, "Hey, do you remember when that vagabond attacked me and Mindy? He was saying something about Opie, like he wanted vengeance on him."

"Looks like Opie had more than one enemy."

A huge gush of wind rushed past them, whipping Karen's beard from her face. They whirled in its direction, upstream. The sound of galloping hooves rushed toward them. Blinking in astonishment, Karen saw a large, glowing object approaching. Its mossy light floated over the path, but the hoofbeats got louder as it came closer. Karen tensed, ready to run, but she couldn't move her feet. The glow raced past them in the hazy shape of a horse, striding along at full speed. A feminine form sat aboard, a mass of curls blowing around her head. She turned to look at the teens, but there were no features on her face. A stride beyond them, the ghostly horse touched down to the ground and then burst into the air as if jumping from a springboard. Among the treetops, the mossy glow brightened dramatically as the horse tucked his legs under him in flight. He took one more stride and then exploded into the night. Tiny flits of light fell to dissipate among the trees. Karen could hear exclamations of awe and disbelief from the direction of Shane's house. The others must have seen it too.

Shane ran to the spot of the spectacular takeoff with Karen breathless behind him. With shaking hands, she took the small flashlight from her pocket. There in the dirt were two hoof prints side by side, gouged several inches deep into the ground.

As she stared at the prints and then back up to where the horse and rider had disappeared, all Karen could think of was her early morning dream.

CHAPTER 10

A Christmas Story

Fall's incredible events bonded the group together. Like clockwork they convened on Saturday afternoons, passing the time with games of capture the flag or board games. However, Shane's yard became the new battleground. They all held an unspoken fear and sense of respect toward the old house. Unsure of the spirit's intent, the teens avoided the grounds surrounding the old house as much as possible, especially at night. Ivy and June complained that working in the dog grooming shop was uncomfortable, although everything seemed normal during the day. The sisters refused to mention the hauntings to Ginny. Firstly, they needed their jobs; and secondly, Ginny would never believe them. The fear of being ostracized seemed to quiet the rest of the group as well.

Karen thought it was curious that the ghostly activity had diminished since Halloween. She reasoned that the spirit was satisfied that her horse's story has been told.

The magic of the Christmas season distracted and comforted her. Gifts and good food and cheer were shared generously. Her father continued his father's tradition of building elaborate train sets that lit up his den. Karen's mother was one of ten siblings. In contrast, Scott was Karen's only brother. However, the siblings had several cousins to share good times with, though they had always been closest to their cousins Jessica and Dave. On Christmas day, Colleen's family congregated at her parents' house in the tiny village of Summerhill.

Scott and Dave separated from their sisters to play Nintendo. Karen told Jessica they had a lot to catch up on. Although they lived close to each other in Johnstown, they were in separate school districts. Jessica was a better student than Karen and more involved in school activities. However, she shared Karen's love of horses. Karen hoped her barn stories would bring Jessica around for riding lessons. As the girls went into their mothers' childhood bedroom to chat, Karen decided to leave the ghost stories out for now.

As they settled on beds, Karen noted that Jessica had changed since the summer. A year Karen's junior, Jessica had been small, skinny, and built straight up and down. Now, to Karen's surprise, a few months had added curves to Jessica's hips. Her skin was olive toned and it maintained a glow, even in the winter, when Karen thought of herself as washed out. Jessica big green eyes sparkled in the light, and Karen couldn't help but envy her hair. It was long, thick, and luxurious, a rich brown in color. Faint blond highlights still remained from the summer sun, and they gave her hair great texture. And next summer, she'd be wearing contacts rather than glasses.

She'll be adding dates to her list of activities, Karen thought.

Thankfully, Jessica's personality hadn't changed, and they immediately started sharing silly stories. Many of the stories were about their own clumsiness. "It must run in the family," they joked. Jessica asked about Mindy, whom she had known since childhood through Karen. The three girls had always gotten along well. Finally, the subject of the barn came up. Karen started by describing Brad's most recent pranks. Jessica scoffed at the thought of meeting him. All the same, his antics were good for laughs.

After they had caught up on their social lives, Karen said, "I do have one more story to tell you. It was pretty scary, so don't tell my mom. She'll start worrying."

"Okay. But maybe I'll start worrying!" Jessica exclaimed.

"Ginny has a gray Thoroughbred in for training. His name is Dorian. This older guy owns him, a friend of Ginny's. This fellow's name is Fred. He used to ride and had racehorses at one point. He found this horse half-starved in a field. He felt sorry for him and convinced the people to sell him for cheap. Well, as the horse got healthier, he started to feel good. Now Fred sees why the people ignored him. The horse is kind of ornery. He'll bite at you when you're passing his stall.

He's hard to ride too. Ginny has a cousin named Mary. Until now, she was the only person allowed to ride Dorian. She has a lot of experience from galloping racehorses on the track. Mary thought the horse was improving, so she told Ginny to try him. Ginny thought that if she could handle him, I could start riding him. So two weekends ago, Ginny, Mindy, and I decided to go for a ride in the woods. Brad had told us about this trail that sits off the Country Club Road, and we decided to go exploring. You wouldn't believe how nice it was that day."

Jessica rolled her eyes and sighed.

"No, I'm serious," Karen went on. "I know you don't like the cold, but something about this day was special. It was cold, don't get me wrong, and there were snow flurries, but the sun was out at the same time, shining right down on the road. It felt so warm, like we had little heaters in our jackets.

"The horses started off great too. They had a spring in their step. Even Cajun was prancing a little and snorting. It was so neat to see their breath blowing in little bursts of vapor. It was really cool.

"So we get to the trail. It was really pretty and everything was going fine. I was in front on Legend, Ginny was second on Dorian, and then came Mindy and Cajun. We came to this little stream. It was running, but in places it was covered with a layer of ice. Well, Legend just stepped through the middle, totally avoiding the ice. But Dorian shied. He stepped toward the side and right onto the ice. Then, excuse my French, but all hell broke loose.

"The ice made this big *crrraack*. Dorian leaped in the air and started bucking. Ginny fell off. I turned Legend around to see if she was okay. She just lay there for a second. I was scared for her, but I didn't have time to help her because of what happened next."

"Oh, man, you're scaring me."

"Dorian bolted toward me, full throttle. Legend whirled around, and all of a sudden we were plummeting down the trail at full speed. Dorian was right at our flank trying to pass, but the trail was too narrow. It was like a real horse race. I'm telling you, Jess, it was like nothing I've ever experienced before. Sure, I've galloped Legend, but never has any other horse been close to keeping up with him. Well, Dorian sure could, and they were feeding off each other. We were going so fast that tears were streaming from my eyes. The wind was searing my face. It hurt! I just froze. I kept pulling back as hard as I could, but nothing helped. They just kept running. I've never heard them breathe like that. It was like they had transformed into two fiery beasts that I didn't know. All I could do was hang on."

"Oh, my gosh!" Jessica covered her mouth.

"We were running and running. It was like an eternity. Then the trail started to drop off into this steep hill. You'd think that would slow them down, but, no, they didn't even break stride. I leaned back to brace myself. My heart was in my throat. Then we came to this log. It was only about a foot and a half tall, but we were going so fast that I thought for sure they'd fall over it. It seemed like that log triggered the start of my luck. The horses cleared it in the middle of a galloping stride. Then the trail got narrower and narrower. The footing became rockier and brush closed in. Legend started to slow down, as did Dorian, still at his flank. The farther we went, the thicker the brush got. I ended up with some scratches, but thank God for jagger bushes! I was able to bring him to a trot and finally a walk."

"Oh, thank God!" Jessica said.

"That's exactly what I did. My whole body was shaking. I jumped off and almost fell to the ground from exhaustion. I was so happy to be alive. Legend was completely quiet. He looked at me as if to say, "What is your problem?" Dorian was calming down too, but the whites of his eyes were still showing. All I could say was, 'Dorian, you're a bad boy.' I took both sets of reins and started to lead them back."

"About ten minutes later, I met up with Ginny. She was running along the trail to find me. Can you believe she said she was worried sick about me? I told her I was okay, just had a wild ride. And I told her I was sorry I couldn't help her after she fell off. Ginny told me that Mindy was the next one to worry about. Despite wearing a helmet, Ginny had been in slight shock and couldn't get up right away. Mindy had ridden off toward the road to get help. Are you ready for the kicker?"

"Oh, man. I don't know if I can take anymore."

"Mindy ran into Shane, the boy I like. He was riding his four-wheeler up the road. Shane and his dad bailed us out when that convict attacked us. Now, he's seen me in trouble again! Anyway, I guess Mindy got him to follow her. Ginny and I got back to the stream where this all started, and there's Mindy and Cajun, huffing and puffing like crazy. Shane is just standing there, looking bewildered. They must have expected to see Ginny still on the ground. He looks up at me and winks. He says, 'Your parents should lock you away. You can't stay out of trouble.'"

Jessica laughed.

"Well, Mindy was mad at both of us for scaring her half to death. It seemed to make Shane uneasy. He said that since things seemed to be under control, he'd go. I told him to stay on call in case I need him again."

Both girls were laughing now.

"I'm sure!" Jessica exclaimed. "You were hitting on him!"

"I have to confess to you, we've hung out a lot over the fall. He's cute. He has wavy dark hair with just a hint of red. He's pretty skinny, but he does have good muscles in his arms. But his eyes are the best. They're huge and icy blue. I've never seen that shade, almost silver."

"Sounds like you have a crush," Jessica teased.

"I guess. We're kind of going together."

"No way! No wonder you spend so much time out there. I see why you're so embarrassed about getting into sticky situations in front of him."

"We've been through something else together," Karen started. She hesitated, but if Jess came to Fox Hollow, the spirits would make themselves known one way or the other.

"I don't think I want to know," Jessica said. However, as Karen described the old house and their incredible experiences with its ghost, Jess's eyes widened in wonderment.

"Wow, I really can't wait to see this place. Spring should be fun."

Karen agreed. The girls went downstairs to join the rest of the family. Christmas cookies were waiting. Soon after, the house shook with the sound of cheer and badly sung Christmas carols.

CHAPTER 11

IMMINENT DREAD

Large snowflakes pelted Karen's eyes with a wintry sting. She leaned back in her sled, desperate to catch Shane in the lane beside her. An icy ramp loomed ahead, daring her to whoosh up it and fly off the other side. Shane leaned to the right, gunning for the ramp. Karen thought better of it, leaning drastically and too late. Shane's sled went airborne, accompanied by his shout of enthusiasm. She caught the bottom of the ramp at an angle, though. The bump combined with her over steering sent her rolling, sled over body, over and over again. Finally, she stopped in a heap, snow frosting her from head to toe.

Cheers and laughter came from the top of the hill. Karen promptly stood and took a bow, her hand extended up at Kirsten and Gage. They leaped onto their sleds and barreled down the same two lanes. Karen collected herself and rushed to the side, hoping they controlled their sleds better than she. Shane approached grinning, his sled tucked under his arm.

Karen wiped the snow from her purple jacket, wishing she had a towel. She whirled away from Shane, embarrassed at how she probably looked after such a spill. She struggled to move her snow encrusted jaw, slurring her response to Shane's question about her well-being. With her back to him, she brushed the snow from her face. Removing her gloves, she felt the top and sides of her hair. Her fingers crunched against the layers. There was still height at the top and width at the sides. That Aquanet was good stuff. She skipped off the sled path and started the climb back up the hill beside Shane. They stopped to watch Kirsten's and Gage's run.

Kirsten and Gage stopped on either side of the ramp. They stood up almost in tandem and trotted back up the hill side by side, talking to each other as they went. Gage ignored Shane's ribbing about avoiding the jump. He and Kirsten made a bee line to the top of the hill.

Karen and Shane lagged behind, Shane teasing her. "All I saw of you was this squall of flying snow. I thought a blizzard was coming."

Laughing at the imagery, she admired his thick dark hair against the background of white. The late day's dull sunlight lit glistening crystals through the snow. "I'm sure I look like the abominable snowman."

He stared at her moment, stopping her momentum with a hand behind her neck. "You're a cute little snow bunny. Somehow, your eyes look gray in this light. You keep me guessing, Karen Mulligan." Her numb cheek tingled back to life with his kiss.

Kirsten and Gage whizzed past again. This time, Gage went right up the center of the ramp. Kirsten came to a controlled stop, avoiding the ramp altogether, and pulling the nose of her sled up. She clapped in appreciation of Gage's successful jump.

They each made several runs. After about forty-five minutes, Karen was chilled. The dark of the late February evening closed in on the hollow.

"Hey, guys, I'm cold. Ready to go in?" she said.

"Yeah. We have hot chocolate inside," Shane said.

The four climbed the steps to Shane's side porch. He cracked the door, but was interrupted by Gage.

"Hey, I think I better get going. I have to work on that engine. See you later." He left so fast that the others had no time to react.

Kirsten blinked away her surprise, shaking her head. Almost inaudibly, she said, "What the heck?"

"Come on in and get warm," Shane said.

Their heavy boots clumped a few steps into the kitchen until they had enough room to remove them. Shane hung the three sets of snow pants on hooks on the wall. A heavy rug would catch any melting snow as they dried.

The dining area and kitchen occupied one large room. Thankful for her comfortable stirrup pants, Karen sat at a long oak table. A large bay window provided a view of the front yard. Kirsten sat beside her, dressed in similar fashion. The girls curled their cold hands under their bulky sweaters. They thawed slowly, thanks to the warmth of a wood burner in an adjacent room. Shane filled a tea kettle and put it on to heat.

His mother, her attractive face framed by thick dark tresses, peaked at them from the hallway. "I see my son has learned something from me. How to boil water."

"Ha, ha. Very funny, Mom," Shane said over the girls' giggles.

Meadow came into the kitchen, her eyes as large and dark as a doe's. Karen always thought they had a soft innocence to them, further instilling a deer-like quality.

"Let me help you." She slipped behind Karen to the antique hutch along the wall behind the table and removed five teacups and saucers. She placed them around the table.

"Do you mind if Jack and I join you?" she asked the girls.

"Of course not. Thanks for having us," Karen said. She noted the deeper skin tone of Meadow's hands. Shane had inherited his darker complexion from her.

Jack walked in, and Karen studied Shane's parents. He definitely got his deeper skin tone from his mother. Jack's lighter complexion was similar to Karen's. Yet the duplication in eye color from father to son was uncanny.

Jack greeted the girls, teasing them about their now wilted hair, and Karen about her run-in with the vagabond the previous summer. That seemed long ago. Karen couldn't believe how much had happened since then.

Meadow and Jack drank half hot chocolates with the teens. They caught up on all the news about the horses, Ginny, Brad, and the sisters. Shane's parents were glad that Brad was acting better. Meadow said that being a part of the group helped him, and stressed how hard divorce was on children. The girls reluctantly agreed.

"Okay, we'll leave you alone now," Meadow finally said. "Come on, Jack, we can finish our hot chocolate in the living room."

The teens thanked Shane's parents, and then Kirsten said to Shane, "They are so nice. They seem so happy together."

"They have their moments, but I know I'm lucky," Shane replied.

"This is so cozy in here," Karen said. "It's too bad Gage is missing out."

"Yeah. What is his deal anyway?" Kirsten asked. "One minute he's cool and hanging out, the next he's practically running away."

"He can be a screwball sometimes," Shane said. "I know he's working on this old Plymouth Satellite. His dad is a mechanic, but I think money is tight. Gage wants to fix the Satellite and sell it. He wants to help with the bills, but at the same time he's obsessed with it. He loves that car."

"What kind of car is that?" Kirsten asked.

"A muscle car from the seventies. He claims it's one of the best street racers around."

"That's too bad about his dad," Kirsten said. "My mom stresses about money too."

"It's a shame, because his dad used to be a race car driver. He used to race at Pocono Raceway. I remember seeing it for the first time when I was real little. Gage and I were five. His dad was a good driver, but never really broke through. Then the raceway got into financial trouble. His dad had to go from driving to repair work to make a steady living."

"You guys are cousins, right?" Karen asked.

"Yes, our mothers are sisters. Their family goes way back in this valley. Supposedly, our great-grandmother was descended from the Indians who lived in these hills. That's why I feel okay about going to the haven. It's my ancestor's legacy."

"So that's how you can make me jealous of your year-round tan," Karen teased.

"Hey, come to think of it," Kirsten said, "Gage has the same skin tone. Anyway, I feel bad about his situation, but I wish he'd leave the car alone on a Sunday evening."

They were on their second cup of hot chocolate when the phone rang. Seconds later, Meadow came into the kitchen, stretching the phone cord from the hallway.

"Karen, it's for you. It's Ginny."

After a few seconds of conversation, Karen almost dropped the phone. With a shaky voice, all she could muster was, "When?"

Legend had been sold. He would leave in a week.

CHAPTER 12

Mysterious Mountain

With surprising empathy, Ginny encouraged Karen to ride Legend once more before he left. Saturday arrived, and Karen suggested that she and Mindy ride to the haven. Mindy agreed wholeheartedly.

"I wish the four of us could just camp out there forever," she said. "I don't want Legend to go either."

An early thaw had melted most of the snow, leaving only dirty piles along the sides of the trail. Wintry breezes intermingled with periods of sunshine, enforcing winter's grip while hinting at the promise of spring. Though grateful for this spring preview, Mindy was saddened to see Karen fighting back tears the whole way up the mountain. Legend and Cajun topped the hill and entered the plateau leading to the haven. They were about a quarter of a mile from the rock walls when the girls decided to pick up a trot.

The horses bounced merrily along at a trot. As they approached the steep walls of the cavernous formation, its magnificence captured Mindy's attention, and her sadness was replaced by wonderment. A hauntingly familiar sound buzzed around her. Determined to deny it, she shook her head, blaming the breeze. But the war drums pounded relentlessly, demanding attention. Indian voices hummed in low rhythms, as if in a trance.

Pale-faced, Karen halted Legend and turned to Mindy. Abruptly, Legend plunged forward, jolting Karen into riding position. He cantered toward the cavern walls and past the thriving holly. Seeming disassociated from reality, Karen sat motionless. It looked like she was floating, peacefully but with no purpose. Mindy urged Cajun to follow, but the older mare wavered with hesitation.

Legend approached the cavern walls. Mindy huffed with the effort of driving Cajun behind him. Something drew her gaze upward. A strange mist rose atop the haven walls. In the center of its highest point, a form appeared. A lean, dark outline of a man stood atop the rugged cliff. His robe fluttered in the breeze. The outline of a feather jutted from atop his head.

Karen gasped. "My God, there *are* Indians up here!"

Legend stopped easily. He raised his head toward the figure and then lowered it, blowing softly. Cajun, on the other hand, slid to a quick stop. Wild eyed, she tossed her head toward the figure. It lingered in the mist with a featureless stare, holding Mindy's gaze for several seconds before fading away. Cajun snorted loudly and wheeled around on a dime. Off balance, Mindy clung to her neck. Cajun bolted off, away from the formation. Barely able to stay on, Mindy fought to pull her up.

After the fight of her life, Mindy turned the reluctant Cajun around. She kicked her toward the shadow of Legend and Karen. To Mindy's shock, the strange mist was surrounding them, engulfing horse and rider in a gray whirl. Mindy rode Cajun into the mist, calling for Karen. Suddenly, the mist dissipated. Cajun slammed to a halt. The scene at her feet was unbelievable.

Legend lay flat on the ground with Karen leaning over him. "No, Legend, please come back. No!"

Legend was motionless. His eyes were closed as if he were sleeping. There was no stress on his face, no pain. Nonetheless, he was gone. Mindy knew there was no saving him. She jumped from Cajun to comfort Karen. After several minutes of sobbing, Mindy pulled Karen to her feet.

"Come, we must go. He's gone." She couldn't imagine what had caused Legend's demise. She thought about her friend's grief and knew she had to say something. "He couldn't stand the thought of leaving you. He knew it was coming. He's at his favorite place."

Mindy looked around. The mist had completely gone. The sun's glow hugged her with warm silence. No dark figures watched from above. Birds chirped innocently in the nearby forest. The haven had returned to normal.

Mindy guided Karen, quiet and listless, away from the scene. The girls took turns riding Cajun halfway down the mountain. Yet the normally stoic mare was nervous and unsettled, prancing and spooking at every shadow. Karen dismounted and handed the reins to Mindy. She walked ahead with her chin buried in her chest. Holding Cajun's rein, Mindy walked too.

Toward the bottom, Karen finally spoke. "It's like Swale. It's the only explanation."

She was talking about the heroic racehorse, the Kentucky Derby and Belmont Stakes winner, who died suddenly from an aneurysm after a routine morning gallop.

"Yes, that's all it could be," Mindy replied, knowing that Karen believed it as much as she. After months of relative calm, the paranormal activity had taken Legend's life. How would they explain this to Ginny?

The girls decided to leave the war drums, voices, dark figures, and mists out of the story. They told Ginny that Legend had simply collapsed.

"You took him up that hill before he was to be sold? I said you could ride him. I meant in the ring! You never risk injuring a horse that close to a sale!" Ginny stared at them in anger. The girls had no rebuttal, only tears. The verbal assault stopped.

"All right, it could have happened anytime. It isn't your fault. Some of them just have an unnoticed weakness. We'll get another nice one for you to ride. You'll see."

Two days later, Karen enlisted Shane's help. She hated the thought of Legend's body lying out in the open. She convinced Shane to help bury the horse.

"You can use the four-wheeler to move him," she reasoned.

"How will we dig a hole that big?" he asked.

Unsure how to answer that, Karen merely frowned.

"Semantics," he said. "We'll deal with them later." And he took Karen up the mountain on the ATV.

They reached the site of Legend's demise. The pressure of having to bury a horse was lifted from Shane's shoulders, but the mystery of the haven deepened. The horse's body was gone. He looked at Karen incredulously.

"Nothing shocks me anymore," she said, and proceeded to tell him the whole story.

CHAPTER 13

KIRSTEN AND GAGE

"I'll tell you, Kirsten, this drive is a drag." Kirsten's mother pulled her Volkswagen into the lot along the Somerset Pike across from June and Ivy's house.

"What do you want me to do, Mom? I love coming here. It's not my fault Dad didn't pick me up."

Her mother's face softened. "Okay then. You meet me back here at four o'clock. Don't keep me waiting. I don't trust your brothers alone."

"Okay, Mom."

As she got out of the car, Kirsten inhaled the clean spring air. Her sneakers barely touched the ground as she skipped toward the barn. She was barely halfway through the back paddock when June came bounding toward her.

"Gage just called for you," she practically screamed. "He wants you to follow him up the mountain on Dawn. He's bringing some lunch for the two of you."

"No way! He wants to have a picnic with me?" Kirsten exclaimed.

"And Dawn too." June giggled. "I guess he's not ready to double up with you on the four-wheeler. You'd have to hang on too tight. He wants you ready by eleven o'clock."

In the barn, Karen was standing with Mary in front of Dorian's stall. When Kirsten told her about her lunch with Gage, Karen smiled for the first time in weeks.

"Maybe he's finally coming around. I hope you guys have fun. It's a beautiful day."

Kirsten paused. "I'm kind of scared to go up there, though. I don't want anything bad to happen."

"Remember we rode up there before and nothing happened? Something tells me it was just Legend's time."

Mary added, "You better go for it, girl! There are more girls than guys around here. Go with him before someone else catches his eye."

"Well, okay, I guess," Kirsten said, unsure of how to react to that statement. She gathered Dawn's tack.

June came into Dawn's stall, brushes in hand. "Let me help you. It's getting late."

"You don't have to. Aren't you going to ride Blondie?"

"I already did. Can you believe she's jumping four fences in a row?" June said proudly. "Ivy can hold down the fort at the shop for a few minutes."

Though grateful for the help, Kirsten knew her date would be prime gossip in the shop for the day. She focused on Karen and Mary's conversation from across the aisle.

"So next week," Mary was saying, "I think you can try Dorian. Just go over in your mind what I showed you. You can learn a lot by watching others ride."

"Sure, I understand," Karen replied. "You said Dorian's owner, Mr. Green, was involved with racing when he was young. Has he ever mentioned a steeplechase course in this area?"

"In this area? No, why do you ask?"

"I just heard there used to be one here a long time ago."

"I'll ask him. Funny he wouldn't mention it, though."

Dawn was clean and tacked, and butterflies started in Kirsten's stomach. Self-conscious, she ran her hand along the top of her head, noting a flat spot. "Karen, do you have any hairspray?"

"Yeah, in the tack room. Just get it out of my purse."

It was almost eleven o'clock. Kirsten left Dawn tied in the stall and jogged to the tack room. Ginny had installed a full-length mirror, mainly so the girls looked presentable when clients came to look at horses. It came in handy now.

She retrieved the hairspray and held her head upside down, fluffing her hair away from her scalp. She sprayed her head thoroughly, sealing the arched feathers of hair into position. Straightening, she studied her figure, assessing the look of her stone-washed jeans.

"If only I could get down two sizes," she muttered. "Karen's a five. She looks good." She pulled her tan jacket down over her hips.

If Gage wanted to be discreet, he was doomed from the start. Not only had June answered his call, but the ATV announced its arrival from a half mile away.

June yanked her from the tack room. "There he is! You're so lucky. I wish someone would pick me up on a red four-wheeler."

"It's supposed to be a white horse," Kirsten said. "Instead, I'm on the almost white horse. Anyway, I thought you said he was some dork you rode the school bus with. You shouldn't be jealous."

"We're growing up, and he's definitely looking better," June said. "Come on, you better go. I'll help you get mounted."

Kirsten really didn't need help getting on and thought it was time June made herself scarce. Mary's comment was starting to make sense. However, she didn't have the heart to shoo June away.

Gage came over the bridge, wearing jeans, work boots, and a red checkered jacket. Kirsten rode Dawn toward him. Their greetings were simple enough. He would lead the way. He explained that he would go slowly, but if she lost track of him, he'd be back.

"I don't know if I can go a snail's pace the whole way," he teased.

"You don't know my horse. You'll be surprised how quickly she'll climb that mountain."

They started over the bridge to where Gage had left his four-wheeler. Before he started it, June dashed past.

"Have fun!" She threw open the door to the dog grooming shop and disappeared inside.

"Let's get going," Gage said. "We'll see what that horse is made of."

Kirsten was right. Dawn was even able to pass Gage a few times when the ATV got stuck in the mud from a recent spring storm. Luckily, there were no storms that day. At times, the bright sun penetrated the trees with comforting warmth.

Nice to thaw out from the winter, Kirsten thought.

Shane and Lance had managed to clear some of the overgrowth that had made the upper forest impenetrable to ATVs. Now, they could ride right to the haven with horses or machines.

They approached the haven's massive walls. Cool air rushed at them from moisture dripping from the sides.

"Have you been here yet?" Kirsten asked. When Gage replied no, she took the lead. She dismounted and led Dawn toward the cave. All the time she had spent with Dawn paid off. The little Arabian fit easily through the passageway. She followed Kirsten's flashlight without protest. Kirsten stopped at the cave painting. Even Gage was enthralled by this piece of history.

"I wonder if any of my ancestors painted that," he said.

"According to Shane, it's a possibility."

"Yeah, our great-grandmother was descended from the Delaware Indians that lived in the area. Most of the Indians were run out of here. However, my great-grandmother's family was able to stay. They worked on my great-grandfather Davis's farm. The Davises were Welsh. They had some old money to start off in the new world. Their farm was on the original site of the golf course clubhouse. My house sits on a tiny corner of the old property. Anyway, my Indian great-grandmother married my great-grandfather Davis. Their daughter had my and Shane's moms."

"Well, that explains your darker complexions. The both of you have white features too. You have the reddish hair, and he has the blue eyes. Where did the Jacobs come from?"

"They were also British. They were working class. Jack's dad actually worked the Davis farm too. That's how he and Meadow got together. It's strange how the tides turn. Now, the Jacobs have a bigger house than we do."

"You never know how or where your fortunes will go." Remembering that Gage's family was struggling, she changed the subject. "I can't believe you know so much about your family history. You sure go way back in this valley. It explains why Shane is so interested in this place." Kirsten thought she would one day research her German ancestry. "So are you and June related? Her grandmother was descended from Indians too."

"No. According to my mom, June's ancestors were Shawnee. The two tribes were mostly friendly, but I wonder about them. There has always been tension between my mom and June's mom. I overheard my mom talking about some kind of skirmish. My dad told her to forget it, that it was ancient history and didn't matter now. Anyway, I wasn't too interested in this place until now. It really makes you think about the elements of fate coming together. It is how we ended up the way we are. What do you make of that horse dying up here? Do you believe there are Indian spirits? I wonder if we'll see them. I never played into the ghost stuff, but after what we saw at Ginny's, and more than once, how can I deny it?"

"I don't know what to make of any of it. I'm glad I wasn't here when Legend disappeared. Karen still isn't over it. June sure believes the native spirits are here. They planted a holly tree to appease them. Anyway, it's a great place to hide out. Let me show you the rest."

Uneasy, Kirsten continued through the cave and into the meadow surrounded by the canyon walls. She hadn't been there for quite some time. Relieved to be in daylight, she was amazed by the meadow in full spring glory. The lush green grass extended for some four hundred acres until it met the sheer cliff walls that encompassed it in the distance. Wildflowers dotted the expanse, bringing a surreal sense of beauty to the untouched area. The mineral springs bubbled from the cliff walls into a fabulous running stream that traversed the valley floor. Dawn dropped her head and grazed contentedly as her human friends surveyed the land.

"This is why they call it the haven," Kirsten said.

"Look." Gage pointed. "There's another cave over there."

"It's by the stream. Dawn could use a drink. Let's check it out," Kirsten said.

After horse and humans got a refreshing drink from the spring, curiosity got the better of Gage.

"Let me see that flashlight," he said. "I've got to check out this new cave."

Water trickled down onto the cave floor. Gage and Kirsten entered with Dawn in tow. Another refreshing blast of cool air hit them. The walls were solid as could be, no loose rock to speak of. The flashlight barely afforded enough light. They continued up a slight grade, proceeding about fifty feet.

"Wait, don't get too far ahead." Kirsten nervously grabbed the back of Gage's jacket.

"Just hold on," he said, but his jacket was suddenly ripped from her hand.

She heard, "Oh crap," followed by a splash and a quick "Ouch!"

"Aw, man, my shins! And I'm soaked."

Kirsten couldn't help it. She erupted into laughter. The release from stress was too much. Breathless, she asked if he was okay.

"Yes," he grumbled.

He scanned the area with the flashlight. He had knocked his shins on a solid bowl of rock. It rose to chest height, forming a basin. It held a pool of fresh, sparkling mineral water. He had practically fallen in.

"How does it taste?" Kirsten asked, still giggling.

"Very funny. It actually tastes pretty good. I guess this is like the caverns I saw with my parents near State College. The rainwater filters down through the rocks at the top. As it passes over the rocks, it picks up minerals, then, obviously settles in this bowl. The recent storms made it overflow. That's why the floor was wet as we came in. But even in drought, this holds enough water for an army. Look, it's huge, like a mini lake." He moved the flashlight back and forth. The true diameter of the pool could only be guessed through the darkness.

"So cool," he said, "but we better turn back."

The path had widened before they reached the mineral pool, leaving plenty of space for Dawn to turn around.

The sun welcomed them as they emerged from the cave. They returned to the four-wheeler outside the cavern walls for lunch. Gage was silent as they prepared for lunch, but Kirsten felt strangely comfortable. Studying his strong jaw and pensive brow, she realized they were reflecting together, in awe and reverence of this extraordinary place.

Shaded by the tower of rock, they sat on a patch of grass. Dawn was tied on a long line to a nearby tree. She munched quietly on the green leaves and grass she could reach. The walk through the meadow had been enough to dry Gage's shirt. He seemed comfortable as they ate the peanut butter sandwiches and chips and drank the soda.

"This was a great idea, stellar lunch." Kirsten looked at him and smiled.

With that he put his arm around her shoulders. Surprisingly, she actually felt him muster his courage. He looked at her, seeming to admire her.

"I guess if there was light in the cave, that crystal pool would resemble your eyes," he said.

Kirsten's heart started pounding. No one had said anything like that to her. He had seemed so shy and standoffish. Before, muscle cars and ATVs had been the only things to spark his interest. Who knew he had this in him?

All she could do was smile. He leaned over and kissed her softly. They sat together shoulder to shoulder, enjoying the occasional warm breeze that whispered past. That was it. She was hooked.

Suddenly, the sound of galloping hooves echoed through the woods. They were coming closer, apparently from the lower trail.

Darn it, June! Kirsten thought. *You just can't let me have my moment, can you?*

She assumed June had convinced Karen to ride up with her. However, she wondered if Karen would have the guts to take Dorian out of the ring? Mary had told her to wait. Yet Dorian was the only horse Karen had to ride. On the other hand, June certainly could be persuasive. Maybe she had pulled out all the stops on Karen in an effort to get the scoop on Kirsten's date.

Kirsten strained to see through the trees. She saw no one. Although the hoofbeats were approaching, they sounded muffled. They should have gotten louder as they hit the rocks on the trail. Instead, they sounded as if they were hitting the leaves and undergrowth of the woods just below the trail. The horse had to be dangerously close to the edge of the hill.

Worried they might be trampled, Kirsten jumped to her feet, pulling Gage up beside her. Dawn was on alert at this point, her head and tail elevated. She snorted, pulling at the end of her rope. Finally, a shadow appeared just inside the tree line. Kirsten craned her neck, straining to identify the figure. The form was of a tall, refined horse, dark in color. It eased to a stop. Silence choked the area with an almost physical hold. Kirsten's skin tingled until she wanted to jump out of it. Although the figure was dark, there was no density to the body. It almost looked transparent, almost unreal.

"Karen, is that you?" Kirsten called out. Maybe Dorian's gray coat looked odd in the shadows of the trees. But why was she off the trail?

"Karen!" she repeated. Then she realized there was no rider. Furthermore, there was no tack. Had a rider been unseated, reins should be dangling and visible.

Kirsten gripped Gage's arm. His body was rigid and his mouth gaped. The dark horse continued to stand motionless. An eerie chill gripped Kirsten's body.

Slowly, the horse turned its face to her. The head bore an unmistakable large white star. She had never seen a duplicate on any other horse. This definitely was not Dorian.

She gasped. "Legend?"

The horse bolted. He was gone quicker than he had arrived. With silenced hoofbeats, he just disappeared.

"O-okay." Gage stammered. "There is no doubt now. This whole area is haunted. Let's get out of here."

This time, the kiss was a quick peck. He hurriedly led Kirsten to her horse, made sure she mounted okay, and hustled back to the ATV. They descended the mountain.

June was waiting for them at the bridge.

"Here let me take her. I'll be your groom, my queen." June smiled and did a mock bow as Dawn approached.

"Okay, fine." Kirsten was still in shock. It was easier to let June help. But seeing June waiting for them answered one thing. She'd had nothing to do with the horse on top of the mountain.

To Kirsten's dismay, June didn't just take the horse. She stood there holding the reins, eyes wide with anticipation as Gage stopped the four-wheeler. June didn't get more to gossip about, though. Her disappointment became Kirsten's with Gage's simple good-bye. He merely squeezed Kirsten's arm and gave her a cockeyed smile.

"I'll see you later," he said.

The four-wheeler headed out, and the girls took Dawn to the barn. Kirsten could only half focus on June's barrage of questions. She gave small details, like where they went and what was for lunch. Distracted, she stood on tiptoes, scanning Ginny's property over June's head and excited face. Beyond the ring in Ginny's yard, Karen grazed Dorian on a lead line.

Walking out of the barn, Kirsten approached Karen. "You mean you weren't up on the mountain?"

Karen looked startled and confused by the question.

"We saw a loose horse up in the woods," Kirsten continued. Dorian dumped you, right? Somehow, you made it back here before me." She paused, and said quietly to herself, "But it didn't look like Dorian. The woods can play tricks on you, though."

She willed herself into thinking she had imagined the star on the horse's forehead. Desperately, she waited for Karen to admit she had been riding in the woods.

Karen looked at her incredulously. "I know he has a reputation, but no, I didn't get dumped today. I've been here the whole time."

"Then, I have to tell you something. I don't think your Legend is truly gone. I'm not sure in what capacity, but he's not gone."

CHAPTER 14

Ambition in a Small Package

Karen took a deep breath as she entered Dorian's stall. Approaching him at an angle, she avoided eye contact. The gray threw his head and pinned his ears, swishing his tail in annoyance. Silently, she went to his head. She rubbed his forehead, simulating the sensation of the mare's body when a foal nuzzles against her. Dorian relaxed his head and allowed her to halter him. She took her time brushing and tacking him, being sure not to crank the girth tightly all at once. She slipped the reins under the stirrup irons on both sides, assuring the horse would not get tangled in them as she left the stall. She hoped Mary would not be too late for their lesson. Ginny had some lessons scheduled for the afternoon, and Karen wanted to be done before then. She stepped outside to watch for Mary.

Ashes ran up to her, doing his favorite trick of leaping into the air for her to catch him. She giggled as she pulled the dog into her arms. An unfamiliar voice came from the back of the barn.

"Nice catch." An elderly man shuffled into the barn. He used a cane haphazardly, carrying it for a few steps and then leaning on it for the next few. He held a yellowed newspaper in his hand. "You must be Karen. I heard you've been working hard with Dorian. He needs it." The man held out his hand to greet her.

"Yes, you must be Mr. Green. Thanks for giving me the opportunity to ride him."

"You're helping me out. Mary does a good job, but she works during the week. The more Dorian gets ridden, the better mannered he'll get.

I'm too old to mess with horses. I just felt so bad for him, I had to buy him. Now I hope we can find him a good home."

"You used to ride and train horses, didn't you?" Karen asked.

"Indeed. By the way, Mary said you were asking about the steeplechase. You might find this article interesting."

He handed her the brittle newspaper. She took it gently and straightened it in front of her. It was from the *Tribune Democrat*, dated April 15, 1960. A headline caught her eye, and she read the article.

North Fork Steeplechase Marred by Injury

> Saturday's steeplechase was highlighted by the five-length victory of longshot Infinity ridden by Stanford Wesley and trained by Paul O'Donnell. The five-year-old bay gelding took the lead after the last fence, overtaking the fallen Loyal Pal. Loyal Pal had taken the lead midway through the three and one half mile race. Infinity sprinted to lead after the incident and won unchallenged. The brave Loyal Pal, owned and trained by William Opie, sustained a fracture to the right front cannon bone and was humanely destroyed on the racecourse. Loyal Pal's rider, Mr. Oliver Milland, sustained serious injuries during the fall and was taken to Mercy Hospital in Johnstown, where his condition is unknown at this time. Three other horses lost their riders as a result of the incident, either tripping over the fallen horse or trying to avoid him. They escaped with only minor injuries. Infinity's win brought his hurdling record to two wins and three thirds out of twelve starts.

Karen's breath caught in her throat. She struggled to maintain her composure. "Oh, my God. How sad."

"It was sad. I was there that day. It was a beautiful spring day. I had the privilege of seeing Loyal Pal race several times. He had a ton of heart. He wasn't always the fastest, but if he'd go head and head with another horse, he'd give them a run for their money. But the best thing about him was that Opie's daughter rode him on foxhunts when he wasn't racing. He'd go just as fast or slow as she wanted. A real lady's horse."

Karen gulped. "What was Mr. Opie's daughter's name?"

Mr. Green paused for several seconds, looking to the southern sky for help. "Oh, blast. My memory isn't what it used to be. I can't think of it. She was a looker, though, with long curly red hair and ivory skin. If I recall, she disappeared a few months after the race. No one ever knew what happened to her. Did you know her family owned this property? It was much larger then. They owned as far as the eye can see, the whole way up to the country club. None of those houses across the way existed." He motioned toward the Country Club Road and Shane's house. "After the old man died, his estate was divided into lots and sold to private citizens."

"So the golf course was the steeplechase course?" Karen asked.

"Yes, it was. It was acclaimed for its beauty and good footing. It was so ironic that one of the few accidents that happened there was Mr. Opie's own horse. It brought bad publicity to the steeplechase. The next year, attendance waned. Opie couldn't afford the upkeep of the course. In a few years, the whole event was cancelled."

"I always thought this land was better suited for horses than a golf course. What a shame." Karen's mind reeled with the new information. Her and Shane's suspicions were true about Loyal Pal.

She struggled with the concept of a father knowingly putting his daughter's favorite horse in harm's way. Obviously, Loyal Pal's injury was more severe than Opie had admitted to the jockey. She fought the urge to run to Shane and share the information. It would have to wait, for Mary had pulled into the driveway. It was time to ride Dorian.

Mary approached, tall and slim in light blue jeans. She greeted Mr. Green and the two conversed for a few minutes. Hoping to move things along, Karen brought Dorian out into the ring. She started to warm him up at a walk and trot. Still talking, Mary set up small jumps. The first combination was a bounce, a low jump set in front of a higher one. They are set closely together, so that when the horse's front legs land, he immediately hops the second jump by pushing off with his hind legs in half a stride. The exercise helps focus the horse on his job, and is great for agility and hind end strength. The second combination was a vertical with two strides between to an oxer. Karen cantered around the jumps, eyeing the lines of approach.

Mr. Green and Mary stood in the center of the ring. Mary instructed, "Bring him to a trot for the bounce. Go through a few times before you go to the double combination."

Dorian approached the bounce on the bit. He hopped through the first time with no problem. The second time, he bucked upon landing. Karen eased herself back in the saddle, pulling the reins firmly but not aggressively. She remembered Mary's instructions from previous lessons. Dorian would take advantage if he knew the rider was upset or tense.

"This time," Mary said, "try turning him in the air, aim for the combination before he lands. We have to keep his mind working. Wait a little longer with your body before the first jump. You're getting ahead of him."

Karen took a deep breath. She squared her shoulders and slowed her posting. Dorian still came into the jump strong, but her body position allowed her stay in sync with his movement. As he bounced over the second jump, she opened her inside rein and looked to the double combination. The horse bulged to the outside slightly, surprised by the change of direction. Karen closed her outside leg, pushing the horse around the turn. He straightened out nicely, taking the vertical and oxer combination like a pro. She stroked his neck as he cantered away.

"Very nice, give him a break," Mary said.

Karen allowed Dorian to walk on a loose rein. He put his head down, but she felt tension in his body. She made loops and figure eights, trying to keep him focused. Mr. Green was generous with compliments for Mary, Karen, and the horse.

After a few minutes, Mary instructed Karen to try the combination by itself. "Canter in between the jumps, then sweep around and come right at it. Don't give him much time to think about it. We don't want him anticipating. That will make him rush."

Karen successfully guided Dorian through the combination once more. She felt him pick up speed upon landing, and was relieved when Mary instructed her to stop. *Best to quit while we're ahead*, she thought.

She walked Dorian around the perimeter of the ring to cool him down. Mr. Green said his good-byes, congratulating her again on a job well done. After a few turns, Karen steered Dorian to the center of the ring, alongside Mary. He stood quietly while they talked. Ginny wanted to start a 4-H club and had asked Mary to help organize it.

"We should have no shortage of members," Karen said.

Suddenly, Dorian raised his head. Pricking his ears, he gazed up at the North Fork Dam Road directly above them. A clattering of hoofbeats echoed from the road. Karen saw two riders through the weeds. In the lead was a red-headed man on a dark bay horse. Directly behind him was a petite girl with strawberry-blond hair. She rode a shorter black horse. The two seemed to glide along the guardrail, the riders motionless. They were not posting as one would to a trot, nor were they cantering or galloping.

"Oh, that's my friend Wendy," Karen said to Mary. "She's the one that might be interested in Dorian." She called to the riders at the top of her lungs. "Hey! Wendy!"

Wendy's head turned. The clattering slowed to a walk and then stopped. Karen waved. "This is Dorian. You should come down and see him."

After a short pause, Wendy replied, "We'll be down in a minute."

"She already has a horse," Mary said. "She wants another one?"

"Her horse is a Tennessee walking horse. Wendy likes her, and says she's a great trail horse. But Wendy really wants to ride English and jump. She's been taking lessons from Sonja Sullivan, the event rider."

"I know Sonja. She's about ten years younger than Ginny and me. We boarded our horses at the same farm for a while. She's good, but she's a tough instructor."

"Yes, Wendy told me that. Wendy is tough too. I don't think I could put up with Sonja's teaching style. Also, Wendy's dad isn't in favor of her changing to jumping. He wants her to stick with the gaited horses. I'll tell you, Wendy's up against it sometimes."

Dorian started to dance as the other horses descended the driveway and approached the ring. Mary held his head and started leading him in circles. When the two gaited horses got to the fence, Mary turned Dorian toward them. Dorian let out a big sigh and stood still, but not before tossing his head in protest.

"Oh, Dad, look how beautiful he is," Wendy said. Her smile emphasized her defined cheekbones in her heart-shaped face. Her blue eyes lit up, in contrast to lightly freckled pale skin.

"Pretty is as pretty does. He seems nervous," her father said, frowning.

"Brian, this is Mary," Karen said. "She's been schooling Dorian. Now she's teaching me how to ride him. The horse has come a long way. You just missed him jumping."

Brian's stern expression faded. Dismounting from his Australian stock saddle, he reached over the fence to shake Mary's hand. "Good to meet you. Should I really listen to this one?" He motioned to Karen. "I've only known her since she and Wendy were cantering around pretending they were horses. Does she know anything about the real thing?" He winked.

Mary laughed. "She's growing up quickly around here. Did you know she has a boyfriend now?"

Brian's eyes widened and he gasped mockingly. Wendy giggled while Karen blushed.

"Not until I approve of the kid," Brian joked.

"Anyway," Mary said, "it's true the horse has come a long way, but he's still a handful. I wouldn't recommend him for a beginner."

"I'm not a beginner," Wendy said. "I have Sonja to help me. She knows Thoroughbreds. Besides, Dorian is started over fences, and he's my favorite color. I couldn't ask for anything more."

Brian turned to his daughter. "I don't get why you'd want to trade in the smooth ride of a running walk for a trotter. That can't be comfortable on a trail ride."

"Dad, I've had it with trail rides. We've been on the same ones a thousand times. I'm ready to show and jump."

Exasperated, Brian turned back to Karen. "You like racehorses, right? Take a look at this guy." He urged his dark bay gelding closer to the fence. "He's a Standardbred. He was a harness racer at the Meadows in Washington, PA. He raced seventy times as a pacer, can you believe that? Many Standardbreds are naturally gaited like him. His running walk rivals any Tennessee walker I've had. Not only is he smooth, but he's fast. Your Thoroughbred would have to canter to keep up with him."

"Really? I had no idea." Karen studied the stout-looking horse. Although he had a roman nose, his face looked quite noble. His crested neck sat high upon wide, sloping shoulders. He stood about fifteen two hands tall, with a short muscular back. His hindquarters sloped sharply from the top of his rump, and they and his hocks were less angular than Karen was used to.

"It's great that he has a new job," Mary said. "Thoroughbreds are hard enough to place after racing, and they can be ridden. I'd hate to imagine where Standardbreds end up when they're done racing."

"You'd be surprised. Most of them take easily to saddle," Brain replied.

"Okay, Dad," Wendy said, "now we know Hanover is a nice boy. Can we please try Dorian out next Sunday? I'll ask Sonya if she can come."

"What will you do with Orchid if you get a Thoroughbred?" Karen asked, admiring Wendy's quiet black filly.

"You can't have two horses," Brian said. "They cost too much."

"Dad, it's my money. I've been working hard at the restaurant. I should be able to spend it the way I want."

"If it weren't my restaurant, you wouldn't have a job. Besides, it's your grandmother's farm you're using."

"Grandma likes the horses. Heck, Orchid is so gentle, she could ride her. It would get her out of the house."

"Your grandmother has plenty to do, feeding the horses when we're not around. Anyway, these people don't need to hear us argue. Try the horse out next Sunday."

"Yes!" Wendy exclaimed. "See you at school, Karen. We'll talk more then."

Karen bid them farewell with a smile, happy that months of anticipation for Wendy would soon be realized. Yet as Karen led Dorian back to the barn, an overwhelming sadness came over her. She missed Legend. If Dorian was sold, she'd have no horse to ride.

With Dorian secure in his stall, she spotted Mindy and Kirsten riding across the bridge on Cajun and Dawn. Mindy's collie mix raced ahead, greeting Ashes with a wagging tail.

"Hey, Smores," Karen said. The dog had been named for her contrasting white and brown coat. She patted the dog's head, and then Ashes and Smores raced around the paddock, taking turns chasing each other.

Phantom Hoof Prints

"How was the ride?" Karen asked.

"Great," Mindy replied. "It's been too long."

"We went the whole way to the dam and down the country club road," Kirsten said. "Dawn was good, except she still spooks going by Gage's garage."

"Speaking of him, did you see him?" Karen teased.

"Well, you might say we rode that way for a reason," Kirsten replied. "We should all go to Skateland sometime."

"That would be great, but why wait to hang out? Shane and I and Mindy and Lance are hiking up to the haven and leaving the ATVs behind. We think they might be disrupting the spirits."

"I'd love to go, but my dad insists on taking me to a matinee today. So you haven't seen Legend since I did?" Kirsten asked.

Karen shook her head. She saw June and Ivy approaching. Ginny had asked her to give them a lesson on Blondie. She called to them from across the paddock.

"Hey, girls, come here. I have to tell you something while everyone is here."

Karen explained the plans to start a 4-H club under Ginny's stable name, Fox Hollow. In addition to the five of them, Karen's cousin Jessica and Wendy planned to join. Ginny was recruiting other kids from local barns. Karen explained that each club in their county puts on a horse show. There was one a month from May through September. Each placing in a class was worth points. Those with the highest points in each division were eligible to compete in regional and then state competitions.

"Shows aren't the only thing involved. Each month there's a meeting where we learn something about horses and we're tested on the information. As we pass the tests, we advance through levels of skill. Each year the challenges get tougher. I think it's a great way to learn about horses."

"I heard Ginny is just doing this to get more exposure for the stable," June said. "She wants to attract potential buyers for the horses."

"That brings up the next problem. We have a shortage of horses. Two people can share a project horse to move through the levels. Only one person can show for points. Of course Kirsten's set with Dawn, June and Ivy can share Blondie, and Mindy can use Cajun. Dorian is the logical choice for me, but if Wendy buys him, it leaves me and Jessica without a horse."

"That stinks, but the club idea sounds great," June said. "Can we start our lesson now? We have to work in the shop in an hour."

"Oh, yeah. And I have to finish the barn work before our hike."

Karen and the others jumped into action.

The bustling activity finally ceased. Karen and Mindy changed from boots to sneakers and walked across the bridge to meet Shane and Lance. Karen took a deep breath of the fresh April air. Ashes and Smores pranced happily, the sunlight gleaming on their coats. With her mood improved, Karen felt lucky to be alive. She waved at Ivy and June through the shop door, pitying them. It was too nice to be stuck inside.

A loud motor fractured the serenity of the day. Karen's back stiffened as if someone had hit her from behind. She didn't need to look back. Brad was tailing them. His dirt bike whizzed past. Spewing gravel from the tires, Brad spun around and faced them.

"Where are you going?" he demanded.

"We're going for a hike, something you're unfamiliar with." Karen hoped he'd speed off in the other direction.

"I'm bored. I want to come." His tone was surprisingly subdued.

Karen and Mindy looked at each other, sighing simultaneously. Their fate was secured as Master and Aries trotted up beside them, tongues flapping and docked tails wagging.

Looking into Master's expectant eyes, Karen said, "Okay, but you leave the motorcycle here. The dogs come with us."

Shane and Lance greeted Brad with playful punches to the arms and gut. Moving on to Karen, Shane winked. Lance and Mindy joined hands. The two streamlined Dobermans and two mismatched mutts lead the way joyfully into the woods as Karen shared the story of Loyal Pal. A somber quietness filled the forest.

CHAPTER 15

BAD LUCK FOR ONE, GOOD LUCK FOR ANOTHER

Sunday would bring Wendy, Brian, and Wendy's instructor Sonya to Fox Hollow, so Karen rode Dorian two extra days that week. The added springtime daylight coupled with her desire for a good showing drove her to put extra effort into his training. He schooled well during the week, his temper tantrums in check, and Karen decided to ride Dorian one last time on Saturday. However, she wanted to reward him for good behavior. She would not drill him in the ring that day.

A short ride up the North Fork Dam Road would loosen Dorian's muscles and provide him with a change of scenery. In theory, the reprieve from the ring would freshen him for Wendy the next day.

Jessica's father dropped Jessica and Karen off at the barn. Reluctant for Jessica to ride her bike the whole way, he had insisted. Tom had barely stopped the Chevrolet before Jessica flung the door open and burst out of the sedan.

"Bye, Uncle Tom." Karen said, giggling.

As the girls walked to the barn, Jessica asked if Karen had seen Legend in the last week.

"No, it was just a nice hike up there. I'd say Kirsten must have been seeing things, but spend any time around here and you won't discount anything. I just wish he'd show himself to me."

They joined June, Ivy, and Brad at the barn. Jessica fit right in with the group. She required little prompting to pitch in with the barn work.

Karen planned on giving Jessica her first riding lesson on Cajun after she rode Dorian. She told Jessica to stand by the stall door while she tacked Dorian.

"We'll get the work done while you ride," Jessica said. "It will give us more time for my lesson."

She had barely finished the sentence before Brad struck. She screamed as he snuck up and pinched her on the side. She swatted at him with her hand but he was too quick. He jumped to the side, avoiding the blow.

"You better watch out," Karen warned Brad. "She's got a brother and several boy cousins. She's used to fighting boys."

Brad jeered. "She can have fun trying to get me."

Karen knew Jessica could take care of herself. Dave had his share of bruises from not so pleasant encounters with his sister. Karen taught Jessica how to lead Dorian and hold him while she mounted. As Jessica returned to the barn, Karen called to Ivy, "Show her the ropes, but keep her safe, okay?"

The lively chatter coming from the aisle way eased Karen's mind. The girls were getting along.

She pointed Dorian toward the road. He walked on a loose rein for the two and a half miles to the North Fork Dam. This was her planned turnaround point, but she yearned to test Dorian's tenuous connection to sanity. It was so beautiful out, and he was being so good, she decided they could go a little farther. A grouse flushed out of a nearby bush. Dorian scooted sideways, but came back to Karen as she collected the reins.

"Okay, boy, you are green. We better quit while we're ahead." She eased Dorian around and pointed him for home.

It was a great theory; however, it was the wrong decision. As soon as she made the turn, Dorian started to get strong. In stark contrast to his passive demeanor on the way out, his mood escalated. He broke into a trot. Karen tried to give and take on the reins to slow him, but upon feeling the pressure, he broke into a strong canter. Before she knew it, he bolted, bucking as hard as he could. The combination of speed and power unseated her. She couldn't stick this one. Scanning the ground for a landing spot, she leaned to the right. The road's grassy shoulder was more inviting than the concrete. She fell off and allowed herself to roll, easing the impact. Eventually her momentum stopped. Her limbs were all intact, but brush burns scorched her elbows. Relatively uninjured, she leaped to her feet, looking for the horse. In dismay, she watched sparks fly from his shoes as he galloped away.

"Oh, my God! I hope he doesn't kill himself."

The sound of hooves on pavement disappeared in seconds. Out of breath, she realized the futility of chasing him and jogged toward the barn. She hoped Dorian found it.

Halfway there, she saw Brad and Ivy jogging toward her. Even Brad had a look of concern on his face.

"I'm okay," she told them. "Dorian's back at the barn, right?"

"Oh, I'm so glad you're okay," Ivy said. "No, Dorian didn't stop at the barn. He headed straight out towards the pike. The others went after him."

Karen's heart skipped a beat. She was horrified that the horse had gone onto the main road.

"Mr. Green's going to kill me!" Karen said in despair. "I hope he doesn't get hit!"

The three ran to the pike. Exhausted, they reached the intersection of the dam road and the Somerset Pike. They looked north and saw nothing. When she looked south, Karen's heart filled with relief. June was leading the excited horse through the parking lot bordering Ginny's property. Jessica followed, face red with exertion. Karen approached the horse.

"How did you catch him?" she asked.

"Oh, man, he was booking!" June said. "If it weren't for a good Samaritan, he'd be in Somerset by now. A lady was driving and saw him. She blockaded the road with her car, jumped out, and caught him. I was so out of breath, I could barely thank her!"

"We ran as fast as we could," Jessica added, "but he just kept getting farther and farther away!"

Karen took the horse. He was still blowing and needed walking. The other girls went to prepare the hose and get antibiotic ointment for a small cut on Dorian's hind ankle. The adrenaline started to leave Karen's body. She was shaking, and tears came to her eyes. Brad approached her, concern furrowing his brow.

"What if he would have gotten hit?" she said. "Worse yet, someone could have been killed trying to avoid him. Now he's got this cut. How will I explain that?" She was almost beside herself.

"Don't worry. It's just a small cut. He'll be fine. We were really worried. It was freaky to see the horse coming down the road without you on him."

He walked along with her as Dorian cooled off. Somehow, Karen was comforted by his presence. When they reached the stable, he ducked into the barn, quickly reappearing with a boom box. He played her favorite song, "Livin' on a Prayer" by Bon Jovi. She calmed down as her rock god carried her away.

Brad was right. The cut didn't bother Dorian at all. Karen called Mr. Green about the incident. She expected to be scolded, but instead he said, "It's all right, young lady. It's all part of learning. It takes a while to train these ex-racehorses. You probably shouldn't have gone out alone though. Remember, your safety in more important than anything else."

With the excitement done for a day, Jessica took to riding like a natural. Despite Cajun's rough trot, she kept her balance and learned the rhythm easily. Karen looked forward to spending time with her cousin at the barn. The day went quickly. The teens only had time for a quick soda in Ivy and June's front yard before Jessica's father was due to pick them up.

Jessica held up her can in a toast. "Thanks for making my first day an adventure!"

The group laughed. Karen picked up a can, handing it Brad. He looked at her in surprise, but then a satisfied grin quickly opened his face.

There was no lack of conversation during Karen's sleepover at Jessica's.

"You wouldn't believe what we thought when the horse ran past the barn," Jessica said. "We were thinking, now why is she passing the barn up? We thought you were just going for a short ride, and couldn't understand why you were headed toward the main road. We couldn't see very well through the trees. Then he passed out of the trees, and we all said together, 'Hey! It's Dorian, but where's Karen?' Then we all scattered like lunatics!"

The girls laughed. Jessica had jumped head first into the unpredictable world of horses. Runaway Dorian would provide a popular topic of conversation in the weeks to come.

The next day, Dorian's jitters were out of his system. Wendy, her father, and Sonya watched Karen ride him quietly on the flat. Eager to try him, Wendy asked to jump him. Sonja took her position in the center of the ring.

Sonja could have passed for Wendy's mother. She had the same strawberry-blond hair, fine in texture, and the same light skin and freckles. But her demeanor was anything but motherly. Sonya verified Wendy's stories about her rough teaching methods.

"Push! Wendy, pay attention! Don't let him die if you want to jump!" Sonya bellowed when Dorian plugged up to a jump.

Wendy responded to the shouting. She was able to focus Dorian's attention, and he jumped the next line perfectly. Karen couldn't imagine being yelled at like that. However, one thing was certain—Wendy responded to Sonya.

Sonya decided she liked the horse. Mr. Green wasn't asking much money because the horse was green. Sonya told Brian that for the money, they wouldn't do much better.

Wendy loved the horse's steel gray color. "Dad, he's young. He'll start to dapple, and he'll be even prettier in a few years."

Karen had reservations, especially after the previous day. She knew Dorian wasn't always this agreeable. Not wanting Wendy to get hurt, she pulled her aside and told her what had happened on the road.

"That's okay," Wendy said "My dad will ride with me outside of the ring. He can help me. You never fell off inside the ring, did you?"

"No," Karen replied, "but he has bucked sometimes."

"That's okay too. If he gets too bad, Sonya can ride him. She's had Thoroughbreds all her life, and she's an event rider. I'm going to work with him every day." Wendy obviously had her mind set.

She does have every imaginable support system, Karen thought. *And I warned her. That's all I can do.*

A brooding Karen fed the horses with the setting sun. Dorian's departure in a few days would leave her horseless. Worse yet, it was Sunday evening and Monday brought another week of school. After tidying the barn aisle, she slammed the rake down. Huffing, she started to the pickup point for home.

"Hey, grouchy," Ginny called from behind her, "don't go away mad. We have a solution to the horse problem."

Karen turned to see Ginny standing beside a petite brunette with short feathered hair. Eyeing the woman's small frame, Karen wondered how she stayed so thin. She had to be in her thirties, and she made Karen feel like a whale in comparison.

"This is Sharon," Ginny said, smiling. "She has two ponies. They're not doing anything this summer and she wants to keep them working. Especially the one I want you to show. She was champion hunter pony at regionals last year."

Taken aback, Karen stuttered, "Th-that's great. But aren't I too big for a pony?"

"Not this one," Sharon said. "You're not very tall, and she's fourteen two hands and bulky. She's a quarter pony, which is just a quarter horse at pony height. Believe me, she'll teach you a thing or two. She's got fire, but she's real honest. Ginny tells me you've been riding these green Thoroughbreds. You have a chance to learn now, instead of teaching the horse at the same time."

Karen's mood suddenly lightened.

CHAPTER 16

PONY TALES

Ginny tiptoed from her bedroom to the kitchen. The sleeves of her white nightgown fluttered as she quietly put coffee on to brew. Brad hadn't developed a taste for it yet, and she hoped its aroma would not wake him. She took a seat at the table and gazed out the window to the barn.

She watched with amusement at the flurry of activity, particularly to the left of the barn. Shane was carrying a large board to where Lance stood at the outside corner of the new stalls they were building. The straps of his faded overalls hung loosely from Shane's shoulders. She guessed they were Jack's. Gesturing to Lance, Shane hoisted the board to the top of the developing wall. He held it steady as Lance hammered it into place. Without overalls, Lance fumbled for nails in the pockets of his tight jeans. Often, he retreated to an old coffee can a few feet away, apparently getting more nails than his jeans pockets held. This prompted looks of exasperation and head shaking from Shane, who was stuck holding the board over his head.

As Ginny kept watching, Karen approached. She was cute and tidy in her riding breeches and trailed by her younger cousin Jessica. Karen looked at the new stalls, her hands on her hips, and then said something that stopped both boys in their tracks. This sent Shane hustling into the main barn. Lance shrugged and then looked down, kicking at the ground while Karen continued talking. Ginny laughed as Shane emerged from the barn. He carried a wooden stall door, struggling with its weight. After Karen took one side and helped him place it in front of the stall, the boys worked to mount it on hinges.

As Ginny sipped her second cup, Karen wheeled two loads of sawdust around, dumping them into the new stalls for bedding. Jessica brought feed tubs and water buckets. Finally, the four teens convened in front of the new stalls. Shuffling from side to side and looking up and down, they analyzed their work. Suddenly, Karen threw her arms around Shane, hugging him tightly and then kissing him. Shane smiled proudly, sticking his chest out. Jessica turned awkwardly and went inside the barn, leaving Lance sitting on an overturned bucket and wiping sweat from his brow.

I guess Karen's happy with the construction, Ginny thought. *I can only hope the whole thing doesn't collapse.* At least Jack had helped the boys with the overhanging roof. He seemed to know what he was doing. *The girls will really appreciate Jack when he finishes putting in the barn water line.* Ginny inhaled with satisfaction. Her dog grooming business had provided the funds for the barn renovations.

As Karen and Jessica started arranging jumps in the ring, Ginny studied Karen's cousin. She was slightly shorter than Karen, but her arms and legs looked long. She would likely grow into them. Her long legs probably helped her keep a good seat on Cajun. If she kept riding, she'd be a force to be reckoned with. This eased any concerns Ginny had over investing money in the new stalls. Good riders meant glory in the show ring. In turn, that would enhance the reputation of her stable, both for sale horses and the lesson program.

This was assuming Jessica didn't mind being an underdog. Earning her stripes with Sharon's raggedy pony wouldn't be easy.

Dawn and Kirsten emerged from the barn. Jessica spoke to Kirsten, eliciting laughter as Karen held Dawn at the mounting block. June entered the ring with Blondie. Looking at the clock, Ginny convinced herself she had time for one more cup. She admired June's grit with the skittish Blondie. While schooling over a double combination, the palomino tried to run out on the second fence. June had good balance and straightened Blondie's head. She drove the pony forward with her legs, avoiding a refusal. Throughout the jumping session, June stuck in the middle of her back, even if the distance came up wrong. No matter how awkward a leap, June stayed in sync with Blondie.

The boys remained steadfast to their task, despite all the action in the ring. As they finished the final touches on the stalls, Lance smiled for the first time that day. Mindy waved coyly to him as she led Cajun past. Ginny's newest recruit, a local ten-year-old, prepared to mount Cajun. Mindy held the gentle mare while Christy got situated. Mindy led the mare around the ring slowly, gesturing the proper hand position. Mindy was the most cooperative about sharing project horses. She voiced little interest in showing, and seemed to enjoy trail riding. Lance played his part in distracting her from serious training. He stuck to her like glue, wrapping his arm around her shoulders as Christy circled them.

With the gang all there, Ginny rose reluctantly from the kitchen table. Just then, the crunch of gravel signaled the arrival of Sharon's horse trailer. Ginny hurried to get dressed.

Stepping out into the warm freshness of May, Ginny called a greeting to Sharon. Sharon waved and then, flanked by the attentive Karen and Jessica, went back to demonstrating the proper unloading technique of the ponies. Ginny joined them, saying, "Pay attention girls. Sharon has offered to haul you and the ponies to the shows so I can take the others. You need to help Sharon with everything and do it the right way."

Grand Moment backed calmly from the trailer. Her chestnut coat glistened in the sun. Warm, intelligent eyes gleamed in her blazed face. The pony could easily be mistaken for a horse. What she lacked in height was made up for in defined, toned muscle. She was certainly compact compared to Thoroughbreds. However, she wasn't overly bulky. Her proportions were perfect, a well-balanced athlete for any discipline.

"She's beautiful," Karen said.

"Wait till you ride her. She's push button," Sharon said proudly.

In contrast, the thirteen two hand Cookie could only be described as cute at best. Her dun coat was dull and rough. A sweet dished head sat atop a ewe neck. A longish back led to a slightly high but well-muscled rump. Her conformation was mediocre, but apparently, this didn't matter to Jessica. She stroked Cookie's tiny face. The pony let out a friendly nicker. A collective "Aw" sounded from all the humans.

"We'll tack them up," Sharon said. "I'll give you girls a few pointers about them before I go."

Sharon had brought her own tack, which she would leave with the ponies. She gave the girls a stern lesson on leather cleaning and conditioning. The girls agreed to follow through.

Ginny said to Sharon, "Don't worry. I'll make sure they keep it sparkling."

"I'm sure you will, but when was your saddle cleaned last?" Sharon teased. "So, Jessica, I know this is an English riding stable, but Cookie's tack is Western. It came with her, and is probably the only thing in the county small enough for her. Ginny said you're just starting. You may like the security of the saddle horn."

Jessica smiled. "That's fine."

Sharon and Ginny watched the girls practice with the new ponies. The ring had cleared by this time, the others undoubtedly scattered to the four corners by now. Indeed, Grand Moment was a special pony. She never picked the wrong lead, and Karen's aids were invisible as she went through her paces. On the flat, the pair would be tough to beat. However, jumping was a different story. Karen had issues with timing, which made Grand uneasy. Still, the pony was honest. Her ears flicked back and forth, asking for guidance from the rider. When she didn't get clear leadership, Grand took control. The pony chose her takeoff spots as best as she could. She snapped her knees clear of the obstacles and gave a beautiful bascule over the fences. Karen was not so graceful. She flopped out of balance onto Grand's neck upon landing.

"You're getting ahead of her," Sharon said.

"I'm afraid to hit her in the mouth. She jumps so round," Karen apologized.

"Sit back a little more. Stay still and let her get closer to the fence. As her front legs come up, let your hip angle close forward and slide your hands up her neck. You'll stay with her and avoid bothering her mouth"

Karen took a few more fences, her brow furrowed with concentration. Finally, she coordinated herself with Grand's stride.

"I'm so glad to have a forgiving horse I can learn on," Karen said as she patted Grand on the neck.

Cookie and Jessica also battled crossed signals. The unrefined pony struggled with the ring work. She ducked in on the corners and hurried along the long sides. Jessica bounced wildly in the saddle as she tried to sit the choppy trot. Finally, both became tired of the ordeal and simultaneously gave up. Pony and rider stopped in the center of the ring, rider puffing with exhaustion.

"You may have to use an English style pull rein until she gets used to this concentrated work," Sharon said. "She needs more support and guidance right now than neck reining can give. It's also fine to post. It will save both of your backs until we can develop a slow Western jog."

Sharon worked with Jessica and Cookie in a corner of the ring, where she led pony and girl through small circles and figure eights. This slowed Cookie and she started to bend through the turns. Although she looked exhausted from the effort, Jessica smiled at the end of the session. Sharon gave encouraging words as the redness slowly dissipated from her face.

"You did fine. I can see why Ginny thinks you have potential."

Jessica thanked Sharon and Ginny. Ginny could only hope this didn't back fire on her. The first show was just two weeks away.

Two weeks' time allowed Karen and Grand to bond. Karen's timing over fences had improved. Jessica and Cookie's partnership had developed as well. However, the collective consensus was for Jessica to skip the first show. She would ride along with Sharon and Karen to observe.

After securing Brad's position as Shane's best buddy for the day, Ginny roared up the highway with her ex-husband's Ramcharger, horse trailer in tow. Running late again, she silently told Dawn and Blondie to hang on. The three girls in the backseat were oblivious. June and Ivy grilled Kirsten about her date at the roller skating ring with Gage.

"Did you hold hands?" Ivy asked.

"Only after *I* took his. He kept looking around, like someone was going to see us. Some kid he knew said hi to him, and he got all red. I don't get him. He asked me to go skating, then he acted like I have the plague. It's not like we haven't kissed before."

"Really?" Ivy said. "Is he a good kisser?"

June interrupted before Kirsten could answer. "Maybe he just wants to be friends."

Ginny cringed. An uncomfortable silence filled the cab before Ginny said, "I'm sure he likes you, Kirsten. Boys are just weird, that's all."

Ginny was relieved to pull into the Cambria County Fairgrounds in Ebensburg. Hooves clopped on industrial concrete as she drove past other competitors. The atmosphere was like a carnival compared to the saddle club. Concrete and steel ride structures replaced peaceful green fields. The fairgrounds embraced functionality rather than ambience. She found a place to park the trailer between a cow barn and the fittings for a carnival ride. They unloaded the horses.

"Kirsten, since you're not showing today, you want Dawn to have a good experience. Lead her around the whole place and let her look at things. After she calms down, bring her close to the ring so she gets used to the loudspeaker. Don't get too close though. The whole arena can be loud and scary. Approach it slowly."

Because of Pennsylvania's unpredictable weather, it was an indoor ring. The rusty steel girders and aluminum siding were loud in the wind. It could be unnerving for the most experienced horse. Ginny took Blondie and June to the warm-up ring. The green pair would practice outside first. Blondie needed to be calm enough to negotiate the tricky sawdust footing of the indoor ring. Its corners were notoriously slippery, and the bad lighting didn't help. Ginny schooled June and Blondie for half an hour, until Jessica came to find her.

"Ginny, Sharon said to tell you the classes are about to start."

"Okay, Jess, thanks."

Ginny guided June and Blondie to the indoor competition ring. Once Blondie had secured a waiting position at the rail, Ginny stepped to the side. Exhausted from a long week's work, she longed for some quiet.

Karen and June were both entered in the pony hunter division. It included three classes: hunt seat equitation, hunter under saddle, and working hunter. Ginny saw Karen ride up beside June on Grand Moment. Karen spoke to June, presumably with encouraging words.

Other entrants of the pony hunter division gathered around the ring. In addition to Grand and Blondie, there were five other competitors. Most notably were Lindsey Suppewicz and Chip. Lindsey had won the champion hunter pony title on Grand last year; this year she was mounted upon another quarter pony. He shared similar qualities with Grand. He too was a chestnut with a blaze. Sharon reported that he had come with an expensive price tag. Lindsey's father owned a car dealership in town, and he had scoured the tri-county area for the most well-trained, well-mannered pony for his daughter.

Another interesting pair waited at the ring gate. Ginny watched with apprehension as June approached a red-headed boy rider. His pony had thick, sturdy legs and light feathering around his fetlocks. Ginny listened to their conversation.

"What a cute pony," June said. "I've never seen one quite like him."

"Thanks. He's a Connemara pony from Ireland." The boy patted his pony's arched neck. The fine-headed bay pricked his ears and angled his head toward Blondie, as if interested in the conversation.

"Oh, I've only read about them. I didn't think anyone around here had one." June nudged Blondie closer.

In typical mare fashion, Blondie sniffed noses with the curious bay. Deceiving everyone, she accepted his gentle blowing into her nose. Suddenly, she grew tired of him and squealed, causing the entire grandstand to look at them.

"June! What are you doing? Don't ride right up to someone like that." Ginny marched up to the annoyed Blondie, leading her clear of the unaffected Connemara.

"Sorry," June said. "I guess I'll see you later." She waved to the boy.

Ginny looked at him apologetically.

"No worries," he said, his hazel eyes twinkling.

Ginny got June settled and started back to her corner. She was stopped in her tracks by another rider in distress.

"Good God! I hope things settle down. I'm stressed enough!" a girl complained to her mother.

The comment came from Tracy. She was another member of Fox Hollow 4-H. This was her first show, and she wasn't very competent. She trembled visibly atop her black and white pinto pony named Bella. Instinctively, Ginny approached Bella's head; sure that Tracy's nervousness would transfer to the pony. Yet Bella barely flicked an ear to Tracy's anxiety. Ginny relaxed as she thought about Bella's rock solid temperament during Tracy's riding lessons. An entire spring of work had yielded little improvement with Tracy's confidence, yet little Bella always soldiered through Tracy's rough hands and almost constant tension. Tracy couldn't ask for a more forgiving mount.

Tracy and her mother, Corrine, were a study in contrast. The only features they shared were their almond-colored eyes and light brown hair streaked with gold from time spent in the sun at the country club. Tiny and thin, Corrine was soft spoken and gentle toward all people and animals. Eleven-year-old Tracy already was as tall as her mother and outweighed her by fifteen pounds. She shared her grandfather's outspoken and sometimes abrasive personality. There was never any doubt about what she wanted or expected from others. Living on Corrine's father's former racehorse farm, mother and daughter lacked for nothing materialistic, but Tracy's insecurities bubbled just under the surface, erupting often into anxiety attacks. Ginny put on her most compassionate face to support this reluctant 4-H club member. Ginny's old friend Corrine looked like she could use some support as well.

"Tracy, just relax," Ginny said. "Go with the flow. You look great, and Bella is groomed impeccably." She determinedly looked away from the brown stain on Bella's white rump. "Have a good experience."

"Thanks, Ginny," Corrine said softly.

The equitation class was first. The rider's general position, control, and grace in the saddle were judged over the horse's performance. The ringmaster opened the gate, allowing the riders to enter. Ginny climbed to the center of the bleachers and joined Mary, who had barely made it on time.

Karen led the way. With a look of concentration, she squared her shoulders. Ginny was glad to see her looking up instead of her usual tendency to look at the ground. Posture played a key role when collecting and guiding a horse. The announcer called for a trot. Karen's brow furrowed as she concentrated on keeping her position. Every so often, Ginny saw Karen glance at Lindsey. Everyone knew the former champ was their biggest competition. Lindsey was the epitome of style in the saddle. Karen would have to perform perfectly to beat her.

The announcer called for a walk. The canter would be next, and Karen lightened her seat in preparation. Lindsey was right behind her. She edged Chip between Grand's flank and the outside rail. Swishing her tail in annoyance, Grand lost concentration for just a moment. The canter command came. With the judge looking directly at her, Karen gave a gentle pull to her inside rein, redirecting Grand. The mare took one stutter step before cantering away. Chip completed his transition cleanly, also within the judge's full view.

"Oh, that transition was a little off," Ginny said.

"The judge will penalize that," Mary said. "Lindsey is almost playing dirty, but she's too smart to make it obvious."

Across the ring, June had her work cut out for her. Blondie rushed around the ring with head high. She snorted past the announcer's booth in wide-eyed fear. June sat stock still, but her face was tensed, as if she was holding her breath. Ginny knew June was trying to emulate their work at home, but this environment was too unsettling for Blondie. The palomino stormed past the other ponies like they were standing still. They approached Bella, cantering quietly on the rail. June had to haul Blondie to the inside, barely avoiding the pinto. Bella couldn't care less, but Tracy nervously snatched up her reins. Sensing her rider's fear, Bella slowed. Ginny had seen this before. Bella was so smart that, to protect herself and Tracy, she steadied her stride. She broke into a trot. Tracy's complaint about Blondie and June could be heard across the ring into the grandstand.

"Man, what a maniac. How does that girl handle that crazy thing?"

The class changed direction. They would repeat the three gaits to the right. The canter request came for the second time. Karen cut across the center of the ring, separating from Lindsey and Chip. Her trot transition was sharp and clean. However, as they came around the lower corner, Lindsey crowded Karen again, this time from the inside. Karen tried to continue onward, but Chip swerved in front of Grand, causing her to take a stutter step again. As Karen's luck would have it, the judge turned to look at her just in time to see it. Of course, Chip continued onward smoothly, as if nothing had happened.

"Okay. That was no accident," Ginny and Mary said simultaneously.

June's ride seemed to be improving. Blondie had settled and actually had a bow in her neck. This frame would impress the judge. The judge watched Blondie as she started to pass the bay Connemara on the rail. Just then, a huge gust of wind burst through the indoor arena, and the steel siding rattled menacingly. The experienced show ponies thought nothing of it, but to Blondie, the sky was falling. She leaped to the outside, breaking the desired frame instantly. The small mare collided with the broad shoulder of the Connemara gelding, which seemed to jolt Blondie back into reality. The Connemara cantered on steadily. He acted as if a mere insect had bounced off him. Seemingly unaffected, June steadied her horse and cantered on until the announcer called for the walk.

The command came for the class to line up in the center of the ring. Ginny saw June speak to the red-headed boy on the Connemara. She assumed June was apologizing. The boy smiled and responded.

"He seems like a cool kid," Ginny said to Mary.

The judge approached Blondie. It was common for judges to give young riders feedback at 4-H shows. The judge gave June an encouraging look and said something with a gentle smile. June nodded.

Predictably, Lindsey won first place. Karen was second. She smiled and thanked the ringmaster for her ribbon, but Ginny thought Karen's gaze would burn a hole in Lindsey's back as they exited the ring. The red-headed boy was granted third place. His name was Carl McNeil. June accepted her hard-fought fourth-place ribbon, followed by a disinterested Tracy in fifth.

Ginny descended the bleachers to join the club. June was apologizing again to the boy.

"Hey, don't worry about it. If Hardy couldn't handle a little bump like that, he'd never hold up during foxhunts. By the way, I'm Carl." the boy held out his hand. June giggled as she told him her name.

Standing between Blondie and Hardy, Ginny looked up at Carl. "You're a good man. Thanks for being understanding."

Carl sat up proudly in the saddle. "Yes, ma'am. It's no big thing."

Ginny turned to June. "So what did the judge say to you?"

"She said I did the best I could with a nervous pony, to keep up the good work, and she'll come around for me," June said proudly.

Ginny proceeded on to Karen and Grand. Ivy was obsessively shining her boots, but Karen seemed oblivious to her.

"How did the judge miss that?" Karen was asking Sharon.

"Lindsey's just using a bit of showmanship. Now you know to watch out for her. Next time, secure your space on the rail. Do what you can to protect your space. You might have to be assertive too."

"Hey Ivy," Ginny said, "Go help your sister. Karen has her cousin to help her. Blondie is your project horse too."

Ivy scurried off. At the far corner of the waiting area, Tracy stood beside Bella, red-faced and panting. Her mother wiped her brow with a wet cloth and held the water bottle for Tracy to sip from.

Hunter under saddle was the next flat class. The horses were again shown at the walk, trot, and canter both ways of the ring, but the focus was primarily on the horse. They were judged on quality of movement, manners, responsiveness, and overall looks. This time, Ginny stood beside Jessica to watch. They eyed Lindsey as she approached the ring in her perfectly tailored navy show jacket. Her thick mahogany hair was tied with a matching ribbon. Freckles danced over her nose and cheeks. She caught Ginny's gaze with her blue eyes, merely looking back at her with confidence.

Sharon whispered advice to Karen. "Grand should be able to win this class. She's a better mover than Chip. You just have to make better use of the ring. Don't cut corners. If you ride close to the rail, her gait will appear smoother. On the straightaway, ask her to extend her stride a bit. A slight extension at the trot will catch the judge's eye."

The tactics paid off for Karen and Grand. They held on to their rail spot. When Lindsey tried to crowd Grand, Karen pressed Grand into Chip, and Grand held her ground against the gelding. She sailed smoothly through all transitions, extending on command along the straightaway. The judge must have appreciated this. Grand placed first with Chip finishing second, despite Lindsey's rolling eyes upon announcement.

Hardy and Carl finished with a solid third again. Blondie had settled down, but she picked up the wrong lead and placed fifth. Little Bella received a white fourth place ribbon to match her spots. Tracy grinned with pride and the members of Fox Hollow congratulated her.

Karen, Ginny, Jessica, Sharon, and Kirsten huddled around June. She was disappointed with her low placings.

Ginny put a hand on June's shoulder. "Don't worry, kiddo. That was great! That pony has never been shown before. You did a wonderful job handling her. It will get better." She gave June a hug. This brought a smile to June's face.

"Hopefully she will settle for the next show," June said. "It would be great if she does well for the show we sponsor. Finally, she should be ready to jump."

"Yikes," Jessica said at the reminder. "Cookie and I will be showing for the first time."

"You picked a great day for your first show," Karen said, teasing her cousin. "We'll be going nuts running it and competing."

June and Tracy left the area to cool their ponies out. Kirsten brought Dawn close to the outer rail, letting her get a good view of the ring and the grandstand. The young Arabian stood quietly beside Grand.

Pony working hunter was the last class for Karen and Grand. Ginny realized her modest jump course at home might not have prepared Karen adequately. She had never jumped so many fences in a row. Members of Ebensburg Area 4-H club had set up the course. Even to Ginny, who hadn't ridden for months, the jumps looked gigantic, although the maximum was two feet six inches. Any pony could jump that with their eyes closed. The rider's challenge was to put the lines together and keep a steady pace. Karen looked nervous.

Karen and Grand entered the ring. They cantered a courtesy circle and approached the first line. Karen seemed tense. She leaned too far forward. Undoubtedly, her nerves transmitted to Grand. She became quick to the first fence. The takeoff spot came up long. Grand had to jump extra big to clear the obstacle. She was an honest pony and continued straight to the next line. Karen regrouped just in time for the second fence. They cleared it and continued on.

"Relax. Just go with her!" Sharon instructed from the sidelines.

The rest of the round went more smoothly. Karen seemed to channel the schooling sessions where she had learned to sit back and wait for the fences. She allowed the jumping arc to close her hip angle for her. Grand was obviously relieved. It was as if she was saying, "Leave it to me. I know what to do, even if you don't." Unfortunately, the rough start knocked them down to third place.

Chip was victorious again, and Carl received a well-earned second place. Ginny congratulated him and then joined Karen and Sharon outside the ring. Lindsey and her family congregated several yards away, just out of earshot. It looked like some kind of silent standoff.

Every so often, one of the Suppewiczes glared at Karen or looked in Grand's direction.

"Wow. Is the whole family involved?" Karen asked Sharon.

"Yes. Lindsey's two sisters ride. One rides in the horse division and, of course, the youngest rides in the peewee division. Their brother acts as the groom during shows. Their father funds everything, naturally. He likes to see wins related to his financial sacrifice. He can be a sore loser."

"I guess they don't lose often. From what I see, they're all good riders," Karen said. Sharon agreed.

Surprisingly, Lindsey walked over and introduced herself, extending her hand. Karen returned the gesture. Ginny thought Lindsey's freckles made her look younger. In reality, she was the same age as Karen. But it was difficult to picture this girl being so aggressive on horseback. The biting tone in Lindsey's next statement made Ginny a believer again. Lindsey approached Grand, caressing the mare's forehead. It was as if she was taking possession of the pony.

"Hi, Grand. You're such a good girl. We had such a fabulous time together, didn't we?"

The gentle strokes turned into a firm pat, almost a push on Grand's nose. Abruptly, Lindsey turned on her heel and strode off.

"What was that all about?" Karen asked.

"She probably feels threatened," Sharon said. "It annoys me that she acts like that, especially toward a horse who's been good to her. We'll work on your confidence with jumping. She's definitely your competition, but we'll give her a run for her money."

An exhausted Ginny slipped under her covers that night, thinking of the day's events. Karen needed to improve her confidence over fences. Lindsey might mess with her in the flat classes, but Karen was her own worst enemy on the jump course. Having a good season was critical if Ginny was to build her business. Yet, she smiled as she thought of June's beaming face on the way home. Whether she spoke of Blondie's improvement or her new friend Carl, the poor coalminer's daughter had had a great day.

CHAPTER 17

Environmental Disruption

"See ya, man," Lance said.

Brad zipped away from the old house on his dirt bike. The sound of the screaming motor faded as he crossed the creek and roared toward Ginny's house. Lance turned to the fountain and mounted his own four-wheeler. He paused a moment before starting it, looking over his shoulder, staring into the dark. Finally, he shrugged and started the machine.

Rather than speeding away, he crept up the hill to the Country Club Road. He almost stalled the motor as he looked behind him several times. At the top of Ginny's driveway, he stopped, silencing the motor, and gazed into the empty windows of the abandoned house. He was certain he'd see Lady Luminess, but only blackness filled the panes.

Something caught his eye on the northeast corner of the property. A yellow glowing ball danced along the lane leading from the house to the Somerset Pike. It hovered and then spun, and then rose until it skirted along the treetops. Lance turned his head toward Shane's, scanning the hillside for pranksters. The only light from Shane's was the dull glow of the television in the living room window. Lance located no other light source that could cause the dancing ball.

Looking to the northeast again, he saw the ball was still. Slowly, it started to expand, like a balloon filling with air, and then it darted away, flying across the Somerset Pike and rising farther northeast. In the distance, it exploded into multiple fragments of light, the pieces floating downward coating the northeast portion of the valley.

"Now I know where to take Mindy four-wheeling tomorrow," he said.

"Thanks, Dad," Lance said after they unloaded the four-wheeler. "We'll meet you back here at noon."

Lance guided his father as he turned his pickup and vehicle trailer around on the narrow, old mining road. The trailer blew dust at them as it pulled away. The teens struggled to breathe as the dust mixed with the humid June air. Mindy pulled her bandana over her nose, jogging backward to escape the dust cloud.

"Are you sure he'll pick us up by noon?" she asked. "I'm already going to be late for the 4-H fundraiser. I'm sure the other girls are going to be mad enough."

As she dropped the bandana around her neck again, Lance admired her pink painted lips. A matching shade of blush highlighted her cheeks. Lined in blue, her eyes captivated him. She leaned on one hip, her long legs sprouting from her denim cutoffs. She tapped the ground with the toe of her cowgirl boot, waiting for his answer.

Pulling himself from the trance, he said, "Don't worry, he won't want me running wild for too long. Besides, I can't think of a more boring way to spend a Saturday, giving pony rides and selling gobs."

"You didn't mind the carwash too much," she said.

"At least I got to see a few cool muscle cars. That black Camaro with the fiery hood was great."

The pair mounted the four-wheeler. Exhilarated, Lance cruised up the wide mining paths that scarred the eastern hillside of Johnstown. The turns were challenging but not impossible to negotiate, and he could accelerate up the straightaways without worrying about low-hanging branches. They traveled about four miles to the top of the strip mine, Lance happily aware of Mindy's tight hold around his waist.

He stopped at a flat area, bordered to the left by a steep hillside dotted with struggling young trees. Below them flowed the Stony Creek River. Despite the barren hills surrounding them, Lance had chosen this spot to look over the river that bordered the Geistown section of town. Behind them, to the right of the path, was an abandoned mine shaft. Large boulders blocked its entrance, but the timber framing the opening remained intact.

Lance took Mindy's hand as the two stood atop the hillside. Stony Creek's shallow current glistened in the sunlight, despite the stains of orange lining the flood walls and covering the exposed boulders along the riverbed.

"If it doesn't rain soon, the river will dry up," Mindy said. "I'm just glad the creek by Ginny's is cleaner than this. Imagine swimming in water like that."

"You never invite me swimming," Lance pictured her in a cute swimsuit.

"Next time," she promised.

He nodded absently as he noticed the ground to their right was tinged in orange. He followed its line with his gaze, losing it as it continued over the plunging hillside.

"It looks like that orange stuff is coming from up here." He released her hand and walked to the orange stain. Looking toward the mine shaft, he noticed the road between it and the hillside was also stained. "Whatever that is, it's coming from the mine." He approached the blockade of boulders.

"My dad says that the orange stain is caused by sulfur," she said. "It drains from the mines into the river. Be careful over there, those boulders could slide."

"Wow! How weird is this?" He crouched to read the inscription on a small steel plate bolted to the rock outside the mine. It read, "Opie Mine Number Eleven."

"That was some family," Mindy said. "They must have owned half the town."

"It would be cool to see what's inside." Lance started to push at a smaller boulder.

"Don't you dare!" She tugged on his arm, pulling him away from the mine.

The two went back to the hillside. The stump of a huge tree stood like a platform at the edge. It was easily big enough for them to sit on side by side, dangling their feet over a four-foot drop. Beyond a boulder at the base of the tree, the hillside took an almost vertical slide to the river.

"I better hold on to you. I don't want you to fall." Lance put his arm around Mindy's shoulder.

She ran her hand along the surface of the massive stump. Starting from its core, she touched each ring, stretching her body to its fullest and coming nowhere near the outer edge. "My God, this tree must have been hundreds and hundreds of years old."

Lance studied the tree rings with mild interest. "Sure, maybe even a thousand years old."

"You know, Karen tells a story about the lumber company taking down a huge tree on this hillside. She said it practically roared when it fell, and she has nightmares about it still. I thought she was kind of nuts, but sitting here on this giant stump and seeing the damage to this area is scary."

"I have a weird story of my own," Lance replied.

He told her about the strange light show over these hills the night before. Her blue eyes widened in wonderment. With her attention focused solely on him, he moved in to kiss her. They stopped talking for a few minutes.

"I don't know what to make of all this," she said when they parted. "It's like the spirit of the old house wants us to know something."

"Every time she shows herself, we find more out about this Opie guy. None of it seems good. Look at what he did to that horse, Loyal Pal." Lance looked at his watch. "We better head back."

He helped Mindy up and held her as they walked across the stump and stepped onto the solid ground just below the mining path. Something caught his eye at the stump's base. Embedded in the soil and jammed against the stump was a piece of tarnished metal. He leaned down to get it, using all his might to pull it from the earth. Mindy crouched beside him as he cleared the dirt from its surface.

He strained to read the shallow lettering engraved into the weathered piece of metal, which looked like a badge. He scraped the dirt from its crevices until he could make out the words in the top row: Pennsylvania Wildlife Federation. The bottom row was undoubtedly a name, but he could only discern a few letters.

"What in the world?" he muttered.

"Lance, there's something else here," Mindy said.

He glanced at her, alerted by her shaking voice. Her face was white and her eyes wide. A few feet from where he'd found the badge, an ivory ridge of teeth poked from the soil. Lance gulped loudly as a wave of fear swept over him. Tentatively, he brushed some of the soil away from the teeth, uncovering a human jaw.

The summer sun had waned as Lance's dad pulled into Ginny's parking lot. A few sedans were still there, parents loading smiling small children into the backseats. June and Kirsten were leading Blondie and Cajun away from the lot along the tree-lined path. Pony rides were done for the day.

Lance helped Mindy out of the pickup truck. As his father drove away, Karen approached, looking over her shoulder at the other 4-H members who were packing things up from the bake sale. Her furtiveness indicated she wanted no one to see him and Mindy.

"Mindy, where have you been?" she whispered when she reached them. "Everyone except Jess and Kirsten has been complaining that you're not here."

"Believe me, Karen," Lance said, "she has an excuse. We've been talking to the police all afternoon."

Karen's face paled and hands trembled as she listened to their story. When they were done, she hugged them both.

"It was right where you saw that huge oak tree fall," Mindy said. She wiped the dust from her tear-stained face.

"The one over Geistown?" Karen said. "I still cringe when I think of it. It's like the voice of that wildlife officer came out of that tree when it fell."

The Somerset Pike yielded no more traffic until Karen's father Tim arrived for the girls. He listened somberly to the saga of the screaming oak.

CHAPTER 18

Always Learning

"Are you sure you're up for this?" Karen asked.

"Yes, it will take my mind off things," Mindy replied.

They were arranging the ribbons and trophies by class inside the announcer's booth of the Ebensburg Fairgrounds. It was the day of the Fox Hollow 4-H club's horse show.

"They say the guy's been dead for decades," Mindy went on, "and that he will probably never be identified. It's still really creepy, though. I'd feel better if his death could be recognized."

"I know what you mean. I could never handle finding something like that. How weird is it that it happened near Opie's mine?"

"The more I know about that family, the less I want to know."

"On top of what he did to Loyal Pal," Karen said, "it sounds like he was endangering wildlife. Why else would an official from the Pennsylvania Wildlife Federation be there?"

"That hillside was totally stripped and the river polluted. All the wildlife was probably run out of there."

"It seems like Lady Luminess was different, though. Maybe she wants the sins of her father to be discovered."

"What about Lady Luminess?" Ivy asked. She climbed the stairs and took her assigned position at the microphone for the first class.

"We'll tell you later. I've got to get going, my class is early. Are you sure you're okay?" Karen asked Mindy one last time.

"I'm fine. Ivy will keep me company, and Lance is around somewhere."

"Yeah," Karen said. "He and Shane are real thrilled about helping set up the barrels, poles, and jumps."

Karen took several hangers of ribbons with her. She would serve as ringmaster for the first few classes of the day. She joined June, who was on gate duty. The two would work together and then leave to prepare for their classes when other club members came to relieve them.

Grooming and showmanship was a halter class that judged overall turnout, handling, and manners of the horse. Fox Hollow's leaders had suggested that Kirsten use the class for Dawn's first show experience. In this halter class, the young horse could experience the sights and sounds of the show ring without the added stress of being ridden. Sharon had worked with Kirsten and Dawn at the farm, and the pair had become proficient with the requirements. From her spot at the center of the ring, Karen noted Sharon standing by June. Undoubtedly, they would be rooting for Dawn from the gate.

Unable to hide her favoritism, Karen winked and smiled at Kirsten as she led the beautifully turned out Arabian into line. Dawn's coat sparkled. Her mane and tail were tangle free and flowed lightly. Kirsten's choice of a black Arabian show halter with a green brow band complemented Dawn's rose-gray coat. Dawn stepped nervously from her spot a few times as she waited to be inspected by the judge. Kirsten applied light pressure to the chain under the filly's chin, and she went back to standing. Her ears twitched curiously at all the activity, but she maintained her composure with each small correction. Her fussiness was the only flaw in her performance. Kirsten and Dawn executed the required trot transitions in hand sharply. Their 360-degree pivot was spot on. The look of frustration left Kirsten's face when she was announced as the third place winner. Karen congratulated her quietly. In contrast, Sharon and June hooted and hollered their approval.

After six classes, it was time for Karen and June to compete in the pony hunter division. Shane joined Karen as she mounted Grand. She gave him instructions on how to set up the jump course.

"Just be sure the heights of the rails and the distances between jumps are correct," she told him as a puffy-eyed Lance joined them.

"I do know how to use a tape measure," Shane said. He looked at Lance. "It's this joker you have to watch."

"Hey, I'm not responsible for my mistakes. I'm half asleep!" Lance said. He opened the gate. "Let's get going."

Karen laughed. "No, silly, we have the flat classes first."

"Flat class? What does that mean?" Lance asked as Shane guided him to the side.

The same competitors assembled for the pony hunter division, minus Bella and Tracy. Karen was not aware of any difficulties between Tracy and Bella and wondered where they were.

As usual, equitation was first. Lindsey gave a quick nod as she trotted past Karen. Karen noted she was steering clear of Grand this time, as Lindsey secured a rail space across the arena. She glanced at Carl and Hardy. The Connemara looked as cooperative as ever. June and Blondie were behind Karen, and she saw Blondie walked with her head cocked sideways and was gnawing at the bit. Although Blondie was walking rather than prancing, her body language gave her away. She was still not entirely comfortable in the ring. The class proceeded as usual.

Lindsey did indeed leave Grand and Karen alone. *She can't intimidate us,* Karen thought as they trotted down the long side of the ring. The thought no sooner left her mind than she saw someone who could. Lindsey's brother stood at the rail. He stared at her intensely, a scowl on his face. The negative energy was almost enough to knock Karen over. She stared back at him, but she couldn't hold his gaze. Later, she couldn't even describe Jude's physical features. All she remembered was the hatred exuding from his eyes. It gave her the creeps. It distracted her enough that she was slow to complete her downward transition when asked.

Again, Lindsey won the equitation with Karen in second. Applause from Lindsey's corner echoed through the arena. As Karen saw Jude congratulate his sister, she told herself to ignore him and pay better attention to the commands.

She left the ring and turned to watch the rest of the procession. A white fourth-place ribbon dangled from Blondie's bridle, and June looked disappointed. However, her expression lightened as Carl greeted her. He patted her on the back and must have said a kind word. Hardy's yellow third-place ribbon complemented the pony's bay color.

The same group reentered the ring for the pony hunter under saddle class. Refocusing, Karen secured a rail spot away from the other ponies. The request for a trot came. Karen asked for more impulsion from Grand as they rounded the corner. Grand responded, and by the time they entered the straightaway, she was in full extension. The wonderful pony moved effortlessly past the judge. To achieve the ideal hunter canter, Karen emphasized collection rather than extension. The pony was to travel in a slow but distinctly three-beat gait in a slightly rounded frame. Grand delivered, taking the class. Lindsey and Chip placed second.

If she was annoyed, Lindsey hid it this time. She smiled politely at Mindy, who was now ringmaster, as she received her ribbon. The judge addressed both Lindsey and Karen as they left the ring.

"It was a tough decision," she said. "Both of these are lovely ponies. The two of you will have an exciting season competing against each other."

Karen's green eyes met Lindsey's blue ones. They simultaneously smiled and nodded at each other. It was just enough to acknowledge the judge's statement.

As she left the ring, Karen smiled when she saw Shane rouse Lance into action. The boys grabbed jump rails and hustled toward the ring. Jude came out of nowhere, bumping into Shane's shoulder. The force almost knocked Shane over, causing him to drop the rail. Turning to confront Jude, Shane yelled something. Karen urged Grand into a trot, hoping she wouldn't have to stop a fight. Yet Jude continued on robotically, without a backward glance. Shaking his head, Shane picked up the rail again.

"That kid is a real jerk!" he said as Karen came near.

"He has a real problem with us," she said.

"Especially when you beat his sister." Shane patted her knee in congratulations.

Karen talked with June and Carl while the boys set up the jumps.

"The judge told me to work on getting Blondie in a long, low frame," June said. "Maybe then we can get a different colored ribbon."

"She seemed more settled," Karen said.

June nodded. "I'm just glad she's not leaping in the air anymore!"

"You're doing a good job with her," Carl said. "Good luck to both of you in the jumping class."

"He is so polite," Karen whispered to June as Carl rode off. "You should hang out with him more."

Chip and Lindsey put in a stellar jumping round. However, Karen's confidence was building. She made only one mistake, which caused Grand to chip in to the second fence. She rode more forwardly for the rest of the round. They finished well. Again, it would be close between Grand and Chip.

To Karen's dismay, Lindsey prevailed again. Nonetheless, she was proud of her round. She would continue working on her jumping skills.

"Someday, we'll beat them," she told Grand as they left the arena.

Shane hustled toward Sharon's horse trailer, thinking that Grand would be thirsty. She deserved a drink right away. As he rounded the front of the Chevrolet pickup, his jaw dropped and he blinked in disbelief at what he saw.

Jude was leaning over the trailer hitch. In his hand was the clasp that secured the trailer hitch to the ball mount on the truck. The clasp was obviously in an upright position, the unlocked position.

"Hey! What the hell are you doing?" Shane said angrily.

His eyes as dark as coal, Jude scowled at him for a few seconds before abruptly smiling.

"I'm glad I noticed this," he said. "Your hitch was undone. You guys are lucky you made it here without the trailer coming off. Look, I'll secure it for you." He pushed the clasp into the locked position.

"No way. I hooked that trailer up myself. There's no way I forgot to lock it."

Even as he spoke, Shane struggled with the idea that he had forgotten to close the clasp. His mind raced, retracing his steps earlier that morning. The shock of barely stopping a possible sabotage dumbfounded him.

"Well, you must have forgotten," Jude said. "See you around."

He nonchalantly greeted Karen as she approached the trailer. Stone-faced, she barely acknowledged him.

"That is one weird dude," she said to Shane as Jude walked off. "What's wrong? You look like you've seen a ghost."

Just then, June approached on Blondie with Sharon and Kirsten in tow. The females chattered about June's toughness and determination, congratulating her for getting the pony around the jump course with two refusals. Shane decided not to ruin the jovial mood, but one thing was for sure. He'd check the trailer hitch himself before each departure.

Karen relished the comfort of Shane's arm around her shoulders as they walked to the refreshment stand. He was the perfect boyfriend, always there for her, patient, kind, and extremely good looking. Who could ask for more?

Not only were they both starving, but Karen wanted to check on her family. She had a strong aversion to housework and cooking, and was glad to leave the concession stand in her mother's and aunt's hands, yet she felt bad that they had to toil in the summer heat.

Her aunt Rose eased her concerns, greeting her with a warm hug. Jessica's mother had always doted on her nieces and nephews, and today was no exception. She asked about Karen's classes and joked with Shane, teasing him about how bored he must have been. Karen's mother added her two cents, teasing Karen about how prim and proper she acted in front of the judge. Colleen's and Rose's jovial natures mimicked that of their Irish mother, in contrast to their more reserved German father.

Sitting in the back of the concession stand, away from the commotion, in her perfectly tailored rose-colored linen pants suit, Karen's paternal grandmother looked far more sophisticated than a regular seamstress. She applied her job skills to make her own clothing fit perfectly, not to mention her family's. Of Slovenian descent, she exuded a casual old-world elegance, yet she was known to voice her opinions freely. When Karen asked if she had seen her classes, her grandmother responded, "Of course. You did very well. You should have won the jumping class. Those Suppewiczes have enough already."

They all laughed. Karen and Shane stayed to chat, until Karen told Jessica it was time for her to get ready for her first show. Sharon had Cookie waiting in one of the barns.

After Jessica received numerous well wishes from her family, Shane and Karen walked with her to the barn. They dropped Jessica off, and then Karen took her place as announcer, allowing Ivy a break. Shane joined Lance to set up the fences for the working hunter class. Mindy looked on as gatekeeper and June sat in the judge's booth, ready to be ringmaster. Karen watched the process apprehensively. Just looking at the size of the jumps made her nervous. The class was for horses, and their jumps, at three feet six inches, were a foot higher than the ones Karen and Grand jumped. When she saw Sonja and Brian along the outside of the ring, she realized Wendy and Dorian must be competing in this class. It seemed kind of soon.

Her heart pounded with anxiety as Dorian entered the ring. He looked beautiful, his steel gray coat gleaming with health. Wendy performed her courtesy circle and approached the first line.

Dorian cantered to the first fence. Karen was surprised at how he had settled. He jumped the first fence nicely and moved on to the second. It was an oxer, and it was right in front of the announcer's stand. The horse glanced off to the side, losing concentration. His stride shortened, and he started to balk.

"Wendy!" Sonya roared from ringside. "Use the crop!"

As Wendy reached back and smacked Dorian behind the girth, the horse got in too close to the oxer. He leaped into the air like a rabbit, catching the rail with his front feet. Wendy was unseated, but managed to stay on.

"Keep going! Drive him!" Sonya commanded.

Dorian had become unsteady and was weaving from side to side. Worse, Wendy had lost her reins and was desperately trying to gather them. The horse had no idea where to go. The last scream from the rail was, "Look where you're going!"

Wendy yanked her outside rein to bring Dorian to the next fence. She got him there with no time for him to judge the distance. He slid to a stop, crashing into the jump. Poles tumbled to the ground, slamming into his cannon bones. Flung forward, Wendy clung to Dorian's neck.

Despite everything, the horse knew he was to jump. As the last pole hit the ground, Dorian propelled himself over the wreckage from a stand still.

Wendy could not hold on anymore. Though she clung to him with all he might, she came off, flipping around backward. She landed hard in a seated position and let out a shrill gasp. It sent chills down Karen's spine. Brian and Sonya ran to her aid. Surprisingly, Dorian stood beside Wendy. His head was down, ears dropped to the side. Wendy didn't move. Brian and Sonya knelt beside her, talking quietly to her. A few minutes seemed like hours. Finally, they lifted Wendy slowly to her feet. They walked three abreast from the ring. Dorian followed Wendy, his head drooping, like a lost puppy. No one collected the loose horse, so Karen jumped from the announcer's booth and went to Dorian's head.

"Poor boy," she said, patting his neck. "You just weren't ready, were you?"

By the time the group reached the trailer, Wendy was walking by herself. She was very stiff, and Karen could see the pain on her face.

As Karen started to untack Dorian, Brian suddenly yelled from behind her, "You worthless piece of garbage! You're going to be dog food before you know it!"

The angry voice startled the horse, causing him to spook sideways. Karen moved quickly to stay with the frightened horse.

"Brian, please!" she said. "I mean no disrespect, but it's not his fault. The fences were too big. He wasn't ready."

"She's right, Dad," Wendy said. Her voice was shaking and weak. "He didn't mean to hurt me."

Brian took a deep breath. "Look, Karen, I'm sorry. Thanks for your help. Please give the horse to Sonya."

Karen reluctantly gave the reins to Sonya.

"I hope you're okay," she said to Wendy, and hustled back to the announcer's booth.

Kirsten greeted her, a sheepish grin on her face. "I thought I'd take over while you were gone. Everyone was complaining that there was no announcer."

Karen blushed. "What was I thinking? Thanks, I was just worried about Wendy *and* Dorian."

"I understand. Hey, I know I'm supposed to help in the concession stand, but Jess's class is coming up. Can I stay to watch her?"

"Of course, I almost forgot with all the drama. I hope things go okay from now on. What could go wrong with a little pony like Cookie?"

Kirsten took a spot in the center of the grandstand. Ivy joined her. Sharon, Ginny, and Mary supervised from the rail. Upon seeing the adults, Karen wondered where Ginny and Mary had been all day.

The pony Western pleasure started. Cookie was less than pleased about the indoor ring. Rather than traveling in a slow jog, she gawked at the grandstand and announcer's booth. Jessica worked hard to straighten her, but Cookie zipped around at a hurried trot, trying to cut the corners. Jessica's face reddened with the effort of controlling the pony. When she hauled her onto the rail, the pony evaded the bit by raising her head. Jessica didn't give up, but the picture wasn't pretty. She started to post, which helped Jessica balance. The overall picture improved, but she would be penalized for posting in a Western class. Nonetheless, Karen was proud of her cousin. Unfortunately, others were not so kindhearted. Rude comments came from the bleachers. Karen looked over to see two women laughing and pointing at Cookie.

"Boy, you'd think she'd be able to handle that pony. Look at her legs dangling. She's way too big for her."

Karen's blood boiled. She wanted to ring their necks. She wasn't the only one. Seated just below the women, Kirsten scowled with distaste. Mindy shot an angry glare at the women from the gate.

As ringmaster, June prompted Karen to call for a lope. A lope is a slow canter, the term used in Western riding. As Karen gave the command, Jessica was forced to struggle again. Cookie trotted briskly away from Jessica's cues, but refused to lope. Jessica tried again, but the little pony looked nervous and off balance. She continued at a fast trot, bouncing Jessica in the saddle. Karen's heart sank as Cookie finally cantered, just in time for the walk command.

The rude women were holding nothing back. The whole grandstand heard them say, "Get a different hobby or take the training wheels off. That pony is no good!"

Kirsten spun around. "Hey! That's my friend down there and that pony is the best she's got. I'd like to see you do better!"

The whole crowed nodded in agreement. Kirsten was the only one brave enough to say anything, but the piercing looks from the others made the women shrink down in their seats. They said nothing the rest of the afternoon.

Karen called into the stands, "Ivy, can you please cover for me?"

As Ivy scrambled up to the announcer's stand. Karen went to Jessica, who was wiping the tears from her face. Kirsten and Mindy were trying to comfort her. Karen took Cookie's reins.

"Don't worry. We all go through these rough spots. She'll get better."

Karen could have kicked herself as she had a revelation. The pony driving class was about to enter the ring. The class was small, with only four ponies entered. She remembered that Cookie knew how to drive.

"Look, Jess. Here's a class more suited for Cookie. Because of her small stature, it's hard for her to balance around the ring with a teenage rider. But if she were pulling your weight rather than carrying it, she'd be golden. Keep riding her on the trails. She has no problem carrying you in a straight line. But look at those driving ponies. The competition isn't that tough! We'll see if Sharon will bring the cart to Fox Hollow. You can show her in harness next time!"

Indeed, the competitors were hardly refined show hackneys. To Karen's surprise, Bella led the group into the ring. Obviously, this was why she hadn't been in the other classes.

Bella was the best looking pony of the bunch. Tracy must have figured she was a better driver than rider. Her size didn't overpower Bella from the cart. Like Cookie for Jess, Karen had seen Bella carry Tracy steadily through the woods. Of course there, appearances meant nothing. Karen adored and respected the pinto with the dished face. She was steadfast and true to Tracy. She kept her owner safe, whether under saddle or in harness.

Now there was hope for Jessica to enjoy her show season. Cookie would fit right into the class profile. Karen could have kicked herself for not thinking of this before.

The day concluded without further mishap. Karen was too tired to question Shane's silence on the way home. She figured he was exhausted too.

Despite her exhaustion, Karen didn't sleep well that night. Brian's words about Dorian becoming dog food stuck in her mind. She called Wendy the next day.

"I'm okay, just a little sore," Wendy said. "I bruised my tailbone."

"I feel so bad. I hope you get better soon," Karen said. "Wendy, did you see how Dorian stood beside you after the fall? They say it's the sign of a good, faithful horse when they don't run away after you fall."

"I know. I love that horse. I just don't know if I can trust him. I don't want to get hurt." Wendy's voice was shaking again. "My dad's really mad at him."

"Wendy, I saw everything. He tried to do what you wanted, but the booth scared him. You lost control, and he didn't know where he was going. He got too close to the last jump. He doesn't have the experience to get himself out of a sticky situation like that. I'm not trying to be a know-it-all, but I think Sonya is pushing you too fast."

"Maybe you're right. He's been relaxing so nicely, especially when I'm riding at home. Sonya thought he could handle the working hunter class. He's been doing so well during our lessons. I guess it's different when they're away from home. I'll be sure Sonya doesn't push us too quickly again. I think the horse has potential. If my dad realizes my fall wasn't Dorian's fault, I'm sure he'll come around."

Karen had to be satisfied with this. Yet again, she saw how horses and ponies provided life lessons for all involved.

CHAPTER 19

LIKE A VOLLEYBALL

Gage waited outside Skateland's girls' bathroom. He hoped Kirsten wouldn't be long. His dad would be there any minute, and they were meeting the others at Shane's for a volleyball game. His school's quarterback rolled up to him. Mike's white T-shirt barely concealed the muscles popping from his arms and chest. He peered at Gage.

"Where'd you find that piece you're with, Gage? She's cute, but don't you think she's kind of chunky?"

Gage's jaw dropped. He searched for words to retaliate with, but his mind was blank. Mike departed with a satisfied sneer.

Anger boiled inside Gage. He replayed the scene in his head, intent on besting Mike with words. Yet all he could think of was, "No, I think she looks great."

Finally, Kirsten emerged from the bathroom. A new coat of lipstick and blush adorned her beautiful face. A soft fragrance filled his nostrils. The urge to take her hand was strong, yet he couldn't touch her as they walked out the door.

The merciless July sun spat its rays over the evergreens lining Shane's yard. The girls congregated in a circle, jubilant about the previous weekend's horse show. Sitting on a log and brooding, Gage listened half-heartedly while Shane, Lance, and Brad set up the volleyball net.

"I'm so proud of you, June," Karen said. "Carl is a good rider, but you nudged him down to fourth place. You're equitation has gotten so much better. You probably don't know how to act, now that Blondie is behaving herself."

"It's been tough, but I can say my hard work is paying off. You have something to celebrate too. You beat Lindsey in the jumping class!"

"That was unbelievable. I almost fell off Grand when they called us first. But even better was how little Cookie did in the driving class." Karen turned to her cousin. "I told you, Jess, the first few shows were rough, but she came around for you. A second place at your third show is great. Bella is hard to beat."

"What about how Cookie keeps up with the bigger horses during trail rides?" Mindy said. "She's a spunky little thing."

"So you're still not interested in showing?" Jessica asked Mindy.

Mindy shook her head and pulled Ivy close to her. "Ivy and I can watch from the sidelines."

"I wouldn't mind having some of the glory too, though," Ivy said sadly.

"Maybe someday there will be enough horses for everyone." Karen paused. "So, Kirsten, how did you like showing Dawn under saddle for the first time?"

"It was okay. I think I messed her up. I was more nervous than she was."

"One wrong lead during your first attempt isn't bad. It will come."

Agitated, Gage butted in. "Equitation, leads, horse shows. It all sounds useless to me." Standing abruptly, he strode to the volleyball net. "Let's just play the game."

Deafening silence swallowed the yard. Gage's stomach turned, and he gulped, bracing for a verbal assault. The continued silence made him want to vomit. The gaze of six girls burned his back. He fought the urge to run home.

The boy's circle was no safe mecca. "What's up with you, man?" Shane asked. He drilled Gage with the volleyball. The thud as it hit his chest bounced through the hollow. Looking confused, Lance and Brad said nothing.

Deflecting the awkward tension, Gage said, "All right, teams are: me, Kirsten, Ivy, Mindy, and Brad facing downhill. So Jessica, Lance, June, Shane, and Karen face uphill. This way, both teams have a real player, Kirsten for us and Jessica for you." Crossing his fingers for brownie points, he credited the girls who played on their high school teams. Quiet prevailed. His next comment would make or break him. "You guys will need all the help you can get with Karen on your team."

Laughter erupted, the happy sound rising to meet the remaining glow from the sun atop the trees. He tossed the ball to Kirsten, winked, and said, "Let 'em have it."

Kirsten's first serve whizzed past Gage's head with a message. It pelted the opposition's ground, leaving Karen flailing on the ground in its wake. Through bouts of laughing at one another, Kirsten maintained the upper hand for several serves. Jessica was the only one to return the ball successfully, finally bringing the serve to their side. It was not without a price, as Jessica shook the sting from her hands for several seconds.

The game became more evenly matched as the others filtered through their turns to serve. The match was tight when it was Jessica's fourth turn to serve. Gage studied Jess's intense gaze. She lacked Kirsten's power, but was dead accurate. She landed the ball just out of his reach. Brad came roaring from the right, but ended up in a heap in the center of the court. Finally, Brad was able to spike the next shot, bringing the serve to Gage.

He surveyed his opponents, looking for the weakest link. Shane was crooning over Karen's scraped knees and elbows, but Gage decided that was just too easy, like taking candy from a baby. He passed over Jess; she was a superior player to him. He locked onto June. She was a weak spot. Without thinking, he let his gaze linger on her developing curves. Though still thin, she wasn't built like a boy anymore. As he aimed for the space between her and Karen, he caught a glimmer in June's eye. She made a slight move toward Karen, as if instinctually covering the weakest link. Their gazes locked for a moment. Gage lifted the ball slowly, drew his serving arm back—and June winked at him. Her fluttering eyelashes distracted him, so he hit the ball more softly than he intended. With a spritely lateral move, June got under the ball, popping it back over the net. Gage barely noticed Brad's game-winning spike. His team rejoiced around him, high fiving each other and mocking the opposition. Yet again, Shane helped Karen from the ground as Jessica laughed. Lance, too, was fighting back his amusement, trying to look disappointed with the loss as June patted him on the back. Gage took a deep breath, looking toward the heavens. Stars of enchantment sparkled in the summer sky. The glow of the full moon bounced back to earth, shrouding June and setting the red of her hair alight. The other girls remained in shadows.

Reality woke Gage with a gasp as Kirsten tickled his sides from behind. "Come on, Gage, what planet are you on? We won!"

They settled around a fire pit as Shane lit the kindling. As the fire rose, the smell of roasting hot dogs and marshmallows filled the air. Gage started to relax, feeling comfortable sitting beside Kirsten. He even fed her a toasted marshmallow after smooshing it playfully against her nose. The others laughed and Lance followed suit, squishing Mindy's cheek with the white goo.

"Hey, don't waste those," she said. "We have to make s'mores."

"We know how much you like them," Karen said, "since you named your dog after them!"

Sitting across from Gage, Brad looked bored. He kicked stones between his feet like soccer balls. Gage knew there would be trouble when Brad got up and said politely, "Excuse me, I have to relieve myself."

"Thanks for letting us know," Lance said.

"Yeah, we really didn't need to know that," Jessica said.

Gage waited in anticipation. After a few minutes, he caught a low shadow creeping up behind Jessica and Karen. Seconds later the girls leaped up, screaming with fear. Brad stood behind them, doubled over with laughter. This put him in a vulnerable position, unable to escape Jessica's charge and double-handed push. She almost knocked him to the ground amidst laughter from the others.

With everyone distracted, Gage pulled Kirsten closer. They smooched for a few minutes while the others settled back down. Suddenly, headlights appeared below the yard and a horn beeped. Kirsten's face dropped.

"Oh, man," she said, "I told my dad I'd call when I was ready. Now, he just shows up. Gotta go."

She looked to Gage as the other girls groaned in protest. He knew all eyes were on him. He felt like a public display. He tried to muster the courage to kiss her good-bye, telling himself just to give her a peck. But he could only shrug and say, "Okay. I guess I'll see you later then."

She looked as if he'd punched her. She rose abruptly and marched to her father's car. Gage watched her leave. As she closed the car door, he shifted his gaze across the campfire. June was staring at him, her head cocked, her eyes twinkling in the fire's glow. His breath caught in his throat.

He was only half aware of the others talking. Something about Karen walking Jessica down to Ginny's so her father could pick her up, and Brad assuring the girls he would protect them as they passed the old house. Despite their rolling eyes, the girls accepted his escort, as Shane felt it best to stay with the fire. Lance and Mindy were going to his house to watch a movie. Ivy was the last to speak, asking June if she was ready to go.

June continued to hold Gage's gaze. "Not yet. You go ahead. I don't feel like going home now."

The group disbanded. Shane strode up the hill, saying something about getting more kindling. Only Gage and June remained at the campfire.

June rose and circled the campfire. She sat beside him, her catlike eyes reflecting the dying flames. Her graceful movements, combined with her sharply defined cheekbones, made her seem fairylike. Enchanted, he stroked her cascading auburn curls from her face. She tilted her head, drawing him in with those fluttering eyelashes. He kissed her softly, pulling her closer by the strap of her tank top. Her skin was smooth beneath his fingertips, and he kissed her more passionately.

Shane cleared his throat loudly. Gage jerked his head around. Shane's piercing eyes ripped through his soul, but Gage wasn't ready to own up to his actions. He whispered to June, "Come with me." Without a word, he led her to a grove of trees alongside the yard.

They sat under the boughs, talking nonsense about schoolmates and neighbors. As the conversation waned, they kissed several more times.

He felt strong next to her petite form, but slowly, guilt and regret crept into his heart. Hearing Shane and Karen's muffled voices, he stood abruptly. How would he explain this? Would Shane cover for him? What if Kirsten found out?

He stood still for several minutes, listening for the movements of Shane and Karen, hoping they would leave. He shushed June when she asked what was wrong. Slowly, the fire's glow diminished. The only sound came from his breathing. Confident that Shane and Karen had gone, he said flatly, "We better go now."

June followed him silently from the grove. Darkness enveloped them as they approached the smoldering campfire. Everything was still. He exhaled in relief. He said a quick good-bye to June and started toward his four-wheeler. His breath caught in his throat again as he passed closer to the fire. The embers cast just enough light to reveal the staring faces of Karen and Shane.

CHAPTER 20

A Fiery August Sunset

June readied Blondie in the barn aisle, her chest tightening at the sound of approaching footsteps. She gulped, realizing that Karen was coming. Though she dreaded facing Karen, she longed for any diversion from her feelings of rejection and embarrassment. Since her brief rendezvous with Gage, her stomach had been in knots. She had barely eaten, and had dreamed up various schemes to get back at him for humiliating her, all the while longing for his touch. Focused on tightening Blondie's girth, she waited for Karen to speak first.

Karen cleared her throat. "Hey, June."

June felt Karen's gaze on her, but she couldn't face her. She greeted Karen in a similar way. Seconds of silence passed. June's heart thundered as if it would burst out of her. Karen's fast and shallow breathing told of her own distress. June started to sweat, and not because of the August heat.

"Roundup is coming," Karen finally said. "Let's start practicing."

A qualifier for the regional 4-H competition, Roundup was the same as any other show, except that each placing was assigned points. Three classes made up June and Karen's division. After the three classes were pinned, points for each competitor were added up, and the competitor with the highest point value was considered the top for that division in the county. Making it to regionals meant that one competed against the best of five counties. The number one horse in a respective region went on to state competition. Karen and Grand were ranked second in Cambria County. They had duked it out with Lindsey and Chip all season. Frequently, Grand took the under saddle class and Chip took the over fences. Grand and Karen had beaten Chip and Lindsey once over fences. Karen had closed the gap in the rankings. Lindsey led by only one win.

June's heart rate slowed. She bridled Blondie, proudly thinking of their respectable fourth-place ranking. She was just behind her friend Carl and his Connemara. Blondie had come a long way, and June had trained her with relatively little help. When she'd first attempted the jump courses, Blondie had been distractible and had a tendency to stop. In the beginning of the season, June had to trot courses rather than canter. Yet during the last two shows, she had cantered her jump courses without refusals.

The girls warmed their ponies up on the flat. Afterward, they took turns setting up the jumps, giving each other pointers along the way. An afternoon of sweat spilled into the evening. Finally, the stalls were done, the horses fed, and June and Karen walked side by side across the bridge.

As if reading each other's mind, the girls sat atop the rim of the old fountain. June had some explaining to do, but didn't know how to start. Seeking a benign subject, she decided to flatter Karen.

"Your last jumping round was fantastic. How did it feel to beat Lindsey and Chip?"

"What a rush. I was soaring for days! I owe it all to Grand and Sharon. Grand gave me everything she had that day. I could feel her rounding her back and snapping her knees under her chin. It was as if she was really trying to create a dramatic picture, trying to win. Everything came together, we hit all the distances perfectly, and I stayed in sync with her each time for once. I only hope we can duplicate it for Roundup. I don't want to prove the Suppewiczes right."

"Forget them. I never saw such poor losers. If their claims about Chip being sick that day are correct, I agree with what you said. He shouldn't have been competing anyway." June continued, "Is Jess taking Cookie for the last driving class?"

"She can't. I feel so bad. Her dad got laid off from the steel mill. Money is tight for her family right now. I can't imagine my dad being laid off. He says almost every dollar is spoken for by the time his next paycheck comes. How do these companies expect people to survive?"

Although working in the dog grooming shop was exhausting, June was grateful to have the extra money to pay for the horse shows. Without her job, she'd be in the same situation as Jessica. She started to say something, when a thud came from the old house. Karen leaped to her feet, scanning the windows nervously. June put a hand on her wrist saying, "Relax. She hears us. Watch this."

She faced the house. "Lady Luminess, are you ashamed that your father's companies have laid off my father and Jessica's father? Now our families are struggling to make ends meet."

Tension filled Karen's body. She strained against June's grip. "Don't make her mad!"

Two distinct knocks shook the third floor window. A flash of light illuminated the blackened inner walls. Karen broke June's grip and rushed up the driveway. June shouted after her, "Karen, wait! I need to talk to you about Gage!"

Karen's spine stiffened. She stopped in her tracks, as if hit by a stun gun. Slowly, she turned back. With her hands acting as blinders to her peripheral vision, she eyed June with apprehension.

"I'm sorry, Karen," June said tearfully. "I don't know what came over me. I was drawn to him like a fly to honey. I'm just so tired of being the odd one out. I want a boyfriend too."

Karen's face softened. "It's not me you should apologize to. Does Kirsten know? I've been struggling all week, trying to decide whether to tell her. I'm sorry you feel lonely, but how could you do that to her?"

Sobbing, June buried her head in her hands. Karen sat back down beside her. She started to say that June wasn't the only one to blame, but headlights pierced the darkening August mist from Country Club Road. A roadster stopped at the top of the driveway. Seconds later, the passenger door opened and then slammed loudly. Surrounded by the pink lights of the descending sun, Kirsten strode toward them. Her father's car stayed there, idling.

June's blood ran cold. A sickening realization swallowed her. Kirsten knew. She fought the urge to run as a horrible combination of guilt and defensiveness gripped her. She got to her feet as the taller girl approached. Her body tensed, preparing for fight or flight. Silent, Kirsten bore down on her relentlessly.

The guilt spoke first. "I'm really sorry, Kirsten. I was lonely, jealous of you with boyfriends. I wanted to feel wanted." The defensiveness spoke second. "Besides, he didn't officially ask you to go with him. I didn't think he was spoken for."

Kirsten's angry stride faltered. Still, she towered over June in the darkness. June felt more than saw Kirsten's face contort with pain. June braced herself.

A sob escaped Kirsten. "I can't believe you." She crumpled to her knees. Karen knelt beside her, saying something comforting. June only heard the deafening thud of her heart.

Seconds passed, and then Kirsten got up and turned abruptly. She stormed away toward her father's car.

"Wait, Kirsten," Karen called after her. "I don't want you to leave so upset. Come back and we'll talk about it."

"I have nothing to say to her. If I stay, I might start talking with my fists! Just call me later." The car door slammed shut, and the MG sped away.

Karen turned to June. "I don't know what to say. We have to fix this. Did you have to say that?"

June broke down, her body shaking uncontrollably. She couldn't look at Karen.

Karen took a deep breath. She put her arm around June. "Come on, I'll walk you home. Shane can wait."

Side by side, they passed the front door of the old house, June closest to it. A blinding light zipped from the porch. With it came a tremendous amount of energy. Before either girl could react, it collided with June, knocking her to the ground. Untouched, Karen stood beside her, gasping. The light disappeared as quickly as it had appeared.

Electricity surged through June's every muscle, rendering her helpless. Her hair stood on end, and she gasped for breath. Karen hovered over her, staring. Finally, June willed her legs to move. Karen pulled her to her feet.

They stumbled toward June's house in silence. As they crossed the Somerset Pike, Karen said, "I don't think the spirits are very happy with you."

Shane woke in a cold sweat. It was the morning of Roundup, and it had not started pleasantly for him. Visions of his nightmare remained as he got dressed. The image of a truck and horse trailer careening over a cliff was horrifying. He could see the whites of a terrified horse's eyes looking at him. Lingering in his mind was the screech of tires and screams from human passengers. He knew it was a dream, but he couldn't shake the horror of it. He left the house to meet Karen at the barn, the ominous feeling sticking to him.

"Boy, you look terrible," she said by way of greeting.

"Gee, thanks. What do you expect? It's very early for a Saturday morning." He would not tell her about the dream.

"Sorry. I'm glad you're coming. June and I appreciate the support. The rest of the girls are going swimming at Prince Gallitzin State Park for most of the day. I get the feeling they're over the horse-show thing for the year. And Kirsten, well …" Karen paused as June entered the barn.

Looking forlorn, June said, "She's still mad at me, isn't she? What did she say when you talked to her?"

Shane saw Karen wince. "Let's just say the two of you have a lot to work out."

"Great, I've lost a friend. On top of it, I don't know why I'm going to Roundup. It's between you and Lindsey." June sounded defeated.

"Don't say that. You could be a wild card for districts. Either of us can have a bad day. Besides, Ginny and Mary are bringing your mom to watch for the first time. I just hope Ginny doesn't sleep in too late."

As Karen and June loaded the truck and trailer, Shane took the opportunity to inspect the trailer hitch. He unlocked and relocked it several times; shaking the apparatus to be sure it was secure. He checked the tire pressure for the truck and trailer, and then rechecked the trailer hitch. Karen peered at him from the trailer's tack room, a curious look on her face.

"What is with you? You're obsessed with this trailer."

Barely looking at her, he told her not to worry. On a whim, he opened the driver's door and pulled down the sun visor. The keys clinked as they fell into his lap. The girls were walking back to the barn. He started the truck and gunned the engine, slamming on the brakes before going into Ginny's yard. He pulled backward and forward a few more times, applying different amounts of pressure to the brakes. Everything felt fine.

Sharon pulled up in her car during his last test. Looking amused, she asked him what was going on.

"Oh, good, you're here," he said. "I see your trailer was inspected in the spring. Have you had any trouble with it since then?"

"Uh, no. I would have gotten it fixed if I had," Sharon said sarcastically. "Is all this horse manure getting to your head? You have a strange look in your eye."

The four squeezed onto the bench seat of the Chevy. Shane only half listened as the girls discussed how June could make up with Kirsten. When Karen asked him how his friend Gage could be such a jerk, Shane merely grunted that he agreed. He drew a breath of relief when they pulled into the fairgrounds safely. The first part of their journey was over.

The day proceeded like any other show day, except that Sharon told the girls to braid the ponies' manes using colored yarn instead of rubber bands. Shane filled the water buckets to keep near the ponies and helped organize the equipment. He wallowed in boredom while the girls discussed how blue yarn would accentuate the brilliant red of Grand's coat and go with Karen's navy jacket. Green would complement Blondie's golden color, and match June's jacket. He seriously missed the company of another guy. After an hour passed, the ponies were ready.

"It won't be long now," Karen said. "Why don't we go watch the pony driving class? I'm anxious to see if Bella wins."

"Okay," Sharon said. "I wish Jess had brought Cookie just for fun. I know Bella's hard to beat, but it's sure fun to watch Cookie pull that cart."

Karen agreed half-heartedly. She didn't tell Sharon the real reason Jess couldn't show that day. Shane realized he missed Karen's spitfire of a cousin. When he picked on her, she gave it right back to him.

They provided hay nets for the horses and left them tied to the trailer before heading toward the arena. They climbed the bleachers, looking for a central spot. Shane felt a dark stare. Standing at the lower level, almost obscured by a steel support beam, was Jude. Shane met his dark gaze, and they stared each other down. In a flash, Jude was gone.

It was if he disappeared into thin air. Shane shook his head and focused again on the steel support. Indeed, Jude was gone. He had a sickening feeling in his stomach and stayed standing, scanning the entire place. Everything seemed fine as the pony drivers entered the ring.

"Bella has red ribbons in her mane," Karen said. "Look how nice it looks with her black and white coat." She nudged him when he didn't respond. "You could at least act interested."

Shane still saw no sign of Jude. He stood abruptly. "I'm going to check the ponies. It's hot. They might need a drink."

"Okay." Karen's gaze never left the action.

Shane hurried down the steps and practically sprinted to the trailer. Adrenaline surged through his veins as his suspicions were realized.

Jude had his back turned, the end of Grand's tether in one hand. He flailed a baseball cap with the other, shooing the mare away. The sensible mare was only slightly bothered. She moseyed away to a small grassy area along the border of the grounds.

"Get out of here, you worthless nag!" Jude flapped the cap wildly, stomping toward Grand.

Shane lunged at him from behind, tackling him. Jude grunted in pain as his limbs scraped on the concrete. Gravel crackled under the struggling bodies. Shane had the advantage, since Jude's body protected him from the hard concrete. He grabbed Jude by the neck, pinning him against the ground, and punched him in the jaw. Jude lay on the ground, stunned. Shane stood up and stared down at him. He was so furious, he had no words.

"Shane! What's going on? Where's Grand?" It was Karen.

He turned to look at her as Jude strained to get up.

"Don't worry. I have her," June said. She brought Grand to Karen.

Sharon raised her voice for the first time since Shane had known her. "All right, boys. You have a lot of explaining to do. I don't like to act like an adult, but you're leaving me no choice." She turned to Karen and June. "You girls don't have time to worry about this. Get ready. Your classes will start soon."

There was little time for the girls to process what happened. Karen inspected Grand, making sure the mare was unharmed. Satisfied she gave her a final brushing and tacked her. A flurry of movement caught her eye, and she laughed at the sight of Sharon dragging Jude by the ear. He grimaced in pain, his elbows bloodied. Sharon's departing comment made June look up from her work.

"Your dad and I are going to have a little talk!"

June and Karen looked at each other and burst out laughing. Shane joined them, looking sheepish and subdued.

"What in the world is going on?" Karen asked.

"I'll tell you later. You have a competition to worry about."

The girls mounted and Shane spit shined their boots. Hurrying to the arena, they barely made it on time. Karen noticed that all of the ponies' manes were braided. Roundup was serious for her competitors also. The judge took her spot in the middle of the ring. She eyed each competitor quickly, noting his or her number. Karen trotted past to secure a rail spot away from the other ponies. She was sure to add extra impulsion as she passed the judge. Ahead of her, Lindsey glanced back and flashed a smile. The announcer called for a walk.

Grand walked on a medium-length rein, using a long stride to show off four distinct steps. Karen sank her heels down and imagined a line going from her earlobe, through the shoulder to the hip, and ending at her heel. This was proper position. She took a few deep breaths and relaxed her elbows and hands, following the movement of Grand's head. She kept the picture in her mind, intent on holding position for the entire class.

The call to trot came. She tightened her calf muscles against Grand's side. The slight pressure kept her legs from swinging out of position. She asked Grand for a forward trot, but didn't ask for full extension in this class. Too much impulsion could bounce her out of position. Since the rider was primarily judged in equitation, she wanted to play it safe. She glanced across the ring to Lindsey. Overall, her position was good. However, she carried her hands too high, with obvious tension through her elbows and wrists. Karen trotted past June on the inside, giving her a quick wink. June's position looked good. Despite what had happened with Gage, Karen was proud to call June a friend. Her hard work showed through Blondie's rippling muscles and quiet demeanor. The class walked again.

Karen prepared to canter. *Don't mess up your lead,* she told herself. The announcer called for a canter. Karen took a deep breath and blew the tension out. Grand picked the correct lead. Karen breathed another sigh of relief. Of all the gaits, Karen had the most difficulty maintaining position at the canter. She reminded herself to sink down into the saddle. She let her hips roll with the motion of Grand's back. Again, she tightened her lower legs. She felt confident her position was right.

Carl and Hardy cantered past on Karen's inside. Carl was not to be taken lightly as a competitor. He had good hands and he took everything in stride. He and Hardy made few mistakes over fences. When they did, Carl kept his wits about him. He could turn a rough start into a solid round in moments. His only flaw was a lack of polish to his riding. It was no secret he preferred riding to hounds. He had told June he wasn't upset to finish third at the shows. Karen understood why June liked him.

The class ended. Lindsey pulled alongside Grand and gave Karen a smug smile. She expected to win. After a few moments, the announcer said, "First place goes to number thirty-three, Karen Mulligan riding Grand Moment."

Karen's jaw dropped. Lindsey gasped and swore under her breath. Applause erupted from the bleachers. Karen looked up to see Shane sitting with Ginny, Mary, Sharon, and Stella cheering. The loudest clapping came from Karen's grandmother. Decked out in her Sunday best, she stood beside Karen's mother, smiling proudly.

Polite clapping continued as Lindsey was announced in second place. She put on a good show in front of the judge. She smiled and thanked the ringmaster as she accepted her red second-place ribbon, but Karen caught the icy look Lindsey gave her while Karen's mother snapped a picture of Grand with the blue ribbon dangling from her bridle.

Carl and June emerged with their normal third- and fourth-place ribbons. Unconcerned, they were involved in an enthusiastic conversation.

There was little time before the group was called back for the under saddle class. Karen's confidence was high. Historically, Grand sparkled during this class. Karen hoped to add a second blue to Grand's bridle.

Grand exhibited her usual splendor during the trot. She lengthened her stride willingly along the long side, directly in front of the judge. Karen could feel the judge's gaze on her and hoped the judge recognized Grand's quality. Again, the walk was requested. Karen had placed herself strategically on the far corner. She wanted space to complete the canter transition. Suddenly, an old friend made an appearance.

Lindsey trotted right alongside Grand. She aimed Chip's head toward Grand's ear, pushing into the mare. Grand pinned her ears and nipped at Chip. *Poor Chip*, Karen thought. *He's an innocent pawn in Lindsey's games.*

"Hey, give us some room," she whispered to Lindsey. She couldn't start a shouting match in the show ring. However, her temper was rising.

Lindsey sneered at her. "Thought you'd like some company."

"Canter please. All canter," said the announcer.

Grand was all class. She was unaffected by Chip's intrusion into her space. She chose the correct lead again and completed a smooth transition. Chip, however, completed a stellar transition also. The judge was looking directly at the pair. Cantering in tandem with Grand to the outside, Lindsey had successfully obscured the judge's view.

"Why don't you get away from me?" Karen said as Lindsey held her position relentlessly.

"Shut your trap."

They were behind the judge's back. Lindsey drove Chip sideways and slammed Grand.

Karen had to get away from Lindsey. She gave Grand a strong half halt. It was risky. If Grand broke stride, they'd lose for sure. Just as she felt Grand's body drop in preparation for a walk, she squeezed her back into a normal canter. Lindsey went on down the rail. She couldn't turn back now. Karen was running out of time. Trying to be noticed, she cut across the ring and subtly completed a large canter circle around the judge. Shortly thereafter, the class was over.

I can't believe the nerve of that little witch! Karen looked into the stands for her friends. They looked annoyed and anxious.

Their anxiety was justified. Lindsey and Chip won first place. Grand's trot must have been memorable, Karen decided. She placed second, despite hardly being seen at a canter. Karen's blood boiled.

With her head about to explode, she rode toward the gate. Fortunately, the next announcement vented some of the pressure. June and Blondie won third place.

"Whew!" June yelled. "The curse of the white ribbons is broken!" She waved to Stella who stood clapping from the stands.

Karen laughed and congratulated her friend. Carl did the same.

"It was only a matter of time," he said. "When she's settled, your pony is quite elegant."

Karen was complaining to Shane about Lindsey's behavior as Sharon joined them.

"I know it's not fair," Sharon said, "but you need to let it go. There's something odd about that family. The father barely flinched when I told him about Jude's prank. I don't know what they're capable of. Let's not start something we'll be afraid to finish. Anyway, you're all alone for jumping. She can't get to you from outside the ring."

Karen knew she was right. She was perplexed by the family's ruthlessness, but she had to forget it. It was time to concentrate on the jumping round.

Lindsey was first to go. Chip came into the ring with his head low. His eyes were dull. For the first time, Karen noticed he had lost some weight. Lindsey and her sister were infamous for overtraining horses. It appeared to be catching up with poor Chip.

The pair jumped their opening line. Chip was steady and true. However, he barely cleared the fences. He jumped flatly and he looked stiff leaving the ground. Lindsey stiffened her jaw and dug her heels into her horse, trying to increase impulsion. Struggling to make Chip round his back over the fences, she overarched her own back and gave him a big release with her hands. Karen had to admit, she was talented. However, Lindsey got only marginal results from her effort. Chip had completed a good, consistent round. However, it was clear he was not himself.

Grand and Karen were up. Karen felt the tension in her shoulders, felt her legs clamp into the saddle.

"Relax," Sharon whispered.

Aware that her toxic tension would ruin the round, Karen took a deep breath. She pictured Jude's shocked face as Sharon dragged him by his ear. Amused, she smiled. Grand snorted softly, as if releasing her own tension. They entered the ring.

Grand skipped lightly into a canter and approached the first line eagerly. Karen fought the urge to hold her back. The pony knew what was best. She took the first fence with a spring. Karen merely followed with her shoulders and hands. She stayed out of the pony's way. Up and over the second jump they went.

This is like flying. She now understood the age-old saying about horses: thou shalt fly without wings.

They continued down the second line. It was a vertical to an oxer. Grand launched herself high over the vertical. She jumped it so dramatically that Karen was almost thrown off balance. She anticipated Grand's rushing to the oxer, but the mare steadied herself. She reached the fence and extended her frame to clear the wider jump. A diagonal line was next. Karen urged Grand deep into the corner, leaving plenty of space to turn. They had to be straight, since they jumped these two fences on the diagonal. Grand completed a lovely flying lead change on the corner. She eyed the last line. Karen felt the energy build in Grand. She did not go faster. However, she engaged all the energy from her hindquarters. Again, she sprang over the jumps in dramatic fashion. They pulled up to applause.

"You are one special girl. You turned it up a notch today!" Karen gave Grand her head and stroked her neck enthusiastically.

Karen met Shane's sparkling eyes as she exited the ring. She threw herself into his arms when she dismounted.

He hugged her. "That was great, no matter where you place."

"Grand was spectacular!" Karen rubbed the mare's forehead and took some sugar cubes from her pocket. Grand munched them happily.

Sharon joined them. "I'm so proud of you both."

June and Blondie were next. They completed their best round to date. It was as if Blondie had picked up on Grand's energy. She basculed over each fence beautifully. Their only mistake was failing to complete a lead change after the diagonal line.

The girls' support group returned to the bleachers, anticipating the announcing of the winners.

Karen didn't want to get ahead of herself. However, going to districts was a possibility. Dare she hope?

"In first place is Grand Moment and Karen Mulligan." Because of the deafening cheers, the announcer paused before proclaiming the runner-up. There was little respite from the noise, though, for June and Blondie placed second. Carl and Hardy were third. Lindsey was pushed the whole way down to fourth!

Leaving the ringmaster holding her white ribbon, Lindsey shoved Chip's reins into Jude's hands. She stormed off in tears.

Through Karen's elation, she felt Jude's heavy stare. He stood stock-still holding Chip. A disturbing anger emanated from his eyes. It gave her the same chills as at Fox Hollow's show. Shuddering, she turned away. Rejoicing with her friends was better.

The fire from the celebratory cookout was dying. The long day had ended with the company of the rest of the gang, minus Kirsten, in Ginny's yard. Despite her exhaustion, Karen didn't disappoint with a clumsy performance during the badminton game. Everyone got their fill of laughter from her follies. The evening ended on a quiet note, as even the boys sat transfixed by John's stories of his homeland, told in his Irish accent. Gradually, the adults drifted away, prompting Ginny to rid her yard of teenagers. One by one they left, except for Karen and Shane. They sat arm in arm on a log by the fire.

"What a day," Karen said. "Thank God Grand didn't run too far. What if she had gotten hurt? You're a hero! I can't believe you took Jude down like that." Her tone changed from concern to excitement by the sentence.

"I didn't do that much. One thing's for sure. That kid's disturbed. If you ever see him, stay clear."

"I hope that's the last I see of that family. Well, forget them. Look at that sunset."

The orange glow of the sun's final rays eclipsed the mountaintops. The light surrounded puffy white clouds, trimming them in magical gold. The couple watched it in humble silence.

Chapter 21

Summer's End

Karen and Mindy pedaled furiously past the old house and across the bridge to the barn. Several people milled about the aisle way, but their energy scattered in all directions. Only two of them seemed to have any semblance of unity. Unsure of where to look or who to greet first, Karen became uneasy. The normal feeling of warmth, belonging, and peace at Fox Hollow was gone. Her shoulders tightened and her jaw clenched. Looking over at Mindy, Karen barely recognized her face of stone.

Kirsten brushed past them, carrying her saddle and bridle, barely grunting a hello. She continued to the tack room, pausing only momentarily when Karen asked if she'd ridden already.

"Yep, all done," Kirsten said shortly.

"So you're not coming on a trail ride with us?" Mindy asked.

"Nope, not with present company." Kirsten stood with one foot inside the tack room, barely looking at Karen and Mindy.

Like a child sitting in the corner for a time-out, June looked out at them from the shadows in front of Blondie's stall.

In desperation, Karen said, "Jess is coming. She was really looking forward to seeing you."

"You know I love you guys and Jess," Kristen said. The sadness in her voice was palpable. "I just can't. I gotta go."

Karen and Mindy sighed in unison. Turning toward the interior of the barn, Karen felt her chest tighten. In the middle of the barn, Shane and Ivy stood cozily close. Although Shane had his arms folded across his chest, he laughed with Ivy. She reached out and squeezed his arm, fluttering heavily blackened eyelashes. Karen had planned this day around Ivy, trying to thank her for all her help over the past two summers. Now a flicker of anger strained Karen's voice as she told Shane she needed to talk to him.

"Hey, babe," he said easily. "What's up?"

Karen exhaled slowly. The warmth in his eyes calmed her. She led him outside the barn. The September sun drove away the shadowy chill of the barn.

"I need you to get Gage down here right away. He at least owes Kirsten an apology. We can't go on like this. She needs some kind of recognition from him to move on. I want us all together again."

Shane sighed. "I can't force him. He knows he screwed up. He just started talking to me again. He thought I'd told Kirsten about him and June. I'm not sure if he believes me, but I told him it wasn't me or you. On top of everything, he's afraid to approach her."

"Believe me she'd rather have him talk to her than avoid her. Acting like he did nothing wrong is not going to cut it. Tell him the 4-H awards dance is coming up. If he wants to mend things, he should ask her to the dance." Karen peered across the bridge to where Kirsten sat on the fountain wall. "Call him now. Her dad will probably pick her up soon."

Shane marched into the barn, past the other girls, and to the phone. Feelings of unrest continued to bounce off the walls. A distraught June leaned heavily against Blondie's stall. She was almost doubled over. Mindy and Ivy hovered over her.

As Karen got closer and heard June, she realized more than the falling-out with Kirsten was upsetting her.

"What am I going to do if those people from Pittsburgh buy Blondie? All my blood, sweat, and tears are wrapped up in this pony."

"I know, I don't understand it," Mindy said quietly, her hand on June's arm.

Karen's eyes welled with tears. She remembered getting the news that Legend had been sold. Trying to hold her composure, she gulped back her emotions, unable to speak.

"At least you're getting a commission," Ivy said. "That's more than I'm getting."

"Shut up!" June said. "Two hundred dollars won't replace Blondie. Anyway, you're the reason Kirsten won't speak to me, you and your big mouth."

"Well, next time Dad conveniently forgets to take both of us and not just you for ice cream, maybe you'll remind him!" Ivy retorted.

Shane stood outside the circle, eyebrows raised in light of this new information. Karen merely shook her head. She only hoped the rift between Kirsten and June could be fixed. Shane moved close to her, whispering, "He's on his way." He added in a normal voice, "Okay, time to fix that fence. See you later." He kissed Karen on the cheek.

The clatter of hooves from the road refocused the girls. "Okay, Ivy," Karen said. "Here comes your ride. She's real smooth. I hope you like her."

Wendy descended the driveway, riding a surprisingly well-behaved Dorian and leading her black Tennessee walker, Orchid. Karen beamed as she walked into the ring to greet her friend.

"Thanks, Wendy. You don't know how much we need a diversion right now. I wanted all of us to ride together at least once before winter, and Ivy is always left out."

Even as she spoke, Jessica's grandfather pulled into the driveway. Karen waved a greeting as Jess got out. "Now we're only missing one."

"The Kirsten situation still isn't resolved?" Wendy asked.

"No, but I'm working on it." Karen had never been so happy to hear the roar of a four-wheeler cruising down Country Club Road. "What I wouldn't give to be a little birdie around that fountain right now."

Wendy giggled. "Let me know what happens."

Karen took Orchid's reins after greeting Dorian with a rub on the forehead. "Look at you, being so well behaved." The gray nudged her gently, as if he agreed.

Jessica joined them, her green eyes glittering, free from the glare of glasses. As happened every summer, her shoulder-length brown hair was streaked with blond. In a more subdued look than her cousin, only her bangs were teased skyward and to the side. The slight curve of her hips emphasized her tiny waist, but her frame was expanding upward more than outward. It had only been since school started that Karen hadn't seen her, but she looked completely different.

Her light, fun personality remained. She entered the barn cheerfully, jolting the others out of their funk with her greeting. "Okay, everyone. Your top rider is here. Where's my steed?"

The others burst into laughter as Jess bowed in front of Cookie's stall.

Karen paraphrased a line from *The Black Stallion Returns*. "Remember, Jess, for every great horse, there is but one rider. You are Cookie's rider." The substitution of little Cookie rather than the majestic Shetan had the girls laughing again.

With the mood lightened, the girls readied the horses. They left the yard, Mindy on Cajun, June on Blondie, Jessica on Cookie, Wendy on Dorian, Ivy on Orchid, and Karen on Grand. Karen stroked Grand's neck as she listened to Wendy give Ivy pointers about riding a gaited horse. Sharon would be picking up Grand and Cookie soon. The pair would spend the cold months at Sharon's farm, on vacation from the bustle of the 4-H club.

"I'll miss you, girl," Karen told Grand. The pony's ears flickered. "You gave me everything you had this year."

Wendy pointed Dorian up the path running parallel to North Fork Dam Road. The horses climbed the rising hillside, blowing softly and snorting as the cooler air of the woods filled their lungs. The first signs of autumn trimmed the leaves shyly, yet the foliage still provided a shield from the sun's bright rays. The trail leveled as the group reached the ridge.

"Everyone ready to trot?" Wendy called.

The horses picked up a trot in their varied strides and tempos, except for Orchid, who demonstrated her breed's trademark running walk.

"Whew, this does feel different. You mean I just sit here?" Ivy clung to Orchid's sides, leaning to the right against the unfamiliar gait.

Wendy looked back. "Relax. Let your hips roll side to side with her. Don't brace against the motion. Find the center of the saddle and let her carry you."

Ivy adjusted her seat and relaxed her body. By the end of the straightaway, she was in tune with the horse. Wendy slowed Dorian as the trail dipped down a hill. Karen recognized the area where she and Mindy had seen the vagabond's camp before he attacked them. It seemed so long ago, but she realized they rarely rode through this way. Her lingering uneasiness told her why.

Dorian protested to being reined in, throwing his head and prancing the first few yards down the hill. Karen held her breath. That was what he'd done before throwing her that time. Wendy half-halted firmly but remained calm. The horse eventually settled.

From her spot third in line, Karen said, "Wendy, he's come a long way. How is doing with jumping?"

Wendy smiled back at her. "Great. After the 4-H show when I fell, we backed off him some. I guess we were asking a lot of him to jump three-foot-six-inch courses so early in his training. Who would have thought the fences in 4-H were so big for horses? Anyway, the schooling shows at J. T. Acres are great. They have jumping classes ranging from cross rails to four foot. The problem is he rushes the smaller jumps because they're so easy for him. Anyway, he's won several seconds and two blues this summer."

"Cool! I hope you're still coming to the 4-H dance. We're all working on our outfits and getting the boys in line to go."

From the rear of the line, Mindy said, "Yeah, Lance is making up every excuse in the book. He better go or I'm going to dismantle that four-wheeler."

Wendy laughed. "I know what you mean about boyfriend problems. I guess mine is the opposite. He always wants to be with me, but my dad doesn't want him within five miles of me."

Karen's eyes widened. "Really? Who is this guy?"

"I'll tell you later. Let's just say he's a bit older."

Cookie's nicker came from last in line, as if prefacing Jessica's statement. "C'mon. You guys worry too much about boys. Let's just go and have a good time!" The group collectively agreed.

The reprieve from boy obsession was short-lived. As the horses descended Ginny's driveway, boys and four-wheelers were scattered about the yard. Right in the center, Kirsten sat behind Gage, apparently in a much better mood than before, talking to Lance. Shane and Brad hovered around a vehicle trailer, strapping Brad's dirt bike in place.

The six horses halted in a row, some snorting at the unfamiliar sights. Kirsten shot a look at June. Luckily for June, looks couldn't kill.

Without a word, June turned Blondie to the barn. Lance approached Cajun. Placing a hand on Mindy's knee, he gave her his sweetest look. Despite the long hair and dew rag, he had a baby face, and Karen knew he could be persuasive.

"Brad's dad is going to ship us all over to the east hill to ride," he said. "Why don't you come along?"

Mindy stared, the color draining from her face. "The east hill? No thanks. Don't want to uncover another crime scene. I'm hanging with the girls today. Maybe we'll meet you later."

Lance walked away, shoulders slumped. Shane put in his bid. "Karen, oh, Karen, won't you come with me for a day of thrills and excitement?"

"Sorry, I made a promise to my loyal helper here." She urged Grand alongside Orchid. "Ivy has helped me for the past two summers at the shows. The least I can do is treat her to Shaffer's ice cream." Thinking back to the morning's revelation, Karen dared not deprive Ivy of her ice cream again.

"Come on, girls," Kirsten said. "Don't stick me alone with these guys!"

Karen dismounted and approached a smiling Kirsten. Despite her pleas, Kirsten hadn't been this happy for a long time. "You need to make up for lost time," she whispered. She raised her voice slightly. "Take care of her Gage."

Jess urged Cookie forward, "Can't we convince you to stay with us? Look at this cute face." She nudged Cookie closer to Kirsten, and the pony practically laid her head on Kirsten's lap.

Kirsten giggled and crooned to the pony. Brad stepped abruptly to Cookie's side. "Jess, you should ride with me. My mom said you're my date for the dance anyway."

Jessica cringed visibly. "What planet are you living on?"

The girls laughed, and then Wendy said she had to go. "I've got my own arguments with my dad and boyfriend. Ivy, bring Orchid over. I'll lead her back home."

"Thank you so much," Ivy said. "Is there anything you need me to do for her?"

"No, we'll be fine. Maybe, if my dad lets me keep two horses, you can use Orchid as a project horse next year."

"That would be great!" Ivy smiled.

The groups disbanded. The boys and Kirsten left with Brad's father. Jessica and Mindy joined June at her house. Karen and Ivy lingered in the tack room. They freshened their makeup and hair in preparation for the two-mile-walk to Shaffer's Frosty Freeze. Stepping back into the sunshine, Karen heard a soft whine coming from Master and Aries' doghouse.

"Why does Ginny leave them tied so much? We're taking them with us." She took two lead shanks from the barn. Attaching them to the dogs' collars, she took Master and Ivy took Aries.

"How cool do we look, leading these tough-looking Dobermans around?" Ivy said.

They walked along the berm of Somerset Pike. With its elusive perfection, the weather had brought out heavy traffic. The sun warmed the air into the mid-seventies, and a pleasant breeze warded off any overheating. Karen was completely comfortable in her cutoff shorts and blue ribbed tank top. As if she had watched Karen pack that morning, Ivy was dressed the same, her cutoffs just a bit shorter. Screams of approval came from the young men in passing cars, yelling out their open windows, their radios blaring.

"I wonder if any of those guys are cute," Ivy said.

"They all looked older," Karen said. "How gross."

The girls proceeded down a long hill and past a chip and putt golf course. A five-acre horse farm sat unoccupied to the left, its quaint red barn shut up. In contrast, at the bottom of the hill were expansive bluegrass pastures fenced with steel. A large barn with a high rounded loft sat behind an acre of road frontage, and a smaller barn topped a rise, surrounded by several paddocks. A manor house crowned the left corner of the property. All the buildings and fencing were painted in steel gray, with the house and barns trimmed in white. A sign showing an elegant-looking horse dangled from the front gate. It read, "Far From Home, Winner of the Mother Goose Stakes." In contrast, the fields were dotted with shorter, stockier equines, including a few Arabians, a quarter horse, and the familiar black and white of Bella.

"Look at little Bella," Karen said. "This makes putting up with Tracy's demands worth it."

"What's the Mother Goose Stakes?" Ivy asked.

"It's a prestigious race at Belmont Park. They must have owned Far From Home. Why else would they hang a sign in her honor?"

"I think Ginny said Tracy's grandfather had racehorses."

"What I wouldn't do for a place like that," Karen said.

Shaffer's renowned soft-serve beckoned. This was the last weekend before it closed for the season. Karen sighed at the length of the lines. All three windows were crowded ten deep. The girls took their spots. The Dobermans sat obediently by their sides, despite the nervous sideways glances from other patrons.

"Man, we're going to be here forever," Karen said.

"I don't mind." Ivy leaned closer to Karen and lowered her voice. "We have a nice view from here." She gestured to their right.

Three teenaged boys huddled in a circle in the line beside them. All were tall and muscular. One had dark brown hair and eyes, another had lighter brown hair, hazel eyes, and freckles, and the third had blond hair. The blond stood parallel to the girls. Every few seconds, he cocked his head toward them and peered at them from beneath a long lock of hair that framed the right side of his face. The rest of his hair was cropped short over his ears and to the base of his skull.

Ivy cocked her head and waved daintily at the boys. Karen had seen her flickering-eyelash move before. Thankfully, now it was not directed at her boyfriend. The blond boy pressed his hands together, making his broad shoulders ripple the thin cotton of his shirt. He gave the girls a sideways smile and then turned to speak to his friends. They looked at the girls also. Subdued chuckling came from their circle.

Uneasy, Karen diverted her eyes. The boys' demeanor made her feel self-conscious. She reached down and petted Master's head. Focused on the dog, she was much more comfortable. Ivy, on the other hand, continued her flirting from afar.

Finally, the boys ordered. The rest of the line shifted forward slowly. By the time they were second in line, the boys were lost in the crowd. Karen sighed in relief.

Her favorite treat was an M&M Flurry with chocolate ice cream instead of vanilla. She preferred Shaffer's to the chain restaurants because they left the M&Ms whole rather than chopping them up. She loved to let them melt in her mouth, enjoying the full flavor of the chocolate. Ivy went for a lighter treat, ordering a medium teaberry cone. Shaffer's was the only ice cream stand in the area to carry that flavor. The order was complete with two small bowls of vanilla for Master and Aries.

Ivy took the dogs while Karen juggled the ice cream. She hustled to an empty corner of a picnic table. Squeezing beside strangers, she plopped the containers down in the nick of time.

The dogs wolfed theirs down in a few bites. Master licked the white from his lips and looked at Karen hopefully.

"My goodness, buddy, you should have made it last. Sorry, chocolate isn't good for dogs. You'll have to wait on us now."

Karen savored every bite, along with the warm, fresh air and the sun on her back. She and Ivy talked about the new school year, teachers, and classmates. When the subject changed to the Fox Hollow gang, Ivy almost admitted remorse about telling Kirsten about Gage and June.

"It looks like they're working things out," Karen said. "Kirsten looked pretty cozy on the back of his four-wheeler."

The crowd started to thin. Soon, Karen and Ivy had the picnic table all to themselves. Reluctant to move, Karen mustered the energy to start their trek back. A voice from behind stopped her as she started to stand.

"Hey, don't leave so soon." The blond boy approached the table.

Karen's line of sight was at the boy's chest. She looked skyward to meet his eyes. She felt like an ant he could easily squish.

"I'm Alex." The boy extended his hand to shake hers, but withdrew it quickly as Master growled a low warning. Surprised, Karen shortened her hold on the leash.

"Shh. It's okay, boy." She jiggled Master's collar.

"Yeah, big guy, I won't hurt you."

Alex offered his hand for Master to sniff. The Doberman's nose wiggled back and forth, taking in the scent. Yet his lowered head, upturned eyes, and bristled back relayed his mistrust. He growled again as Alex took a step closer.

"Okay, maybe it's better if you don't pet him," Karen said. "I'm Karen, and this is Ivy."

Ivy stepped forward with a smile, dropping Aries's leash mindlessly. Aries belly crawled to lie beside Master, mimicking his body language.

Karen picked up her leash, securing both dogs. An odd, sinking feeling overwhelmed her, and she was glad to be surrounded by the Dobermans.

From behind the safety of her canine fortress, Karen noticed Ivy was in full flirt mode. She squeezed Alex's bicep while she smiled and giggled. Apparently, Alex was a varsity quarterback for Westmont, an affluent community atop the hills over Johnstown. His crooked smile enhanced his attractive, angular face. He glanced at Ivy sideways, appearing only half interested in what she was saying as his gaze shifted back and forth between Ivy and Karen. Although his eyes were a brilliant blue, a broad brow overpowered them, giving him an inscrutable air. Finally, he took a cautious sideways step, positioning himself between the girls, but not too close to the dogs.

"So, I live at the top of Shaffer Road, within walking distance," he said.

"Oh, wow!" Ivy said. "There are some nice houses up there."

He nodded in acknowledgment. "So where are you from, Karen?"

Karen answered him politely, and Ivy added, "She doesn't spend much time in town though, between her boyfriend and our riding club." Ivy was sure to emphasize the word *boyfriend*.

Alex looked down and kicked the gravel of the parking lot. "Riding club? Where do you do that?"

Ivy described Ginny's place enthusiastically, and told him about the relative success of Fox Hollow's first show season.

"Interesting," he said. "That's my great-grandfather Opie's old place."

Karen's heart skipped a beat. Her stomach turned. She looked around, as if needing to plan an escape.

"Have you ever found anything, uh ... valuable around there?" Alex asked.

"Valuable? What do mean by that?" Karen asked.

Alex paused, shifting his weight uneasily. "Oh, I don't know. Never mind, that house was completely gutted by fire."

Ivy redirected him again, boasting that the rumored ghost of the house was real and they had all seen her. Alex's eyebrows lifted and he seemed to hold his breath. He glanced at Karen, looking surprisingly vulnerable. He held her gaze for a moment and then snapped back to his previous persona.

"Well, isn't that funny. I don't know if I believe you. You'd have to prove it to me." He yelled to his friends, who were hanging around behind Shaffer's. "Nigel, Brighton, come here. They say my family's old place *is* haunted."

The other boys approached. The words "Westmont Football" were branded on their white T-shirts. Their cocky expressions mimicked Alex's. The dark-haired one was Nigel. He stood beside Alex with his arms folded over his broad chest.

"If that's the case, you should take the place back. We could make a bundle on Halloween." Nigel refused to look directly at the girls.

The freckle-faced Brighton was slightly friendlier. "Don't worry, girls. We'll let you in on the deal," he said, smiling.

His openness put Karen's guard down, and she allowed herself a giggle. "Well anyway, we better get doing. It's a long walk back." She held out Aries's lead to Ivy, prompting her to take it.

"Okay," Ivy said, sounding put upon. "I guess Karen wants to get back to Shane." Nigel and Brighton made an indiscernible comment when they heard Shane's name. Ivy stepped between Nigel and Alex. "Anytime you want to hang out, just come by. We're always around."

"I'll think about it," Alex said casually.

Karen couldn't get a word in during the walk home. Ivy ranted nonstop about the rich football players. The easy chore of feeding the horses still awaited them. Karen allowed Master and Aries to stay with them until the last moment. The Dobermans looked at her soulfully when she returned them to Ginny. She felt them watching her leave and for a moment wished they were hers. She and Ivy crossed the bridge, guessing the others were at Shane's. The old house was enveloped in shadows, with just a dying ray of light highlighting its third floor.

Ivy looked upward. She paused, staring into the empty windows. "What do you think Alex meant about something valuable?"

Reluctant to linger around the house at night, Karen said dismissively, "Who knows? I personally wouldn't want to be involved with that family's business."

She heard Ivy gasp and turned to her. "Are you okay?"

Ivy stayed focused on the upper floors. Distracted, she said, "Yeah, sure. I'm fine." She followed Karen up the driveway, but kept looking back at the house every few steps until it was hidden behind the trees.

CHAPTER 22

WHAT GOES AROUND COMES AROUND—THEN LEAVES

Karen watched sadly as the new aluminum horse trailer ascended the driveway, the top of Blondie's golden rump and her flicking ears visible above the closed ramp. She would start her new life in suburban Pittsburgh. Her new eight-year-old owner could barely contain her excitement. She told Karen and Ginny of the massive indoor ring where she trained. She would ride all winter. Blondie would enjoy top-class care, and her trainers competed at rated horse shows. The girl's parents boasted that they would not have to ship to schooling shows, as the facility hosted their own series. Yet the father assured them that when Blondie was ready for the rated shows, he'd spare no expense and haul her as far as was needed.

Ginny acted as if the freshly written check was burning a hole in her hand. "Okay, see you tonight," she said to Karen. "I've gotta get this in the bank and do some shopping!" She bounded toward her old Cadillac.

Drawing a deep breath, Karen looked around the silent barn. Dawn and Cajun were in their stalls across the aisle from each other. They nodded and nickered in unison, as if realizing they were the only ones left. Sharon had picked up Grand and Cookie picked up minutes before Blondie's new owners arrived. Cookie would return next year, but Sharon's niece wanted to show Grand. Karen felt June's pain. Not only had she lost Blondie, but Grand would be unavailable for next year's show season. Karen only hoped June would attend the 4-H awards dance that night. As she exhaled, her breath caught and shivered in her throat. The normally vibrant energy of Fox Hollow lay dead on the ground.

"Jeez, don't look so depressed." Shane rolled beside her on a beat-up BMX bike. "You got me out on this dumb thing instead of something with a motor."

She smiled as he came to an awkward stop, the bike tipping from side to side before he plopped his feet to the ground.

"Good thing you have holes in the knees of those jeans," she said. "You'll need some ventilation to keep up with me. Let's ride up to the dam. The leaves should be at their peak now."

Shane agreed. The two peddled through Ginny's property to the North Fork Dam Road. Karen took a leisurely pace, yet her relaxation was short-lived. The road rose insidiously upward. She bore into her peddles, pushing strong with each rotation. She glanced back at Shane, who appeared to be out of his element.

"Are we there yet?" he panted, the BMX weaving from side to side as he strained on his pedals.

"Come on, that ATV has you spoiled. A little exercise won't kill you."

The October day was phenomenal. It was the ideal temperature for any outdoor activity. The sun welcomed them as they emerged from the shaded road. There was one more hill to climb, and it was a doozy. Their trek ascended the land parallel to the rise of the dam. Karen stood on her pedals and dug into their resistance. Now she was panting. She glanced back at Shane to see him walking his bike. She chuckled to herself.

The couple topped the hill, and Karen dismounted. A walkway spanning the dam's crest invited them. Horses were not allowed on it, so Karen had never crossed it. At this moment, not having a horse wasn't so bad.

"At least the bikes won't get nervous and impatient," she said. "We can stay as long as we want."

They left their bikes at the end of the walkway. Hand in hand, they dawdled along, crossing the dam's crest. When they neared the center, Shane faced the lake and put his arm around Karen's shoulder. Both breathed deeply and gazed across the water. A light breeze danced along its surface, and tiny waves caught the sunlight. The show was mesmerizing, and they watched it for several minutes in silence.

Suddenly, Shane shifted his weight uneasily. Looking down at the ground, he kicked little pebbles from the walkway into the water. His fidgeting pulled Karen from her moment of peace.

"You know," he said, "it's okay that you made a mistake at districts. It happens to the best of athletes. It doesn't make you a failure."

Karen bristled. "It does make me a failure! I had the perfect pony, I was given every advantage. She deserved a better representation. I made Grand, myself, and the whole club look bad!" Her voice shook. "Anyway, I didn't make just one mistake, I blew every class! How will I be an equestrian if I freeze under pressure?"

Her anger brewed. She had swallowed and buried her disappointment from that day. Who was he to bring it up? She pulled away from him and faced him defensively.

"Calm down," he said. "You haven't been yourself since districts. You need to let it go. Tonight you're being recognized as the top pony hunter rider in Cambria County. That should tell you something. You did well all year."

"I shouldn't even be going to this dance. Lindsey may be rotten, but she's a talented rider. She would have never tanked like that. She would have qualified for states. Cambria County would be proud of her representation."

"You don't know that. She and Chip were looking pretty disjointed by the end of the season. She's not perfect either."

"Shane, I blew a simple canter transition! Grand and I could do that in our sleep. I must have looked like a raw beginner, hanging onto poor Grand's mouth and kicking her like she was a mule. Do you know that we went around an entire corner like that? Grand had no idea what this crazy girl wanted. What an embarrassment! Then, to make things worse, I could have gotten her hurt, crashing into a jump like that. Grand had never knocked a rail down in her show career. But what do I do? I put her at an impossible distance to that fence. She's so honest. She'd never refuse. I'll tell you, when she scrambled to clear those flying rails, I thought we were going down for sure. I never want to hurt a horse, and I came close to hurting a wonderful one." The pain of those moments flooded her. She pictured the looks of shock and disappointment on Ginny's and Sharon's faces.

Tears welled up in her eyes. "How can a great year end so badly?"

"Come here." Shane held her close until she stopped crying. "You have to chalk it up to experience. You can't change it, so don't dwell on it. Just the other day, Ginny told me how proud she was of you. She said her friends still talk about your rivalry with Lindsey. They loved it! Most of all, Grand is not hurt. You saw for yourself the next day. She didn't have a mark on her."

Karen wiped her eyes. Shane was a great support. She actually felt better. They found a place to sit, and Karen laughed as they reminisced about the summer's follies with their friends.

"It's been great," she said. "I can't believe 1987 is almost over."

Shane looked at his watch. "We better get going. My mom said you could use her room to get ready. We're still going, aren't we?"

"Yes. I wouldn't miss the Gage/Kirsten reunion for the world."

They rode back to Shane's house. Karen felt like a weight had been lifted from her shoulders. Her whole attitude had changed. Cheerfully, she utilized Meadow's shower and bedroom. After achieving record heights with her hairstyle and doing her makeup, she squeezed into her fuchsia tank dress and stepped into her white pumps. She even snuck a squirt of Meadow's expensive perfume.

Lastly, she topped her look with a white fringed leather jacket. She admired it, cognizant that it would stick out against the usual black of the others' leathers.

She looked forward to a night with her friends.

Colleen's car was big. It was a good thing, because she spent plenty of time hauling kids around. Whether it was just Karen, Mindy, and Jessica going to the barn, or boys added when going to the movies, the Pontiac LeMans was well used. The monster could easily hold a driver and two teenagers in the front, and four skinny bottoms in the back.

However, it could not hold the entire 4-H club. Mindy's dad had been recruited to chauffer also. His tan Dodge Caravan was parked beside the LeMans at the chosen departure point along the Somerset Pike. Teenagers milled toward the vehicles from all directions that crisp autumn evening, while the parents were immersed in adult conversation, oblivious to the squabbling teens.

"I'm sitting by Jess," Kirsten stated firmly. The white ruffles at the bottom of her jean skirt fluttered in the breeze.

"I want to ride with Mindy," Ivy said. "I never saw such a cool van before. Look how the door slides sideways," she said to Lance, who rolled his eyes. "But I'm not riding with her." She pushed her sister away with two-handed force.

Caught off guard, and not used to her mother's black heels, June stumbled into Kirsten.

"Well, I really don't want to ride with her either," Kirsten said through clenched teeth.

"This wouldn't be a problem," Gage said, "if my dad had helped me finish the Satellite. I should be driving us."

"Oh, man, that's right," Lance said. "You're almost done with it?"

Had Shane been a horse, his ears would have pricked. He joined Gage and Lance in a huddle. They spoke excitedly about Gage's project with the muscle car, ending the conversation chanting, "Mopar power!"

Karen looked at her watch. "Okay, guys, we have to go." She whispered to Kirsten, "Can you cut June some slack? Blondie left today. You got the guy anyway, and you look darn cute tonight."

Kirsten nodded begrudgingly, and Karen asked Shane if he'd take one for the team and sit up front beside June.

"I guess. That means more leg room for me anyway. C'mon June, you're on the hump." He urged the petite June into the middle of the bench seat beside Colleen.

Jessica sighed heavily. "Finally, let's go. At least we don't have to ride with Brad."

"Amen to that." Mindy grabbed Ivy's arm and pushed her into the van.

In the back of the LeMans, Karen and Gage took the window seats with Jessica and Kirsten sandwiched in between them. Colleen stepped on the gas, the V8 engine roared, and the car sailed along the pike. Several minutes passed in awkward silence, until Colleen cleared her throat.

"You kids act like you're going to a funeral rather than a dance."

Taking the cue, Jessica turned to her cousin. "Karen, do you remember when we were spying on Shane? We were being sneaky, and I slipped and fell down the hill."

Short, nervous jiggles escaped tight-lipped mouths.

"Yeah," Karen said. "We laughed so hard, he found us out anyway."

"Why were you spying on me anyway?" Shane asked.

"We heard there was a voluptuous brunette at your house. You were seen talking and laughing with her. You're lucky she was your brother's girlfriend."

"I wonder who told you that," June said sarcastically.

"Speaking of your sister, what were you two fighting about?" Karen asked.

"Mom let me wear her heels, and Ivy was stuck with flats. It was only fair, though. You should see the jewelry Ivy has on. It's gorgeous! She wouldn't say where she got it. I can't believe she bought it with her grooming shop pay."

"Wow, can't wait to see it," Karen said.

The silent tension returned. Kirsten cleared her throat a few times, as if she wanted to say something, but didn't.

As the Pontiac topped the mountain from Johnstown to Jackson Township, the last rays of the autumn sun illuminated the crimson leaves. All the teenagers noticed it. No matter how they felt, it was a great time to be alive.

"You know," Shane said, "every October the Indians looked to what we call the Big Dipper. They called it Great Bear. They believed that in the autumn, three spirit hunters and a dog kill Great Bear. It is his blood that drips from the sky and colors the leaves."

"You are such a dork!" Gage said. "How do you dream this stuff up?"

Surprisingly, the ribbing worked to break the ice. Karen was upset that the bear died in the legend. The blood dripping from the sky offended Jessica. Kirsten told Gage to leave Shane alone. Finally, they arrived at the dance.

The group found their seats and Mindy's group. Ginny, Sharon, and Mary arrived with John, the Irish horseman, and Brad. Ginny sat down and immediately pulled a dark bottle from her purse. She mixed its contents with several plastic cups of soda, looking up from time to time like a naughty schoolgirl. She gave a cup to each adult. John instantly came to life with his first sip. A renewed energy radiated from the group. Couples mingled, and Brad actually complimented Jessica on her outfit. She hammed it up, twirling in her black pleated skirt. Over her crisp white button-down shirt she wore a black vest with red trim that emphasized her tiny waist. Everyone in their group applauded and cheered, garnering looks from others in the room.

Karen relished the jovial atmosphere, but she noticed that Ivy was nowhere to be seen and June sulked in her seat. Karen scanned the room, looking for help. Finally, she spotted a shock of red hair bobbing around another group. She walked over to Carl, congratulating him on his overall third place status for the year and complimenting his Connemara's fortitude.

"Can you do me a favor?" she said. "June could really use a friend right now."

Carl grinned, gave Karen a mock salute, and marched over to June. As soon as he sat beside her, she smiled, her face lighting up. Her royal blue dress accented her auburn hair. With Carl beside her, her whole aura was now transformed.

Karen spotted Wendy across the room. She took Shane's hand and brought him over to her.

"Wow, he does have awesome eyes," Wendy said, smiling. "I didn't get to look the last time, with Dorian dancing around."

"Oh, man." Shane blushed and covered his face.

Karen blushed also and changed the subject. "And you must be Bob?" she said to the young man sitting beside Wendy.

"Hey, what's up?"

A true bad boy, Bob sat with his biker boots on top of the table. He lounged against the back of his chair, which was propped against the wall. A chain extended from his black belt to, presumably, the wallet in his back pocket. He wore a biker bandana, and a black Harley-Davidson T-shirt with a black leather vest. He stared at Karen, making her uneasy.

She barely noticed the rest of his features, only that his eyes were blue. Long brown hair fell to his shoulders.

"Nice to meet you," she said as Shane's hand tightened around hers. She turned to Wendy, who had toughened her look as much as possible, wearing black jeans, cowgirl boots, and a black tank top. Yet her dramatic dark makeup couldn't disguise the blue of her eyes or the delicate features of her heart-shaped face.

Grasping for something to say, Karen asked them how long they'd been there.

"Oh, just a few minutes," Wendy said. "What a cold ride up here on the bike, but it was some kind of feeling! You know," she added with obvious delight, "my dad would kill me if he knew Bob and I were together. He already threatened to beat Bob up. He thinks I'm here with Sonya." She nodded toward the corner where Ginny and Sonya chatted, mystery drinks in hand.

"Just don't get caught." She decided to change the subject again. "How's Dorian? He really came around for you. That seems to be a theme this year. We all had to overcome something. It took me awhile to jump decently, June had to persevere with Blondie, and you had to pick yourself up out of the dirt. In the end, we all ended up with decent points."

"Yeah. The best thing I did was ease off on Dorian. Sonya hated to admit it, but his performance at the schooling shows spoke for it. He did so much better in the green hunter division. We'll see how next year goes for the hunter horse division at 4-H. He's a cool horse, but his attitude is a lot to deal with. It's like he's never truly happy to perform. You always described Legend as being so willing to please. I wish I had a horse more like that. Anyway, we'll see what happens."

"Maybe I'll buy you a decent horse," Bob said. He pulled her to him and started kissing her as if no one else was there.

Karen cringed. She cleared her throat, and Wendy came up for air. "I think I'm going to find Ivy," Karen said. "Rumor has it that she's wearing the crown jewels. I want to see them."

"Okay, cool. I haven't seen her." Wendy barely got the words out before Bob kissed her again.

Karen and Shane hurried off. With the elusive Ivy nowhere to be seen, Karen abandoned the search. Seeing Sonya still talking to Ginny and Sharon, she walked over to them. She was curious about something else.

"Hey, Sonya. I don't see Lindsey. Do you know what's going on?"

"I heard the whole family boycotted the awards. After Roundup, people started talking about Chip's appearance and his lethargy. Rumors spread about them overworking him. The owner of their boarding stable started analyzing her training techniques. She put limits on both Lindsey and her sister's time in the ring. Word got around. We think they're trying to save face, hoping it will go away if they lay low."

"I'm glad someone is looking out for poor Chip. It's kind of surprising they're not here, though. Didn't Lindsey's sister win the hunt seat horse division?"

Sonya verified this fact. Karen was relieved. Running into Lindsey was the last thing she needed. She was just starting to feel better about 4-H.

The lights dimmed and an announcer asked them to be seated. Karen settled into the crook of Shane's arm. Ivy slipped into a chair three seats to the left. Through the dark, Karen could only see the outline of a large necklace. Intrigued, she squinted to make out the details. Shane nudged her in the ribs. It was time to award the pony hunter division. Karen stood sheepishly when she and Grand Moment were announced as champions. She took her trophy shyly to the roar of her supporters and then hustled back to her seat as the announcer begged for quiet. He continued with Lindsey as reserve champion. Virtual silence filled the room. Carl received plenty of applause from his club and Fox Hollow for placing third. June received honorable mention of the year. Her heart and dedication during the show season hadn't gone unnoticed. She walked past her peers, grinning. Karen gaped as Kirsten stood up and greeted June as she returned to the table. Extending her hand, Kirsten said, "You deserve it." June thanked her. Karen caught Kirsten's eye and pumped her fist lightly in the air, acknowledging Kirsten's gesture.

With that the dancing began. There was plenty to laugh at as the group did the Locomotion. The girls flashed across the room as they formed a train, holding each other's waists. In the lead, Ivy ran wildly, twisting and turning around the dance floor. Expectedly, Karen and Jessica's feet became tangled as they made a sharp turn. The whole back end of the train tumbled to the ground. A tangled mess of arms and legs flailed around amidst wild laughter. The boys cowered in the corner, burying their heads.

After picking herself off the floor, Karen saw her chance to check out Ivy's jewelry. She spotted Ivy standing alone by the front of the room and walked over. As Karen neared, she realized the hype was well deserved. Ivy wore an emerald necklace, the large, rectangular emeralds separated by sparkling diamonds in the top two strands. In tasteful contrast, the bottom strand was made of oval-shaped emeralds and covered Ivy's collarbones. The necklace glistened with the flashing strobe lights from the dance floor. Her simple black dress cowered under its splendor. Karen bowed her head in reverence as she approached.

"My God! Ivy, where did you get that?"

Ivy's eyes shifted uneasily. She continued to look toward the door. "I shouldn't tell you, but I found it in the old house. The other night, I noticed this dangling from the third floor window seal." She pinched her earlobe. A large pear-shaped emerald earring dangled three inches down the side of her neck. It connected to a smaller emerald stud. "I snuck upstairs, and the other earring was under this piece of old carpet. Something told me to keep looking. It was like I was being pulled to this spot. I kept pulling up the carpet until I found a loose board. I pried it up, and there, between the floorboard and the ceiling, was this spectacular necklace! The walls were charred all around it, but it was as if the fire stopped right before this spot. It's the find of a lifetime. Please don't tell anyone."

"Ivy, you could have fallen through that floor! But more importantly, don't you think that could be Lady Luminess's? Weren't you afraid to take it?"

"I'm telling you, I was drawn to it. I think she wants me to have it. Do you think this is what Alex meant when he asked if there was anything valuable in the house?"

Karen shuddered. She had a strange feeling about Alex. Now she wondered what he knew about the old house and Lady Luminess. "I guess it could be," she said slowly.

"Karen, please. Promise me you won't tell."

"Okay, fine. I just hope we never see Alex again. You probably don't want him to find out." She stared at the necklace for several seconds in awe.

"We may find out if Alex knows about this sooner than later," Ivy said.

Just then the lights dimmed. Couples streamed onto the dance floor to Bon Jovi's "Never Say Goodbye." Karen tried to follow up on Ivy's statement, but was pulled away by Shane.

"Come on," he said as she looked at him in confusion. "I thought you loved this song."

He held her close and they stepped slowly around in a circle. Immersed in the lyrics and the scent of his musk, she quickly forgot about the necklace and Alex. Shane joked with her, pointing out that even she could dance in such a simple way. Through her laughter, she looked contentedly around the floor. Mindy and Lance, Kirsten and Gage, and June and Carl were all dancing. Her eyes widened in shock as Brad twirled Jessica around playfully. Jessica waved at her cousin and took a dramatic backward dip. The others yelled their approval to the applause of the adults, watching from the sidelines.

Finally, the music ended and the lights came on, signifying the end of the dance. Karen saw Bob take Wendy's hand as the two rushed to the door, straining to kiss each other as they walked. Still by the door and looking dejected, Ivy acknowledged Wendy as she passed. Suddenly, an athletic blond boy appeared in the doorway, scowling at Bob as they brushed past each other. Alex stepped confidently through the doorway, the collar of his Izod shirt sticking straight into the air. He was shadowed by Brighton and Nigel. Nigel tucked his hands into his brown bomber jacket, nodding curtly as Ivy greeted them. Wearing a green turtleneck and dress pants, Brighton scanned the room.

Alex accepted Ivy's hug, yet the necklace caught his attention almost immediately. He pushed Ivy back with both hands on her shoulders, staring at her neck. He spoke to her, but Karen was out of earshot. Feeling uneasy, she left Shane in the Fox Hollow huddle and walked over to Ivy and Alex. Alex's voice was getting louder as he stared intensely at Ivy's face. Karen walked as quickly as she could in her white pumps.

Someone touched her arm. She turned to see Brighton, his freckles scrunching together as he smiled. "Hey, Karen, nice to see you again." He put his arm around her shoulders and gave her a sideways hug.

Their exchange brought Alex's gaze to her and he let go of Ivy's arms. After an awkward silence, Karen said, "I'm surprised to see you guys here."

"Ivy mentioned the dance to me," Alex said, "but I guess we missed all the action."

"You sure did miss it," Ivy said, her voice a high-pitched whine. "Why were you so late?"

Nigel rolled his eyes and sighed impatiently as Brighton stifled his laughter.

Alex took a deep breath. "I'll make it up to you." His gaze returned to the necklace. "So, Karen, I was admiring Ivy's necklace. Where did she get such an exquisite piece? I can't get her to spill the beans."

"Umm, I don't know. Wasn't it your grandmother's?" Karen asked Ivy.

"Oh, yeah, that's it. It was my grandmother's," Ivy said.

Ivy's face was pale, and Karen doubted Alex believed her. Alex turned his gaze on Karen, and his eyes looked black as he glared at her, although she knew they were blue. She felt her face redden, and then Brighton's touch distracted her.

"So, did you have a good time?" he asked as he stroked her upper arm.

Karen felt like a lamb in a lion's den. She was fighting the urge to hightail it out of there, when she heard someone clear his throat behind her. Turning to see Shane, she practically fell into him and latched onto his side. Gage and Kirsten approached, Gage's arm around her shoulders, Kirsten bubbling with laughter and her face pink with happiness.

Karen felt the spiked icicles shooting from Shane's eyes to Brighton. Kirsten's giggling stopped as she and Gage came shoulder to shoulder with Shane.

After a few seconds, Brighton extended his hand. "Hey, you must be Shane, good to meet you."

Shane shook his hand firmly. "And you are?"

"Brighton here. This is Nigel and Alex." Brighton said cheerfully. We met your girlfriend and Ivy at Shaffer's, thought we'd check out this 4-H thing."

"All right then," Shane said. "We better get going." He motioned to Gage and started to guide Karen out the door.

"Hold on one minute," Karen said. "I need to make sure Ivy's okay, and I have to round up June and Jess."

Shane left reluctantly with Gage and Kirsten, but not without giving the three preppy boys a scowl. Karen interrupted Ivy and Alex.

"Okay, Ivy, I'm sure Mindy's dad is waiting. We have to go."

Ivy smiled flirtatiously at Alex. "I was hoping to catch a ride with these guys."

"No, really, Ivy," Karen said. "You need go. Mr. York won't appreciate you going off on your own."

"Don't worry," Alex said to Ivy. "This won't be the last you see of me." He kissed her on the cheek.

"It better not be," she said. "You owe me a dance!"

Alex only nodded. He turned to Brighton and the yawning Nigel, and the three of them stood together, as is they were in a huddle planning a football strategy. They looked confident and smug as the rest of Fox Hollow's group filtered past. Karen grabbed the reluctant Ivy and urged her along behind Mindy and Lance. As they headed for their respective rides, Karen heard Ivy's excited babbling across the parking lot.

"Who the hell were those jocks?" Shane asked her.

"I don't think I want to know, but it seems Ivy does."

CHAPTER 23

SNOWFLAKES FOR WINTER

June burrowed her chin into her coat collar, pushing like a battering ram through the November wind. As she walked along the tree-lined drive toward the old house, branches creaked eerily. They groaned in protest at the relentless wind, sending a shudder of foreboding through June. She thought of her father, working underground in the mines that day. He might actually prefer the mine rather than being out in this chill.

The unease in her stomach intensified with the sight of Dawn's gray tail swishing past her. Kirsten looked down her nose at June, barely nodding an acknowledgment.

"Riding out alone?" June asked quickly.

Kirsten halted, "Not for long. I'm meeting Karen and Mindy at Lance's. Seems that his sister has a horse she can't handle. Karen's checking him out for Mindy as a project horse next year. Anyway, I miss those girls. Gotta go."

At least she's speaking to me. June listened to the departing clip-clop of Dawn's hooves. She burrowed deeper into her collar and trudged on to the barn. Sliding open the door, she was grateful for respite from the wind. Warmth from the horses' bodies greeted her, along with the smell of molasses as the horses finished their last bites of breakfast. Surprise stopped June in her tracks. Two horses were heating the barn, rather than just Cajun. She approached the stall on the right and was greeted with a nicker and a nudge from a velvety nose.

A small blood bay mare looked inquisitively over the stall door. A tiny white star sat high on her wide forehead. Her longish ears flicked forward and back with each stroke of June's hand along her neck. June crooned to her happily, following her conformation lines to her hindquarters, which were blanketed with white flecks. She guessed the mare to be fourteen two hands tall and of medium build.

"You're an Indian pony," she murmured. "Grandma Kakowa would like you."

After a few seconds of quiet, June flinched, sensing a faint vibration in her ear. Static tingled the tiny hairs of her ear canal. The vibrations became more tangible, rattling softly at first and then building into a clearly audible rhythm. Now every hair on June's body stood up. She looked over each shoulder and into all the barn corners. No one was there.

Suddenly, the front barn door rolled open, bringing a flurry of light snow whisking through the aisle way. Ginny strode in, smiling from ear to ear.

"How do you like your new project?" she asked.

Still reeling from the mysterious rattle, June stammered, "I—I love her."

"Bet you can't guess her name."

"Snowflake?" June replied.

June led Snowflake back into the barn after their successful first schooling session. Ginny followed, blocking out the breeze and lingering flurries with the door. Snowflake stood patiently in the cross ties while she was tended to.

The Appaloosa's ears pricked at hoof steps approaching from the back paddock. Dawn halted just outside the barn. Kirsten dismounted, smiling at Ginny as she put Dawn into her stall.

"So, how'd it go?" Ginny asked her. "Does that palomino look worthwhile?"

"Oh, yeah, he's a pretty horse. He has good substance but isn't real blocky. He has the cutest blaze too."

"Can he be ridden? I can't give them a stall if I can't get some kind of commission from his sale."

"Well, Mindy just hopped on him with a halter and rode bareback around the yard, so I guess he can be ridden." Kirsten laughed. "But I've never seen a horse not take to Karen. She tried the same thing, and he refused to go. He dragged her back to the shed like a little kid!"

Ginny chuckled. "Karen doesn't have the strongest driving leg. She's better with the Thoroughbreds. They move forward willingly. What else are you up to today?"

"Karen and Mindy have their dogs with them. I guess they're going for a hike and then hanging with Shane and Lance. As for me, I have the honor of riding in Gage's Satellite for the first time. He and his dad just finished it, and Gage is taking me cruising. It should be fun."

"Just make sure he doesn't go too fast," Ginny said. "We need you back in one piece. I wish Karen would get her own horse already. I miss having all of you around here. Maybe I can push the issue a bit. Anyway, you'll have a better afternoon than June and I. We have two dogs to groom, and apparently Ivy is taking off. What did you say, June? She's meeting up with one of those jocks from Westmont?"

Her head down, June kicked at the floor. "Yes, she's meeting the blond one. I don't know what he wants with a coal miner's daughter. I don't trust him."

"Come on, he's cute and rich," Ginny said. "Be happy for your sister." Seeing that Snowflake was brushed and cool, she added, "All right, let's get to the shop before my envy of you young girls puts me back to bed!"

Ivy bowled her last set, cheering for herself as she landed a spare. Alex winked at her from their booth. He said something inaudible to the lounging Nigel and Brighton, sending them into laughter. She sat down to take off her bowling shoes, careful not to show too much as her short beige skirt rode up. Her white button-down shirt covered her well. To date a Westmont kid, she had to look the part. Thank goodness for Goodwill.

Slipping on her penny loafers, she fondled the emerald necklace idly. The three boys huddled just behind her, yet she felt utterly alone.

A hand patted her shoulder. Expecting Alex, she turned to see Brighton's lively smile. "Not bad. At least you scored better than Alex. Good thing he throws a football better than he bowls."

"Okay, funny man," Alex said. "Let's go. My parents are in Ligonier for the afternoon. Let's move this party to my place."

He grabbed Ivy's arm, barely giving her enough time to get her coat on. The four proceeded to his silver BMW coupe. Although he opened the passenger side door for her, he pushed her inside firmly, catching her off guard.

Annoyed, Ivy glared at him as he took the driver's seat. He grinned at her, brushing her hair back. He rubbed her neck, letting his hand brush over the clasp of the necklace. Her anger subsided.

Nigel and Brighton groaned in protest as they contorted their legs and muscular bodies into the backseat. "Dude, I'm glad you don't live far away," Nigel said.

Alex zipped through the five gears of the 325 ES until he was well above the thirty-five mile an hour speed limit of Menoher Boulevard. The ancient oaks lining both sides of the parkway blurred past. Alex drove like he owned the road. Unfazed by the solid double line, he spurted past slower traffic, barely clearing the other cars as he jerked the BMW back into the lane. Ivy braced herself as the car sped along descending turns, waiting for them to spin out at any moment. Somehow, it stayed the course. She exhaled audibly as Alex slowed before turning onto a narrow, wooded road.

They descended out of the woods to an area cleared recently for homes. The houses sat on a ridge to the left, huge, new houses with brick or stone facades, intermingled with crisp siding. Large windows—bay, rectangular, or stained glass—overlooked the dark woods of the steep hillside to the right. Alex pulled into the wide driveway of a house with pure white siding. Its roof peaked into a high point at the entrance, with the lower levels extending away from the center from both directions. Alex pressed a button on his sun visor, opening the garage door effortlessly.

Unsure why, Ivy shivered as the garage darkened with the closing door. A mix of awe and uneasiness filled her. The boys were unusually quiet as they exited the car. Ivy was left to open her own door this time. Alex opened a door in the left corner of the garage, and the boys funneled through ahead of Ivy. She smiled at Alex, assuming he was being polite by holding this door for her. Again he grasped her arm a bit too firmly and led her into a game room. A pool table sat across from a large bar. A dart board and foosball table stood against dark-sided walls. Alex walked behind the bar and poured whiskey into four glasses.

No prompting was required for Nigel and Brighton. They scooped their glasses from the bar and placed them along the sides of the pool table. Brighton broke the balls lackadaisically. He and Nigel hit the balls around between sips of whiskey.

Alex remained behind the barn, staring at Ivy. She settled onto a bar stool, unnerved by his strange behavior. She turned sideways, watching the lackluster pool game and eyeing the room at the same time. Alex's eyes burned a hole through her. She mustered a smile and looked at him. He pushed a glass of whiskey toward her.

"No thanks," she said. Her father's behavior when drinking while he'd been out of work soured her to the idea. "This is a great house," she said quickly. "Can I have a tour of the rest?"

"Maybe, after you drink that." Alex smiled charmingly. "It won't hurt you. It will help you relax."

"Really, no thanks. That's the strong stuff." Unconsciously, she traced the tiers of the emerald necklace with her forefinger.

"Well, maybe you'll change your mind." Alex walked out from behind the bar abruptly. He joined Nigel and Brighton at the pool table, but not until saying, "That sure is a nice necklace."

The boys downed several more glasses of whiskey between random games of pool and darts. They became louder and louder as an hour wore by, then two hours. Ivy winked away the boredom anytime Alex made eye contact. She was desperate at first for his attention, yet as time wore on, despair settled in. It was clear he wasn't interested in her. She pictured Shane's doting on Karen and Lance's attention toward Mindy. Her stomach tightened in knots and every muscle longed to spring her out of there. She became angry and confused, wondering why he'd invited her there.

Finally, she cleared her throat. "Alex, I better get going."

Crouched over the pool table and ready to shoot, Alex glared at her, his mouth tensing as if he was going to yell at her. He looked to Nigel, who stood with pool stick in hand, looking unsure. Standing at the bottom of the table, Brighton seemed uneasy too. Alex abruptly laughed.

Ivy felt an intense flash of heat at her back. Out of the corner of her eye, she noticed a fleeting glow. As it dissipated, another flash of heat practically pushed her to her feet. She started quickly for the stairs. The urge to leave was undeniable now. She felt Alex's presence behind her. Before she knew it, he was blocking the stairway, his hot breath heating her face and filling her with fear. His eyes were narrow slits, but the glare from the bar lights bounced out of them like fire.

"Of course I want you to go," he said, "but not before you give me that necklace!"

He seized her left shoulder, his fingers digging into her trapezius muscle. Ivy crouched to escape, but he grabbed her right arm too, holding her in front of him.

Breathless and quivering in fear, Ivy said, "What are you talking about? The necklace is mine."

Nigel and Brighton laughed. Alex squeezed harder, gritting his teeth, his upper lip lifting in a snarl.

"We all know that wasn't your grandmother's. You found it in that crappy old house of my great-grandpa. My mother is his last female relative and that necklace is a family heirloom. Now give it to me before I take it off you!"

Ivy felt the individual strands of the necklace as its weight pushed into her skin. She pictured the way it glistened and shone in the light, and how everyone gasped at its beauty. The rich girls at her school had once snubbed her, giggling over and criticizing her used clothes. Now they stared in awe of the necklace, even speaking to Ivy in short sentences. She pictured her father's face after a long day at work, blackened with coal, his fingers gnarling more and more by the year.

Fire ignited inside her. She felt the power building in her left leg, the muscles firing in perfect coordination and accuracy, ending in a devastating blow from her knee into Alex's crouch. He crumbled to his knees, gasping and groaning in pain.

"Finders keepers!" she screamed, and dashed toward the door leading into the garage. It was the only exit she knew. Hearing the fast approaching footsteps of Nigel and Brighton amongst an onslaught of yelling, she slammed the door behind her and locked it. As they pounded on the other side, she scoured the wall for the automatic garage door opener. Breathless, almost panicking, she searched in vain. Heavy thuds came from the other side of the door, as if the boys were trying to break through. Suddenly, a flick of light appeared on the wall close to the banging, then another, and another. Ivy's breath caught in her throat. She saw the garage door button. She slammed it with her hand, just as she heard Alex shout, "Go around the front, you idiots!"

Ivy sprinted from the garage as she heard the boys bang back up the stairs inside the house. The gray skies of November were darkening. A cold wind blew squalls of snow into her face as she ran down the road. Unsure of where she was, Ivy cringed as her loafers became soaked in muddy puddles. A car started in the distance, and fear gripped her. Eyeing the woods to her right, she remembered the day at Shaffer's. Alex had told them he lived just up the road. The sound of gravel spewing from speeding tires pushed her down the bank and into the woods. She could only hope to find the Somerset Pike from there. Branches cracked and leaves crunched under her feet. She stumbled and slipped constantly on the unforgiving rocks and steep, downward terrain.

A car zipped past on the gravel road above. She continued south, deeper into the woods. With any luck, she'd end up in Tracy's backyard. Alex would never think to look for her there, and certainly Corrine would help. She plummeted on toward the faint light of the houses below the woods.

"Okay, kiddo," Ginny said. "See you later. Time to round up Brad, drop him off at my mom's, and go party! It's been a long week. You'll finish feeding for me?" Ginny didn't wait for June's response. She waved and disappeared through the front barn door.

June sighed and shivered as a blast of cold air blew through the barn with Ginny's departure. At least the grooming shop was warm. She pulled gloves from her pockets before opening the feed bin.

Enthusiastic nickers made her smile. The horses tossed their heads as she fed them one by one, ending with her new love, Snowflake. Uncharacteristically for a hungry horse, Snowflake paused as June dumped the feed into her tub. The mare cocked her head to June, lowered it, and rubbed against June's arm.

"Aww, you sweetie." June rubbed the crest of Snowflake's neck.

Suddenly, Snowflake raised her head, staring into space with ears pricked at full attention. Tingles ran up June's spine, and again she felt the static inside her ears. She knew what was next. She tried to run, but her legs would not move. The rhythmic rattling encompassed her, along with the overwhelming scent of frankincense.

Ivy stumbled up the manor house steps. A lone porch light was all that illuminated the area. She pounded on the thick oak door. The heavy brass knocker landed in dead thuds against the impenetrable wood. No light crept past the curtained windows. Her legs and feet were numb with cold, her pantyhose torn and riddled with burrs. Against hope she banged the door knocker once more. Tracy and Corrine were not home.

The sound of an engine and headlights pierced the encroaching darkness of the Somerset Pike below. Ivy jumped into a corner of the porch, away from the light. Cowering in the corner, she saw the silver BMW slow, pause, and continue on. She waited several seconds, listening as the engine sound became faint and eventually disappeared altogether.

As she peeked around the corner, she saw the rear lights disappear over the hill, moving south toward her house. She shuddered in fear, choking back tears of dismay. Her only solace was that she had met the boys in Ginny's parking lot before they went bowling. They only knew she lived close, not the specific house. But how would she get home without them seeing her?

She scanned the road, waiting to see the headlights doubling back. Staring south, she remembered the small abandoned barn she and Karen had passed that day they'd walked to Shaffer's. A side road ran parallel to it and the Pike. It was dark and surrounded by fields. She sprinted toward it.

June woke with a start. She gasped, blinking away her visions and looking wildly around Snowflake's stall. She was still standing and Snowflake was peacefully munching her hay. June darted from the stall, shut up the barn hastily, and sprinted through the darkness toward the bridge.

A powdery but steady snow blew into her face, stinging. Breathless, she stepped off the bridge and turned left, away from the old house and toward the tree-lined lane. From the corner of her eye, she saw a flash streak from behind her. Seconds later, more flashes of light sparked in front of her, enough to light the path. A larger streak exploded like an arrow, heading north to the Somerset Pike and disappearing.

June continued toward her house. A dim light shone through the living room window. Her mother was home. June plunged on, crossing the Pike and standing in her front yard, her chest heaving with her heavy breathing. The driveway was empty. Her father was still in the mines.

Now what? June thought through the scenario. She goes in, tells her mother she had a premonition that Ivy is in danger, her mother flips out, but then what? They call the cops? Have them look for Ivy on the basis of a premonition?

"Shane," she said aloud. "Maybe Shane can help." She had turned toward Shane's house when a loud motor rumbled from the north. June stopped in her tracks.

Four bright orbs illuminated the Pike, cutting a path through the darkness to reveal the hulking, low stance of a 1970's muscle car. With a growl, the beast headed down the slope toward June. She ran into the center of the road, jumping up and down and waving her arms wildly.

"Gage! Gage, stop!"

The growling motor eased into a low rumble. Tires screeched while the driver braked. The Satellite slid to a stop, forcing June to jump back.

Through the driver's window, Gage gaped at her. Beside him, Kirsten looked equally surprised.

"June, what the hell are you doing?" Gage asked. "You're lucky I saw you!"

"Quick, it's Ivy, she's in trouble. Take me to the abandoned red barn, please!"

Gage's eyes widened. "Okay, get in."

June ran to the passenger's side and flung open the door. Without hesitation, Kirsten slid over toward Gage and yanked June into the front seat beside her. The Satellite spun around, the hind end skidding from the force. Gage straightened the wheel, stomped on the clutch, and roared through the gears, plastering the girls back against their seats.

Gage didn't slow until they reached the side road that ran parallel to the pike and beside the abandoned barn. He kept the car in low gear, scanning the road through flurries of snow.

"You think she's walking along here?" he asked.

"I think she's inside that barn." June's voiced quivered as the scene came to her mind's eye. "Hurry, please."

The dusty air of the old tack room encompassed Ivy. All she felt was the cold dankness of the corner she huddled in. She stifled a sneeze down to the volume of a hiccup, but she knew it had betrayed her as cold air zipped through the opening door. Alex stood in front of her, blocking any chance for escape.

Ivy's breath rattled uncontrollably with fear. Unable to speak, she cowered in the corner, waiting for his next move. He stood there for a moment, silent. Although she couldn't see through the dark, she felt his eyes beaming holes through her. She squatted lower, trying to slow her breathing and preparing to rush him again. Just as she readied herself to explode into him, he was suddenly upon her. This time both hands clasped her throat with just enough pressure to make breathing difficult. He pulled her to her feet.

"I tried to do this the nice way," he said. "Why did you make me resort to this? My aunt never deserved that necklace, always whining to my great-grandfather about him damaging the environment or being cruel to those race nags. She constantly criticized my mother, calling her materialistic. What's the point of having money if you don't use it for nice things? The only reason my great-grandpa gave the necklace to her was to shut her up after her horse broke down. Then she threatens to donate it to a race horse charity? You've got to be kidding me! This necklace is going to stay in my family. Any longer with your family and it'll be ruined by coal dust. Now take it off and give it to me!"

Defeated, Ivy raised her hands and reached for the back of her neck. Alex released some of the pressure around her throat. Her fingers numb, she found the clasp but struggled to unhook it. Her fingers slipped and fumbled uselessly, unable to discern the release from the hook.

"Hurry!" Alex yelled.

Suddenly, Nigel's voice came from outside. "Alex, someone just pulled up."

"Get rid of them." Alex clasped his hand over Ivy's mouth and kicked the door shut behind him.

After a brief silence, Ivy heard Brighton say calmly, "Everything's okay. We're just checking out a party spot. You know what I mean, man."

Another male voice said something. Ivy couldn't hear the words, but its low quality struck her as familiar. A female voice came stronger and demanding.

"Where is my sister?"

Ivy screamed into Alex's hand, "June! Gage!" She heard a rustling outside, a shuffling of feet and then a bang, as if someone had hit the wall of the tack room with force. Alex's grip lessened on her mouth as he spun his body away from her. There was more scuffling and slamming outside. June yelled, and there was a thud against the door. Alex released her completely, rushing to the door. It burst open, smashing into Alex. He groaned and his body thudded on the floor.

A dark, petite form jumped on top of Alex. He groaned again as the figure kicked him in the ribs.

"Ivy!" It was June. Ivy ran into her sister's arms. They held each other, sobbing, for a few seconds. Ivy looked over June's shoulder to see headlights from the idling Satellite. They illuminated the aisle way of the barn, revealing another scene.

Blood dripped from Nigel's snarling lip as he scowled at Gage, who was restrained against the wall by Brighton. Nigel pulled his fist back, ready to land a direct blow on Gage's face.

"Stop!" Ivy screamed. She dove out of the tack room. Just missing Nigel's legs, she landed prone on the dirt floor. A sudden clunk sent Nigel staggering sideways. Ivy looked up to see Kirsten brandishing a shovel. She aimed its tip at Nigel's head.

Everyone stood stock still, eyeing each other. Kirsten had her shovel at the ready, staring intently at Nigel. Nigel stared back at her over the bump in his nose, his dark hair wild from the fight. Brighton kept a tentative hand on Gage's chest, but he kept looking from Nigel to Kirsten. June walked over to Ivy, placing a hand under her arm and helping her to her feet. There was another groan and a rustling from the tack room. Alex was on his feet.

Ivy grabbed June's arm and yanked her past Nigel. The sisters stood beside Kirsten. Staring down Nigel and Brighton, they raised their chins and squared their shoulders. Nigel's gaze darted back and forth as he looked for weakness in the wall of femininity. Finally, he just stared at the tip of Kirsten's shovel.

Alex hovered in the doorway and then suddenly rushed out of the tack room.

"Stop right there!" Kirsten said. "I'll take your friend's head off, I swear!" She swung the shovel back high over her shoulder.

Alex stopped. Gage slapped Brighton's hand from his chest and pushed him to the ground.

"Okay, everyone," Brighton said. "This is out of hand. Let's everyone just leave. Alex, man, this isn't worth it, not for a stupid necklace."

"Shut up!" Alex said. "I told you that's a priceless family heirloom. I should have that piece of trash Ivy arrested for theft."

Ivy turned on him. "You tried to hold me against my will, chased me down, and almost choked me to death. You should be going to jail, all of you!"

"You did what to her?" Gage lunged at Alex, hitting him firmly in the face with a right cross.

Instead of rounding on Gage, Alex laughed. It started low and slow, but built in intensity until he was practically cackling. "You gave me just what I wanted. My dad's an attorney. My black eye is all he'll need to nail you on assault charges." He looked from Gage to Ivy. "Keep the necklace, you slimy little rat. Maybe I won't say your friend hit me. Maybe I got in a fight with some random dude at the mall. But remember, I have witnesses. I go way back with these boys."

Brighton rose slowly to his feet. "Okay then, you guys leave first, all of you. I want to see you all in that old piece of junk before we go."

Ivy met Gage's eyes. Nodding, she motioned for him to leave. He paused as he passed Brighton, pushing him slightly in the chest.

"That 'piece of junk' will blow the doors off that Beamer any day of the week."

Kirsten backed slowly out of the barn, her shovel still poised for action. Ivy held June's hand and they backed in unison with Kirsten. Gage followed slowly behind the girls, never taking his eyes from the jocks.

The sisters piled into the backseat. Gage got in the driver's seat and placed a comforting hand on Kirsten's knee. She put her head in her hands for a moment, and then took Gage's hand in relief as they pulled away.

Ivy threw her arms around June. "How did you ever find me?"

"Let's just say I had some help from beyond. I think Grandma Kakowa's people gave me the sight. But there were also these flashes of light coming from the old house again."

Ivy hugged Gage and then Kirsten, wrapping her arms around them from the backseat. "I owe you guys. Thanks."

"I thought they were going to be trouble when I saw them at the dance," Gage said. "I don't even want to know what they want with your necklace."

"I don't know why," Ivy said, "but I feel like I'm meant to have this necklace." She looked at June, who was staring at Ivy's neck.

"Look," June said, "the necklace is glowing! Lady Luminess does want you to have it!"

Chapter 24

Christmas Spirit

"Where is she?" Brad muttered. "The car's here and the lights are off. She's always going out somewhere, meeting somebody. Can't she stay home for once?"

His hands and feet were numb. His plan to hitchhike from town had yielded no good Samaritans. The four-mile walk had left him cold and blistered.

Brad burst into each room of the trailer again, as if it were possible to miss his mother the first time. In his bedroom, a two year-old picture caught his eye. Christmas lights twinkled behind his parents, who smiled brightly in what was now his father's house in town. There he was, front and center, grinning, with his parents' hands on his shoulders. He yanked the picture from the wall and smashed it on the floor. Walking back into the living room, he looked around the dim, silent trailer. The small artificial Christmas tree by the window did little to comfort him. A baseball bat behind the door beckoned him. He snatched it up, barely controlling the urge to use it inside. He darted out the door and across the yard toward the riding ring. The crisp dark air chilled his lungs and clung to his already cold, wet feet and hands. Fury blinded him, white streaks racing across his eyes. He got to the fence, and the bat splintered a top board in two.

Emboldened by the release of rage, he continued along the outside perimeter, smashing another board on the way. Still no signs of life around the entire property, not even a rustle from the stupid horses his mother liked so much. He strode along through the dark, looking for anything else to smash. As he crossed the creek, the bridge's iron rails reverberated from the bat's abuse. He stormed toward the fountain in front of the old house. Breathless and shaking, he lifted the bat over his head with both hands and let it slam into the rock wall of the fountain with all his might. The granite didn't flinch. Instead, shock waves vibrated up his arms, diffusing his anger with pain. He crumpled against the fountain walls, hyperventilating and fighting back tears.

Why were they so against him? He didn't want to move to Indiana. He was sick of his dad telling him what to do. He was always jumping down his throat about something. His mom wasn't like that, but where was she? The holiday picture flashed through his mind.

"I'll never see her or my friends if I move. Why can't they just be together?"

Familiar in every detail, another picture crept into his mind. A newborn, he was wrapped in a blue blanket, coddled in a white bassinet, with the shade of his dad's maple tree shielding him from the June sun. His parents grinned from where they knelt on either side of the bassinet. Again their smiles and warm eyes, his mother's darker than his father's, revealed the falseness of their relationship. Brad jumped to his feet, hot with rage again. He thought about ripping off his flannel shirt, but it would take too long. He needed to break something now.

The darkened house of the elderly Mrs. Smith sat across Country Club Road. Her long driveway buffered the house from the road, but there was no buffer for her mailbox. Brad's steel-toed boots thudded up his drive, the mailbox in his sights.

As he reached the road, a flickering caught his attention, along with an onslaught of evergreen wafting up his nose. A faint clip-clop came from a distance and dim flashlight beams cut the night. Suddenly, the outline of Shane's house was illuminated with red, blue, orange, and green. The lights almost whitened the gray house. A large evergreen wreath hung on the door, a red ribbon bow in the center. Shane's mother peered out the bay window, her smile highlighted by lipstick the color of the bow. Her dark hair grazed her shoulders as she looked up the road. Brad stood still, staring at Shane's mother as she spoke to someone and made a gesture. Shane came into view beside her, and then the two disappeared from the window. The door opened, and Shane and Meadow stepped onto the porch. Their smiles both sickened and warmed Brad.

The clip-clopping was louder now, with a jingling to accompany it. Three horses came into view, the darkest carrying a fully turned out Santa Claus. Brad recognized Cajun, who turned up Shane's driveway. Dawn followed, blowing ghostly clouds to float among the Christmas lights. Karen smiled from under her Santa hat, her cheeks blushing from the cold. The lights glimmered gold against her skin. Brad had never seen someone sparkle like that before. Snowflake carried June beside the other two, so that the three horses stood side by side in Shane's driveway.

The carolers opened with "Silent Night," sang "We Wish You a Merry Christmas," and belted out "Hark! The Herald Angels Sing." The horses shook their heads occasionally, ringing the bells on their bridles. After the singing stopped, Meadow gestured for the riders to wait and ducked into the house.

Shane approached Karen, who leaned over and kissed him. June rolled her eyes. The door opened again, and Meadow and Jack carried steaming mugs, cookies, and carrots. They divided the treats among themselves and the horses. Talking and laughter echoed through the barren trees. Jack said something to Santa, and Brad heard his mother's unmistakable laugh in reply. He dropped the bat to the ground.

The horses turned their heads, ears pricked, in Brad's direction. Ginny stared into the darkness. After a moment, she started with recognition.

"Brad! My God, what are you doing? You're supposed to be with your dad."

With a gloved hand, Shane motioned for Brad to join them. "Come on, don't tell me you're shy all of a sudden. There's plenty for everyone."

Brad was frozen where he stood. Remnants of adrenaline buzzed through his muscles. His head was foggy and his breathing shallow. He wanted to crumple into a ball.

Shane went back inside his house while Karen called to Brad.

"Don't just stand there in the dark, silly. Come over!" Her face remained golden, her cheeks still crimson.

Brad willed his shaky legs to move. Slump-shouldered, he joined the others, choosing a spot beside Cajun's shoulder. Shane came back out and thrust a steaming mug of hot chocolate at Brad, slapping him on the back.

"You came at the right time, buddy. They just finished singing."

The girls protested as Jack and Meadow laughed. Shane walked back over to Karen and June, leaving Brad beside his mother.

Seeing his mother wearing a Santa hat and beard pulled a smile from Brad. "Mom, you look ridiculous."

Ginny smiled. "Hey, it's all in good fun." She pulled the beard down and looked at him cautiously. "So, did you and your dad talk?"

"He talked. He didn't give me a chance. I'm not moving! How could you dump me like that? I love it here. All my friends are here." Brad spoke through clenched teeth, aware of the others. "Look at this. Shane has everything." He motioned to the merrily decorated house. "His mom would never send him away!"

"Easy, easy," Ginny said. "It was just an idea. Brad, your dad and I have problems. Sometimes parents don't get along. I didn't think you were happy here. You fight me on everything!"

"So you just throw me away." Feeling the tears, Brad turned his back on his mother.

"No, that's not true. You don't have to go, okay?" Ginny reached down from Cajun and squeezed his shoulder. "Now drink your cocoa. Ivy's meeting us at the house. You'll have friends all around you."

"Hurry up and drink that before it gets cold," Karen said, looking at him over Dawn's neck. "You shouldn't waste good chocolate." She rarely spoke to him, except to complain about his pranks.

Brad followed the horses home. They easily outpaced him, and he fell behind as they passed the old house. Karen scuttled by it quickly as usual, urging Dawn to a trot. June looked unconcerned, glancing at the house intermittently. Brad scanned its top floor, unable to quell his curiosity. A tiny light shone in the center of a window. It darted out, hovering outside the third floor and growing in size and brightness. Brad stood transfixed, his heart racing again. The light morphed into a five-pointed star the size of a basketball. Although it had no features, Brad felt it was staring at him. He stared back, prepared to run. In a flash, the star zipped skyward. It hurtled into the heavens and stopped abruptly, as if taking its rightful place among the other stars. There, it shone brightest in the cold, clear night.

CHAPTER 25

Galloping in the Snow

Winter brought a blanket of white. Riding Dawn, Karen looked behind her to see Snowflake following willingly, a content June aboard. The mood around the group seemed enlightened and invigorated. Karen shivered at the thought of Ivy's ordeal with the Westmont boys. Yet it appeared to have been catalyst for change. June and Kirsten spoke openly now, even teaming together to get the barn work done. Ivy willingly helped her sister, setting up jumps and helping tack and care for Snowflake. Gage demonstrated a new air of self-confidence, organizing sled outings for the group. This day, he had taken Kirsten to a matinee, freeing up Dawn for Karen to ride. Karen wouldn't have known how to contain her excitement otherwise. This was the eve of the day she had waited for her whole life. Tomorrow, she would travel with Ginny to Waterford Park and pick out a horse all her own. Elated, she pushed Dawn along behind Cajun and Mindy, while June followed on Snowflake.

They topped the mountain and looked upon the haven and surrounding white-covered treetops. Everything seemed fresh and awe inspiring. Upon entering the clearing, the girls stopped abreast of each other. Stray snowflakes dotted the little Appaloosa's coat, matching the pattern on her rear end. The girls sat in rare silence, mesmerized by the beauty of the February day.

Karen checked her purse for the fifth time, assuring herself that the four hundred dollars was still there. She jumped into the back of the borrowed Ramcharger beside Wendy.

"I'm glad you're coming" Karen said. "Everyone says you're small enough to be a jockey. This way you can decide if you're interested."

"I'm just glad to get away from the restaurant for a day," Wendy said. "It's driving me nuts!"

June took the shotgun position in front as Ginny slipped into the driver's seat, chewing her gum vigorously. With the horse trailer in tow, they were off.

As she drove, Ginny told of her time spent at the track in her late teens. She was a groom, hot walker, and even galloped a few horses. "You can't imagine how strong they get. It takes every fiber of your strength to hold them. Sometimes you just can't and they run off. The trainers get real upset when that happens. Horses can easily damage themselves from overexertion."

Hoping to secure the teens' interest, she went on to describe the backside of the track, the stable area where the horses lived and were cared for.

"All you see is rows and rows of horses' faces looking out at you. I fell in love with it from the start."

"By the way, I have a special guest coming with us. You girls like John's stories, and I want his opinion on the horses. Karen, you can learn from him. He'll be a second pair of eyes for me as well."

"You're getting a horse too?" Karen asked.

"Of course. You'll pay me back for bringing yours back by schooling it for me."

"I'd love to!" Karen smiled as she thought of John. He never ran out of horse stories from Ireland. Tales sounded so exciting and romantic with his stamp on them. He was also a good judge of horses. He'd ease the agony of the three-hour drive to Waterford Park in West Virginia.

Ginny drove south, although it seemed like they were headed for the sky. The truck strained to top Ligonier Mountain. They hit Route 30 at the quaint town of Ligonier. The town had been the site of battles during the French and Indian War during the country's infancy. Now it was a classy refuge for the wealthy. John worked and lived at the Rolling Rock Hunt Club.

Huge fenced pastures sat on hillsides edged with old hardwood trees. Immaculately constructed stone barns burnished the countryside. They had stood the test of time. Most had been built early in the century. Countless generations of horsemen had enjoyed this land. It was the perfect combination of open fields and woods. The girls gasped as they drove past the old steeplechase course and saw the remnants of a jump.

"I can't imagine approaching that at a full gallop," Karen said.

"It's huge," Wendy agreed.

"Here is the Colonial Barn," Ginny said as they turned down an evergreen-lined lane. "They used to stable the chasers here. Now it stables the hunt horses."

The barn was well named. Indeed it was colonial style, with Dutch doors and pure white pillars supporting the roof to the shed row. The living quarters were smack in the middle of the shed row. They were framed in red brick. A small tower extended above the roof of the stalls.

"That's where the jockeys used to get ready," Ginny explained.

"What a great place to live," Karen said. "Talk about being close to the horses." She liked the idea of living at such a historic place.

"Why did they stop the racing?" Wendy asked. "I would have loved to see it."

"Yeah, how great would that be? We live so close. Imagine having such a spectacle in your backyard."

"They stopped it after a rider got killed in a race," Ginny said. "The powers that be worried about their reputation. Steeplechases are very dangerous."

Karen nodded, remembering the plight of Loyal Pal. It had been over a year since his spirit had leaped past her. He seemed so free now, but what he had endured and Mr. Opie's cruelty were unthinkable. Silence filled the cab.

John waited in front of the living quarters. He shooed June into the back, took the front seat, and immediately lightened the mood. "Oh, you lasses look comfy back there. You're all huddled together like my hounds when I haul them in the back of the truck." He greeted Wendy, whom he hadn't met before. "And you, my sweet. I've never seen a real life angel until today," He smiled at her with twinkling eyes.

Wendy indeed could have passed for an angel. Her fair skin and crystal blue eyes fit the bill. Her reddish-blond hair fell straight to her shoulders. With her slight build, she seemed light enough to fly away.

She laughed at John's compliment. "My dad would argue that point."

"Are you in trouble again?" Karen asked Wendy.

"A little. One night Bob was kissing me good-bye on my doorstep, and my dad caught us. Bob barely escaped with his life. I barely see him now. My dad's watching me like a hawk."

"As he should," Ginny said. "You're too good for that creep. Focus on something else. You're too young to be so involved."

"You don't need some useless boy," John said. "Look at you. You're the perfect size for a girl jockey. There's more and more of them. Some trainers prefer girls, especially to ride their more sensitive horses. They have a lighter touch than the lads. Some say girl riders try harder. They think they have something to prove."

Wendy nodded. "I'm considering it."

The truck headed west on Route 30 toward Pittsburgh. The busy, fast Interstate 276 took them past skyscrapers, over the Fort Pitt Bridge, and through mountain tunnels. The scenery slowly changed to countryside as they descended the mountain leading into West Virginia. Chester was located in the panhandle of West Virginia, a thin sliver of the state that divided Pennsylvania and Ohio. Compared to lovely Ligonier, Chester left a lot to be desired. It was mainly an industrial working-class town along the Ohio River. Huge river barges trudged slowly along the banks. Billows of smoke rose from towering factories. Karen couldn't picture horses in this setting.

"I guess this isn't Belmont or Saratoga," she said.

"Far from it," John said. "These horses couldn't run a half mile with Belmont horses. They're lower quality."

Karen's reservations were quickly forgotten as they drove past the shed row. Countless beautiful faces looked over stall doors. The cold air produced clouds from their nostrils. Ginny was right. It was like a wonderland.

How will I ever choose? She wondered.

"We'll start front side," Ginny said. "Let's watch a few races so you girls can get a taste of it."

They walked into the grandstand and out to the rail. They were just in time to catch the first race. Lower quality or not, the thunder of hooves flying past at forty miles per hour made their hearts beat faster. Every muscle of the horses tensed and exploded with unbelievable power. Manes and tails blew along with snow flurries as the horses raced past at maximum exertion. To Karen, there was nothing more magnificent than a Thoroughbred horse, especially when stretched into a full gallop. What wonderful creatures.

"Wow. I wonder what that's like," Wendy muttered.

Of course, John was tuned into everything the girls said. "You can easily find out. I can teach you a thing or two. If you're serious, I can hook you up with some trainers who can teach you how to gallop. Once you do that, race riding should come naturally."

"Well, I do have the summer off," Wendy said. "It looks like an exciting life."

Ginny took the girls to the paddock area. This was where spectators watched the runners being saddled and walked as part of the warm-up. Some people placed bets based on what they saw in the paddock. Karen studied the different types of horses. Some were tall, strong, and beautiful. Others were scrawny and underweight. Some held their heads proudly with fire in their eyes. Others dangled their heads listlessly. She felt as sorry for these as she revered the others.

"I wish we could take them all home," she said.

"Yeah, I know," June said. "How can people look at those skinny horses and think they're all right?"

"Some people," John said, "say a horse can't run well if their ribs aren't showing. Of course that's not true. They need good flesh for strength. It all depends on who you learn from and what you believe."

"Wow, look at some of these." Wendy pointed to a muscular chestnut walking past. "They look more like quarter horses. Dorian seems twice as tall and long as that one."

"Most of the shorter, more compact horses are bred to sprint," Ginny said. "They are usually faster than the classic looking Thoroughbreds, but they also only race three-quarters of a mile or less. The type you're used to is the type I prefer. They're called route horses. They race for a mile or longer."

The girls took it all in. After a few races, it was time to go to the backside. Two lucky horses would get new homes that night.

Ginny went to barn twelve. She knew the trainer and had bought horses from him before.

"What do you have for me, Ed?" she asked the gray-haired man.

Ed's assortment of horses matched the less desirables that the girls had seen front side. After viewing six horses, Ginny was disappointed. She had to be particular about the horses for resale. Show-horse people liked tall horses, at least sixteen hands. They had to have an attractive head. White markings were preferred. Many racehorses had hard bumps on the inside of their legs called splints, and larger ankles than normal called osseletes. Those conditions could cause lameness at first, but with time they healed and didn't bother the average show horse. However, if the growths were too large, it scared off potential buyers.

"Oh, Ed, don't you have anything a little more suitable. You know what I like," Ginny said in her sweetest voice.

"Not really. This is about it—" He stopped mid-sentence and took a deep breath. "Well, maybe there's one more." He sighed. "Since it's you, maybe I'll consider selling him. I wanted to get one more race out of him, but he's been good to me. He might not have another chance at a second career if you leave. He deserves it. Blue Darter's a nice horse."

Ed was obviously a tough *trackey*. They didn't get too attached to horses. The minute a horse couldn't pay for itself, trainers got rid of them. Sadly, many were sold at auction for slaughter. However, even trackies developed soft spots for the better horses. Obviously, Ed felt that way about Blue Darter and was willing to let him have his shot.

He walked to a stall a short distance away and led out a regal-looking gray. "Here's the old boy."

The horse's body was almost white, but a silvery mane and tail highlighted his muscular neck and rear end. He was a medium-built horse, somewhere between the stocky sprinter and long-legged router. He was well balanced, with a short, strong back. A crested neck sat high on sloping shoulders.

"He's a dressage prospect with that build," Karen said.

"Oh, you're a nice old boy." Ginny rubbed his forehead and the horse leaned into the pressure, appreciating the attention.

"Yeah, he's won his share of races," Ed said. "He's eight years old, but he's still sound. He's just lost that desire. He's been doing this a long time. He has a good temperament. It's what kept him in the game so long. He knows when to protect himself."

"I think he'll do," Ginny said, and she and Ed settled on the price. Eight hundred dollars bought the horse.

Word spread quickly about potential buyers on the backside. Everyone had horses to get rid of. A heavy-set man came up to the group and spoke with a Cajun accent.

"I hear you're lookin' for a horse?"

"I am," Karen said, "but it's got to be cheap."

"Well, I have one for you. She might need some work, but she's a looker. I know show people are picky about looks."

The group followed the man to his barn. He directed Karen to a stall. Just as she got there, an exquisite face emerged. It was refined and delicate. Intricate veins wove from the eye to above the cheeks, defining centuries of breeding quality. A wide forehead separated soft eyes, thought to be a sign of intelligence. A well-shaped star and a snip on the nose decorated the mahogany bay.

"Can I see her out of the stall?"

The filly's energy rose as she was lead from the stall. Her eyes brightened with awareness, as if to ask, "What are we doing next?" She was tall, with a body as graceful as her head. A hind sock completed the picture.

"Now that's a Thoroughbred," Wendy said.

"Now we have to see her move," John said. "This young lady wants to clean the shows of their ribbons. She must move properly." He motioned for the filly to be trotted in hand.

The man scooted off clumsily, but the filly made up for it. Her neck arched and her eyes sparkled with life. She floated along the ground. With each step there was a special cadence, a little extra suspension that caught the eye.

"Okay, that will do," John said. He whispered to Karen, "There's your champion."

Karen had her horse.

CHAPTER 26

A New Spring

Fox Hollow Stables was quiet no more. Karen's new filly made sure of that. As the man had said, she needed a lot of work. Karen sought advice frequently from more experienced horsemen. She wasn't sure how to contain and control the filly's exuberant energy. The horse also created a stir in the form of visitors. Family members celebrated the long-awaited arrival of Karen's first horse. Her numerous aunts and cousins made a point to visit the barn on weekends. The filly received loads of carrots and sugar cubes, and seemed to eat up the crooning and compliments on her beauty as well. Karen didn't hesitate to boast about the filly's Olympic-level rated gaits. She was very athletic, jumping at will when turned out in the ring. Karen credited John for recommending the four-year-old filly.

On the other hand, the filly's temperament could be explosive. She was the cliché of being female. One day she was calm and complacent, the next she was all fire. Karen loved the challenge. However, it was clear she would not be able to show the filly that year in the 4-H jumping classes.

"Don't worry," John told her. "The best of them develop slowly. Take it one step at a time. You have to get into her head. This is no robotic lesson horse. She is extremely sensitive. You'll have to work with her and not against her. Make her think everything is her idea." He was generous with his time, coming from Ligonier once a month to help Karen school her new project.

Something else added to the ambience of the barn. It was the good cheer of Karen's mother, Colleen. She often stayed to watch her daughter work the filly. Apparently, Karen's ownership of the horse spiked Colleen's interest in the training process. Also, John's presence was a draw. Everyone was a sucker for his accent.

Colleen played a part in nicknaming the filly too. The Jockey Club had her registered as Get Excited, but as apt as it was, that didn't translate well when addressing the filly at home or in the field. One day, Karen was speaking softly to the filly while working with her in the cross-ties.

"It's all right, babe," she said.

Colleen overheard her. "That's what you can call her. She's strong physically, but so sensitive emotionally. It's a good name."

During the first month, Karen followed John's suggestion and worked Babe in long lines. She bridled the horse, and then two lunge lines were placed on the bit on either side and run through the stirrups. The trainer stood on the ground and drove the horse from behind. Turning and stop and go commands were taught in this manner. It kept the trainer safe on the ground while the horse got used to the new behavioral expectations. As in Babe's case, many ex-racehorses became stiff and unresponsive to a rider's commands. All they seemed to remember was to run fast. The excitement of race training overrode basic dressage. Also, a human could never out power a horse. Attempting that while mounted could be dangerous and exhausting for the rider. Using the long lines allowed greater mobility for the trainer. By eliminating the association of a rider with speed, most horses could be successfully retrained. It was like breaking them all over again.

After a month of slow but steady ground work, Karen started Babe under saddle. Setting a foundation through the ground work proved invaluable, for Babe transitioned seamlessly under tack. There were times when she became nervous or rambunctious, especially while cantering, yet for Karen, this was her nirvana. It didn't bother her that the filly was years away from jumping the three-foot-six-inch courses of the 4-H working hunter division. She could continue to relish in the success of the previous year. Grand had taught her a lot. Now she would take on the role of trainer for the green thoroughbreds.

Through Wendy's recommendation, Karen planned on attending schooling shows at J. T. Acres. These shows were developed specifically for young or green horses and riders. They offered a variety of flat classes, and the range in the jumping classes was huge. They varied from cross rails to two feet, two foot three to two foot six, two foot six to two foot nine, and up to three feet to three foot six. Wendy had found these shows to be essential in Dorian's training. Karen looked forward to taking both Babe and her other training project, Blue Darter.

Darter had indeed proven himself a good investment. Of course, he could not compete in working hunter classes either. Yet he required much less ground work and was less anxious than Babe. Karen was confident Darter would be her 4-H project horse. Between the flat classes and hunter hack, she would stay active in 4-H and provide Darter with valuable training for Ginny. Hunter hack was a class that combined flat work with jumping a simple double combination. Horses were judged on manners and suitability for the foxhunting field. Darter took to his new lessons with the wisdom of a regal eagle.

One March day, Wendy's father brought her to Fox Hollow. Wendy and Brian watched John teach Karen lower-level dressage techniques, aiding her with keeping Babe on the bit. Circles and figure eights, shoulder in and haunches in, turn on the forehand and turn on the haunches, all promoted suppleness and submission to the bit. He advised various stretching exercises before and after the session, teaching Karen how to do these by applying steady pressure to the bars of the horse's mouth. Horses were taught by giving to pressure, so as soon as the horse gave in and lowered its head, the rider released the pressure. The horse learned to drop its head on command. This also promoted relaxation by triggering the animal's parasympathetic nervous system. When the horse was in this frame of mind, its natural fight-or-flight reaction could be overcome if the horse became upset. At the conclusion of the session, Karen smiled at the railbirds. The new techniques boosted her confidence while dealing with her anxious horse.

"I need to try that with Dorian," Wendy said. "Maybe his attitude would improve."

"I don't think anything can help that old crank," Brian said.

"You'd be surprised, sir," John said. "Not only does this promote relaxation, but it stretches the top line and can relieve muscle aches. They're like any athlete. They feel strain and pain as we do."

Brian nodded. "That makes sense. Actually, I wanted to talk to you about my daughter's future. She told me you had suggested she become a jockey. She's been involved with a guy who will only ruin her life and nothing better. I'm not about to let that happen. I think she could stand to broaden her horizons. Sending her out of town bothers me, but I think she needs some perspective on her future. Can you teach her the basics of race riding? After all, her horse used to be a racehorse, so I think she can learn the galloping technique on him. Then you can tell if she's got any potential."

Wendy stayed quiet during Brian's talk, though Karen saw tears well up in her eyes. She knew Wendy was at her limit. She was afraid of losing her father because of Bob. Karen bit her lip in sympathy as Wendy hid her tears.

"It would be my pleasure to help," John said. He smiled at Wendy. "Just don't forget me after your first Kentucky Derby win."

"We have plenty of gallop mates around here too," Karen said. "I bet Darter would like to take on Dorian."

"One step at a time, lass. It's a lot harder to gallop these guys in company than you think. Darter is coming along great, but put him head to head with another horse, and you'll have a race if you're not careful. I'll work with both of you. Karen, it won't hurt you to learn this. Wendy, I'm sure you'll be a natural. I saw you riding that gray crank of yours at the show. You have good hands. I'll teach you both individually. After that, you'll gallop together and see how you fare. This will be a nice change of pace. Whipping in at the hunt is fine, but I miss the excitement of racing. This darn back of mine …" John's voice trailed off as he clutched his lower back, seemingly unconsciously.

"I'll beat you all with my spotted pony!" June chimed in as she entered the ring with Snowflake. The group burst into laughter as they compared the tall, streamlined Babe to the sleepy-eyed pony. Babe's legs alone were almost taller than Snowflake's back.

"I don't know about that," John said, "but your spotted pony's coming along well. She may be fit to come with the hunt someday. You'll be my personal guest."

"How exciting that would be," June exclaimed, "to ride with hounds!"

Ivy led Cajun into the ring and stopped her in front of the mounting block. An annoyed-looking Mindy helped the young 4-H member Sara mount the quarter horse.

A wave of discomfort seized Karen. Ivy barely acknowledged Wendy and Brian. Withdrawn as of late, this was the first time Ivy had been to the barn in weeks. Karen cleared her throat, looking at Wendy.

Wendy's eyes brightened, as if a light bulb had gone off in her head. "John, could a Tennessee walker keep up with the hounds? Ivy's been working hard all winter and barely gets to ride. My filly Orchid is available. Ivy needs to have some fun too."

John put his hand over his chin and pondered. "Hmm, I'm not too familiar with that breed. We gallop a good bit, but she can hilltop. We have a bunch of hunt members who follow at an easier pace, sometimes taking shortcuts from the main route and viewing the hunt high points." He motioned for Ivy to come closer. "Sure, why not? Look out Rolling Rock, the Hausemann sisters are coming!"

He threw his arm around Ivy's shoulders, jostling her gently. She giggled. "Thanks, Wendy."

Wendy and Brian left then, and Karen led Babe toward Mindy in the center of the ring. Now how could she make this friend smile?

Mindy's face lit up as Karen approached. "Great news. Lance just brought Saint down. Ginny's going to consign him for his sister. In the meantime, he's my project horse and I get to ride him anytime. That is, after you get him going. I was hoping you could start today. The warmer weather is coming soon." Mindy clasped her hands over her heart and gave Karen her sweetest look.

"Of course. I'll get Babe settled and we'll get started."

"Good. That will give me time to finish helping Sara. You know Ginny doesn't do anything without a price," Mindy joked.

"That's right. I haven't seen her yet today. Must be catching up on her beauty sleep," Karen suggested.

Karen opened the barn door to see Kirsten brushing Dawn in the cross ties. The girls talked about Gage while Karen untacked Babe and Kirsten tacked Dawn. After a fun winter spending Saturday evenings together, Gage was back to his backward behavior. His father had bought another muscle car to fix up, and Gage hadn't called Kirsten for two weeks.

"Unbelievable," Kirsten said angrily. "I held a shovel to someone's head for him and he can't even talk to me for ten minutes!"

"He gets so obsessed with those cars," Karen said. "What kind of guy chooses a car over his girlfriend?"

"That's another thing. He never officially asked me to go with him. Maybe he doesn't think of me as his girlfriend."

"Let's get everyone together at Shane's soon. Maybe he just needs a kick in the butt." She at least got a laugh from Kirsten with that.

Kirsten took Dawn into the riding ring and Karen approached the stall with the new occupant. Karen remembered having trouble controlling the horse when she tried him at Lance's, but blamed that on the fact that she had only a halter and two lead ropes to steer and was trying to ride bareback. The golden palomino stuck his head over the door. He was fifteen hands tall. A wide blaze decorated his slightly roman nose. She stroked his strong, arched neck and rubbed his forehead. He nodded his head, shaking his long mane.

"You seem friendly enough. I hope you live up to your name, Saint."

Karen brushed and tacked the gelding. He stood motionless and apparently unbothered. Mindy led Cajun in as Karen led Saint out of the barn and into the ring.

"I'll be right there," Mindy said.

Saint stood beside her with head lowered. There was no fidgeting as he watched Dawn and Snowflake walk around the ring together, their riders in deep conversation.

"Good boy," Karen said. "You shouldn't be a problem." She rubbed his forehead again. "And look, June and Kirsten are getting along."

Mindy arrived at the mounting block. She held Saint as Karen mounted, and then led him for a half turn until Karen was ready. Saint plodded along, weaving away from the rail and cutting corners. Karen took a firmer hold of her outside rein and applied pressure with the inside leg. Saint continued to push to the inside. Karen thudded him harder with her leg, which prompted him to trot. She took back on the reins as a correction.

"Easy, boy. You need to stay on the rail and walk at the same time."

Karen completed a few misshapen circles, attempting to limber the horse and get him on the aids. His neck was like iron, and she had difficulty driving him into the corners. Frustrated, she asked for a trot, hoping the forward momentum would help steer him. She squeezed and squeezed, but it was like squeezing an empty tube of toothpaste.

"Mindy, can you hand me the crop?" Mindy ducked inside the barn and handed it to Karen.

Karen took Saint back on the rail. She asked again for the trot with no response. "C'mon, you lazy thing."

She raised the crop and hit him firmly behind her leg. Saint reacted instantly. He dashed away, tucking his head between his knees and bucking wildly. Unprepared, Karen was thrown onto his neck. She gripped his mane, trying to right herself, but he bucked again, sending her off sideways. She landed hard on her shoulder. Gasping for air, she lay there for a few seconds, her lungs working overtime. Saint moseyed around the ring with his head down, picking up small bits of new grass along the way. He paid no mind to Snowflake and Dawn as their concerned riders approached Karen.

"It's okay. I'm all right." Karen huffed as Mindy helped her up and June and Kirsten dismounted. "Let's catch him. I have to get back on."

"Maybe we'll get out of your way," Kirsten said. She and June took their horses inside the barn.

Mindy caught Saint easily. Karen put on a brave front and mounted him again. "Why don't you keep a hold of him?" she said to Mindy. "Put us on the rail, I'll tell you when to start jogging. Give me some help to start."

Apparently, Saint was satisfied with his antics. He trotted alongside Mindy willingly. At Karen's bidding, she released him after two turns around the ring. He continued on lazily, but maintained the trot with some leg pressure. He even completed two twenty-meter circles. Taking a breath of relief, Karen slowed him to a walk. She joined Mindy by the barn door and halted.

"Whew, that's enough for today." Karen was more exhausted than she was after riding two Thoroughbreds. "I think he'll come around. I must have hit him too hard or something."

"He'll get the hang of it."

Mindy had barely finished her sentence when June opened the barn door. Saint honed in on the gap like a missile to its target. Karen tried to turn his head, but he resisted. He stormed into the barn, almost running June over. Karen's attempts to stop Saint were in vain. Her head barely missed the rafter as Saint barreled into his own stall. Immediately, he settled into eating hay, as if he had never been taken from the stall.

Mindy stormed into the stall and snatched the reins from a heaving Karen. "Enough is enough!" She smacked Saint in the rear with the crop and led him back into the ring. She stopped him beside the mounting block and climbed aboard the horse.

"Mindy, wait!" Karen stumbled after her with June and Kirsten behind.

Mindy dug her heels into Saint, practically whirling him from a stop into a canter. She hollered and drove him, flipping the reins from one side of his neck to the other, slapping him on the shoulders. Saint galloped around the ring, sending clouds of dust in his wake. After four rounds, Mindy turned him down the center line and pulled him to a stop. The palomino held his head high at attention, his eyes shining brightly. He stood like a statue as a final vast cloud of dust caught up to him. It engulfed him like a giant wave, blowing past him and into the horseless girls' faces.

Karen coughed and blinked the dust from her eyes. June wiped her face. Kirsten sneezed and pulled her shirt over her nose before saying, "That's some cowgirl!"

CHAPTER 27

HORSES OF A DIFFERENT COLOR

It was the first Saturday of April and the last fox chase of the season for the Rolling Rock Hunt. Foxhunting or more accurately, fox chasing, began in the fall, continued through winter, and ended in early spring. This allowed the foxes to have their young uninterrupted during the warmer months. Unlike in Great Britain, American hunts rarely caught and killed the fox. It was all in the thrill of the chase. Furthermore, there wasn't an overabundance of fox. Maintaining a healthy population of fox was vital to the survival of the hunt stables.

This particular hunt boasted the best turnout all year, and the weather was exceptional. It was pleasantly warm, and bright sunshine illuminated a clear blue sky. It was the perfect day for three newcomers to join the hunt.

John had honored his invitation to June. She and Snowflake would be tested during the chase, galloping across rough terrain, mostly in the woods. They would jump some intermediate obstacles. It would be fun and challenging for both horse and rider. After complaining about hauling June and Snowflake to the hunt early on a Saturday, Ginny changed her tune. John knew of a family seeking a reliable pony for their youngest daughter. Ginny jumped at the chance to showcase Snowflake as a prospective pony hunter.

John had also invited Wendy. She would showcase her horse, Dorian. Howard, the huntsman, was looking for a new horse for the next season. His faithful old horse was due for retirement, and with Wendy's new goal of becoming a jockey on the horizon, she would have little time for Dorian. All involved felt that open gallops and cross-country riding might suit Dorian.

Wendy's preparations for the race track had gone well. She and Karen had galloped Dorian and Darter together in a small field. Both girls had relished in it. They had shown the ability to control and guide their horses at speed. John taught them how to manage a cross hold of the reins. The techniques used for lateral movement were different when using the cross as opposed to pull reining. Wendy and Karen demonstrated good general ability with these techniques. However, Wendy had the most potential to become a jockey because of her size and fearless attitude. She would have to practice her galloping skills further on a training farm. If she was successful there, she would progress to racetrack riding and then jockey training.

Ivy was simply grateful for the opportunity to ride Orchid at a leisurely pace behind and beside the hunt, take in the beautiful scenery and landscape of Ligonier, and watch the drama from afar. She and the other hill toppers sat atop their horses along the long shed row of Colonial Barn, waiting for the body of the hunt to move out.

The huntsman trotted away from the kennels, his red coat afire in the spring sun. His white Irish draft gelding pranced with arched neck and light, feathered feet. Forty hounds howled and bayed in excitement behind him, their tan and white bodies leaping with joy. John flanked the pack astride a stout bay, also sporting the feathered feet. John's head twitched back and forth like a hawk's as he analyzed and anticipated the hounds' every move. The occasional stray was sent back in place immediately by the crack of John's whip beside it and the whisk of feathered hooves. A petite blond woman controlled the other side aboard a brown and white pinto. The pinto's short but powerful limbs propelled him back and forth deftly, as he stopped, turned on a dime, and accelerated with his rider's slightest touch. White feathering decorated his legs in contrast to the neat and unmovable bob under the helmet of the huntsman's wife.

The field followed, comprising of horses and riders of all sizes, types, and ages. Front and center, just behind the whips, was Dorian. He almost cantered in place, his nostrils flaring as if blowing fire. He lunged and spurted away, coming quite close to a few of the slower hounds.

"Uh-oh," Ivy said aloud. "Here we go. John told Wendy never to pass the pack and to avoid the hounds at all costs."

A heavyset woman named Sue stood beside her on a chestnut quarter horse mare. "You better hope she doesn't run any of them over."

Near them was an elderly man atop a red and white pinto. The short, sturdy horse sported the same feathering as the others. "Now there, well done," he said in a pleasant tone. "She's got him now."

Wendy was strongly centered in a two-point position. Using a cross hold on the reins, she seesawed back and forth firmly. Dorian came back to her. She sent him forward again into a controlled canter.

Ivy strained to recognize Snowflake among the colorful array of horses. Normally, she stood out amidst the bays and chestnuts of Fox Hollow. Twenty horses cantered past. Some riders chatted casually across withers. Others were focused on the pack in front of them. Finally, the sea of painted horses was broken by a solid bay. Ivy studied his rider, noting the red curls peeking beneath his helmet. As he came closer, she saw the sprinkling of freckles across his nose. It was Carl from 4-H, aboard the Connemara pony, Hardy. Ivy noted his friendly smile, and then saw June's olive-colored jacket on Carl's far side. With Snowflake glued tightly to Hardy's side, June appeared to float in midair.

"Tallyho!" the huntsman shouted.

The group stormed off and banked a right along the tree line, eventually disappearing among the softly budding branches.

Sue squeezed her chestnut into a trot. "Okay, folks, we'll top the steeplechase course. We'll have a great view from there."

Orchid's running walk, unconventional as it was for fox chasing, carried Ivy effectively with the others. The gentle thud of hooves murmured amongst the fresh blades of grass. They followed the ascending outside tree line of a huge open field. At the top, they all halted at Sue's chosen vantage point. Looking down into the immediate field, Ivy could see several manicured paths twisting through taller grasses. They formed figure eights with various escape points that led up or down the hill and into other paths. Intermediate level jumps dotted the straightaways. Some were post and rail, others chicken coops, with a few roll tops. Ivy breathed the fresh air and raised her face to the sun's warmth. The entire valley stretched below, uninterrupted except for the occasional mammoth brick or stone barn. Vast open fields were divided by sections of woods. Post and rail fences contained horses the size of ants. It was like a scene from a movie set in Colonial times.

Twenty minutes passed with only songbirds breaking the silence. Then the hounds bayed in the distance. Orchid pricked her ears and stared off to the left. Ivy followed her gaze to the lower corner of the steeplechase course. A dirt road appeared to meet the woods leading into the course. The baying became louder. Orchid tossed her ebony mane. She flung her head and snorted at the sight of a red dot hurtling from the road into the steeplechase course. It was doglike, but exceptionally swift. It sailed headlong into the tall grass. Its fluffy tail flapped white underneath as it disappeared, as if waving good-bye.

Ivy and the elderly man chuckled as the lead hounds milled around the spot of the fox's disappearance. After a brief pause, the hounds rushed along the cleared path, away from the correct spot.

"Outsmarted again," Sue said, cracking a smile.

Ivy gaped in awe. The complete wave of hounds caught the leaders, and the entire pack sailed along the bottom of the field. Meeting a set of post and rails, some hounds leaped over the entire three-foot height with ease. Others slid between rails, some ducked underneath, while still others slipped past the jump completely. The entire mishmash was across in moments. The leaders hung a left and negotiated a roll top before disappearing down the hill and into the woods below.

On the other hand, the horses had only two choices: over or skip the jump altogether. A ghostly glimmer emanated from the huntsman's white steed as the sun highlighted his brilliant jump. John and the bay followed close behind. Howard's wife, called Caroline according to Sue, slid past the side of the jump, urging a stray hound back into the pack. Dorian came next, a tenuously controlled locomotive. Eying the jump, he pricked his ears and sped toward it. Wendy sat back and braced herself, releasing at just the right moment as Dorian took off. Although he took a long spot, the gray cleared the fence effortlessly. The rest of the hunt followed, some jumping and others going around. Finally, Snowflake cantered into view. She cruised along in tandem with Hardy, jumping the fence in unison. June never stopped talking, her head turned to Carl even in midair.

"Jeez, June, don't let a little thing like a jump distract you." Ivy said aloud.

Her companions laughed. "That is quite a nice pony your sister has," the elderly man said.

"If only she was ours. She may be going too well today." Ivy said.

At Fox Hollow, Karen was planning her own ride. She felt Babe was ready to be ridden outside the ring. A short jaunt up Country Club Road would do. Karen had been frustrated by ring work lately, and Babe felt it. The frustration was carrying over into Babe's performance, and both horse and rider had become stiff. They had worked so hard on achieving a lateral softness, yet they were no longer in sync. Karen was feeling tense about riding in general these days. Her attempts to train Saint had been ineffective, and she took her failure to heart. Inadvertently, she took it out on Babe by becoming rigid and short on patience. She hated to fail, especially at something she loved.

As she crossed the bridge into the back paddock, Karen's frustration mounted. *How can I be so weak?* She thought. Babe poked her beautiful face over the stall door. Approaching the filly, Karen told her, "Yes, just a short ride." She stroked Babe's face. "Afterwards, a matinee with Shane."

She noticed a flash of gold streaming past a small crack at the barn door. It was Mindy and Saint working together. Karen scooted into the ring to watch. Not only was he jogging along the rail, he looked relaxed and happy.

"What in the world did you do to that horse?" she asked her friend.

"I did some reading. I learned about this technique to use when they act up. You teach the horse to disengage their hind end. This is the motor of the horse. Controlling it gives you control over the horse. You just bring your hand across your chest toward your opposite shoulder." She started to demonstrate. "When he starts to give his head to the side, you squeeze with your inside leg. He'll step across with his hindquarters because he's slightly off balance from his head being turned. That way, you can stop whatever bad behavior you don't want. It breaks the behavior cycle. You regroup and start over again. Each time he misbehaves, you ask him to do this. Soon he gets tired of going in circles all the time. Going forward becomes more appealing. He learned it really quick. He's very smart." She patted Saint's muscular neck.

"Yeah, he's too smart. He really got my number."

As if the tension in Karen's voice set Saint off, he started to wheel around, toward the barn.

"Oh, no, you don't." Mindy laughed as she repositioned his head and applied leg pressure. Saint disengaged his hindquarters as quickly as he had wheeled. Mindy used her long, strong legs to drive him forward. Off they went, jogging quietly around the ring.

"Good job." Karen was sincerely happy for her friend. A wave of relief came over her, yet feelings of self-doubt still flooded her.

"Kirsten should be here soon," Mindy said. "You're riding out with us, right?"

Karen looked at her watch. It would be great to have company. Yet hearing Shane's voice in her head about being on time for the movie, she replied, "I'd love to wait, but Meadow's giving Shane and me a ride to the movies. I better go for a quick ride now."

"Yeah, Shane's been whining to Lance about you spending too much time with Babe," Mindy teased.

Karen quietly readied Babe. The filly stepped across the bridge without hesitation, and up North Fork Country Club Road they went. Things started out well. Like most racehorses, Babe was unbothered by the sights and sounds of the country road. Vehicles passed, and she didn't flinch. Flags fluttered in the wind. Her walk was quick, but she maintained a flat gait.

"Stay relaxed," Karen told herself and the filly.

They topped the dirt road in this manner. Karen looked at her watch.

"Oh shoot. I don't have time for the whole circle. I'll have to turn back."

As if someone turned a switch, Babe's demeanor changed with the direction. She jigged nervously, arching her neck and snorting.

"Whoa, easy."

Karen tried to steady Babe with the reins. Tension from her hands made the sensitive filly brace against her rider. Her head came up, and the bit was no longer effective. Like a row of falling dominoes, Karen was out of control. The jig became a fast trot and then a full gallop. They were plummeting headlong down the dirt road. The hill became steeper as they raced down. The terrible clamor of uncontrollable hoofbeats was deafening.

Oh my god, she'll break a leg! Karen thought in horror.

It was just like the runaway experiences with Legend and Dorian. The harder she pulled, the faster Babe went. Turning was out of the question. They'd roll off the bank. Karen was again paralyzed with fear. Her body braced as she held on for dear life. The wind whipped her eyes. She could barely keep them open.

What if a car comes? She thought this could be her last day on earth.

Babe sailed over the rolling terrain. Whether they were going up or downhill, she continued at full speed. There was no tiring her. Her breeding went back to the great English Triple Crown winner Hyperion, a king of stamina. They reached the bottom of the hill, hitting the hard macadam. Exhausted, Karen tried one more time to slow the filly. Again, her offer to stop was ignored. Ahead, Karen saw two figures approaching. Babe continued to eat up the ground as Karen recognized the movement patterns of the two riders' heads and the gold of Saint's coat.

"Look out!" she screamed. She knew Mindy and Kirsten wouldn't hear over the clatter of their own horses' hooves, but Saint and Dawn raised their heads, alerting their riders to the impending danger. Mindy and Kirsten snapped to attention.

Karen approached the meadow preceding Gage's property. Maybe if she steered into the grass, she could circle, or even jump off. She knew galloping straight toward the other horses would mean disaster for all of them. Somehow she guided Babe's furious energy off the road and onto the grass.

She heard Mindy shout, "Holy crap! She's out of control!"

From the corner of her eye, she saw her friend boot Saint into a gallop and head straight for Babe. Instead of balking, Saint put his head down and ears back. He charged his target like a warhorse, Dawn close behind.

"I'll try to cut her off from the front!" Mindy yelled into the wind. "You try to block her from the side!"

Babe's pace had slowed slightly when she saw the other horses. Exhausted, Karen mustered up one last once of energy. Guessing Mindy's intentions, she opened her left rein and guided Babe precariously close to the edge of the meadow. The bank dropped off steeply into a creek.

I hope this works!

Saint arrived with the intensity of a bullfighter. Babe's ears pricked as Saint's flattened. He surged in front of her, blocking her motion nostril to nostril. Both horses slid on their haunches to avoid collision. Mindy braced herself, staying seated. Karen was unable to do so, and flew forward on Babe's lathered neck. She slid off to the side, rolling onto the spring grass of the meadow and precariously close to the bank, barely avoiding being stepped on.

As Karen came off, Babe attempted to dart off to the right. Her momentum was stopped by Dawn. The bright, little Arabian stared Babe down, her expressive eyes blocking her as much as her body did. It was as if Dawn was saying, "Calm down, sister!"

Saint leaped ahead of Babe. Now the palomino and Arabian formed a ninety-degree angle, a barricade around Babe. Mindy grabbed Babe's reins and all equines became still.

Karen slowly got to her feet. With her knees shaking, she approached Saint. "I never thought I'd be so glad to see you. You're a regular cowpony!" She marveled at his apparent herding instinct as she stroked his noble head.

She turned to Dawn and rubbed her head too. "You guys saved my life."

"Don't mention it," Mindy said, gasping for breath.

With Mindy holding Babe and Saint blocking her, Karen remounted. Mindy kept a hold of Babe as she rode Saint one handed back to the barn. Slowly, Karen caught her breath. She couldn't fight with Babe if she wanted to. The other horses seemed to help the filly, but she still pranced nervously alongside Saint.

"I guess I just have to ride it out," Karen said.

"Don't worry. We've got you," Mindy said.

Saint knew he had done well. He held his head proudly as his ears flicked back and forth with the girls' voices. He stepped out at the walk, showing surprisingly good gaits. Karen giggled at the look of achievement in his eye. She was starting to think this horse had a future. She also wondered about his past.

Most palominos in America were quarter horses. Although this horse was solidly built, he didn't have the short, blocky muscles that were typical of quarter horses. His high crested neck met a good sloping shoulder. His back was strong and level, meeting with smooth hindquarters. As Saint continued to sail along at an extended walk, Karen continued to study him. Unintimidated by a large, charging horse, he had shown the fearlessness of a bullfighter. Karen thought about the Spanish horses she had read about. They were the first to come to America, and they had an extreme influence on American stock. Because of his color, she picked Lusitano or Barb horses as his ancestors. Andalusians were the most famous of the Spanish breeds. However, they were most commonly gray, with occasional bays and blacks. Since Saint had no registration papers, they would never know. He certainly had redeemed himself that day. Maybe he was entitled to the name Saint.

Previously, Karen had looked forward to an afternoon alone with Shane. Now, she felt bad that Mindy and Kirsten's ride had been cut short. She called Shane and told him to make it a triple date by inviting Lance and Gage to the movies.

"I won't change either," she told Mindy and Kirsten. "We'll all smell like horses."

"The boys will love that," Kirsten said. "I hope Gage agrees to ride with you guys. He's still high on the Satellite."

After Shane twisted Gage's arm, the six teens stuffed into Meadow's car. Goofing around with her friends and the action movie temporarily eased Karen's mind. However, her bad decision with Babe haunted her conscience. She hoped the filly was not ruined. That road had to be hard on her legs. More importantly, she had learned to run off. Karen would have her work cut out for her. She only hoped to fix the emotional damage both she and Babe had sustained.

Orchid sailed along the wide wooded path. The fresh smell of spring filled Ivy's nostrils. The last daffodils of the season brightened her way, and small white buds on the trees promised a lovely future. Sue urged her chestnut to canter alongside Orchid.

"Maybe you can come back when they're in full bloom."

In these lowlands, the hill toppers were forced to follow the hunt rather than ride ahead for a full view. Completely satisfied with this, Ivy relished her time on hallowed ground. The honor of mingling with western Pennsylvania's elite would be short-lived.

An intersection loomed ahead. The trees cleared enough to the left to reveal another large field. Ivy saw a sprinkling of parked cars along the tree line. Several people stood scattered about in small groups, chatting and drinking a dark red liquid. Standing along the field's edge, right beside the path and slightly apart from a beautiful auburn-haired woman in her forties, was a tall, muscular teenaged boy. In a salmon-colored polo shirt with a white cardigan tied around his neck, he looked over his shoulder stealthily. Quickly, he slurped a bit of the red liquid from a cup, and then covered it discreetly between his large hands. The sound of hoofbeats alerted him, and he looked up.

Freckles splashed over his nose. His wavy light brown hair arched back from a prominent brow. Practically on top of him, Ivy looked into his hazel eyes. A jolt of recognition straightened her spine, enough that Orchid scooted forward abruptly.

"Brighton?" she gasped.

Orchid's running walk swooshed them past Brighton in the blink of an eye, leaving Ivy with her head turned back and him watching her with a look of disbelief.

The terror of the night in the abandoned barn gripped her. Absently, she rubbed her throat as she had done while wearing the emerald necklace. It was tucked away in her dresser drawer, as it had been since that night. What could Brighton be doing here?

She relinquished her lead and finished the ride apprehensively. She looked behind every tree, bracing herself through every gate, sure Brighton had been sent by Alex to wrestle the necklace away. She was so withdrawn, that Sue asked if she was all right.

As she assured Sue she was fine, the hill toppers turned back into Colonial Barn's yard. The body of the hunt stood scattered about, some sitting atop their horses, others leading theirs as they greeted friends. Hounds scurried playfully among the polished boots. Having handed his steed off to a groom, Howard strode to the center, a whiskey bottle held high overhead. He motioned to all, and Caroline held a large tray of shot glasses as Howard poured celebratory drinks. Glasses were raised to a chorus of cheers.

With Sue and the elderly gentleman celebrating, Ivy looked around for June. She spotted Wendy leading Dorian along the shed row on a loose rein. Howard approached her, and he and Wendy had an apparently pleasant exchange. Ivy continued to scan the mass for June and her Appaloosa. Finally, she spotted June holding Snowflake under a tree across the yard. She nudged Orchid's sides to walk across to her sister. June smiled, and Ivy frowned suspiciously. June was never that happy to see her. She halted Orchid abruptly just as Carl walked over to June. Oblivious to Ivy's approach, Carl wrapped his arms around June and kissed her sweetly.

"Give me a break," Ivy said, but she couldn't help feeling happy for her sister.

Someone called her name, snapping the tension back in her spine. She looked to her left to see Brighton approaching cautiously. Barely able to look her in the eye, he took hold of Orchid's rein. The filly tossed her head and started sideways.

"Look, I don't have the necklace," Ivy said. "T-tell him if he wants it that bad, I'll give it back."

Brighton looked up at her dumbfounded. He turned Orchid's head to him and gave a gentle but firm pull of the rein. Orchid stood still, but her nostrils flared.

Ivy wanted to dismount and run. Her heart racing, she whispered, "Let go. Don't you see all these people around?"

"You've got it all wrong," he said. "It's fine. I don't want the necklace. Listen, I feel horrible about the whole thing. I never should've let Alex take it that far, much less be part of it." He paused. "When I saw you ride past, I knew this was my opportunity to apologize. I've wanted to for a while. I just didn't know how." He released the rein and looked at the ground.

Ivy took a deep breath as Orchid lowered her head and chewed the bit. She stared at the top of his well-groomed head. Bewildered by his humbleness, she said, "How can you be friends with someone like that?"

He chuckled and then sighed. "It's not so simple. He's my cousin." He finally looked at her sheepishly.

"Oh, great, you're in the same family. Someone else with claims to the Opie emeralds."

"No, no, we're second cousins. My mom's dad was the son of old man Opie's brother. Old man Opie owned the property where you found the necklace. Since Alex's mom was the old man's granddaughter, if anyone had any claim to the necklace, it would be her. My mom's claim would be far removed. Anyway, I don't think my aunt Jennifer is concerned about the necklace, and Alex has gone on to his newest blond obsession." He took a deep breath and smiled at her. "Of all the times for me to watch the hunt, you happen to be riding as a guest."

"How did you know that?" she asked, bristling again.

"It's okay. I just asked around about you. I know these people. My dad's over there. See the tobiano draft cross?"

Brighton pointed across the yard. A tall, thin man held a large black and white horse with a roached mane. His hair was slightly darker than his son's. He gulped down a final shot before shaking hands with his acquaintances and leading the tobiano to a smaller cluster of people close to where June and Carl stood.

"He's a member of the hunt?" Ivy asked. "Why didn't you tell me? It would have been something to talk about. It was awkward as hell at Alex's that time."

Brighton winced. "Sorry. I'm sorry. Let me make it up to you. We'll hang out at the mall or something. I'll buy you a cinnamon roll at Cinnabon."

"Well, maybe." Ivy couldn't help smiling. "I hope you're a better driver than Alex."

"Way better."

Brighton patted her knee and then looked across the yard again. His father was joined by the auburn-haired woman. Her yellow dress fluttered in the breeze, and she held the hand of a young girl with the same colored hair. Brighton's family started toward the tree where June still stood, holding Snowflake. Ginny walked from the opposite direction, greeting them with a handshake. There was a brief exchange, and the group turned to Snowflake. Even from this distance, Ivy swore her sister's face turned white.

"I may have more to apologize for," Brighton said. "Looks like the pony your sister was riding is the one my parents are buying for my little sister."

After the movie, Karen, Mindy, and Kirsten returned to the barn to complete their work. They saw Ginny pull up with her horse trailer, but she went straight to her house. June got out of the truck, but didn't unload Snowflake. She walked toward the barn with her head low, Ivy close behind.

Where was Snowflake? Karen wondered.

"Hey. How was the hunt?" she asked. She had no interest in chasing animals through the woods, although she knew it was an honor to ride with the hunt.

"Oh, the hunt was great," June said. As she got closer, Karen could see her makeup was smeared from tears. "Snowflake did everything right. We galloped up and down hills. We ran in front of horses and behind horses. Wherever we ended up, she was perfect. You should see the jumps. We went over big logs, post and rails, even chicken coops." Her voice lightened briefly as she described them. "But Snowflake was too good. A family bought her on the spot for their daughter. Her new home is at Rolling Rock."

"Oh, I'm sorry." Karen hugged June as Mindy and Kirsten patted her on the back. "You went from the greatest experience of your life to one of the saddest."

"Her day wasn't totally bad," Ivy said. "She got a kiss from Carl."

The girls gasped and crooned in delight. Giggling, Kirsten asked if Carl was a good kisser.

"He's a great kisser!" June smiled for a moment, but it faded and silence encompassed the girls. "You won't believe whose family bought Snowflake."

After she told them, groans of outrage spilled from the girls. Karen bit her lip. The thought of a rich brat taking Snowflake away was bad enough, but for it to be Brighton's sister was a real kick in the gut.

"First they want Ivy's necklace," she said. "Now they take Snowflake. Unbelievable jerks!"

"Oh, Brighton's not that bad," Ivy said. "He apologized. Alex is a bad influence on him. Brighton can't help that they're cousins."

"I don't know about that," Karen said.

"Ivy," Kirsten added, "he helped corner you in a barn where Alex was ready to rip that necklace right off you. Brighton did nothing to stop it. Who knows what would have happened if we hadn't showed up."

"Whatever, he was really sweet to me today. He had nothing to do with his dad buying Snowflake either. We should focus on June right now."

Karen cleared her throat. "Ivy's right. I'll help you with Blue Darter, June. Certainly you can handle him. At least you'll have something to ride."

June nodded, and then she broke other news regarding Wendy and Dorian. Howard was impressed with Dorian's strength and spirit. He bought him and planned to school him over the summer to lead the hunt.

"I hope she knows what she's doing," Karen said when she learned that Wendy had regrets about agreeing to sell Dorian. "Hopefully her riding career will take Dorian's place."

No matter how much trouble Babe gave her, Karen would always have a horse. She relished this silently, grateful that the filly could not be snatched from under her.

The day had been draining for all, including the horses. Not only did many of the horses show their true colors, but their careers had changed too.

CHAPTER 28

ON THE FAST TRACK TO CHANGE

It was an early June morning. An inviting nicker from a small pony welcomed four girls into the barn. Cookie had arrived a few weeks earlier, with Jessica returning to Fox Hollow for the second year. As anticipated, Grand did not return. Sharon's niece would be showing her that summer. June's small hope of using Grand for the show season fizzled. She would have to make the most out of another green horse.

June would get her project horse that day. She just had no idea what it would be like. She was not the only one for whom change loomed on the horizon. With Ginny and John as escorts, Wendy would travel to Waterford Park to begin her apprenticeship as a jockey. The trip gave Ginny the opportunity to buy another horse; June would have an ex-racehorse to ride.

Jess, Karen, Wendy, and June stood in the aisle way, talking quietly while waiting for Ginny.

"Well, I wish you the best," Karen said to Wendy. "You're one brave girl,"

"Yeah, you've always been tough," Jessica said. "I'll always remember the first time I met you at Karen's eighth birthday party. You were this bundle of energy, kicking up your heels and squealing like a horse. You've always been assertive. Keep that in mind if the guy jockeys give you a hard time."

"Thanks. I'm kind of scared. John said Todd would look out for me. He's the trainer I'm going to start with. That makes me feel a little better. I guess Todd is young, and he gets along with the jocks." She described another concern. "John said I'll have to get a lot stronger to ride races. I've practiced working horses at speed on a training farm, but he says it's nothing compared to pushing a horse and weaving through traffic in a race. I hope I can do it."

Her eyes were still red from a tearful good-bye with her father. He had been loving but tough with his words. He expected her to do whatever it took to be successful.

"You'll be fine," June said. "We'll check out the situation for you." She was going too, and she, Ginny, and John planned to approve the living quarters and help Wendy settle in.

Finally, Ginny arrived. "You two hold down the fort," she said to Karen and Jessica. "And Jess, be easy on Karen and her mare. You and Cookie may end up waiting for them to catch you."

Jessica smiled "I'll keep everyone in line."

There was some truth to that. Since Karen's runaway experience with Babe, Cookie had become her mascot. There wasn't enough space to put horses out together, but the small pony fit anywhere. If Babe started to fret, Karen put Cookie out with her. Now, Babe hated to have her out of sight. Jessica frequently grazed Cookie in the front lot while Karen rode Babe. The lot was close to the Somerset Pike, and there were many distractions around. However, as long as Cookie was there, Babe stayed quiet. Jessica also took advantage of Cookie's ability to drive. Riding in the cart was a lot easier on her backside than dealing with the pony's short stride. Also, the cart was advantageous for Cookie. Although Jessica was very light, Cookie was quite small. At longer distances, it was easier for the pony to pull rather than carry Jessica. The unlikely foursome had ventured out on short excursions away from the barn. Today, they planned on doing the Dam Road and Country Club Road loop.

The horse lovers finished briefing one another on their plans for the day. The girls hugged Wendy good-bye and wished June luck with Ginny's choice of horse. Karen felt gratified with June's progress as a rider, and Darter had been the ideal step up from ponies for her. He was kind and sensible, with just enough spirit. June required little guidance while adapting her riding style to Darter. Despite having to back off her strong driving leg, June must have learned through osmosis. She transitioned from pony rider to the subtle elegance of Thoroughbred riding without a hitch.

After the others left, Jessica and Karen prepared their steeds for exercise.

The wheels of Cookie's cart hit the gravel of Ginny's driveway. The crunching sound sent Babe scuttling up the driveway toward the road.

"Oh, great, here we go," Karen muttered.

"Don't let me see that horse come back without you!" Brad yelled from the window of the house trailer.

"Great, she left him behind?" Karen said as Jess caught up with her.

"He's actually been pretty nice since I came back. The other day when you went to Shane's and I was waiting to get picked up, Brad brought me a soda and his boom box to keep me company. Do you like that new Def Leppard song?"

"'Love Bites?'" Yes, it's cool." Karen hid her surprise regarding Jess's attitude toward Brad. "I just wish I knew what he says at the beginning."

The girls proceeded with the ride. To Karen's surprise, her fears about Babe running off were unfounded. As they hit the blacktop, Babe lowered her head and strode along at a relaxed walk. Karen took a deep breath and enjoyed her filly's ground-covering stride. Babe's delicate ears flicked back and forth as she listened for Cookie's cart behind her. She had learned that the noise from the wheels meant her buddy was not far behind. The little pony had to jog most of the way to keep up, and Jess made her walk to catch her breath every so often. If Babe got too far in front, she stopped, chewed on the bit, and looked behind her for Cookie. Often, she sighed deeply, as if to say, "Come on, little legs."

As the girls topped the hill and turned left to connect with Country Club Road, Karen became nervous. Soon they would pass the area where Babe had run off.

"I need something else to think about," she said.

"How about we sing 'Pour Some Sugar On Me,'" Jess suggested. "We know all the words to that."

The girls belted out the Def Leppard tune. Babe's ears again started to flick, this time more quickly. The strange and out of tune sounds held her attention. They passed the runaway spot and Babe's gait remained unchanged.

Before they knew it, the girls had recited several Def Leppard songs. The combination of badly sung rock and a pony with a cart calmed Babe's worst tendencies. The foursome arrived back at the barn without incident.

"Wow!" Karen said. "That was awesome. You deserve some good grazing for that." She patted Babe as she dismounted. The beautiful filly rubbed her head on Karen's arm. There wasn't one hair turned with sweat.

"You deserve a treat too," she told Cookie, approaching the pony with a sugar cube.

Cookie was more affected by the outing than Babe. Her small face was wet with sweat. However, her eyes remained bright, and she too rubbed her head on Karen.

"Poor thing, she has to work three times as hard to keep up," Jess said, joining the petting. "You do realize where the best hand grazing is, don't you?"

Karen nodded. "Right in front of the old house. Actually, things have quieted down lately. Maybe Lady Luminess is satisfied that we discovered Loyal Pal's fate and honored his memory."

"Do you believe Ivy's story, that Lady Luminess lead her to find that necklace?" Jess asked.

"If you'd asked me that when we first came here, I'd say you were nuts. But we've seen too much, and I've felt that compulsion too. It's like she wants to show us everything about this place, good and bad. Of course, it's really scary what happened to Ivy. Kirsten said Alex looked crazed, like he would do anything to have that necklace. I'd get rid of it if I was her, but on top of everything, now Ivy's made up with one of Alex's friends. Brighton was there that night and let Alex practically attack her. Now Ivy says Brighton's cool. I don't get it."

"Weird for sure," Jess said.

Indeed, the best grass grew in front of the porch, where the supernatural light had engulfed Mindy and Lance. Karen led Babe to the green patch, with Jess and Cookie behind. Despite her saying she wasn't scared, the hairs stood up on her nape. Tiny jolts of electricity buzzed up her spine. The buzz rushed to her head, and a slight, steady pressure pushed her entire body forward. Karen stared at the porch steps, fighting the urge to climb them, fighting the undeniable beckoning. She stumbled forward, barely catching herself and spooking Babe.

Jessica giggled nervously. "You're the only one who can trip over nothing."

Karen shook her head as if a fly had buzzed in her ear. As she stared vacantly at Jess, the tingling stopped. She turned slowly to Babe, who blew nervously from her nostrils. Karen blinked and focused on her cousin's confused face.

"Whew. Sorry, I lost myself for a minute."

After a few minutes, everyone relaxed. The horses ate grass at the end of their leads and the girls chatted about the newest movies. Karen and Shane had gone to see *The Naked Gun* during the winter, and when they had gone with Kirsten, Gage, Mindy, and Lance, saw *Die Hard*. Jess and Karen laughed about the slapstick comedy of the first movie. They agreed that *Die Hard* was a good movie, but it was violent. They continued comparing notes about the school year and Jessica's volleyball team. Her team had played Kirsten's during the season. She and Kirsten had been so busy making faces at each other from across the net; neither had played a good game. But it had been fun, and that was what mattered. There was no rivalry there.

As time passed, the girls were lulled by the peaceful sounds of birds chirping, butterflies seeking out flowers, and the warm touch of the sun. The horses shook off the occasional fly, but seemed to enjoy the day. Then Babe's head rose slowly. Her ears pricked toward the front door of the old house, she started to walk toward the porch. Karen thought about redirecting her, but somehow she couldn't. She was too curious. Babe's expression and body language eased Karen's fear. Her eyes were soft and inquisitive. Her walk was purposeful, not hurried or nervous. Cookie was unaffected. She kept her head down, concentrating on the grass.

Babe stopped at the bottom of the porch steps. She craned her neck forward, eyes focused in front, looking into the foyer through the door. The door was made completely of glass, leaving a clear line of sight to the inside. The soft sunlight gave the area a warm, homey look, completely different from the glaring, intrusive light they had seen two Octobers ago. The beige walls and white countertop actually looked inviting. Babe's nostrils fluttered and she blew softly. She was curious about something just inside the doorway. Strange orbs of yellow light danced around the room. Some started at the ceiling and fell slowly to the floor. Others bounced lightly from the floor to the height of the counter, then down again. They repeated this in rhythm. Babe and Karen stared at them. Karen was mystified. Babe still showed no signs of fear, but Karen could hardly resist the urge to run. She looked around the house, searching for an explanation. There was no breeze or movement outside the house. No shadows reflected into the foyer. There was nothing to cause the light show. Finally, she managed to motion for Jess to come over.

Dragging Cookie from her grazing, Jess walked over to Karen and took in the sight, her mouth agape. The girls looked at each other in astonishment. Even Cookie took notice now, staring trancelike at the house.

The orbs continued with their lively dance for minutes. The girls were so absorbed they never noticed Brad approaching.

"What in the world is that?" he said. He jumped onto the porch, pointing inside.

The several small orbs joined together one by one, until there was only one ball of light the size of a basketball. Karen tensed and tried to run away, but her legs wouldn't respond. The orb started its gentle bouncing again, but this time it bounced toward them. The teens stood transfixed, although the horses remained unaffected, watching calmly. The orb bounced through the glass door as if it wasn't there. It continued toward them, bouncing about five feet up and coming to earth slowly, like a balloon being hit up into the air. Finally, it took one last jump. It left the porch and slowed its flight even more. It hovered over Babe's head. Slowly it descended, landing on her forehead. It illuminated her brown face and then disappeared. Babe tossed her head casually, as if waking from a nap. She yawned and then lowered her head, She licked and chewed her lips, a sign of relaxation and endorphin release in horses.

"To answer your question, Brad," Jess said, "I don't know what that was," Cookie had pulled herself to the end of the lead and was grazing at the bottom of the steps.

"I was coming to scare you," he said, "but that stopped me in my tracks. It sure turned the tables on me."

"Good," Jess said. "We would have killed you if you had scared us."

Karen spoke as if she hadn't heard either of them. "Hold her." Robotically, she placed Babe's lead in Jessica's hand. She glided up the stairs, across the porch, and into the old house.

"What? Karen, come back!" Jess flung her hands in the air helplessly, a horse's lead in each. She glared at Brad, whose chest heaved under his white T-shirt with his quickened breathing. "Don't just stand there. Go after her!"

Inside, she found the reinvigorated small light orbs clustering into a gentle wave. Rolling like a calm sea, they led Karen through the foyer and across the living room to the east wall and the old fireplace. The orbs whirled like a cyclone to the center of the mantel piece, where they hovered and blinked intermittently. Karen crept closer, her focus on the orbs. They slowly dissipated the closer she got, until only one remained at a particular spot of the wall.

Just above the mantel, the plaster was broken, revealing the brick of the outer wall and a shallow hole behind the mantel. Karen strained on tiptoes, reaching inside the hole. Her fingertips scraped across the top of a smooth wooden box. She grasped the edge of the mantel with her left hand, trying to steady herself. She tried to grab the box, grunting in disgust as her fingers slipped uselessly across the top.

"Here, let me help."

Karen turned around in surprise. Brad stood behind her, and she realized he was now several inches taller than she. She stepped aside willingly, and he easily pulled the small box from its hiding place. He handed the box to her.

Though obviously quite old, the box was made of fine mahogany. An intricate tulip was etched into its cover, and a heavy brass clasp sealed it shut. Expecting it to be locked, Karen fumbled with the clasp. It slid open with surprising ease. Holding her breath, she lifted the lid. Beside her, Brad watched nervously.

The box opened with a tiny creak, releasing a loud whoosh of wind. It blew into Karen's face, lifting her hair and spraying the dust from the neglected floor into her nose. She started, and Brad took her shoulders.

"Okay, enough," he said. "Let's get out of here."

The wind whirled around them, rushing like a dust devil, yet never touching them. Karen buried her nose under her T-shirt while holding the box open with just a finger. After choking back the dust, Brad took one hand from her shoulder and covered his face too. The torrent slowed a bit. He nudged Karen with his other hand, and the two rushed through the wind toward the door. Karen could hear Jess calling. "Karen, come out now! What is that noise?"

Karen and Brad jogged down the porch steps and into the fresh, sunlit yard. Babe and Cookie grazed peacefully. Songbirds continued their calls. Jessica still held the two lead ropes, looking anxious.

"What were you doing in there? It sounded like a whirlwind. Brad, you were supposed to get her out of there!"

"It's okay," Karen said. "He tried. I had to find this."

She extended her arms to her cousin, the box perched like a baby bird in her hands. Her one forefinger protected its contents from another dive into darkness.

Brad shook his head as she moved to open the lid farther. "Hey, I don't know if that's the best idea. I don't need another wind storm."

Karen flung open the lid.

"Fine," Brad said. "Don't mind me, I'm just invisible here." He raised his hand and waved his fingers.

The girls stared at a pile of neatly folded papers inside the box. With the air still, even Brad looked inside. Karen took the top paper and handed Brad the box. It was a typewritten letter, and she read it aloud.

Dear Mr. Bjerne La Cour,

> I understand through a mutual friend, Neb Hoyle, that you are close to producing a megawatt wind turbine capable of supplying a substantial amount of power. Neb and I share a mutual interest in bringing wind power to Pennsylvania, and eventually the entire United States. With his skill in engineering and my artistic hand, we have developed some diagrams upon which we plan to develop our own wind turbines. May I present the diagrams to you for review? Neb

and I wish to compare notes between our design and what you have succeeded with in Denmark. Also for consideration is a joint venture between the three of us. The ravages of fossil fuels and waste from the steel industry have scarred our landscape and polluted our rivers. Clean energy production is the only hope for conserving our future.

Sincerely,

Deryn Opie

"A wind turbine," Karen said. "Is that like those old-fashioned windmills you see on TV?"

Brad shrugged. "Who knows. What kind of funny name is Deryn? Weird."

"She sure had some new ideas," Jess said. "Wind as a power source?" Her brow furrowed in confusion. "What else is in there?"

Karen carefully refolded the letter and placed it underneath the remaining papers. She unfolded three more documents, which revealed drawings of tall windmills with various shapes and sizes of blades. Some were squared off at the ends, others pointed. Some had three blades, others five. The sketches contained various dimensions for the turbines, the largest being three-hundred feet tall with blades one hundred and fifty feet long.

"Wow, she really wanted to make a difference," Karen said. "This makes me believe even more that she and her father were at odds. Can you imagine the daughter of a steel tycoon pushing for the development of clean energy? I wonder if this letter and the sketches ever made it to that guy in Denmark. Did she ever get this program off the ground?"

The three teens stood and stared at each other for a moment. Karen took a deep breath, filling her lungs with the fresh air. She looked into the blue sky and noted the lush green leaves of the surrounding trees. Babe and Cookie stood fetlock deep in grass.

"Well, Lady Luminess," she said, "we finally know your name."

"Really? What is it?"

Karen whipped around to see Ivy coming toward them. Her ash-blond bangs challenged the sky, with the sides of her hair teased outward. She wore a white collared shirt that tapered at her waist and ended in triangular tails in the back. A stone-washed jean skirt hovered several inches above her knee, and new white flats completed her outfit.

"Hey, where're you going all dressed up?" Karen asked, hoping to divert her.

"I have a date. Now what were you saying about Lady Luminess?"

Jessica bit her lip and Karen cringed as Brad took the box and its entire contents to Ivy. He explained everything with excitement, including the wind storm inside the old house.

Ivy stared blankly at Brad. After a few seconds she said, "Deryn? What kind of name is that? I expected her to be called Natasha or something mysterious like that."

"I know. I don't get it," Brad said.

"Don't worry, guys," Karen said. "I'm sure Shane can look it up and tell me." She cleared her throat. "So anyway, Ivy, who's your date?"

"Oh, just Brighton. We're gonna cruise the mall." Ivy twirled her hair.

"You're kidding me," Brad said. "You're hanging out with that loser? That rich punk can stay in Westmont!"

"You're lucky your sister is in West Virginia," Jess said. "She'd kill you for going out with him."

"Easy, guys," Karen said. "Maybe he's not so bad. At least Ivy has something better to do than us. Look at us, we're crawling around an abandoned house looking for dusty old diagrams."

A dark gray Range Rover slowed at the top the driveway, coming from North Fork Country Club Road. It paused a moment and then bounced down the uneven pavement, coming to a stop beside the group. A tinted window rolled down with the low, smooth sound of a motor. Karen happened to be nearest the car, so she was greeted first.

"Karen, what's up?" Brighton smiled, sending the freckles jumping about his face. He reached out the open window to lightly touch her arm.

She glared at him but the smile never left his face.

"How's Snowflake doing for your sister?" she asked.

"She's cool. Audrey really likes her, spends all her time at the barn. What have you been up to?" He continued to stare at, holding her gaze like a hypnotist.

Karen cleared her throat uncomfortably. "Umm, nothing, just riding."

"Hey, what about me?" Ivy bounded to the window.

Brighton finally looked away from Karen. "Oh, hey, you ready to go?"

Ivy scurried in front of the vehicle and hopped into the passenger seat. She waved good-bye to Karen and the others enthusiastically. The Range Rover pulled away slowly, pausing in front of the fountain. Karen saw Brighton looking the old house over, pointing to its third floors. Ivy leaned across the seat and pointed as well, and the two stayed there for a minute, talking.

"All those jocks are creeps," Brad said when they finally drove away. "What a weirdo."

Karen lay on the floor of Shane's bedroom, her feet propped against the wall. It felt good to stretch her back after a long day of riding, barn work, and mystery solving. She studied her thighs flexing underneath her jean cutoffs, wondering if they looked fat. Shane sat at his desk, poring over a book on Welsh history. The mahogany box sat next to the book.

"Bird," he said. "*Deryn* is Welsh for bird."

"That works," Karen said.

CHAPTER 29

A Midsummer's Dip

The July sun rose over the hill at J. T. Acres. It was the morning of their monthly hunter schooling show. June and Karen were there with two prime prospects. Blue Darter had made the switch from racing to jumping without a hitch. He was much less complicated than Babe; and although this was disconcerting to Karen, she was proud to unload the noble white horse from the trailer. She would pretend he was hers that day. June also held her head high as she unloaded her mount. Bailey was even more agreeable to a career change than Darter. The red bay gelding had left Waterford Park only six weeks earlier. June had said good-bye to Wendy that day and hello to the most cooperative and genuine horse she had ever ridden.

Both June and Karen were excited about the show. Wendy had been right about the variety of classes. It was the perfect situation for green horses and riders.

Ginny separated from the others after unloading. Groggy and grumpy from a night out, she clutched a cup of coffee under her chin. Karen and June couldn't help giggling as she plopped in front of a tree, rested her head against it, and pulled her shades over her eyes. Her deep breathing suggested she was out for the count.

The girls' demands for an early arrival had compounded Ginny's woes. They wanted to take full advantage of the schooling time before the show. Darter would be competing in the special hunter division. Each division included two jumping classes, and for Darter, the fences would be set at two feet three inches over a variety of jumps. Karen knew the height was insignificant to Darter, but putting a small course together at this stage of his training would be a challenge. In the hunter classes, a horse was judged on rhythm. His pace should stay steady, with no speeding up or slowing down. It was the rider's job to make the subtle adjustments in pace that brought the horse to a good spot to jump from. Getting too close to a fence could cause a horse to chip in, which could make for an awkward bunny hop that interrupted the overall smoothness of the round. Taking off from a long spot meant the horse was too far away and usually was a sign of rushing. She would have to ride consistently to give Darter a good experience and prevent bad habits. In addition, Darter had not seen the fancy brick patterned walls, chicken coops, and the announcer's stand. She would have to school him over these jumps before the class. On the other hand, Karen felt confident about the flat class. After jumping, Darter would have to be calm and submissive to show off his best gaits.

Bailey would compete in the long stirrup division. This included jumping two courses over plain white rails at two feet. Of course, a flat class followed. Because of Bailey's inexperience, this was a perfect spot for him to build confidence. June's class would be held in the small lower ring; Karen's would take place in the larger top ring.

Darter's warm-up went fairly well. After some flat work, Karen walked him around each jump so he could examine them. At the same time, she had to watch for traffic. Warm ups at these shows were a matter of controlled chaos, with everyone wanting to jump every fence several times. One young rider failed to call out her jumping line and almost barreled into Darter's rump. He scuttled away, tucking his hind end beneath him and propelling Karen backward. Luckily, he settled quickly. Karen moved him to the outside of the next line, realizing she'd need to look out for others and herself.

Traffic problems were not the only issue in the schooling ring. Instructors were bellowing commands, trying to be heard amidst the mayhem. Karen noted that Sonya had a few new students. She barely nodded at Karen as she rode by. Rumor had it, Sonya was angry about Wendy leaving for the track. She was Sonya's best pupil. She needed Wendy to develop her reputation as an instructor. Karen couldn't worry about it.

She progressed to trotting Darter over each fence. He hesitated a few times, but when she closed her leg, he hopped over all of them. Next, she cantered to all the fences. Darter became slightly fast and strung out between fences. He jumped from a few long spots. Karen practiced some half halts between jumps. She stopped the session after the horse relaxed, realizing that drilling him would only make him nervous. She rode down to the lower ring to watch June.

Bailey showcased his amazing good nature as he trotted over cross rails. It appeared things were going smoothly, but as they headed down the long side in front of the announcer's booth, Bailey shied. Darter had been unbothered by the announcer's booth. He was older and had seen a little of everything in his career. Bailey had raced only a few times, and it was his laid-back nature that hurt him on the track. That same nature only accentuated his potential as a show horse. The battle was half won due to his good temperament. However, the show-ring environment was foreign to the four-year-old horse.

Karen rode Darter into the ring and instructed June to walk on the outside rail. She kept Darter just to the inside of Bailey. As they approached the announcer's booth, Karen put Darter into a long, low frame. On the outside, Bailey gawked at the booth, but the presence of the older gelding prevented him from ducking to the inside. They made a few laps in each direction. Karen stopped the group in front of the announcer's booth and told June just to let Bailey stand a few minutes.

Bailey seemed to relax about the booth. The show officials gave the ten-minute warning. Thankfully, Ginny had woken up long enough to hold Darter while Karen set up some easy jumps for June to practice over.

"You might be better off trotting the jumps," she said to June. "You'll have more control, and if you make it look smooth, you'll place over someone who canters and has a rough round. This is a schooling show for a reason."

Reluctantly, June agreed. The girls had to groom their horses and change into their show clothing before their classes. It would be a busy day of hurry up and wait.

Relief from some of the duties came in a 1982 Chevrolet Malibu. The blue sedan had barely stopped beside the horse trailer when its rear doors were flung open. Jessica bounded out, followed by Mindy and Kirsten. Karen waved to her uncle Tom. He waved back with a look of relief. He wasted no time driving away.

"Your dad looks happy to drop you guys off," Karen said to her cousin.

"We sang for forty-five minutes straight!" Jess said.

"We're trying to perfect our rendition of 'Youth Gone Wild,'" Kirsten said.

Karen giggled. "Something tells me Skid Row won't fire Sebastian Bach and hire you."

"Oh, but what I wouldn't do to meet Sebastian." Mindy wiped her brow dramatically.

"He is so cute," Karen agreed. "It makes me mad when guys have better hair than me, though."

Their chatter and giggles subsided as the girls shined boots and polished horses. Good old-fashioned showmanship came into play when the competition was tough. They had learned in 4-H how to turn out horse and rider. Karen emerged from the tiny dressing room in her gray pin-striped show coat, gray breeches, and white shirt. Mindy helped place her collar and gold pin properly at her throat. Kirsten did the same for June.

"I'm glad we made up," June said, "especially since you have a pin at my throat."

The girls giggled, but soon an awkward silence crept around them. Kirsten broke it by saying she didn't know if Gage was worth getting upset over.

"Sorry," June said. "I didn't mean to bring him up."

"Don't worry about it. Anyway, your olive coat and beige breeches will look good against Bailey's red hair."

Jess helped both riders step into their snug boots, and then June and Karen stood outside the trailer, crops in hand and ready to go.

"Oh, just one thing." Mindy pulled out a pink blush from her purse and swept both riders' cheekbones. She freshened their mascara and offered a light pink lipstick.

"Not too much," Ginny interjected from behind. "Subtle is the key. This isn't date night. Karen, you better get up there. Looks like your class will run before June's."

Ginny gave Karen a leg up onto the snowy white gelding. Jessica and Kirsten went to the upper ring with Darter. Mindy planned to go between rings and help as needed. For now, she'd stay with June.

Karen found a space to the left of the gate to wait with Darter and her friends. She hoped it wouldn't be long, as the July sun continued to rise and burn off the morning dew. Already she felt the heat collecting on her back. Whose bright idea was it to wear this attire in the summer? The waiting got to her and her nerves kicked in. She needed something to take her mind off it.

"So, everyone's coming to Shane's pool party after we get back, right?" she asked.

"Yeah. I'm gonna need cooling off." Jess wiped some perspiration from her brow.

"I hope we're invited," a barely familiar male voice said from behind them.

Karen turned to see Brighton and Ivy walking toward them. They were hand in hand, both in khaki shorts and polo shirts, hers pale yellow and his mustard. Most noticeably, emeralds and diamonds glistened against Ivy's summer tan. The necklace had come out again.

"Hey, Ivy," Karen said in surprise. "You made it."

"We wanted to support you and June," Brighton said. Ivy merely smiled.

Kirsten's face reddened, and she scowled at Brighton. Karen raised an eyebrow at her, and she got the hint. She distanced herself from the new couple, moving to the rail to watch the horse show.

With Jess left holding Darter's head and tapping her toe nervously, Karen searched for something to say.

"So, you never answered my question," Brighton said. "Can we come to your pool party?"

Karen looked from his expectant face to Kirsten's stiff back.

"Karen!" Ivy said in an insistent whisper. Her expression was that of a child pleading to go play outside.

"Umm, okay, sure. You guys can come." Karen regretted the words as soon as they tumbled from her mouth.

"Great," Brighton said. "You're looking good, by the way."

He patted her knee, and she frowned down at him. His warm, friendly smile diffused her annoyance. Along with an extra splattering of freckles from the summer sun, he looked completely innocent.

How much of a threat could a kid like this be? Him in his mustard polo shirt. She fought the urge to acknowledge that he actually pulled the color off well, and that she too freckled more in the summer.

Ivy dragged Brighton away, heading for a picnic table on higher ground. "Let's watch from up there. We'll see everything."

Karen felt as if a boulder had rolled off her back. "Kirsten, you're coming to the pool party, right?"

Kirsten rejoined the group. "I'll come. There's nothing better to do. And I don't know what to make of Gage. He better straighten up. We went to play pool last week. In the beginning, he was all lovey-dovey and affectionate. We got a few games in. Of course, I was bad, so he won every time. I didn't care, though. Then some guys he knows came in and wanted to play against us. He started cutting up with them and ignoring me. It was like I wasn't there. To make things worse, I lost the game! He left in a hurry and acted mad. He hardly said a word to me on the way home. He didn't even hug me good-bye, much less kiss me. I've had it with him!"

"Oh, I'm sorry," Karen said. "What a jerk. Who cares if you lose a pool game? Maybe you should ditch him. You deserve better."

Jess nodded in agreement.

The conversation eased the wait. When the announcer called Karen's number, she took Darter into the ring for the first jumping class. He paused and raised his head, scanning the ring, ears pricked toward the obstacles. Karen felt some tension in his back and decided she should practice what she preached and trot the first fence.

This proved to be a good strategy. Darter landed in a relaxed canter and she pointed him toward the next rail fence. He took that easily. She continued around the other outside line, making only small half halts to control his speed. He was doing well for his first class. She jumped the brick patterned wall. He took it a little high, and she became slightly off balance. She steadied herself, thinking that the jumps came up quickly.

The coop came next. Darter's head came up and his pace quickened. He started to drift left. She steadied him with her left leg and right rein.

He was going faster now. She braced herself for a long spot. He took the jump in a galloping stride, landing on the wrong lead to take the next line. She brought him back to a trot, preventing his rushing. Cantering on the wrong lead around the turn would throw him off balance. She trotted into the last line, and Darter came back nicely. Again, he landed in a relaxed canter and jumped the last fence well.

"Good boy." She rubbed his neck while leaving the ring. She wasn't so pleased when she saw Ginny at the gate. She would have seen that rather rough round.

Surprisingly, Ginny greeted her pleasantly. "That was a good warm up. Now try to let him go at his own pace. He's seen them now and shouldn't be afraid. You just sit back and let him jump up to you. Don't get ahead of the motion. When you come down the diagonal line, open your new inside rein while you're in the air. This will help him get the right lead."

Karen's butterflies eased. She followed Ginny's advice for the second round and the horse jumped everything well. It felt fast to Karen, but his pace was consistent. A judge would rather see consistency than abrupt changes in pace. Darter would make a nice horse.

The end result was rewarding. Darter placed fourth in the first class, and second in the later jumping class. Karen was a more confident rider on the flat and pulled off the blue ribbon. The duo finished second in the division overall.

Coming down the hill, Karen, Jess, and Kirsten caught the end of June's first jumping class. Ginny had hurried down to see her and was standing with Mindy outside the ring. June started trotting as they had planned. Bailey took a slight look at the announcer's booth, but an open rein and leg pressure kept him moving forward.

"Look up!" Ginny yelled to June.

June focused between Bailey's ears and guided him to the next line. He hopped the first and continued around at a canter. June went with her instinct and allowed him to canter the rest of the course.

When they were done, Karen congratulated June.

June also had a good day. She finished fifth, third, and second in her classes. It was a respectable showing for a horse just off the track.

Ivy approached her sister with a hug. "Good job," she said. Brighton trailed behind, hands in his pockets. He didn't look June in the eye, but mumbled congratulations.

June's eyes narrowed. She grabbed Brighton's forearm, forcing him to look at her. "Hurt my sister and a whole bunch of hurt is coming your way."

"Yes, ma'am," Brighton bowed. He put his arm around Ivy and started toward his Range Rover. "See you all at the pool."

As Brighton drove away, Karen and Mindy turned to June. "What did you do with your eyes?" Karen asked. "They were gleaming like a tiger's when you spoke to him!"

"Yeah, you scared me," Mindy said. "He must be quaking in his shoes!"

Stunned, June replied, "I don't know. I just wanted to make a point."

"What did I miss?" Ginny asked. "What a ride that kid has! How did Ivy land that one?"

"You don't want to know," Kirsten said.

In an improved mood, Ginny bought the girls' lunch. She spouted rare compliments to Karen and June about jobs well done with the former racehorses. Jessica took notes as the group discussed their upcoming sponsored 4-H show. Mindy volunteered to run the pony rides fundraiser that year. Kirsten would run the car wash. Finally, they loaded the horses, five girls squeezed into the Ramcharger, and Ginny headed east to Fox Hollow.

"Man, I feel gross after a day at the horse show," Karen said as she and the other girls arrived at Shane's.

"Tell me about it," June said. "We're going to the right place to cool off, though."

"Always nice to see the boys when we're at our best," Mindy joked.

Kirsten scowled. "I don't know if my boy is even here."

"You'll have a good time without him," Jess said.

Shane greeted the girls as they walked onto the deck. "It's about time. I never thought you'd never get here."

"Well, here I am. Give me a big hug!" Despite changing into a red and white striped bikini with tassels at each hip, Karen was clearly sweaty. She lunged at Shane, eager to add to his complaints.

"Oh, no, get washed off first!" He deflected her charge and sent her flying into the pool.

With that, Karen was the chosen prey. As she came up and tried to climb out, Brad rushed her, pushing her back into the pool with a splash.

"Thanks, you creep!"

Karen hopped out as Brad laughed. She grabbed his arm and spun him toward the pool. Teetering at the pool's edge, Brad lost his balance. Karen's plan worked, but he had a grip on her too. She plummeted in with him for a third time.

Shane gave her his hand and helped her out. "Okay, you better give it up."

"Hey, what about me?" Brad asked.

"You're not pretty enough," Shane said.

The atmosphere settled. Karen and Shane sat by Jess at the edge of the pool, dangling their feet in the water and relaxing.

"I don't know when Brad will grow up," Karen said, but then she thought about Brad's concern for her in the old house and his sticking by her through the turbulent dust storm. Her urge to bash him was quelled as she watched him start a splash battle with June.

"He doesn't pick on me anymore," Jessica said. Looking lean in her red and black one piece, she closed her eyes and turned her face to the sun. Her rich brown hair fell in ringlets against her shoulders, the result of a spiral perm. The summer sun had heightened her natural golden streaks.

Suddenly, her ringlets whooshed up in a torrent. She flung her arms upward in surprise and was underneath the water in a heartbeat. Brad came to the surface first, laughing hard. Jess came up after, exhaling like a bellows.

"You jerk!" She leaped at Brad, grasping his shoulders and wrestling him underwater.

"See, Jess?" Karen yelled over the splashing. "Just when you trust him, he strikes!"

"Don't turn your back on him," Kirsten called. She sat across the pool with Mindy and Lance. There was no sign of Gage.

Suddenly, a flurry erupted beside her. "Whirlpool!" Lance and Mindy shouted, jumping into the pool hand in hand.

The group followed their lead. They waded furiously along the outside edge, making several revolutions. Soon a circular tide formed from the energy. The teens lay on their backs and rode the tide with arms outstretched.

As the current died, Kirsten stood up. She scanned the pool and deck for Gage. Karen, Shane, Mindy, Lance, and Jess were standing in the middle of the pool talking. June and Brad were nowhere to be seen. A silent rage started to boil inside her. Everyone else had someone to buddy up with. Where was Gage and why was he blowing her off? Shane had invited him, after all. She struggled to keep her anger under control. Trying to make the most of it, she joined the others in the middle of the pool.

The heat of the day dissipated with the lowering sun. The girls rubbed their chilly arms and talked about getting out. Kirsten was still hoping Gage would show up. Suddenly, a pair of hands yanked at her calves under the water. It startled her, but it had to be Gage. At least he was playing jokes on her. It was a start. As she screamed and turned to face him, she was disappointed to see the mischievous Brad.

"Will you stop!" she snapped.

The girls convinced the guys to leave the pool. They sat around a picnic table, the girls donning T-shirts as the sun sank lower. As they chatted Kirsten noticed a shadow creeping toward the deck steps. She saw June's face, barely illuminated by the porch light. June put a finger to her lips, gesturing for Kirsten to be quiet. Brad tiptoed behind her, a devilish expression on his face.

Flashes of light came from the steps, shining against the wall in front of Karen. Both she and Jess saw them. The cousins looked at each other, and they both screamed.

"There're back!" Brad jumped down from the steps, whipping a flashlight beam back and forth across the wall.

"The ghostly lights are coming to get you!" June shouted as she zigzagged her own flashlight across the other teens.

Everyone except Karen and Jess were laughing. Shane was in stitches, hanging onto Karen's shoulders, trying to stay upright. Brad ran up to him and gave him a high five.

"That's the last time I tell you guys about the ghost!" Karen said, and pushed Shane over. She targeted Brad next, chasing him around the pool.

The chase was interrupted by the sound of the deck creaking under someone else's weight. "What did I miss?"

Kirsten turned to see Gage.

"Hey, man," Shane said, getting up. "Where you been? We're having a blast scaring Karen and Jess."

"Huh," Gage grunted. "Easy pickings."

He sauntered toward the picnic table. Kirsten got up and approached him with outstretched arms. He brushed past her and sat beside Lance.

Kirsten turned her back to the group, biting her lip and choking back tears.

Brad stepped back onto the deck. The look of joyous mischievousness was replaced by annoyance. Scowling, he plopped beside Jessica as two other latecomers arrived.

"Hey, everyone, sorry we're late. Hope we didn't miss everything."

Brighton spoke for him and Ivy. Kirsten wondered if he had let Ivy's hand go once that day.

With apparent reluctance, Shane approached Ivy and Brighton, hand barely extended.

"Shane?" Brighton said. "Hey nice to meet you. I've heard a lot about you. You grew up with this one?" He shook Shane's hand as he nodded toward Ivy.

"Yep, sure did. She's something else," Shane said through clenched teeth.

Gage was staring at Brighton in disbelief. Pounding his fist on the table, he said something to Lance. Lance grunted something in reply.

Karen nudged June's arm, and the two walked over to Brighton and Ivy. As they talked politely, Shane lit the grill and gathered some hot dogs. Kirsten took a deep breath and headed toward Gage's side of the bench.

She sat beside him. "What's going on? Why didn't you call me back?"

Gage broke from glaring at Brighton to glaring at Kirsten. "I have things to do, Kirsten. You know I sold the Satellite and I'm working on the new Charger. Plus, my dad is training to drive again. He's teaching me how to race too. Any more questions?"

"You're the most ignorant jerk I've ever met!" Kirsten yelled.

Gage stood. "I can't be here right now." He stormed off, knocking shoulders with Brighton on the way out.

Shane tried to stop him, but Gage continued down the steps. A motorcycle revved to life and roared away.

Mindy walked over to Kirsten, but Kirsten turned away. The others were all in cozy groups. Ivy, Brighton, and Karen had separated from the others and were on the other side of the pool. Jessica was heading in their direction. June skipped merrily back to the table and got a smile from Brad. A feeling of isolation tore at Kirsten. She rushed to the steps and an escape.

"Hey, hey, hey." Shane moved in front of her, stopping her. "Come on, Kirsten. Stay with us. Gage is being a total jerk, but it's not you." Turning her around, he sat her beside the grill. "He's under a lot of pressure."

On the other side of the pool, Karen stiffened as Brighton stroked her cheek. Despite the humid summer evening and her long T-shirt, a chill crept over her. Ivy stiffened beside him, but her painted smile remained intact.

"So you see," Brighton said in a low voice, "those diagrams are part of my family history. I'd really love to have them."

Karen sensed Jessica at her side, but she couldn't look at her. Unsure of what Brighton was capable of, she didn't want her cousin involved. Yet a sense of duty came over her. Clearly those wind turbine diagrams had been important to Deryn Opie, and she had important plans based on the diagrams. Moreover, Karen was convinced Deryn had paid for them with her life.

Across the pool, conversations buzzed between intermittent fits of laughter. Karen yearned to dive in and swim to the pack's safety. Hesitant to ruin the night, she held her ground.

"I understand," she said, "but there's something more to the story, and I want to know what. Give me a little time."

Brighton laughed. "There's nothing to the story except that she was thinking ahead of her time. I think my family deserves to celebrate that. Now, are you going to give me what is rightfully mine?"

"Actually, Ginny owns the property now. So technically, they're hers."

"Yes, but Ginny doesn't have the diagrams, does she?"

"Not exactly, but they're in a safe place." Karen was shaking now. She looked to Ivy, who looked back with a blank stare.

"Karen, you will give me those diagrams!" Brighton grabbed her upper arm, squeezing tightly.

A rush blew past Karen. Shane barreled into Brighton, pushing him against the deck's outer railing. "Don't ever touch my girlfriend!"

Shane braced a flexed elbow against the bigger boy's throat, barely keeping the football player contained. Ivy tried to push Shane off Brighton.

"Come on, Shane. Let him go!"

Brighton smiled calmly. Shane was breathing hard, but Brighton didn't have a hair out of place. Lance and Brad had squared off behind Shane, and Jessica stood quivering at Karen's side.

"No problem, man." Brighton's voice was steady and smooth. "You don't understand. I'd never hurt your lovely lady. It's cool, really. Ivy and I will go."

Shane slowly lowered his arm and stepped back. Daggers came from his icy eyes as Brighton gathered Ivy to his side and the two walked past Lance and Brad.

"Watch yourself," Lance called after them. Brighton gave no response.

Shane put his arms around both Karen and Jessica. They started toward the other girls, who were huddled by the grill and staring as Brighton and Ivy passed.

"Stay away from him," Shane said to Karen.

CHAPTER 30

The Rescue

It was Saturday night. The first race at Waterford Park was about to start. It would be Wendy's last race for the summer. Looming ahead on Monday was her senior year of high school. The summer at the track had taught her about the racing business. Some aspects were good. There was nothing like riding a good horse to victory, the ultimate high. Yet many aspects of the racing business were heartbreaking. The saying "the agony of defeat" now had new meaning to Wendy. Tonight, she would close this chapter of her life. She would make decisions about her future during the next year, and the lessons she'd learned at the racetrack would undoubtedly influence those decisions.

The starting gate sprang open. Wendy grabbed a handful of mane and stood in her irons. Silver Sickle broke casually. The gentle gray was never too interested in running. He was better suited as a pet; nothing bothered him. He preferred to lope rather than gallop. His workouts were as slow as molasses. Given the chance, he would stand for hours at the rail. He preferred to watch rather than join other horses during morning exercise. A tap of the whip was required to make him get into the game and train. Wendy knew she would be lucky to place fifth that night. It would take all the power she had to drive him to the finish.

Sickle trailed the field at barely more than a hand gallop. He was well named. His hocks formed a sickle shape. That meant there was too acute of an angle to the hock. Most people didn't mind a slightly sickle-hocked horse. Some people believed it actually helped the horse bring his hind legs under himself for added propulsion. However, poor Silver Sickle had the most pronounced sickle hocks Wendy had ever seen. In theory, it would be hard for him to stay sound. With his wonderful temperament, he'd make a nice light riding horse, but no rider with ambitions of competition would buy him. Wendy had shown the horse to a few potential buyers. Everyone said his conformation was too bad. Now he was stuck in a senseless cycle. He raced every other week, barely scraping in enough minor prize money to pay his way. Time was running out. She could tell his rear end was starting to bother him.

They were halfway through the backstretch. The dirt from the other runners pelted Wendy's goggles and stung her face. She moved Sickle out toward the middle of the track. If he had it in him to close tonight, he would need racing room. They passed the half-mile pole. Wendy noticed the riders on the front runners were using their whips. The front end speed was fizzling. She resisted the urge to make her move. Her only hope was to save Sickle's energy till the end. Maybe she could pass a few tiring horses. They entered the far turn, and Wendy asked Sickle for a little more. He extended his stride slightly. Still, he traveled fifteen lengths behind the front runners.

They cruised through the straightaway. The speed horses were fading back toward Sickle. Their nostrils flared as they tried to take in more air. A sprightly little chestnut accelerated from mid pack, pulling away to win. Wendy was giving it everything she had now, pumping the reins and using the whip intermittently. Sickle barely extended into a full gallop. He dawdled past the exhausted front runners and two others that looked lame. The best he could do was sixth place. As they passed the finish line, Wendy stood in her irons and pulled the horse up. He broke into a trot immediately. The rest of the field pranced up ahead. Many fought their riders. They would gladly go around again. To the contrary, Sickle was glad to return to his stall for a rest.

Fortunately, Wendy's other mounts over the summer had more talent than Sickle. She had won 8 percent of her races, and placed second and third in 20 percent of the rest. In a rough business, that was a good record. Even experienced riders had cold spells when they won less than that. Everything had to come together perfectly to win a race. The horse had to feel good physically and be stable mentally, and the rider needed perfect racing luck. Traffic problems caused countless losses. Sometimes a track favored a certain type of running style, and the best horse in the race could end up dead last. So, with all things considered, Wendy had had a good year. She was able to buy a new truck and trailer with her winnings. It had taken most of her money, but a truck and trailer were vital to starting her own horse business. At home, she would work for her dad. It would be hard, especially after experiencing the excitement of being a jockey. She would live rent free and be able to save more money over the school year. By next summer, her future would be open.

She had time for a quick good-bye. Todd was her primary trainer. They had experienced some success together. Wendy thought he was hard on his horses, but they shared a mutual admiration. Wendy had a weak spot for tough guys. Obviously, Todd liked pretty girls in general, but he made her feel special, complimenting her beauty, intelligence, and riding skills. He had clear intentions with her. He was manipulative, and she had fallen for him for a short time. However, intuition had warned her about Todd. Something wasn't right about him. She liked the attention he gave her, so that made it difficult for her to resist his advances. Dating older men had gotten her into trouble before. It was good that she was leaving. The situation was just under the boiling point.

Despite her apprehension, she felt obligated to say good-bye. Maybe it was because he had taught her so much. However, she had another reason to talk to him. Todd had threatened to send Sickle to auction, where most horses ended up in slaughterhouses. Broken-down racehorses were a dime a dozen. The killers, as they are called, bought them cheaply for a few hundred dollars. Wendy despised this horrific part of horseracing, and her ambitions for a future in the racing business were tainted because of it. Now, she would try to save a special horse from this cruel fate. Surely, Todd would give Sickle to her. She couldn't pay for him. However, she would make Todd understand. The few hundred dollars Sickle could bring at auction were inconsequential. Todd should realize the horse deserved a good home.

She pulled up to the barn with her truck and trailer, facing her rig toward the exit. Something told her to be ready to leave in a hurry. Todd tipped his cowboy hat to her as she hopped out of the truck. His nearly black hair peeked from under the hat's brim. His cowboy boots scuffed the gravel as they approached each other. She reached up and hugged him.

"Well, girl," he said, "we had a good trip together." Sorrow emanated from his blue eyes. "You can stay and keep riding. You have talent. Who needs high school?"

"I know, but I love my dad and want to fix things with him. Besides, I can't handle the things that go on with the horses. It's awful to send them for slaughter. They don't deserve it."

"Hey, I don't like it either. It's reality. If they don't pay for themselves, most owners want out. They'd rather invest money in ones that can win. These people aren't millionaires. Neither am I. Horses cost money. I can't keep them if they fail on the track. I couldn't feed them or myself."

"Well, I can help save one. Give Sickle to me. You know I can't buy him, but I can find him a home."

His face reddened instantly. "Are you nuts? A few hundred bucks pay the feed bill for a week! Where do you get off asking me that?"

"Sickle has paid his share of bills. The horse has no talent, but still he tried. Please, he's so sweet. Let him be someone's pet."

Todd paused for a moment. He placed his hand on his chin and gazed downward. When he spoke, his voice was low.

"If you're willing to stay, maybe we can work something out. You have to move in with me, though. You'll be my girl, no ifs, ands, or buts." he knew she was desperate. He also knew how naïve young girls could be. Bagging this young prize would raise his status at the track. He would be hailed as king.

Sensing danger in his tone, Wendy could feel her heart pound. The intensity in his voice and face frightened her. She wanted to run. She knew he thought she was naive, easy prey. Her eye caught movement from inside the barn. Sickle stuck his head over the stall door. His eyes met hers and he nickered softly.

Wendy took a deep breath, "Okay." She hugged him again. "Why don't you go and open a bottle of wine to celebrate? I'm not used to drinking, so this should be fun. We can look up at the stars and have a nice night."

Todd practically leaped up the porch steps. He rummaged through the refrigerator, pushing aside cheap beer. He found a bottle of strawberry wine left over from his old girlfriend. Now he had to find an opener. He rifled through the drawer.

"Man, why can't she just drink a can of beer?"

Finally, he found everything he needed and walked back onto his porch. The wine bottle fell from his hand as he took in the scene. Taillights glimmered halfway down his driveway. The setting sun barely illuminated gray tail hairs trailing over the trailer ramp.

"That little hag! She stole that nag and made a fool of me. She's not getting away with this."

He ran to his pickup and tried to crank the key. His fingers fumbled aimlessly upon the empty ignition.

"Shoot! It's always in the ignition. What's going on?"

Todd would spend an hour in the weeds looking for his keys.

CHAPTER 31

The Mountain Calls

What a strange morning, Karen thought. First, Gage had shown up, completely out of character. He gave Kirsten a bouquet of flowers and practically begged her to ride up the mountain with him. Since when was he romantic enough to pick flowers? She had lost her riding buddy to some wild daisies. Then Shane called about some horse trailer sitting at the top of Country Club Road. Who would be up there? There were no horse farms up there.

These thoughts jumbled together with other matters. Karen felt as if her head would explode as she hustled to finish the morning work. Unable to shake the desire to dig more deeply into Deryn Opie's past, she and Shane had scoured the old house for further clues. The house had been eerily silent, despite Karen's nearly pleading for further signs from Lady Luminess. Research into Deryn's life at the county library shed no light on the situation, simply identifying the woman as William Opie's daughter. Probes into wind-energy research within Pennsylvania yielded no results.

Karen's thoughts drifted to Ivy and the strain between them. Ivy rarely came to the barn anymore, and left abruptly when Karen was there. Karen considered giving Brighton the diagrams, yet the thought seized at her chest. She wished Ivy hadn't walked up on her, Jessica, and Brad when they found the diagrams. Brighton would not have known about them had it not been for Ivy.

Kathleen Parker

A red ribbon hanging on Darter's stall fluttered with a light breeze. Karen's gaze locked on it as the breeze picked up, sending the ribbon's ends twisting and slapping against the stall.

"Oh, man," she said aloud. "I need to call about our ribbon order tomorrow. Crap, that judge never got back with me. She better not stand me up. Our show is next week!"

She peeked in at Darter dozing in the corner. Thinking of the friendly rivalry between the noble gray and Bailey, she welled with pride and enthusiasm. The difference between cumulative placings for the two in flat and hunter hack classes was indiscernible. It was unlikely for either gelding to qualify for districts, but the Thoroughbred breed had a real-life poster child in Darter or Bailey. Babe put her head over the stall door, tossing it impatiently. Karen went to the tack room.

As Kirsten had figured, Dawn topped the mountain ahead of Gage's four-wheeler. The thick vegetation of late summer clung to the wide vehicle as it struggled over rocks and roots. The agile Arabian picked her way through with silent accuracy. Kirsten reminded herself how proud she should be of Dawn. The young mare went practically everywhere. Few things rattled her anymore. On the other hand, Kirsten felt apprehensive about coming here with Gage. They hadn't spoken since Shane's pool party a month ago. His romantic gesture with the flowers had swept her off her feet at the barn, but now she wondered if he would break her heart again.

They entered the clearing leading to the haven. Pristine as ever, its majestic walls towered skyward, and the green of the trees at the pinnacle glistened in the sun. They approached the cave entrance and its cool, comforting greeting.

Kirsten took a deep breath and tried to sound cool and nonchalant. "Now what?"

"Let's take another look at those cave drawings. I need something to humble me. Then we'll go through and sit on the canyon floor. I brought my famous lunch."

He didn't sound like his backward self, and Kirsten unknowingly shared Karen's thought about it being a strange day.

He led the way with his flashlight. Kirsten led Dawn, who didn't hesitate to follow them inside. No doubt Dawn remembered eating lush grass on the other side. Gage stopped at the cave drawings.

"Look at this scene in particular," he said. "It looks like the man is protecting the woman. My grandmother would be ashamed of the way I treated you. In their community, Indian women were treated with great respect. I left you alone with what became another crazy situation with that weirdo Brighton that night. I don't know what was wrong with me." He wrapped his arm around her shoulders and gave her a gentle squeeze. Kirsten stiffened, and an awkward silence followed.

"Forget it," she said. "Let's go out." She would savor this moment later.

They continued on to the meadow, emerging into bright sunlight. The smell of fresh wildflowers greeted them.

"I never get tired of this place," Kirsten said as she gave Dawn a loose rein to eat.

Gage unpacked his knapsack and handed Kirsten a sandwich. They talked idly about plans for the school year. Finally, he held her hand.

"I was a real schmuck. I really don't care about a stupid pool game. I just used your pathetic performance as an excuse." He smiled and nudged her side. "My dad has been on me about finishing the Charger. On top of that he wants to do Indy car again, but he's getting old for that. My mom has been stressed and they've been fighting. I can't deal with it all." He paused, taking a deep breath. "All I know is that I miss you. Do you want to make this thing official? Will you go with me?"

Kirsten struggled to gulp down the excitement welling up in her throat. She had given up hope she would ever hear those words from Gage.

"Of course I will." She punched him on the arm. "By the way, you are a schmuck."

They sat arm in arm for a while, observing the birds soaring overhead.

"Look," Gage said. "There's a red tailed hawk." He pointed to the sky. They sat admiring the skillful flier when, slowly, a feather fluttered down toward them. It landed in front of Gage.

"I hear my school goes all out for our Halloween dance," he said. "Will you be my Indian princess?" He brushed her sun-lightened hair behind her ear and stuck the hawk feather among her curls. She smiled. Her heart was his again.

The morning sun beamed into the cavern. Although it was early September, the heat intensified. Kirsten noticed that Dawn was sweating. Reluctantly, she prompted Gage to go.

"On the way down, I'll show you what I've been working on," he said. "I'm trying to connect Shane's trail with one that will bypass the road, cut through the woods, and end up at my house. That way Dawn can stay off that scary road with those garage doors." He was referring to when they had met. Ironically, he and his friends spooking Kirsten's horse had brought them together. The pair laughed at the memory.

They descended the mountain the way they came. Gage stopped Kirsten at a point halfway down. To the left was a new trail.

"I'll show you how far I've gotten," he said.

Kirsten was happy for any additional riding space. She would show Mindy this new trail. If it wasn't finished, she knew Saint could help clear it. The sturdy palomino would push through anything.

They continued for another half mile. The bramble and bushes grew thicker. The woods became impenetrable to the four-wheeler.

"Wait," Kirsten said. "Karen described this kind of brush. It helped slow Legend and Dorian during their impromptu race. I bet this leads to the same trail." She lined Dawn up with a stump. "Here, climb on the back." She motioned for Gage to sit behind her.

"Are you nuts?" he asked.

"Do you want to find your house or not? Dawn can pick her way through this place with no problem."

Despite the extra weight, Dawn continued on her way, staying parallel to the bramble. Her ears pricked forward, attentive to her task. Soon indeed, the bramble cleared and they were on the infamous trail of the runaways.

"That brush saved Karen's life," Kirsten said, "but it has to go now."

Gage agreed to enlist Shane and Lance's help to clear the trail completely. Kirsten savored the feeling of his hands around her waist as they descended from the woods. Meeting the macadam, they turned right on Country Club Road toward Gage's house. It loomed ahead, filling Kirsten with separation anxiety.

"Let's meet at Shane's later," Gage said. "I'll have him give me a ride to get my four-wheeler. You'll be about done at the barn by then."

A wave of satisfaction eased Kirsten's anxiety. "Sure."

The steady clip-clop of Dawn's hooves was interrupted. Spotting something ahead, Dawn pricked her ears. Blowing gently with curiosity, she continued onward. Someone was walking along the road ahead of them. As they got closer, the petite blond turned and looked behind her. She approached them without delay.

Kirsten's eyes widened with surprise. "Wendy? Are you all right?"

"Hey, guys. Do you know anybody around here with a phone? I need Karen's help with something."

"I think we can arrange that," Gage said.

CHAPTER 32

Light My Way

The barn phone rang again. "Man, I'm never gonna get to ride," Karen muttered, saddle in hand. She plopped it beside Babe's feet. Restrained by the cross ties, the filly stamped her foot.

Stomping to the phone, Karen answered gruffly. There was a pause at the other end, and then a meek, shaky voice said, "Karen, it's Wendy. Are you alone?"

"Hey, Wendy, great to hear from you. Yeah, I'm alone. Everyone else has plans today. Get this. June and Carl from 4-H are on their first date!"

"Oh, that's nice," Wendy replied impatiently. "I'm with Kirsten and Gage, but I need your help. I got myself into a real mess."

Karen's stomach knotted. This was a different Wendy. "What happened?" she asked apprehensively.

"I stole a horse." Karen gasped as Wendy continued. "I know. I think you'll understand why, though. Todd was going to send him to the killers. I asked him to give me the horse, but he refused. The little bit of money was too important to him. Sickle is such a sweet horse. I couldn't let that happen. I really didn't think things through. He's been standing in the horse trailer all night at the top of the road. I haven't been home, so my dad is probably worried sick. But I know if my dad finds out I took this horse, he'll make me give him back. I can't take him to my farm. I realize Ginny knows Todd, so I can't bring him to you. To make things worse, John set me up with Todd. He'll have my hide when he finds out that I stole from his buddy."

"But does Todd know where we live?" Karen asked, while questioning John's choice of friends.

"Todd only knows we live in Johnstown. He doesn't know specifics. I hope he'll just let it go. He's busy enough. But still, I have a bad feeling. I need a place for this horse. Do you know of anyone who will take him?"

Karen's mind whirled in a thousand directions. How could Todd be so cold? Yes, the fiery side of the Irish would show itself when John found out. Who could take the horse? Mentally, she went through her short contact list. Everyone's barn was full. What could they do? Suddenly, a light bulb went off in her head.

"I know just the place. We'll have to wait till Ginny leaves for the night. I don't want her to get suspicious. She has a date tonight and she convinced Shane to keep an eye on Brad. Hopefully, Brad will keep Shane occupied. The less people who know the better. Put Kirsten on the line. Hopefully, Gage will let you hang out there for a while. Call your dad. Let him know you're all right, but don't tell him where you are. Babe and I will show you the way. I'll call you when the time is right. You'll have to bring the horse down here."

Karen briefed Kirsten about the situation. Before riding Dawn home, Kirsten arranged for Wendy to hide out in Gage's garage. There was a couch there. Although it wasn't the most glamorous of accommodations, Wendy could get some rest. Gage would pick Kirsten up after she settled Dawn and he retrieved his four-wheeler with Shane's help.

Karen pondered her plan. The haven could easily support one hundred horses with its plentiful grass. There were fresh springs and clear pools for water. Various caves along the interior walls provided natural shelter. There was just one problem. How would she keep the horse from following them back? She would have to blockade the entrance to the main cave. It was the only way in and the only way out. She remembered a pile of small boulders that had fallen not far from the entrance. How in the world would she move them? She looked at her watch. It was three o'clock. She knew who to call.

Riding Babe would have to wait. Karen busied herself for hours at the barn. She cleared all the cobwebs, and every piece of tack shone with extra polish. The tack room floor was clean enough to eat from. Daylight slowly dwindled. Feeling like a stalker, Karen interrupted Ginny several times during the evening, checking her progress. Finally, Ginny was ready to leave for her date as the late summer sun shot pink rays over the mountaintops. It was setting in a blaze of glory. Shane arrived for his "babysitting" duty. Karen lingered as Ginny gave Shane his instructions.

"Just try to keep him out of big trouble," Ginny joked, as if a little mischief was okay.

"I think I have enough to keep him occupied." Shane held up some VCR tapes, including *Terminator* and *Indiana Jones and the Temple of Doom*.

"I know he'd behave if Jess were here," Shane said to tease Brad. Brad's face turned red.

"Shut up, man," Brad said.

Finally, Ginny drove off. Brad and Shane went inside to watch the movies and Karen headed back to the barn. A slim figure came through the paddock on the other end.

"Perfect timing," Karen said to Mindy. "I'll call Wendy. We'll have to move quickly. It's getting dark. I have all the flashlights I could find. The moon will be full too."

"You don't know what I went through to get down here this late," Mindy said. "You know, it's the night before the first day of school. My dad is mad."

"Sorry. I need Saint's power and the western saddle horn. We're going to drag those boulders and block the cave off temporarily. We'll come up with something better later. Although, I bet when this horse gets used to his new digs, he won't want to leave."

She called the number that connected with the phone in Gage's garage.

"Wendy, is everything still a go? How are you feeling?" she asked.

"I feel better. Gage has actually been really nice. I'm so exhausted that I slept, even on his old couch. Everything is set. Kirsten told him to give me a ride up the hill to the horse trailer. He's starting the four-wheeler now. I'll be there with the horse as soon as possible." Wendy sounded invigorated.

"How much does Gage know?" Karen asked. Shane hadn't acted suspicious, and Karen knew he and Gage had ridden together that day to get Gage's four-wheeler.

"Nothing," Wendy said. "Kirsten just told him I was having daddy issues."

Brad looked out the house trailer window toward to barn. "The lights are still on down there. What is Karen doing so late? I thought she was going to watch the movies with us."

"Don't worry about her," Shane said. "I'm used to taking second seat to the horse. Watch this!" Shane was enthralled in Arnold Schwarzenegger's portrayal of a killer robot from the future.

Brad wasn't the only one who noticed the barn lights. A pickup truck with West Virginia plates sat along North Fork Dam Road. With his headlights off, Todd had a perfect vantage point. A casual call to John was all it took. He had found the headquarters of Fox Hollow 4-H club. Todd knew Wendy was a member of the club and a friend of the group's leader. If Wendy needed help, she'd certainly come to Karen.

"There you are," he said as a horse trailer entered Ginny's drive in front of the decrepit house. It stopped at the bridge, and a girl with a blond ponytail bounded out of the truck and to the back of the trailer. The sound of hooves coming down the trailer ramp carried up the hollow. Sickle had arrived.

Babe's head lifted and ears pricked as the new horse approached. She snorted the cooling air. She must have wondered why she was being saddled so late. Karen tied Babe and approached Wendy and Sickle.

"Oh, he is sweet," she said as the gray nuzzled her hand. "You couldn't leave him behind. We'll make this work, but it will be a long ride. I called Mindy to help. Saint will make sure Sickle doesn't stray from his new home. As soon as he gets used to it, he'll think he's died and gone to heaven. We better get going. You can use Ginny's tack."

Saint and Babe were ready to go. Saint's saddle was adorned with a network of ropes to move the boulders.

Hurriedly, the three girls tacked Sickle. Over the horizon, the last fragments of light faded. It was completely dark. In minutes, the trio was ready to leave. The girls gathered behind the barn and prepared to mount. Suddenly, a noise from the hillside startled all six creatures. A dark figure stepped out of the brush.

"Not so fast. Wendy, what do you think you're doing?"

The calmness in Todd's voice was scarier than if he had shouted. Chills of terror gripped all three girls. They stifled the urge to scream.

"Look, Todd," Wendy said. "I know I shouldn't have taken him. You wouldn't listen to me, though. I'll make it up to you. I'll ride for you for free next summer. Can't we just forget about it?"

"Yeah, right. As if I believe you after the stunt you pulled in my driveway? No one makes a fool out of me. Give me that nag!"

Todd lunged for Sickle's reins. Wendy kicked at his shins, and he winced as she nailed him on the bone. Now he went after her.

"You rotten little thief!" He grabbed her arm, shaking her.

Karen handed Babe's reins to Mindy. The startled filly danced and circled. It was all Mindy could do to hold her and Saint. In contrast, the intuitive Sickle stood still, waiting for his next cue from his saviors.

"Let go of her!" Karen said as she approached Todd. "I'll call the cops!"

"You stay out of it." He backhanded Karen across the face, sending her to the ground.

Suddenly, out of nowhere, a shovel slammed Todd in the shoulder, knocking him off balance. He lost his grip on Wendy.

Luckily for the girls, Brad's curiosity had sent him out to the barn. "Get off my property!" he told the man.

"I'm not going anywhere until I get what I want." Todd turned on Brad, who wielded the shovel to keep him at bay.

"You girls better get out of here!" Brad yelled.

The three girls leaped onto their mounts. Babe picked up on the excitement and galloped off before Karen had her second stirrup. All fear left Karen. Focused on the task, she balanced herself in two-point position. She found the stirrup as Babe led Sickle and Saint over the bridge. There had been no time to get the flashlights out. Thankfully, Babe's self-preservation instincts were high. They hit the dark driveway in front of the old house, and Babe steadied herself as they plunged into the darkness. But Karen didn't know how they'd see in the woods.

Amazingly, someone other than Brad had their backs. As they passed the old house, a large ball of light zipped in front of Babe. Karen's eyes widened with disbelief. The light took on the curvy form of a woman. She levitated at galloping speed, just ahead of Babe's nose, illuminating the driveway and the road ahead of them.

"Deryn, protector of Fox Hollow," Karen said. Emboldened by this extraordinary support, she drove Babe onward. Cruising over the ground, the brilliant light resembled a spotlight. As long as the spirit was with them, Karen knew they'd make it.

Already terrified at Todd's appearance, Wendy stared in shock at the bouncing light. Frightened out her mind, she hyperventilated. She clung to Sickle's mane, hanging on for dear life. Instinctively, the sensitive gray slowed his pace.

"You have to keep going!" Mindy yelled over the roar of a motor.

Someone spun out of Ginny's barnyard. She didn't know who was on Brad's dirt bike, but she had a bad feeling it wasn't Brad.

Sickle continued to pull up, trying to protect his rider. Saint almost clipped heels with him from behind. Babe and the precious light grew farther and farther away.

"Wendy!" Mindy said. "Snap out of it and go!"

As if splashed with cold water, Wendy regained her senses. She drove Sickle toward the glowing light and the sound of Babe's hooves as Babe powered up Shane's hill toward the wooded trail.

———⁓⁓•∽⦁⧖⦁∾•⁓⁓———

Brad lay on the ground outside the barn, knocked silly by the shovel handle. He struggled to come to his feet as his dirt bike tore away.

"Shane told me to quit leaving the keys in it," he muttered.

Todd eased the throttle, figuring the girls and the horses couldn't run all night. He'd just sit back some, make them think they'd lost him. Then he'd get what he came for.

The climb to the haven was tough at a conservative pace. Now the horses' cardiovascular systems were being pushed to the max. Babe traveled like a monster horse, scaling the mountain trail and skipping over rocks as if she were in an open field. She reveled in the challenging run. Her powerful hindquarters reached under her body with incredible efficiency. All Karen had to do was hold on. Like headlights, the spirit stayed just in front of Babe's nose.

Sickle and Saint weren't having such a fun time. Sickle was still recovering from his last race, barely a day earlier. He stumbled and strained to navigate the unfamiliar territory. A lingering consequence form the race, fluid was stuck in his lungs, decreasing their air capacity. He was running out of steam, but they had at least a half mile to cover. Saint was faring better from behind. His stride was shorter than Sickle's, but he was not suffering from lactic acid buildup. Again, Saint came close to colliding with Sickle as they reached the pine forest flats. Wendy pulled the exhausted gray up for a breather. The light and the sound of Babe's hoofbeats diminished. It was so dark that Saint's white face was the only thing visible.

"We can't stop," Mindy said.

"I'm sorry. He just can't go anymore." They could barely hear each other over their heavy breathing and that of the horses. "How far is it?"

"Just over a quarter mile. Can he walk the rest of the way? We can't go much faster without the light anyway."

"Leave it to Karen to take a joy ride through the woods in crisis time." Wendy actually saw humor in the situation. With Babe's history, Karen might be over the next mountain range by now.

Wendy urged Sickle to move on. The thick pine branches brushed their faces. Picking their way through would be difficult. Thankfully, a dim glow filtered through the branches. Seconds later, Sickle and Babe were nose to nose.

"Are you all right?" Karen asked.

"Sickle has had it. He just raced last night. I couldn't push him anymore."

The girls stood in the pine forest and took some deep breaths.

"I think she's losing her energy." Karen nodded toward the fading spirit light. Its womanly form had faded to an indistinguishable haze. "We need to keep going. We're almost there."

Suddenly, the roar of the dirt bike shattered the silence. A single headlight pierced the woods.

"He's coming!" Mindy shouted.

"Come on, Sickle," Karen said. "One last sprint!"

Karen wheeled Babe around toward the grassy plateau. First, Babe had to clarify something. Instead of charging off, she made a complete pirouette. It brought her face to face with Sickle again. She snorted at him and tossed her head. Arching her neck, she blew into his nostrils and then struck at Sickle with her front leg, squealing loudly. Sickle's ears pricked and energy flooded his body. The final motivator was a well-placed nip at Sickle's throat. Then, as quickly as she landed the bite, Babe wheeled and galloped away.

Without further ado, Sickle engaged in the game and took off after her. Saint gave a little buck as he took off, as if to say, "It's about time!"

The spirit light was indeed fading. She held on long enough to lead the trio out of the woods and into the clearing just before the haven. Moonlight illuminated the pathway, but another light was gaining on them. The dirt bike roared behind Saint. Karen looked back, noting the danger, and opened Babe up. Sickle continued trying to keep up. Saint dug in with all he had, but the bike wasn't tired. It was on his heels.

Todd gunned the bike. The front wheel scraped the end of Saint's tail. The feisty gelding was not putting up with this. He kicked hard at the bike, smashing the headlight and bending the handlebars. It slowed Todd's manic pace for only a moment. Babe reached the canyon walls. To the left loomed the immense rock formation; to the right lay the steep mountain cliff. Directly in front of them was a thick, bramble-filled forest. This was the end of the line. What would they do next?

The bike started to shimmy and careen off to the side as everyone slowed down. Significantly damaged, it couldn't stay straight at a slow pace. It rumbled to a stop.

The three horses stood in a line, cornered. They and their riders stared down at the half-crazed man who got off the bike and approached them.

"We can run him down," Mindy said, her voice shaky with fear.

"He carries a gun most of the time," Wendy said. "I wouldn't risk it. I've never seen him like this. I don't know what he's capable of."

Todd continued toward them with unnerving silence. He held something in his hand. In the clearing, the moonlight glinted on steel. He did have a gun. The girls' hearts were in their throats. They stared incredulously at one another.

Karen heard a noise. She thought it was her heart pounding in her ears. However, the rhythmical melody got louder and louder, and the sound became unmistakable. The war drums had returned. They had foretold Legend's collapse. This spot was very close to where he had died. The drumbeats got faster and faster, and the distinct chanting of an Indian war party filled the air. All the girls heard it now. Wendy looked around wildly, wondering who else was up there and how much worse could things get? She noticed that, strangely, the tension had left Mindy and Karen. They were almost in a trance.

Todd seemed oblivious to the music. He got closer, stopping a few yards from the horses.

"Now, Wendy, you know what I have with me. You don't want anyone to get hurt, do you? A friend's blood spilled would be worse than your own, wouldn't it? I know you, girl. You couldn't live with yourself if you caused either of these girls to get hurt. Just come with me."

Wendy knew he was right. She couldn't bear it if something happened to Karen or Mindy. She pulled her feet from the stirrups, ready to dismount.

Karen and Mindy simultaneously came to life. "Wendy! Don't go!"

"I have no choice." Wendy raised her hand to give Sickle's reins to Karen. "Just take care of him."

Before Wendy could release the reins, the Indian music intensified. Even Todd heard it this time. He jumped in surprise, scanning the rock walls, his gun at the ready. A shrill whinny echoed through the night. The dark form of a horse emerged from the shadows beside the cave. It was moving fast but silently, running up behind the disoriented Todd. The horse reared high, striking Todd from behind with its foreleg. Todd fell to the ground, out cold.

The horse paused. Babe nickered to him. The horse took one step toward them, and the moonlight caught the large white star on his forehead.

"Legend!" Karen called. Tears flooded her eyes, her body shook, but she mustered enough strength to urge Babe toward the ghostly figure. Through her tears, she saw the white star fade slowly. She urged Babe on, but by the time Babe got to the spot, he was gone.

All three girls dismounted and sobbed together, holding each other tightly. The horses stood stock still, seeming as shocked as the humans. Finally, the girls gathered their composure. They had to figure out what to do with Todd.

Another noise jolted them. This time it was the moan of two ATVs struggling to climb the mountain. The girls could see the headlights bouncing through the thick pine forest.

"I hope these are the good guys," Karen said.

Minutes later, Shane's headlights found them. He was followed by Gage.

"Karen! What the hell is going on? Are you nuts?"

"Shane stop, you'll run him over!" Karen yelled.

Shane jerked to a halt. He stared at the body lying on the ground. "This guy was after you? Why?"

"I knew you girls were up to something strange," Gage said, "but this takes the cake."

"Be careful!" Karen said. "I don't know if he's dead or not." She couldn't believe she'd said those words.

Shane took a baseball bat from the back of his four-wheeler. "You have a lot of explaining to do," he said to Karen as he carefully approached Todd. Karen handed Babe's reins to Mindy. Indeed, an explanation was warranted.

Shane and Karen hovered over the body. Karen started to explain the whole thing as they checked for signs of life. By this time, Mindy had found the flashlight in her saddle pack and shone it on Todd. His chest rose up and down. As Karen finished her explanation, Shane positioned himself over Todd's head, bat at the ready.

"You could have gotten Brad killed," he said.

"Oh my God, Brad. How is he?"

"His ribs are pretty sore, but I think he'll be fine. But if Gage hadn't called me, I may not have found him for another hour. I was too engrossed in the movie."

"I guess we owe you thanks for telling on us," Karen said to Gage.

"I'll face Kirsten's wrath for sure, but obviously you needed help."

"We need to set Sickle free," Karen said. "I didn't go through all of this to have the horse end up in the wrong hands. I'll get some rope. You need to tie this guy up." Karen hurried over to Saint and retrieved some of the rope from his saddle.

Shane and Gage secured Todd at wrists and feet. After tying Babe and Saint to a nearby tree, the girls scrambled to untack Sickle. They gathered the three flashlights and planned the release.

"Once we get Sickle through the cave," Karen said, "two of you will have to hold him at bay while Saint closes up the gap with the boulders."

The girls formed a single line of flashlights and entered the cave. Sickle hesitated, nickering to Babe. Surprisingly, she didn't answer. She remained quiet, encouraging Sickle to go. Without other horses to mimic, Sickle looked for guidance. Wendy's presence was strong, so he followed her as herd leader.

They emerged into the open field of the haven. The bubbling of the springs could be heard and it had a calming effect on everyone. Wendy unbridled Sickle, who snorted softly, taking in his new surroundings. The girls prepared to block the escape route, but heard a whinny in the distance.

"Oh, Babe," Karen said. "Now you're going to foil our plans. He'll really want to get out now."

"That didn't come from Babe's direction," Mindy said. "Look over there." She pointed across the meadow.

Under the trickling moonlight, a dark horse stood in the center of the field. He whinnied again, as if greeting Sickle. Sickle bounded away, kicking up his heels like a young colt. He met the dark horse and the two cantered into the darkness.

"We don't have to blockade the cave," Karen said. "Thanks, Legend."

The girls returned to Shane and Gage, who were deep in an interesting conversation.

"No, I tell you, man," Todd was saying. "I don't know my name. I can't tell you anything. Holy hell, what happened to me? Where am I? This is weird, man. Why am I tied up?"

"You mean you have no idea who you are or what you're doing here?" Shane asked him.

"No, my mind is blank. Literally, I see white when I close my eyes. I have no idea who I am."

"Do you know me?" Wendy shined the flashlight under her chin.

"No, absolutely not. Why would I be with a bunch of teenagers?"

"Gage, keep an eye on him." Shane handed him the bat.

Shane and the girls huddled together, and Shane asked if they thought he really had amnesia.

"He did take a hard hit to the head," Karen said.

"Knowing his temper," Wendy said, "he'd never sit there quietly without a fight. To be tied up and incapacitated by a bunch of teenagers would be unbearable to his pride. He'd go down fighting."

"I took care of the gun," Shane said.

The girls convinced Shane to go with the flow. Of course, Todd could be put in jail for assault, but Wendy was on the line too. Theft was no laughing matter, and Karen and Mindy could be accused of conspiracy.

"All right, buddy," Shane said to Todd. "We'll get you some help."

Shane gave Wendy a crash course in driving a four-wheeler. She would follow Babe and Saint down the mountain. Gage would follow Shane and Todd as they walked down.

"You girls get a head start," Shane whispered to them. "Don't fool around. I don't want to see any lights when I come off the mountain. He doesn't need to see where you go."

Lance stood in front of his parents' idling car. He was grateful they allowed him to take it out this late, but wished for a different occasion. Shane and Gage guided a man with a cowboy hat into the passenger side of a pickup with West Virginia tags. Gage hopped in the truck from the driver's side, and scooted to the center to sit beside the man. Shane took the driver's seat and flashed the headlights to signify all systems go.

Lance followed the pickup closely, focusing on the strange man. Everything looked quiet inside the pickup and the ride to Memorial Hospital was uneventful. Lance pulled behind the pick up outside the emergency room entrance. Shane got out, opened the passenger's door, and guided the man onto the sidewalk. Gage followed closely and the trio entered the emergency room.

Minutes later, Shane and Gage rushed out and jumped in Lance's car. Shane said, "Okay man, let's get out of here."

CHAPTER 33

THE END

It was the morning of Conemaugh Township's Halloween party. Everyone was going, but Kirsten knew her costume would be the best. She had searched far and wide for the most authentic Indian maiden costume. At the last minute, she had found it. The costume was simple enough, comprised of a knee-length skirt with a belt at the waist, and a tunic made of leather. A length of fake fur was to be worn over one shoulder. The garment was decorated with shell beads throughout. Jewelry consisted of a necklace and bracelet made from deer antler with wampum decorations. Of course, she had moccasins for her feet, and a black wig. Gage would have his Indian princess.

"Indian spirits, I honor you by wearing your clothes." She spoke the prayer aloud, thanking the spirits for saving her friends.

She walked over to June's, and the two of them headed for the barn. June spoke excitedly about Carl coming to the dance as they walked across the bridge and into the back paddock, which bustled with activity.

Jessica stood proudly at the helm of a harnessed Cookie. Behind the pony was a modified cart. The bed was extra-long, but its width was contracted across the axle. Two child-size BMX tires supported the cart. With Ashes at her heels and Master and Aries milling about the yard, Karen heaved a bale of hay onto the cart. Shane and Lance followed with bags of grain.

"How can we help?" Kirsten asked.

"We need four more hay bales," Karen said. She smiled. "The boys can get the grain."

Lance frowned. "How come we get stuck with the heavy part?"

Mindy snuck behind him, pinching his sides. "Get to work, wimp."

Lance stomped away in mock displeasure. Kirsten followed Shane into the barn for the hay. June was close behind.

"Looks like you did a good job with the cart," Kirsten said to Shane. "How'd you figure it out?"

"A lot of do overs. I about trashed it a few times. But that loser over there"—he raised his voice, ensuring Lance would hear—"gave me some ideas. It almost ruined our friendship, but Sickle will have plenty of food over the winter because of this cart."

Shane lifted another feed bag, straining to get it to the cart. Lance unmercifully knocked into him, making Shane stagger to rebalance the load. Laughter buzzed around the paddock.

"What about when it snows?" June asked.

"I started on blueprints for a sled," Shane said. "We're just not sure Cookie has the horse power to pull it through the snow."

"Hey, don't you doubt my Cookie. She's small but mighty!" Jess retorted.

Just then Brad buzzed by, flipping Jessica's hair across her back and over her shoulder.

Jessica's green eyes glimmered. "Leave it to you to show up when we're almost done!"

"I don't know if I should be lifting," he said, "what with my hurt ribs and all."

"Nice try," Karen said. "You're healed by now. But I'm glad your mom doesn't know what happened. How did you hide sore ribs from her?"

"I made sure I did what she said. I'd give myself away if I fought with her. I couldn't move very fast without wincing. So I struggled through cleaning my room in silent pain. You girls really owe me."

"Hey, we made you king for a day. What more could you want?"

The girls had agreed to let Brad dress as a king for the Halloween dance. Karen would dress as his servant, and Jessica would dress as his queen.

"Yeah, man," Shane said. "How do you get my girlfriend to act like your servant? She sure doesn't cook and clean for me."

Phantom Hoof Prints

The group laughed. However, everyone knew Brad was a hero. He had stalled Todd, giving the girls a chance to escape from the barnyard. Otherwise, the results could have been disastrous.

"Hey, Mindy," Brad said. "I'm glad to hear you and Lance are going as Bonnie and Clyde. You could easily have a criminal record."

"Shh!" Jess warned. "Don't say that too loud."

"Yeah, we have to keep Mindy out of jail." Karen patted Jess's shoulder. "She needs to train Saint to pull this cart too, just in case Cookie needs back up."

"How's Wendy doing?" Mindy asked.

"Can you believe she's still grounded? The girl was practically on her own all summer, bought her own truck and horse trailer, and has ridden races, and her dad punishes her for disappearing for a day. The main thing is that she has nightmares about Todd, even though she never heard from him after that night. On top of that, she was frightened for a while because of our ghosts. She was in shock. Can you imagine just coming into that all at once? At least we were introduced to all the spirits little by little."

"Without that brave girl, Sickle would be dead," Kirsten said. "At least she's not grounded from waitressing. I'm sick of fried fish, but at least we see her at the restaurant."

"Yeah really," Karen said. "Actually, without Gage, we'd be struggling to feed Sickle. It's so cool he collected donations at the Pocono Raceway. He's a good guy after all."

"He hopes to bring more donations back tonight," Kirsten said proudly.

"What about me?" Shane said. "Everyone's getting credit when I have to hide this silly cart."

"Don't worry," Karen said. "You're the coolest of them all." She hugged Shane and kissed his cheek.

Appeased, Shane hoisted the last grain bag onto the cart. The group smiled at one another with satisfaction and pride. But then June looked at the ground, blinking back tears.

"One of us is missing," she whispered.

"Not anymore," a girl said from behind them. "Can someone give me a ride to the dance?"

"Ivy, where have you been?" Karen asked as June hugged her sister.

"I've been around. The Westmont scene isn't all it's cracked up to be." Ivy looked at the ground, kicking pebbles.

"You're always welcome," Shane said, "but I don't want Brighton anywhere near us."

Now Ivy fought back tears. "Don't worry. We're done."

The girls crowded around Ivy with concern and relief. Ivy said little about the reason for the breakup and quickly changed the subject.

"Well, Captain Jessica," Karen said, "we better get going."

The other girls went to finish the barn work, and the boys buzzed away on their four-wheelers. Jessica climbed aboard the cart and urged Cookie onward with Karen walking behind. Ashes, Master, and Aries loped along happily, sniffing every interesting spot they could.

Karen settled into stride, happy for the exercise and the crisp autumn air. Looking at the loaded cart, Karen knew Sickle would greet them happily. He had settled into the haven instantly, never venturing out of the tunnel. Karen was sure that the grass and spring water sustained him, but Legend's spirit nurtured his soul. She had seen the dark horse spirit several times, hovering close to Sickle during twilight grazing. Karen knew Legend had knocked Todd over that evening. She, Mindy, Wendy, and probably all the horses owed him their lives.

The wagon headed up the hillside and into the woods. Karen and the dogs followed close behind. Despite the effort, the woods relaxed Karen. She hoped for Deryn's peace too. The spirit had been quiet since the night of the rescue.

Karen mused over the extraordinary events of the last two and a half years. So many things had happened. She had a great group of friends. A wide variety of horses had given her valuable experience. Her own horse was proving to be special. She had learned there were still great mysteries in the world. How many people got to interact with spirits? Yes, she was very lucky. What else lay ahead?